FORBIDDEN FREEDOM

THE FORBIDDEN SERIES: WOMEN OF THE BOOK OF MORMON

MECHEL WALL
R. H. ROBERTS

CONTENTS

FORBIDDEN FREEDOM

A Novel

By
Mechel Wall & R. H. Roberts

❀ Created with Vellum

DEDICATION

To those whose lives have been forever affected by the poor choices of another,
we extend our arms of love and support.
To those who have lost children tragically, our tears join yours as we mourn
with you.
To those enduring abuse in any form, your cries are heard by a loving God
who will one day make things right.
Not all things are fair in this life. Not every story has a happy mortal ending.
We believe that our loving God knows each person's struggles and allows
others to minister in His name to render aid. Where it is possible, we can be
His hands to protect, uplift, comfort and care for one another.
This book is dedicated to the women in the Book of Mormon – a book of true
scripture. We know you were there and played important roles and someday,
we will ask you to share your stories with us. For now, we do our best to
honor your courage, fortitude and faithfulness in spite of incredible
persecution and hardship, in this fictionalized account of a true story.

DINAH, 145 BC, CITY OF SHILOM

*D*inah breathed in deeply. The cool crisp air was refreshing and the smoke from inside their home had long since cleared. She draped her arm across Limhi's chest. She smiled. *My husband.*

Limhi's eyes fluttered open. "Good morning, my queen."

"It's going to take some getting used to, being called queen."

"You'll be a wonderful one."

"Except for learning how to use the fire pit in this new home," she said with a pout.

"It was humorous to have everyone come racing to save us from the fire when it was just a simple mistake. It'll be a funny story to tell our children one day."

Dinah pushed up on one elbow. "What a different life our children will have. One father. One mother. I understand now, how your mother must have felt, having to see Noah with so many other women." Dinah paused, then looked into Limhi's face. "I will be your only wife, right?"

"I promise you; I will honor my word." He combed his fingers through her hair. "I saw my mother weep when she thought she was alone. My Father broke her heart." Limhi touched her cheek, stroking it with the back of his hand. "Never will I treat your heart with such callousness." Limhi placed a kiss on her satin cheek. "I'll not cause you to weep."

Dinah's contented smile accompanied the next question. "Do you wish to live here, always?"

"I'm happy to live here, where I grew up," Limhi stated firmly. "Noah's wives and children can have the palace. We don't need it. I want my children, *our* children, to grow up how I did." He moved his hand from her soft cheek to place his hand over hers.

Dinah lay back down beside Limhi, his strong arm cradling her head. "As much as I love being here beside you, I need to tend to my morning duties." She tugged the soft woven blanket off her slender frame and stretched her feet toward the cold baked clay floor. Before her toes met the rough tiles a slow, dark form caught her attention and she beheld the largest spider she had ever seen. She jerked her feet back on the bed and drew them up to her chest. "Limhi," she whispered. "Can you make that wolf spider and her babies go away?"

Limhi slowly slid out of bed and crept around to where the palm-sized spider moved silently, stealthily across the floor. Her back was covered thick with babies and appeared to be a pile of fur in motion. He stooped over and picked up a twig from the fire pile and then walked over to where the giant spider had paused for a moment. Limhi pulled the tapestry door back and tapped behind the spider.

The spider picked up the hint and moved her legs quickly toward the morning light, moving faster with each tap from Limhi's stick behind her.

As she exited their quarters, Dinah sighed. "I don't think I'll ever get used to sharing space with so many of God's creations. I'd prefer a fewer number, personally." Her tiny feet slid to the floor again, and she scanned the area before walking over to put on her sandals, outer dress, and shawl. "I'll be back soon." She gave Limhi a quick kiss. "Thank you for taking care of me." Then she slipped out into the cool morning.

∾

TAMAR WAS ALREADY UP and working in her herb garden. "Good morning!" Dinah cried as she ran to her. Tamar rose and spread her arms out wide to embrace her daughter-in-law — the new queen.

"What a joy to see you this morning!" She took the young bride into her arms. "What will your first day as queen be like?"

Dinah's joy seemed to wane slightly. "I don't know. Is there something in particular I *should* be doing?"

Tamar smiled gently. "Let's start by taking a walk, and we can talk. Have you had breakfast yet?"

"No, I will buy some fruit from one of the shops."

They pulled woven cloth shawls over their heads and left the old palace courtyard with its relative privacy, and made their way toward the old Temple where a crowd gathered around Gideon and Helam.

Gideon's voice rose above the murmuring, "...each family must have arms and be prepared to defend their families against the Lamanites." His face flushed with emotion.

Helam clearly disagreed. "When we are righteous, like Alma taught, the Lord will bless us."

"He doesn't expect us to not defend ourselves, though. What if the Lamanites break their oath of peace? What then? Will we be slaves now and slaughtered later?"

Many in the crowd commented at once, and the overall tone became louder, the people uneasy.

Limhi slipped up behind Tamar and Dinah. He placed one hand on each of their shoulders. Both turned and smiled uneasily. He moved to stand beside Dinah.

"We will establish a peaceful society."

His voice, though coming from the back of the crowd, was easily recognizable as their king. He slipped his hand from Dinah's shoulder and grasped her hand, drawing her through the crowd with him.

People parted to let them come to the center of the disagreement where Helam and Gideon had come face to face. "We are a captive people now, but we have the freedom to worship the true and living God. That is a miracle and a blessing. We will trust in the Lord and do

3

our best to follow what Alma taught." Tamar had also slipped through the crowd and come to the center with Limhi and Dinah.

More citizens joined the crowd and it swelled to several dozen people. "Not all are believers," one person added. "What about them?"

"The rain falls and waters our crops, those of the Lamanites, and all who are here, whether they believe in God or not." Limhi's face took on a serious look. "Noah's wives, their children — all who were part of Noah's wicked life will be treated as children of God." He turned and scanned the crowd. "We must decide, each in their own hearts, to have peace and unity. No divisions and classes. We must all work together in this new life of captivity if we are to survive."

Many nodded.

Limhi's voice became a whisper as if he was thinking out loud. "The Lamanites have not taken our arms hidden beneath the burial mound — if we must defend ourselves, we can."

Limhi stepped away from Dinah and up to where Gideon and Helam stood. He moved to stand between them and clapped both men on the shoulders. "These are both great men. We are blessed to have them here among us." He pulled them close.

"Helam was first to be baptized by Alma. My heart is heavy that I was not also able to be baptized, but know that in the Lord's time, someone with authority will be sent to our people once again. My soul longs for that day." He pressed his hand over his heart. We have the words of Abinadi that Alma wrote. We are not without hope."

Limhi continued, "Helam has been ordained a teacher. We will gather on the Sabbath to hear him read from the scrolls." Limhi nodded to Helam as a signal to speak.

"Alma taught us to bear one another's burdens that they may be light. Many of our women, even the women and children of King Noah, are without support. We must care for them in love and minister to their needs as Christ would do. It matters not if they belong to the Church of Christ."

Tamar put her arm around Dinah and whispered to her, "I was baptized also at the Waters of Mormon. One day, you will have your chance. Wait on the Lord with Limhi and be faithful."

A cry came from someone near the back of the group as several Lamanites made their way through the city street. Limhi moved quickly to the back of the crowd to stand between the people and the approaching soldiers. Any Nephites who had emerged from their homes quickly retreated back into the relative safety of their cottages.

The remnants of their recent battle still stained the dirt and rocks in the city streets, in spite of the women's efforts to erase the evidence and the painful reminders. Children cried out in fear, the memories of seeing their family members cut down by the Lamanites' swords still fresh in their minds. Fear hung thick in the air as the tensions sparked again.

The soldiers scanned the area side to side, warily approaching the crowd with spears at the ready. They moved closer to the group gathered at the temple. Limhi stood boldly, unarmed, arms raised as they approached. Dinah slipped up to stand beside him. Tamar and Helam stood on either side of the king and queen.

"We are unarmed," Limhi said to the leading soldier.

Silence fell over the group. Soldiers with weapons drawn moved first to the rear where Limhi stood, then moved in front and behind them as they surrounded the Nephite gathering.

"Our king sends a message to you, the new king of Shilom." The head Lamanite soldier's voice rose with each phrase till he was shouting. "You are our captives. You may worship as you please. You may hunt beasts in the forest just beyond your city but no further. If you cross the river, we will find you, and kill you." His steel gaze burned hot with anger. "Your king Noah is dead. We saw the evidence of his death. We seek the priests who defiled our women for so many years." He spat on the ground. "They, too, must die."

There rose a gasp from a number of people.

Limhi lifted his hand as a sign of calm. "Can they repair their wrongs?"

Gideon then spoke in a harsh voice, "God may forgive, but their sins are great. They ran like cowards. I don't see them ever wishing to change their ways."

"All who repent must be forgiven." Limhi chided him in a hoarse whisper that only he, and those standing nearby, could hear.

The Lamanite soldier raised his spear. "If we catch them, they will die. If they come to you to hide, and we find them, you all die. It's your choice." He then pointed toward a home at each end of the city. "My soldiers will live in those huts. You will give them half of your grain, your meat, your cloth, and everything they need to live. They will guard you and make sure you don't escape like the others did."

"Did you see them leave?" Limhi questioned.

"We watched them for some time. We know the direction they traveled but, when they took to the river, we no longer saw them." Then with a hard look, he warned, "You will not go on the river. You are our slaves. You will stay."

LIMHI WALKED with Dinah through the city toward the burial mound and potter's shed. They passed by the shop that, for so many years, Mera, his grandmother, and Tamar, his mother, had created beautiful works of pottery. It sat mostly empty, except for a few apprentices that had come to clean it up after the battle.

"The Lamanite soldiers are coming with their families today. We need to find a place for those who must move from their homes."

"We will rebuild," Dinah said with confidence. "Should we keep the city name, Shilom, or change it back to Lehi-Nephi?"

"We are Nephites, but it matters not what the name is now. It's just our home."

They approached the last hut at the edge of the city where children were placing things in baskets and on woven rugs. A woman, Judith, stepped out to greet them. "Where will we go?" Her eyes were weary. "My husband is dead, my oldest son, dead, and I alone am caring for my family." Her chin quivered.

Dinah put her arms around her. "Will you come and live in the old palace with us?" She smiled. "We have room for you there."

Judith's tears spilled forth, accompanied by halting sobs. "The palace? You'd give us a room at the palace?" she said with disbelief.

"If you don't mind sharing that wing with the other family that has to move for the Lamanite soldiers. We are happy to let you live there."

"Children," Judith said with renewed energy, "we will live by King Limhi and Queen Dinah!"

The children now moved with new excitement. "Can we go to the palace now?"

Tamar, who had moved up behind Limhi and Dinah, stepped into the small hut. "What can I carry?"

A neighbor, who had been nearby tending to her small garden, stepped over. "Judith, I'd love to help with the move."

"Thank you," Judith embraced her friend. "Can you walk with my children and carry the blankets and skins while they carry their baskets?"

Tamar and the neighbor woman stepped inside the hut and emerged with a stack of items each, children carrying baskets following after them. One child's face was hidden completely. "Be careful walking like that. You can't see, can you?" Tamar asked the little girl.

"If I watch your feet, I will follow where you walk." The child's eyes peered out from behind the basket. "I can trust you to lead me."

Dinah's throat, tight with emotion, kept her from speaking. She just nodded. She reached out to grasp Limhi's hand, squeezed it, then smiled. "We will weather this storm together."

Not long after the invitation was extended, Limhi, Dinah, Judith, Tamar, and other neighbors and children were all walking side by side in a long line leading to the palace. Baskets, blankets, and pottery filled with grains and corn were carefully transported to their new rooms in the old palace. Within a short time, the emptied home was ready for its new occupants: the Lamanite guard and his family.

"Shall we go help the other family move now?" Judith asked.

Dinah smiled. "What a great idea. Let's go see."

Leading the growing crowd of people, Tamar moved to the far end of town to the small hut tucked in the trees at the end of the road.

There didn't appear to be activity at all. Tamar stepped up to the door and pulled the tapestry to the side with a greeting.

A woman, with her children napping on some skins on the floor, sat with her head in her hands, her body slack. Tamar and Dinah stepped in. The woman slowly looked up at them. Hopelessness was etched on her young face. Everyone else waited outside.

With a weak whisper, the tiny woman sputtered between sobs. "I'm despised in society. Now I will have no home. What am I to do?"

Dinah's tears returned as she whispered, "I understand."

"How could you possibly understand the shame of being one of the wives of Noah's priests; of being abandoned, left behind to be killed by the Lamanites? He just left us!"

Now the tears came in force. "He left us... and now I have nowhere to go with my children." Her last words came out as a whisper. "They're so young -- and don't know why they don't have a father anymore. I can't say he's dead, like other women. I can't say he fought boldly to save them." A new wrinkle formed between her brows. "He ran away. I am ashamed and will become an outcast." Her shoulders rose and fell as sobs wrenched her frame.

Dinah sat on the dirty, baked clay floor and wrapped her arms around her. "You're now part of our family. Please come live at the palace. We will help care for you and your children."

"Why would you do that for me?" She whispered as tears streaked down her dirt-stained cheeks.

"I told you, I understand." Dinah took a deep breath, her mind flying back through the years spent as one of Noah's concubines and her narrow escape from being taken as one of his wives. "I was in the palace too."

The woman turned her face, squinting at Dinah. "You were? And now you're the queen?"

"Yes."

She reached out a shaking hand. Dinah stood and helped the woman stand, wrapping her arms around the young woman's shaking frame.

"Thank you."

Tamar also reached out a hand and steadied her. "You'll be welcomed in the old palace, with our family."

Dinah took her outside to where the crowd of people waited. "Can a couple of you strong men carry the sleeping children to their new home? As for the rest of us, let's do this one more time." She hugged the disbelieving woman as the crowd began picking up pottery, blankets, dishes, clothing and bedding. Before long, the move was complete, both families sharing a space in the old palace with new neighbors — the ruling family of Shilom.

LISHA, 145 BC, JOURNEYING

The sounds of animals rose around Lisha—the clatter of sheep's hooves, the mewling of kittens in a basket, and the braying of donkeys heavy with blankets and food. Lisha gripped young Alma's hand, lest her son trip over loose stones and scrape his knees yet again. After eight days of fleeing through the wilderness, he had far too many bumps and bruises. But this was the only way to escape the king's wrath.

Lisha had never felt more proud of her husband, Alma the Elder, when he challenged King Noah, pleading for the life of the prophet Abinadi. Nor had she felt more terrified. In the chaotic months that followed, her husband went into hiding. They'd spread Abinadi's words in secret. Now the Lord had warned them to flee. This was a life she'd never expected, fleeing her childhood home with four hundred refugees, including Mera, the king's mother. Lisha glimpsed her up ahead, clinging to the arm of her new husband, the master weaver. Mera was too old to be hacking through the thick woods, starting a new life in a strange place.

With new life growing inside her again, Lisha shouldn't either. She paused for a moment to catch her breath, leaning against a crooked tree while young Alma poked at its roots. At least she wasn't sick so often anymore. But how was she to manage hiking through the wild, sleeping in tents, and caring for her active son when she felt so, so tired? If it weren't for King Noah, they could go back, reclaim their homes and live in Shilom in peace.

A firm hand gripped Lisha's shoulder. She looked up into the broad, open face of her husband and smiled. "Not much longer," he said. He brushed her cheek with a kiss. "We're far enough from Shilom that Noah's men will never find us."

Lisha nodded, though she couldn't claim quite the same surety Alma felt. She was always glancing over her shoulder or peering into the woods at night, vigilant for intruders. Murderers. That's what Noah and his men were, bent on satisfying their own passions, no matter whom or what they destroyed in the process. "You'll send out scouts, won't you? To make sure we haven't been followed? And to see when it's safe to return? You made that map. We'll have no problem—"

"Lisha, as long as Noah's alive, he'll hunt me. We can never go back."

"He'll die someday," Lisha said. "If Abinadi's prophecies come true, it's only a matter of time."

"Lisha."

"What?" She frowned, mentally chiding herself for the hateful sentiment, and resumed walking.

A shadow crossed Alma's face. "You're angry with me?"

"How could I be? You've led us to safety." She tugged their son's arm, helping him skirt a bramble. "Well, almost." Alma crunched through the thick underbrush without seeming to notice, his gaze unfocused. Lisha wondered if he was staring into the future or the past. His mind always drifted to one or the other. Never the present. At least, not often enough to satisfy her. His hand closed around her wrist and he nodded toward the woods. "Hold up," he breathed.

Lisha tensed, her heart thumping. "Noah's men?" she whispered. "Or Lamanites?" She peered through the thick, pungent cedars. Her legs felt shaky but she could still run, and, if it came to it, fight. She kept a tight grip on young Alma.

"Steady, Lisha," her husband said, still holding her arm.

A tangle of vines rustled, and Jesu, the baker, jostled through.

Alma relaxed. "No sign of pursuit?"

"Nothing," Jesu said, nodding gravely. "Not for days."

"Good work," Alma said.

As Jesu jogged off to rejoin his family, Lisha felt her shoulders loosen.

Nearby, a man called Samuel herded sheep and goats along the trail with the help of ten or twelve young men, all fairly scratched and worn. Some of the caravans started humming a familiar song—softly —but loud enough to warm hearts and swell courage. It reminded Lisha of the lilting music once used as the signal for the call to gather to hear the words of the Lord. Yoseph's daughter, Hannah, walked nearby, her light brown braids swaying. She was middle-aged, almost a decade older than Lisha and one of her close friends.

Lisha returned her half smile, then looked around again. She didn't see anyone who shouldn't be there, but Alma still stared into the woods. Maybe he saw something she didn't. He was a prophet, after all. Before she could ask, he spoke.

"I haven't always been a good man, Lisha," Alma said. His fingers tightened on her arm, but his gaze remained distant.

At first, Lisha felt relief; Alma hadn't spotted warriors in the woods. But as she studied him, she wondered if maybe he'd sensed a different sort of danger. His face bore signs of strain, deep grooves she rarely saw in other men under thirty. "You've changed, Alma. You're a different man from who you were when, back when..." She didn't want to say it.

"When I was a priest of Noah? When I shared his...ways?"

Lisha felt her whole body flush. Alma never spoke of these things. He'd repented. He'd changed. "Why now, Alma? Why think of this now?"

He cradled her hand in his. "I taught the people in Shilom. But I was forced to hide while everyone else lived their lives. Now they look to me to be their leader. This morning, Daren asked my advice on how to make peace with his wife. Apparently, he'd complained when she burned their evening meal."

Lisha laughed.

"Sarika asked for my help loading her donkey after her rope broke," Alma continued. "It's a lot for her to manage, traveling through the wilderness with a small child and no husband."

Sarika had been one of Noah's women. One of the few who'd fled with the believers, claiming she believed, too, that she'd had no choice but to live the way Noah and his wicked priests demanded. Even if that were true.... Lisha took a deep breath, trying to redirect her thoughts. For years, her time with Alma had been brief and in secret. They'd not wasted their precious moments on arguments, remorse, and accusations. But sometimes, she felt the weight of unsaid words and how they could divide their marriage.

"How can I lead all these people when I'm no better than they are?" Alma's voice remained low, compelling as always.

Lisha shook her head, forcing her uncomfortable thoughts away. "Abinadi taught of the atonement. He taught us to repent, and that forgiveness is real. I don't think that applies to everyone except you."

Alma squeezed her hand and nodded.

"Daddy?" Young Alma piped up, raising his arms. "Hold you?"

Alma leaned down and scooped up their small son, slinging him onto his shoulders. "I'm supposed to be their leader."

"Even leaders aren't perfect," Lisha murmured.

Alma nodded again, deep in thought as they pressed their way forward. "When we find our new home, I won't live as King Noah did. I won't live a wild life. Nor will I have the people labor while I live a life of ease."

"You're nothing like him," Lisha shook her head.

A voice called out from up ahead, "There's a valley down below. It could be a place for us. We need you, Alma."

Alma blinked and raised his head. "I'd better go see." He slipped Young Alma off his shoulders, transferring him to Lisha, who slung the child onto her hip.

She felt a confusing mix of emotions as she watched him hike away, the lowering sun streaming over his shoulders. She shifted Young Alma and pressed forward, ignoring a persistent ache in her back. The climb up the hill was arduous, and her small son was too tired to continue on his own. By the time she reached the zenith, most of the group had already descended to the other side. She saw Mera making her way down the hill, her face alight.

Lisha breathed a sigh of relief. A beautiful scene stretched as far as she could see, rich fields woven with crystal streams and thick groves of trees. She marked it off in her mind. The main clearing, large enough to be visible from the hilltop, would make an ideal gathering place for evening songs, shared meals, and worship. The forest shielding the clearing might need to be pushed back a bit to make room for tents and thatched homes, but it would provide shelter from storms. The scrubby grasslands would become pasture. And the farmlands—Lisha scanned the valley—there were several options to consider there. This would be a good place to call home, at least until they could return to Shilom.

Down below, a few families spread out and started unloading deerskin tents and supplies. Most massed around a central figure, asking questions, seeking guidance.

Lisha sighed again. Bleating sheep streamed around her, led forward by Samuel and herded from behind by the gaggle of tired boys. Young Alma lifted his head from her weary shoulder and leaned down to run his fingers through their soft wool. They snagged in a tangle. He cried out and yanked his hand away from the heaving, curling masses flowing by.

Lisha took her son's hand and carefully looked it over. The skin was red and swollen but did not appear to be broken. She pressed a kiss to his fingers. "All better."

He turned a tear-stained face up to his mother. "I want Daddy."

Lisha nodded, sweeping a stray lock of hair out of his eyes. "So do I, sweetheart. So do I."

WATER DRIPPED down Lisha's face. She brushed it aside, wiping her face with the sleeve of her rough woven blouse. It didn't help much.

She was soaked through. All she wanted was to huddle in her tent next to her miniscule fire. Even the wayward smoke that didn't quite make it through the escape holes in the top wouldn't bother her now. But no.

Instead, she was out under the heavy, storm-strewn skies, trying to pound a loosened stake into the ground with a broken mallet. The sharp handle slipped in her grasp, slicing her palm. She threw the useless tool aside, tore a strip off the cleanest edge of her skirt and wound it around her hand. The side of her tent had caved inward, the guy rope fluttering uselessly in the stiff wind. Overhead, tree branches creaked and swayed, not providing near as much shelter as Lisha had hoped.

A thin voice wailed.

"It's alright, son," Lisha called. "Stay on the side near the door flap, where I showed you. I'll have this fixed in a moment." She gritted her teeth. Where was her husband when she needed him? If she had a blossom for all the times she'd thought that in the past few weeks, she'd have enough to open her own flower shop, not that she had a building. No one in the village did, if it could even be called a village, more like a camp, a pitiful camp full of sick, tired fugitives. She shook her head. No point in dwelling on things she couldn't control when her home was about to collapse. She searched around, kicking aside tall grass and fallen branches. There had to be something here that would work.

Inside, Young Alma whimpered again.

Lisha's leather-wrapped foot hit something hard. "Ouch!" She reached down to rub her toe then looked to see what she'd kicked. It was a flecked gray stone, smooth and round, half a size larger than her fist. Perfect. She dislodged it from the soil, picked it up, and slogged back through the mud to grab the end of her limp tent string. As she pulled it tight, the deerskin stretched taut. The long poles slipped into the proper position. Lisha shoved the wooden stake into the firmest patch of earth she could find and then pounded with the rock. It was slow going, despite the soft ground. She pounded again. The stake skittered sideways, scraping aside the topsoil, revealing an unyielding slab of dark stone.

Lisha groaned. Then she lost her temper. She banged her rock against the slate. Sharp pieces ricocheted back at her, leaving tiny cuts on her arms and face. She stopped. This was pointless. Pointless. She was alone, her home falling apart, her body tired, her spirit spent. She sank to her knees. "Lord, I need your help. You promised you'd take care of us!"

This wasn't exactly what Alma had said when the Lord warned them to flee but surely this is what he meant. She turned her face to the heavens. *Rain may pour and I may bleed. But I will* not *give up.* A deep warmth bubbled up within her. *The Lord is with me—I am* not *alone.*

With renewed determination, she picked up the tent stake and sought a new spot to secure it. She stretched the leather rope to the right and scraped at the earth. Did the slab extend this far? Would the soil be too soft to secure the stake? The tent wobbled as she pulled then settled in its new position. Lisha took a deep breath and hammered. With each strike, she felt the stake slide deeper into the mud. It ground along the edge of the unyielding slab, which provided enough extra stability that, this time, the stake stayed. Lisha gave it a sharp tug when she'd finished, to see if it would hold up against stronger winds, but, even then, the stake did not move.

She dropped her makeshift mallet, wiped her hands on her muddy skirts, and trudged back inside to console Young Alma and build up their feeble fire. When she opened the flap, she found him curled up on a dry buffalo fur, his thumb in his mouth, and his eyelids fluttering in his sleep. She tucked another, thinner fur over him for added warmth. She then changed out of her filthy clothes and into a warm, homespun sleeping gown. She hung her wet things on a rack made from branches and sheep gut. Then she built up the fire, adding sticks and small logs from the pile she'd stacked inside before the storms came.

Once she finished, she ladled water from her small barrel into a clay pot. She added dried onions and spices from a jar, along with strips of dried meat, a couple of shriveled potatoes, and a handful of grain. She took a measure of dried corn, ground it into a meal in a little stone bowl, and mixed it with water and a pinch of crushed rock salt before spreading the thick mixture on a stone by the hearth.

While dinner cooked, Lisha settled onto a rough chair Alma had made from a tree stump and a taller stump he'd split. Nicer furniture would come later. She rested for a moment, her wounded hand cradling the soft rise of her rounded belly.

A reed basket rested against the foot of her chair. After a while, Lisha reached into it and withdrew a ball of wool. She shook off a few specks of ash, then spread the wool over a wooden card with metal prongs. She drew a second card across it, aligning the fibers. She kept working until the wool fibers all faced the same direction. Then, taking care not to disrupt their perfect symmetry, she teased the wool from the card and placed it onto a stack for spinning. Once that task was complete, she'd take the thread to Mera—once she had a real home—where her husband would dye it and weave it into cloth.

Lisha's arms ached from the day's work. The tiny cuts freckling her arms didn't help. But she remained focused, gathering the wool, spreading it on the brush, carding it until it was just right.

On the pallet near the door flap, Young Alma stirred in his sleep, rolling over and tugging the furs to his chin. Lisha studied him for a moment as she stretched a new piece of wool across her brush. She saw so much of his father in him, in the high planes of his cheekbones and the dark curls at the nape of his neck. She wondered if Mera had seen Noah's father in him, too. The thought gave Lisha a pang of sadness. What heartache Mera had endured at the hands of her wayward son. What cruelties she'd witnessed. It had torn her family apart, resulting in the death of Abinadi. How had she borne it? How had the Lord succored her grief?

The door flap rustled, and Alma stepped inside, water streaming down his sheepskin coat. With a tender glance at their sleeping son, he walked past Lisha to warm himself by the fire, pausing to drop a kiss on her head. He peered at the bubbling stew. "Smells wonderful. I'm famished." He cast her a fond smile. "It's nice to be home." He rubbed his hands together and then spread them over the crackling fire. Lisha had managed to keep it going even when the storm almost blew the tent down.

She started to tell him all about it, but he spoke first.

"Everything's coming together," he said. "The tents are up. We've chosen the gathering place."

"Yes, by that bend in the stream."

"Exactly. Most families have chosen where to build homes. Several widows and single women are building close to one another or are sharing homes for extra support." He waved his right hand. "They'll need help with building, of course, but that won't be a problem. Malachias wanted to locate his forge right by the main river because he likes the view, but Sarika was concerned the runoff might foul the water, so washing won't come clean." Alma ran his fingers through his damp hair. "It got a little heated, but Sarika was in the right. I helped Malachias see that. He's agreed to build the smithy on the southwest side of the village now, not far from the river. He can tote buckets in to cool his hot metals." He beamed at Lisha.

She offered a tired smile in return.

"Were you about to tell me something?"

Suddenly Lisha felt insignificant as if her work were invisible. It would only be noticed if she left it undone. Alma hadn't seen her grand battle defending their home against the storm. He didn't see her cut hand or the blood flecking her arms. "It was nothing," she said, not quite sure why she was keeping this to herself, except she felt vulnerable somehow, and not just because she feared Noah and his men would find them. This need was different, a primal urge to safeguard what was hers. She wondered how Alma fit into that. Sometimes he seemed so far away.

CHANNAH, 145 BC, CITY OF SHEMLON

The corn stalks stood well over her head, with dry husks crackling in the breeze. Channah weaved through the fronds, peeking through each row, searching for her mother. She had seen her well before entering the field, but now all the dark heads looked the same.

"Mother, Mother!" Channah called from across the field of corn. Several heads turned. The spent stalks cracked and snapped as she crossed row after row. A few scolding voices called out, telling her to be careful. Being in the midst of the field was so disconcerting. Channah had never been good with directions and always seemed to get lost. "Mata!" She called louder than before. The queen, Mata, was gathering dry ears of corn and turned as she heard her name.

Worried, Mata called back. "What is it?"

With a huge smile, Channah parted the last few rows separating her and her mother and ran to her arms. "I can go with you to the lake!"

"Wonderful!" She picked up her daughter and spun her around, her long braids flopped against her round cheeks. Every stalk of corn near her feet got knocked down in the wake of her happy spin. "I'm so happy for you!" She took her daughter's face in her hands and kissed her forehead. "My princess."

Channah wrapped her arms around her mother's shoulders and kissed her cheek. "Can I wear the new dress you've been working on?"

Feigning surprise, Mata responded with a mock frown. "You aren't supposed to know about the dress."

Channah dropped her eyes. "I watched you working when I was sleeping."

"Then you weren't sleeping."

"No, mother, I wasn't."

"Maybe it's for Isa."

"No, it can't be! I became a woman first. She doesn't need one yet."

"She doesn't have a mother to make one, so maybe I will wait and give it to her."

"What about my dress? What will I wear?" Channa's eyes began to fill with tears.

"My princess, it is for you. Next time, though, when it's time to be asleep, you better do just that." She hugged her daughter again. "Now go find Isa and tell her to bring her father and come eat dinner with us to celebrate. I must finish gathering corn or we won't have much for our dinner."

Channah turned and started running toward the end of a row, stopped, looked at the trees at each end, then sheepishly went the other way, passing her mother as she went.

Mata shook her head, "yes, the village is that way."

Channah was careful to run straight down a row before leaving the field. Women nodded their approval as she passed, some clicking their tongues as a cautionary warning to not damage any of the crops yet to be harvested. She burst out of the field at full speed and followed the well-worn path back to the city of Shemlon.

Smoke curled slowly from the huts and hung in the still air of the protected valley. Channah scanned the faces as she ran through the city, looking for her dearest friend. Children played catch with spent corn cobs as chickens scratched in the dirt. Large brown hens scurried out of her way as she ran, flapping their wings as they hovered just above the ground for a moment, irritated at being interrupted. Dust filled the air as their wings fluttered, accompanied by loud clucking cries. Channah passed through it, determined to find Isa as quickly as possible.

A crowd had gathered in the middle of town, blocking her way.

Channah skirted the mass of people, dodging back and forth, searching for Isa. After making it all the way around the group, she saw her mother coming in from the fields and ran to her.

"What's all the commotion about?" Channah asked her mother as they walked past the row of huts leading to the city center.

"I think some soldier families are moving to the Nephite city."

"Why?"

With disgust, Mata replied. "To guard them and keep them from leaving."

"I pity them. I wouldn't want to live with Nephites."

"I'm glad you don't have to, but be kind to those that are leaving. I'm sure they don't want to go."

Channah nodded, "Will we see them again, or do they have to stay forever?"

"Maybe someday we can make the Nephites leave, and we won't have war with them anymore." She blew out her breath. "They should go back to where they came from and leave our lands."

"Why are we guarding them and holding them captive? Just let them leave!" the young princess asked.

The queen shook her head. "I'm going to ask your father."

Upon entering the village center, the log structure that sat at the heart of the Lamanite city was churning with people. Some coming, others leaving! One angry exchange took place away from the main group as Channah and her mother passed by.

"I don't care if they will pay us well. I don't want to go."

"The king promised to make me captain of fifty if we would guard the Nephites."

"They aren't my people. I don't want to live in their city."

"Our children are young; they won't know the difference."

"Of course, they will know. The Nephites are pale and strange.

And look at us." She held out her arm. "They'll hate us because of our dark skin."

"They are our slaves." The Lamanite soldier beat on his chest as he spat the words. "We are their masters." Raising his fist high above his head, he repeated, "WE are masters." Then with a touch of softness, he added, "Bring your mother or your sister. What else do you want?"

His wife clutched the rough woven fabric covering her chest and cried, "I want to stay here in Shemlon."

"You can come and visit. You can meet up with them when the women go to dance at the high lake. Will that help?" Wrinkles appeared above his worried eyes.

Mata stopped beside the couple. "Can I speak with your wife for a moment?"

The frustrated soldier threw up his hands, nodded and stepped back.

Mata gently put her arm around the tearful woman's shoulders. "Channah will be going to the lake for the first time this moon. There will be an especially large group of us since it's the king's daughter's first." Mata beamed with pride as she reached out to pull her daughter closer. Channah smiled.

"Come celebrate with me and the rest of our women. Come every moon to be with us. We will all be one."

The woman smiled weakly. "That would be nice." She nodded and continued, "At least it would give me some time to sing and dance and be with my people."

She turned to her husband. "I'll go, but you must keep your promise."

He nodded his head vigorously. "Let's tell the king."

Mata and Channah followed the young family to where the king stood, surrounded by soldiers. They parted to allow them all to enter the circle.

The soldier put his hand on his wife's shoulder and stated loudly so all could hear. "We will go to the Nephite City to guard them as our slaves. We will serve our king and our people and honor our ancestors by standing up to the oppression of the Nephites who have long sought for power over us and stolen our right to lead."

A loud cheer erupted with fists pointing toward the heavens. "We will walk with you to the borders of our land." The king announced. He, Mata, and Channah led the way back to the huts of the soldiers who would be moving to Shiloh. Each carried something as a token of their support for the soldiers and their families.

THE MOVE to the City of Shilom didn't take long. Each Lamanite in the throng did something to help. Even the children herded chickens, doing their best to keep them from running back to their familiar roosts. Luring them with crushed corn strewn along the path, they kept them moving toward their new home.

The procession ended at the catacomb. Many hands, carrying the goods for their Lamanite brothers, placed them at the beginning of what was termed the "pathway of death". Then they backed away, warily. The Nephites had built a serpentine pathway at the north end of the city between Shemlon and Shilom. It was the only way in, aside from a steep climb over the mountain, or a vulnerable trip down the river, which cut through the Nephite city. Any entrance into the city was treacherous. The Lamanite soldiers to be stationed in Shilom placed packs on the backs of their wives and children and kept their bows knocked, ready for the attack as they entered the pathway leading to the Nephite city.

The king and queen, and their only daughter, Channah, watched them disappear. "When will we see them again?" Channah asked.

"Soon. They will come with us to the high lake." With fists clenched, Mata added, "And they can return to the city when we drive the Nephites out of our land. Why do we make them stay?" she questioned the king.

Darkness spread across his face. "To maintain the city, provide food for our people, and build our nation with slave labor. There is much work to do and the Nephites are skilled and hard working.

Shilom is a growing city and we will take it over and let the Nephites build another city for us. Our power will grow as long as we keep the Nephites as our slaves. We must endure it." The king spat on the ground. "If I never see another Nephite as long as I live, I will consider myself blessed." He hissed. "Noah ruined many of our people, spoiled our women." He ground the spittle into the dust. "We will crush them if they rebel."

"Have your scouts seen any sign of the men of Noah that escaped?" Mata asked.

"They steal for their food. We see their fires, but then they move." He sneered. "They hide like jackals and filthy cowards." He straightened his cloak. "We will find them and slay them."

Channah shuddered. All her life, she had been taught about the evil fair-skinned traitors who stole the right to rule from her ancestors. "They can't take anything else from us, can they?"

"No. What is ours is ours."

"How will the soldiers live?" Mata asked.

"We will take half of everything the Nephites produce. The soldiers won't have to do anything but guard the people and collect the tribute."

All three nodded in agreement to the King's insightful arrangement.

THE NIGHT of the full moon arrived and the men took their women to spend a week at the high lake. Donkeys, with food and tents, carried their burdens happily to the lush resort in the mountains. They knew the grass would be green and thick, the water clean and pure, and the days would be spent in the shade of trees surrounding the lake. They knew the way and walked briskly along the well-worn path.

The long procession of women and girls, who joyfully joined their ranks because their time of maturity had come, were together to celebrate. The tinkling of cymbals and instruments of music accompanied their walk. The youngest girls ran up and down the trail, chattering with excitement, unable to contain their glee at finally being able to travel to the lake with the rest of their women.

"How are you feeling?" Mata asked Channah.

"I feel good. Mostly good." Channah responded.

Mata took some herbs from a pouch she had tied around her waist. "Chew on this as we walk. It'll help with cramps."

Channah took the piece of root her mother offered and began sucking and chewing on it. "It's hot!" she exclaimed, breathing quickly in and out.

"Suck and chew lightly." Her mother offered.

When Channah had consumed the root, and gone a while up the trail, she paused for a drink from the skin pouch her father had given her for the journey. "It does feel better, thanks, mother."

"Try this next." She took some dry seeds from another pouch. "They are sweet."

Channah again chewed and enjoyed the strong flavors. All the while, the discomfort decreased as they walked.

"Will I get to dance this month Mother?" Channah asked.

"Watch the other women and girls. I'll let you stay after I go home, and you can learn the dance from them. Come back home with them when you've learned it and you can dance next month."

"I can't wait!" Channah said enthusiastically as she ran ahead to talk with some of her friends.

The group arrived well after sundown, with the full moon high in the sky. They set up their tents and went to bed for the night.

The next morning was foggy and raining. The mist hid the far bank and made the mountains disappear. Fires were small and smoky since the wood was wet. Channah shuddered as rain began to fall again. The women stayed mostly in their tents and waited out the rain. It continued through another day, but, toward the end of the afternoon, the sky cleared and the blue skies returned.

One after another, tent flaps opened and girls emerged carrying their flutes, drums, and cymbals. They all wore new dresses made for the occasion and the women were dressed in their finest. The shoreline was quickly crowded as everyone made their way to the water's edge for the celebration. After the singing and dancing had ended, the ritual cleansing began. All dresses were set aside and the women bathed in the lake. From head to toe, they scrubbed and cleansed. When they were finished, each put on new dresses.

"I see now why all of the men were so happy to see you all come home." Channah mused. "Everyone smells so clean and beautiful."

"You are beautiful," Mata added. "I'm so happy for you, my only daughter." She teared up, "I wish I had a dozen just like you, but truly the Gods have given me the finest one as my own." She took Channah in her arms and held her for a long time. "Are you sure it's ok for me to stay?" Channah asked her mother.

"I'll be waiting for your return tomorrow. I'll wait by the city wall. Just sing for me as you near the city, so I will know you are coming."

Channah gave her mother a quick hug. "I'll learn the dances perfectly, and you'll be so proud of me!"

The main group of women, clean, rejuvenated, and renewed, returned to the city of Shemlon, leaving 24 of their daughters to have one more night of singing and dancing. Channah watched her mother, waving until she could see her no more. Then she returned to the lake's edge where some of the older girls were sitting on large stones along the bank. Some had small drums; others had cymbals. Some made sounds with wooden sticks and hollowed-out logs. It was wonderful.

The drums beat; the rhythmic clicking and tinkling filled the air. Channah danced and danced until her moccasins could no longer disguise the fact that the stones were sharp and her feet were getting bruised.

She sat down along the edge of the forest and took her moccasins off. She lay back on the soft grass and closed her eyes, taking in the sweet smell of the mountain air. Night was approaching. The donkeys grazed lazily on the green shoots of grass. She sighed and looked at the puffy cloud shapes taking on the deep pink colors of sunset.

Channah wrinkled her nose as a pungent scent filled the air. She sat up. A rough hand pressed across her nose and mouth, making it impossible to breathe or scream. A strong arm roughly whisked her up off the ground and she found herself slung over a man's shoulder, still unable to breathe. She bit his hand. He cried out. She screamed. The normally peaceful quiet lake had become a place of terror. Shouts. Cries. Grunts of pain.

Her next recollection, in the increasing darkness, was that of being carried through the trees, mile after mile until her poor back could take it no more. She wept. She begged to be put down, until she realized her moccasins were back at the lake. When the blackness of night engulfed her upside-down world, and she gave in to her exhaustion, she found herself flopped down into some tall grass in a clearing. Dizzy as the blood returned to her head, and her eyes focused on objects in the moonlight, she saw shelters, rudimentary structures lining the open grassy clearing where she had been deposited. Men huddled in quiet conversation near the edge, joined by each one that emerged from the woods carrying their captives.

One by one she saw her friends carried, dragged, and marched into camp. She shuddered in revulsion. They were the white-skinned Nephites.

DINAH, 144 BC, CITY OF SHILOM

*D*inah felt the warmth leave her as the skin blankets shifted. Cool air chilled her legs. Limhi was standing near the door with his sword in hand. He had kept it beside their bed, as he had quietly advised the other men in the city to do. "So much for a promise of protection." He whispered in anger as his hand slipped over the cold metal sword that lay beside his bed.

"What is it?"

"Shh, listen."

They heard the sounds, muffled yelps.

"Laminates?" Dinah whispered.

"We have met their demands, obeyed their commands, submitted to their rule, and not fought back." Limhi blew out his breath as he stood by the open door of their home. "If they choose to attack us unprovoked, then we will defend ourselves."

Over the past months, as captives of the Lamanites, with guards posted at every exit of the city, they had adjusted. Dinah made sure every family had a place to grow food for their families, organized meaningful labor for each woman to do, and made sure each single mother had an older woman to teach her necessary skills. She was exhausted. Her days as queen had kept her extremely busy and, being with child, she was even more weary than ever.

Limhi walked from the door to where Dinah sat on a pile of skins. He reached over and took her face into his hands. He ran a hand over her smooth dark hair and gave her a kiss. "I love you. Your goodness takes my breath away. Thank you." He listened again. "Pray for us."

Dinah got up from her bed, wrapped a shawl around her shoulders, and stepped out into the courtyard. She could see shadows moving all throughout the city. Limhi wasn't the only one who had heard the Lamanite cries. Limhi stepped quickly through the gate, paused and glanced back. Then he was gone.

Other men were running toward the weapon depot. A tall dark silhouette of the Laminate soldier stood at the far end of the city where the old palace sat. With a spear in hand, he was poised to attack. Helam was fixed like a statue facing the catacomb, face to face with the Lamanite soldier armed with a sword.

Dinah cautiously made her way down to the city street from the elevated platform of their palace compound. She saw Gideon emerge from his home, armed, and Rachel's form filled the doorway, worry etched deep on her face. "Be careful, my son. You're all I have left." Gideon paused partway down the road, turned and placed his fist over his heart with a thump as it hit his armor. Then he trotted toward the tower.

Every male in the city, even those who were not believers, understood it was time for unity, not division. There were a few lined up at the burial mound to access the hidden cache of weapons. Some had not retrieved theirs, as Limhi had suggested the previous day.

Dinah held her breath as she heard Limhi's voice carry back down the city street where she stood.

"Men, we must fight like dragons or die."

The war cries of the Lamanites had grown louder. The all too familiar sound made her blood run cold. She shivered as the night chill made its way through her thin shawl. From the increasing volume, Dinah knew the soldiers were nearing the catacomb of death.

Again, Limhi's voice rang clear and strong. "Defend your homes, your wives, your children, and your city." The Nephites roared their reply. "For our Families!" Dinah watched as Gideon scaled the tower with a bow and a quiver of arrows slung over his back.

The armed Nephites ran toward the network of barriers they knew the Lamanites would have to pass through. Their voices filled the early morning air with encouragement to those who were in the front, for they would face the enemy first. Dina scanned the city until she spotted the two Lamanite guards. Both held back, poised for war but unwilling or afraid, to attack the Nephites from inside the city. She hurried back to her home, encouraging the women and children to stay inside. This battle could end up at their very doorsteps. She quickly dressed and returned to the temple mound, standing where she could see all that was happening.

Those who went first into the catacomb disappeared, and others hid behind trees and disguised themselves behind bundles of corn stalks, lying in wait. Gideon's silhouette in the emerging morning light showed he had nocked an arrow. As if a signal for battle, the morning sun cast its warm glow over the tops of the trees. In an instant, the first Lamanite spear glinted in the sun. Gideon shouted the warming. The battle had begun.

Dinah could hear them now. The crisp air filled with shouting and cursing. She envisioned them charging down the hill toward the Nephite city. A sick feeling crept into her gut.

The sounds of battle woke each person in Shilom, including the little ones. Their frightened cries mingled with the angry cries of Lamanite soldiers. Gideon let a few arrows fly from the tower before coming quickly down to aid his brothers in a hand-to-hand battle. Limhi's voice boomed above the melee as he shouted encouragement to those defending their city on the front lines.

The battle had started in the catacomb but now emerged into the city, and, one after another, the Lamanite soldiers fell. It seemed the more they lost, the angrier the rest became. Her stomach clenched in fear. "God help us all." Dinah choked out. She clenched her eyes as she whispered a silent prayer for the safety of her people and the protection of her husband.

Her stomach roiled in protest as anxiety and morning sickness churned inside of her. She struggled to keep her composure. Each strike she witnessed made her shudder in pain for those she knew well.

Some Lamanite blows hit the Nephites with such force it shattered their armor. Her hands trembled as she clenched her fists and balled them under her arms. "Please, Lord, protect us."

A finely dressed Lamanite with beaded adornments, fought with Gideon and fell. As he did so, a different cry came from the Lamanites and they began to retreat.

The sounds of metal against metal decreased while the volume of those mortally wounded increased — and then silence. A cry of victory from the voices she recognized. *Had they won, so quickly?*

Dinah stepped down from the temple steps as Tamar and other women cautiously emerged from their homes. Children, jolted from a troubled slumber, were unusually cranky. Mothers soothed their children as they slowly made their way toward the battle scene. Rachel stood outside of her home, clutching the tunic that had been worn by her deceased husband, Melek. Tears streaked her weathered face but she stood stoically awaiting news of her son.

Very few Lamanite bodies could be seen. Few had actually made it into the city. More of their bodies were dragged out of the catacomb entrance to allow the Nephite soldiers to get into the passageway leading to the outer wall of the city. They lay, unmoving, heaped up like a pile of discarded blankets. Dinah moved closer and saw the soldier dressed in finery, unlike the rest, with beads and jewels adorning his loincloth. His feet, shod with stitched, beautifully decorated moccasins lay still, unmoving. Her mind drifted off toward the Lamanite city as she gazed on the bloodied bodies of men who would not be going home. Their wives would weep, as she would, if Limhi went to battle and didn't return. Her heart broke for them.

"Why did they come up against us?" she said in a sad whisper.

"I will find out," a voice from behind her answered.

Limhi took his wife in his arms and held her tight. "I could not bear to see anything happen to you: not you or any of the other women who have endured so much."

"I'm glad you're alright." Dinah breathed. "I just don't think I could go on…" Her eyes stole another glance at the still bodies lying on the ground. "Let us tend to our wounded." Together they turned and walked toward the place of the fiercest fighting.

As they walked among the wounded men, there were many shot with arrows, but none had perished. The Lamanites, on the other hand, had lost so many men.

Gideon emerged from the catacomb to meet his king. "All are counted; three of the lost were our men. I killed the king of the Lamanites and there are over 200 enemies counted as dead. We are taking their bodies to the hill for their people to bury according to Lamanite tradition."

All who were not wounded carried litters with Lamanite bodies through the weaving catacomb where they had met their fate.

A cry came from the city. Gideon and Limhi both turned toward the commotion. "You continue on. I'll go see what is wrong," Gideon shouted as he ran.

"Dinah, help the women. I'll be back soon." Limhi said as he disappeared into the catacomb.

IT WAS NOW midday and the trees no longer shaded the rows of those who perished that had been laid on the grass. A Lamanite soldier stood over the heap of bodies with sword in hand. The Lamanite's other hand held a spear, which was pointed at Helam.

The women helping tend to the Nephite wounded all stepped back. Dinah came up behind them.

"Stand down?" Gideon cried. "What is the meaning of this?"

"My king!" The Laminate shouted. "He is among the dead, but he is not dead!" He pointed at the well-dressed but bloodied body heaped among the others. "He moves." All eyes rested on the one that was obviously the king. His arm moved, and he moaned. "See, he lives!"

The soldier cried. The bloodied, dirty arm of the Lamanite king shifted, and a second louder moan escaped his dusty lips.

Helam and Gideon moved swiftly to pull the king out, but the Lamanite soldier beat them to it. He sheathed his sword and spear and reached down to lift the broken body from among those who had perished. Gideon took a strip of his cloak and tied it around the bleeding arm of the king, then another for his head. The wound on his head gushed profusely, and the king's body went limp in the arms of the Lamanite.

"Bring him to the shade of the temple where we can have the healer bind his wounds," Helam ordered. The soldier moved quickly to get his king to a place of refuge. "Call for a healer!" Gideon shouted. The group moved in unison to the protection of the temple, where the king was placed on the soft grass and tended to. Gideon ordered a soldier to go get Limhi. "He's at the front lines. Tell him the Lamanite king is alive. We will treat him and question him. Then we will execute him for breaking his oath."

The king, still unconscious, was breathing and seemed to be resting more comfortably despite the death sentence just pronounced upon him. Gideon stood nearby, sword drawn. The Lamanite soldier also stood guard, spear in one hand, sword in the other.

Dinah, Rachel, and others had come to give aid and offered their shawls for bandaging. Someone handed the healer a skin filled with water from the stream.

Breathless from exertion and sweating from his demanding labors caring for the wounded Nephites, he dragged a bloody sleeve across his forehead and dropped to the grass beside the wounded king. He drew a cleansing breath and wiped his hands on the bloodstained cloak that lay across his lap. "Has he spoken or moved on his own?" His hand reached for the neck of the king and felt a spear point scratch the side of his cheek. Slowly he turned as his hand rested gently on the king's neck, checking for signs of life. "I must feel if life flows through his veins. I'll do him no harm." The Lamanite guard locked eyes with the healer and slowly lowered the spear, while still holding his sword at the ready.

"He lives, but the wound is causing the life blood to flow weakly through his veins. We must stop the bleeding." He took a strip of his already torn cloak and ripped it lengthwise, adding another layer to the bandage on the king's head. Drawing it tightly around the wound caused the king to wince.

Gideon stood by the healer's side and took the skin pouch, pouring water slowly so the healer could wash his own hands. The healer then took a clean corner of his cloak to wash the drying blood from the face and arms of the Lamanite king as he searched for additional wounds.

The healer removed the heavy skins and beaded necklaces and adornments from the king's arms. He found several more wounds and bound them with strips of cloth. Soon the king was clean and resting peacefully, with both Lamanite and Nephite guards poised over him, waiting for him to wake.

DINAH, 144 BC, CITY OF SHILOM

*S*everal women, who hadn't lost family, were doing their best to clean up the signs of battle. The worst part was blood that stained the dirt. It was impossible to clean, so it got covered with straw. Patches of dry grasses littered the street leading to the catacomb. Beneath each large tree where there was shade, Nephite soldiers received treatment for their wounds.

Miraculously only a few had died. Dinah again closed her eyes for a moment and whispered a prayer of gratitude for those spared and a prayer of comfort for those who would now be mourning. She stopped for a moment beneath the shade of a flowering plum tree and surveyed the activities, then moved through the grassy patches of shade, looking for the one that she knew was King of the Lamanites.

Unaware of the drama unfolding below, the sun continued through its path, making it necessary to keep moving the king to a better spot of shade. He stirred as his soldier carefully laid him down on a fresh patch of cool grass. Dinah stood back a little to give the Lamanite guard and the healer their space to work. The king moaned. In spite of wounds, his eyes fluttered open, then fell closed. Then they flashed open again. His hand reached for where his sword had been. He tried to roll over, but stopped, moaned and let his wounded arm flop back to the grass. "My king!" The Lamanite guard called to him. The king's eyes opened with recognition and focused on his loyal protector standing over him.

"I thought I had gone to the world beyond." He murmured. "We were not victorious?" He asked his comrade as his eyes darted from Lamanite to Nephite guards beside him.

"Our army ran when you fell. I found you among the dead." The soldier smiled weakly, "You were not dead."

Gideon stepped over to where the king lay. "You were not dead then, but you will be soon. You broke your oath and attacked our city." Gideon spoke through clenched teeth. "Good men died today protecting their families from your unprovoked attack."

The king's eyes grew hot with anger. "Unprovoked? We had every right to slaughter you all." His chest rose and fell quickly as his breath caught in his throat. "You've taken our daughters! My daughter!" The king choked on his words, "I… want my daughter back." His clenched jaw barely allowed the remainder of his words to hiss out, "All of the women you took must be returned, or we will kill your women and daughters."

Fire burned in his eyes, and Dinah retreated slightly to give the men space to get answers from the king.

"Noah did, in the past. That's not our way. We are NOT like Noah and we don't live as he did." Gideon's face flared with anger. "You'll face the king and answer for your crimes. We've done nothing to any of your daughters." Gideon grabbed the king's good arm and pulled him to his feet. The king's head lagged behind his body, flopping backward, then forward. His guard quickly braced him to keep him from falling.

"He's not well," the guard cried out. "Can it not wait?"

"No. It can't." Gideon pulled the king and his attached guard toward King Limhi's palace. Dinah, Rachel, and a few of the other women followed. Gideon shouted, "We have the Lamanite King! He lives!"

Limhi stepped out of his quarters as he finished wiping his freshly washed arms and face. Helam stood at readiness and kept pace behind the king. They stopped to face the wounded king that stood in the palace courtyard. He stood, supported by a fierce-looking guard. Limhi glared at the king, his hands clenching and unclenching. "Why, oh king, have you done this great evil? Why have you broken your oath?"

"It's not I that has broken the oath…you have stolen our women yet again." The hatred in his eyes seemed to give him strength. "You shall pay for this." He stood on his own and rose to his full height. "My daughter is among the missing, and I'll not rest till she is found."

Limhi recoiled with shock apparent on his face. "We will search our city, house by house, until they are found. Those who did this deed will be punished." He turned to Gideon, then to Helam. "You'll see to the search. Do it immediately. Search every home. The guilty will perish."

Helam's face clouded and his lips drew a tight line. He turned to his king and spoke with clenched teeth. "Lay not this to our people's charge, for they would never have taken the daughters of the Laman-ites." He paused, "There is but one who would have done this, and he is dead." Color rose in his cheeks and his face flushed with fury. "Those who followed him live, hide like jackals in the hills, stealing whatever they need to live. I would put this awful deed at their feet."

Limhi absently massaged his forehead, looking past the men who stood ready to act on his orders. Both of his hands slid over his moist hair, smoothing it down around his ears and rested on the back of his neck. His head bowed. "Even his death does not end the evil he began in life." He quietly cursed. Resolutely, his gaze rose and met that of his fiercely loyal friend Helam. Dinah moved around the crowd to stand beside her husband.

She spoke hesitantly but gained confidence as the words left her lips. "There has been a wrong committed. We pledge to search and find those who are missing." The guard and king still seethed with anger.

Helam interjected. "King Limhi, the Lamanites at this hour are gathering their forces yet again, preparing to come against us in battle. Their hosts are numerous. Plead with the king to pacify our enemies that they will cease killing our people, for we are innocent." Helam's voice rose in volume, "Are not the words of Abinadi fulfilled? We suffer because we would not hearken unto the words of the Lord and turn from our iniquities!" He turned to the king and continued in a quieter tone, "It is better for us to remain in bondage than lose our lives. Let us put a stop to the shedding of so much blood."

Limhi pulled his kingly robes over his shoulders and stood strong. Speaking both to his people, who had gathered to watch the interrogation and to the Lamanite king. He shouted so all could hear. "My father, King Noah, was a wicked man. You know what he did to your people and mine. He fled when he saw your army advancing and took his wicked priests with him, leaving their wives and children unprotected. They are cowards." Limhi declared, "King Noah is dead, put to death by those who followed him. Now they hide in the woods, stealing from us, living in caves in the wilderness. They would be the ones to have done this terrible deed." With a wave of his arm, sweeping across the crowd, "My people have done nothing wrong."

The Lamanite king nodded his head. "Take me to go meet my people. Unarmed. I will plead on your behalf that my people will not slay any more Nephites this day. I swear an oath that you will be safe."

Helam's expression softened, and Limhi nodded. "Soldiers," he said with a voice of authority, "we will cast down our weapons and let the Lamanites see that we are unarmed."

Slowly, each soldier deposited swords, spears, bows, and arrows at the feet of their king in a pile that grew quite large. One by one, they lined up in ranks, following the injured Lamanite King and their own Nephite King, unarmed to meet the gathering enemy. Through the safety of the catacomb, they followed until all emerged unprotected outside the walls of their city. The Lamanite King rested on the arm of his faithful guard until the approaching army of Lamanites came close enough to see him. Led by Dinah, the Nephite women observed from the path at the top of the catacomb to witness the encounter.

"Stop" the king cried, with hands held up. He then knelt down upon the ground. The soldiers leading the attack came slowly up to where their king was prostrate in the dirt. He raised his tear-streaked face to them. "The Nephites are innocent of the kidnapping of our daughters. We have broken our oath with them and they come without arms to plead for peace."

Puzzled, the soldiers' eyes passed quickly over the ranks of the Nephites. Helam, Gideon, and Limhi stood like stone statues behind the Lamanite king. The approaching leader reached down to help his King to stand. "Put your weapons away. The battle with our brothers this day is ended."

Lamanite guards took their king, but before turning toward Shemlon, the Lamanite king met the gaze of Limhi, and their eyes locked. He nodded sadly. Turning for their home, the host, too numerous to count, returned to their own city.

LISHA, 144 BC, CITY OF HELAM

A rustling sounded outside Lisha's cottage.

"Alma!" a voice shouted. "We have news!"

Alma strode to the door flap and swept it open. Three men ducked through the doorway. Lisha recognized Asher, one of Noah's guards, who had converted and fled with their people. He'd been close with Helam, who had remained behind in Shilom. The other two men were somewhat younger, in their late teens, old enough to marry. They looked familiar, but she couldn't place them. They looked travel-worn, their clothing torn, their hair tangled and filthy.

"Who are these men?" Alma asked Asher.

Asher clapped his lean hands on the young men's shoulders. His dark eyes glowed. "Refugees from Shilom. This is Taavi." He nodded toward the taller and thicker of the two boys. "This is Rafa. They've brought news from Shilom. We no longer need fear Noah or his men."

Lisha dropped her wool cards to her lap.

"Is this true?" Alma asked the young men. "What's happened?"

"The Lamanites have attacked Shilom," Taavi said. "Noah and his priests, they, well…" The boy glanced to his companion.

"Noah made the men abandon their families and flee into the

wilderness," Rafa said. Both boys looked uncomfortable, as if they were standing a bit too close to the fire.

"What?" Lisha rose from her seat. Her wool brushes tumbled to the floor. "The men left their wives and children behind?"

The boys exchanged glances again. "It wasn't like that. It was chaotic, so much was happening."

"All the men left?" Alma asked in a quiet voice.

A flush colored the tawny skin of both boys. Taavi looked down, but Rafa replied, "No. Many stayed with their wives. But we don't have a family. We fled with the priests and hid deep in the woods."

"We felt horrible," Taavi blurted. "We may not have families, but we shouldn't have left." He squared his shoulders. "We're not cowards."

Alma nodded to the boys. "You're not the first to be led astray by King Noah." He blinked, lost in thought. "But you say we need not fear him any longer?"

"A lot of us wanted to return to Shilom and fight, to protect those we'd left behind," Rafa said, his expression darkening, "but Noah wouldn't let us. The second night in the wilderness, a fight broke out between Noah and the rest of us who wanted to go back. Noah's priests ran off. Noah's dead. The men burned him, same as he burned Abinadi."

Lisha gasped. "Abinadi's prophecy..." It was horrible. But it was also a relief. She turned to Alma. "We can return to Shilom. We can go home."

"We may not want to share the fate of Shilom." Alma said. "Abinadi prophesied many things. He said Shilom would be enslaved if the people didn't repent."

"But they will, after all they went through—"

"Noah corrupted the hearts of many," Alma said.

Taavi shook his head. "Shilom has already fallen. Limhi and Dinah are King and Queen, but they rule in slavery."

"The Lamanites conquered Shilom?" Lisha sank back to her stool. "What about Tamar? Is she all right? Helam didn't abandon her?"

Rafa flushed. "Helam was one of the few who stayed behind. When the others returned to their families, we decided to search for you instead. As we have said, we have no family in Shilom, no reason to enter bondage."

Bondage. Tamar and the others enslaved. Lisha shuddered. She remembered Tamar's kindness to her when Alma had lost his way, Tamar's burning faith and quiet patience. She didn't deserve slavery. But then, no one ever did.

"How could you possibly find us when Noah's men couldn't?" asked Asher.

Lisha felt the blood drain from her face.

Rafa shrugged. "I believe the Lord led us, although it took months. We hid for a long while. After many weeks of searching, we crossed your path. A large caravan leaves its mark on the forest. We found signs of sheep and goats. From there we followed the animal trail. It was nearly grown over, but we made it."

Lisha cast Alma a worried look.

"Noah is dead. His armies will no longer seek us."

She nodded, wrapping her arms around herself. Even with Noah gone, her dream of returning to Shilom was shattered. She'd never see Tamar again; never see the towers and hills of the land of her birth.

"There's more," Taavi said, reaching into an inner pocket of his tattered coat. He pulled out a heavily creased parchment. "It's a letter for Mera. We found it among Noah's things."

LISHA AND ALMA pressed through the rainy night, keeping to the relative shelter and more stable footing of the tree line as much as possible. They circled the clearing to the west, Lisha clutching Alma's arm. When they'd gotten as close as they could without leaving the woods, they plunged across the clearing, where mud sucked at their leather shoes, and rain sheeted down like the waterfalls pouring from the bluffs across the river.

The weather matched Lisha's mood. She felt washed clean of worry about Noah and his men. At the same time, she felt a heavy sense of dread for her future, scraping a life from the wild. Not to mention her dread of the task she currently faced. She'd volunteered to bring Noah's letter to Mera, to break the news that her eldest son was dead. Now all Mera's children were dead. Lisha swallowed and picked up her pace.

Alma had insisted on coming with her to comfort Mera. She also sensed he felt a need to protect her from the storms and whatever might lurk in the darkness. A nice sentiment. A loving sentiment. She let go of Alma's arm. She didn't need protecting.

"Lisha! It's muddy. The footing is unsteady here. We'll do better together."

"You should have stayed home with Young Alma. I would have been just fine."

"Asher will calm him if he wakes. Besides, Taavi and Rafa seemed pretty happy finishing off the stew."

Lisha tightened her fists and stalked ahead.

"Don't you want my help?"

She whirled on Alma, her skirts, heavy with rain, clung to her body, weighing her down. "Where were you when we first came here when the stakes came loose and our home collapsed on our heads? Where were you when our son was crying and I was beating myself bloody trying to keep our home together? I can't do this myself, Alma!"

Alma stopped in the middle, staring at Lisha. "The people look to me, Lisha. I can't help that. The Lord has called me."

"I know," she said quietly. "But He hasn't called you to neglect us. Has He? Has He, Alma? Because if He has, I don't know that I can follow Him."

Lisha turned and continued toward Mera and Yoseph's tent, suppressing a sick feeling of guilt. For so long, she'd been the one to be strong, stoic in her heartaches, determined to cling to her beliefs while her husband led a wild life. Now that he'd changed, it was like her world had turned upside down. She was happy, relieved, but somehow her grip on her faith had loosened, now that she didn't need to cling so tight. She shook her head. Lord, help me, she thought. Help me through all of this.

Alma reached Mera and Yoseph's tent just behind Lisha. Their eyes met, and an understanding passed between them. They would set their troubles aside. That was what it meant, wasn't it, to serve the Lord?

Lisha rapped on a tent pole. Moments later, the flap opened. Orange firelight poured out, revealing Yoseph's wrinkled face and gray-streaked hair. His eyes widened when he saw who stood at his door. "What's happened?"

"May we come in?" Lisha asked.

Yoseph parted the flap wider, inviting them in. Mera was soon at his side, offering them mint tea.

"We're fine, thank you." Alma waved away the offer. "This may take some time."

Yoseph gestured to a pallet of furs since they did not have enough furniture for four. As they sat together, Lisha marveled at the changes that had come over Mera since they'd started meeting at the spring in Shilom so many years before to hear the words of Abinadi and, later, Alma. She'd gone from angry to peaceful. She'd found love again and remarried. Would this reopen old wounds? Could Mera survive that?

Lisha turned to Alma, knowing her unspoken concern would be clear to him. He gently informed Mera and Yoseph of all that had happened since their group left Shilom. When he came to Noah's death, Mera paled. Her hand tightened in Yoseph's, her muscles cording on her thin arms. But she did not cry. Lisha wondered whether this was incredible self-control or if her grief would come later. Maybe she'd already cried all the tears she had for Noah and felt wrung completely dry.

"He left you a letter," Alma said. "Some refugees found it in his things."

At this, Mera flinched. "He wrote me a letter? What could he possibly say that he hasn't already?"

"We haven't read it," Lisha said. She moved closer to Mera, slipping her arm around the older woman's shoulders.

Alma handed Mera the parchment.

Her hand trembled as she opened it. She scanned the letter and then passed it to Yoseph, blinking. "Read it aloud for me, will you?" The look she gave him was so vulnerable, so trusting, that Lisha felt she was intruding.

"We can leave if you'd like privacy."

"No." Mera's answer was swift and her gaze direct. "I want you here."

"Then we stay," Alma said.

Yoseph cleared his throat and began reading, *"Mother, I know I have scarcely called you such in recent years. For that, I am sorry. I am sorry for many things. I have lost my kingdom. I am alone in the wilderness, surrounded by men who hate me. Even my priests resent me, blaming me for their hardships. These men abandoned their families as surely as I did. The fault lies with them.*

If this letter should reach you, you must return to Shilom. You must find me and restore me to my rightful place as king. Our family will rise again. So long as you follow Alma, the people will be divided. Already some here claim that he should be king, that you support him in this. Is it true, mother? I would never have thought it of you. Of course, I never would have believed you'd defy me in all the ways you have.

But I digress. If I am not to be found, Limhi must take the throne. See that he is not prevented. You have my love, Mother. All I ever wanted was yours."

Mera shook within Lisha's embrace. She turned and buried her face in Yoseph's shoulder. "He never understood." She looked up at Yoseph, her face teary. "As much love as I tried to show him, he could never see it. He twisted everything I did to support his doubts."

"He said he was sorry," Yoseph offered, but clearly, this was a mistake.

Mera pulled back. "Sorry for what? Losing his kingdom?" She gulped, her breath thready and weak.

Yoseph patted her knee. "He's in the Lord's hands now."

Mera nodded, then began to cry in earnest. "That's what I'm afraid of. My little boy. That horrible, terrible man was once my little boy. What will become of him now?"

Lisha stroked Mera's back as she wept. For many years, Mera had been mother enough to her, second only to her own. From now on, she would honor Mera the way Mera's children should have. Mera and Yoseph were family now. They would face what was coming together.

LISHA, 143 BC, CITY OF HELAM

A long single blow on the shofar horn. A pause—then three broken notes. A trill of nine more. Lisha had woken to the shofar that morning and heard its blasts off and on throughout the day. Now, seated inside the cool stone sanctuary, she shifted little Eva in her lap and smiled across Young Alma to her extended family—her mother, Avi, her mother-in-law, Naomi, and her unofficial parents, Mera and Yoseph. They returned easy smiles. These shofar blasts did not signal battle, nor were they a call of warning.

This was a time of celebration, the Festival of Trumpets marking the beginning of the annual High Holy Days. They'd held them twice since they'd built their new home in the Land of Helam, as they'd chosen to call it. The City of Helam in the Land of Helam, after the first believer Alma had baptized. When they'd fled Shilom, Helam had stayed behind with Tamar and Limhi to protect them from King Noah's wrath. It was fitting that the new settlement be named after him, though he'd never see it or take part in the ceremonies here.

That first year, their celebrations had been minimal—a burnt offering, a communal meal of lamb, corn cakes, and berries, hymns, and spoken words in a damp clearing where believers listened from split-log benches or woven mats.

In the second year, the High Holy Days were more respectable. They'd built a house of worship by then, at the edge of the gathering place, close to the stream, but not so close that spring rains would swell water into the building. But they hadn't counted on fierce storms toppling the wooden church and their thatch huts before the year's end. In the muddy, heart-wrenching aftermath, Sarika had proposed moving deeper into the woods for shelter. She'd nearly convinced Alma, too. But Lisha brought him to his senses. It had been Lisha whose voice held sway in the community, much to her surprise.

By then, she'd accepted they were never returning to Shilom. But she wasn't about to pull up roots again just because of a storm. Storms would rage no matter where they lived. It was better to stay here where the land was fertile. The cave-hollowed cliffs provided some refuge, and streams brought fish and freshwater almost to their homes. Lisha was never moving again, and that was that.

Instead, she pushed for rebuilding with stone for the chapel, and mud bricks for their homes. Alma had agreed. He'd taken her hand and quietly praised her courage and determination. Two moons later, the worship house was well underway. Lisha's hands bore calluses evidencing her role in the process.

"Why must you labor with the men?" Alma asked her one morning as she strapped Baby Eva into a halter on her back.

"I'm teaching our son to be a man," Lisha said. Young Alma, then only three years old, puffed out his chest and chose a stone hammer from the tool box in the corner of their small home.

His father was all smiles. He picked the boy up and swung him around. "You'll be a fine man someday."

"I already am, Daddy!"

Alma set him back down. As the boy scurried off for shoes, Alma frowned at his wife. "There's more to being a good man than swinging a hammer, Lisha."

Lisha had moved away, securing a thin leather apron across her front. "Well, while you're busy teaching, he can learn hammering from me." She knew she wasn't being reasonable, that Alma spent his fair share of time working on the sanctuary, that he was needed in so many places and for so much time. But just because she was unreasonable didn't mean it was right for him to be gone all the time. It wasn't right that she should be mother and father, both.

Now another year had passed with Alma leading the people, working too hard, and meeting so many needs that he often fell asleep the moment he sat down to dinner at night. As part of the festival, he stood up front in the finished House of God, robed in ritual white linen, his gold skin aglow beneath his dark hair. Watching him, Lisha felt a flush of pleasure, even after all this time. She glanced down at her white gown and tugged the folds out of Eva's fist, smoothing the wrinkles away.

Alma sang the first lines of a hymn. His voice reverberated in the sanctuary, calling the believers to join in song. As Lisha sang alongside them, her mind flew back to that afternoon when they'd gathered beside the great river and read the closing chapter of Micah. Israel had rebelled, but the Lord would have mercy on them. *He delighted in mercy...he will have compassion...cast all their sins into the depths of the sea.*

She thought of Helam, Tamar, Limhi, Dinah, and all the people of Shilom, suffering in bondage. Some refugees had made it to her city, with dire tales of slavery and Lamanites daughters captured by Noah's priests, the reason the Lamanites attacked Shilom in the first place. Noah's choices had a ripple effect, harming so many even after he was long gone. Could the people of Shilom celebrate the High Holy Days? Did they even want to? How long must they suffer before God lifts their burdens and sets them free? Abinadi had said they must repent and turn their hearts to the Lord. Had they? Lisha knew from experience that trials came to the righteous as well as the wicked. Hadn't Alma turned to God then had to flee from King Noah? Hadn't Abinadi died, clinging to his faith and testifying to the King even as the flames rose around him?

Trials came to everyone, one way or another. But what was the difference, then? Did repentance and faithfulness protect from some heartaches, but not all? Was the Lord more able to help if you listened for his voice? Were you better able to bear your burdens with the grace of the Lord?

With hymns of praise swelling around her, Lisha reflected on the blessings in her life—her beloved children, her husband, her mother, Naomi, Mera, Yoseph, and the strength of their little community. She rejoiced in the freedom they shared—they could choose to stay or go, to worship the way they believed, and to care for their own. Her eyes flicked down to Sarika, seated with several other unmarried women and widows. Her small daughter, Shoshannah, sat quietly beside her. Lisha studied the girl for a moment, searching her face for some sign of who her father might be, some familiar tilt to her eyes or firmness to her jaw, but she could never be sure of what she saw. While they sang, Sarika shared a joyful look with the woman beside her. Her glance slid across Lisha as if she weren't even there.

Lisha's voice faltered. There had been nothing in that look, no challenge, no flicker of connection, nothing. A sense of emptiness crept over her, like the cold fingers of frost reaching down from the North in late autumn. Somehow, amid the upraised voices of family and community, Lisha felt small and alone. The people respected her, loved her, listened to her. So why did she still feel alone? The hymn came to a close. The musician blew the shofar horn again, a long, extended note that played to the very end of his breath. The final trump quivered in the air, powerful yet tender, a symbol of redemption.

To Lisha, it sounded forlorn.

WHEN THE SERVICE ENDED, Lisha shook off her unease. She took Young Alma's hand, slung Eva onto her hip, and left the sanctuary amid a stream of people headed for the gathering place. Earlier in the day, portable wooden tables had been assembled there for the feast. Round *challah* bread had already appeared on polished oak platters, courtesy of Josu the baker and his many apprentices.

Lisha entrusted Eva with her mother, and Alma with Naomi, then hurried home to retrieve warm bowls of beets and spinach. She added these to the growing spread. By the time she took her seat alongside

Alma, the tables groaned with ritual dishes - stuffed squash, leek fritters, black-eyed peas, dates, whole fish and lamb's heads, representing the head of the year and the prayer, 'let us be the head and not the tail.'

Alma offered a blessing over the feast, closing with the prescribed phrase, "May it be Thy will."

Lisha ladled food onto their plates, feeling a sense of relief that all she need do at the moment was take care of herself. At a far table, her mother and Naomi wrestled with Young Alma and Eva, who was already throwing handfuls of peas. "It was a beautiful ceremony," she said.

Alma nodded, lost in thought. He took a bite of fish and washed it down with a mug of warm cider. "I know the Lord works through me. I don't doubt that. I just hope what I give is enough." The *rodanchas* pastries turned dry in Lisha's mouth, the pumpkin filling clumpy. How could Alma possibly give more? He was already gone all the time. "I've given great thought to the previous year," he continued, "and I think we've done well." He rested his hand atop Lisha's. "Our family is growing. Our community is coming together."

"Ho, Alma!" Asher called from down the table. "A good year and a good life to you!"

The cheerful sounds of feasting and celebration rose around them, but Lisha scarcely heard it. She took a bite of an apple. This early in the season, it should've been tangy, crisp, and perfectly ripe. Instead, it was tasteless and mealy. She forced herself to swallow.

Alma waved back to Asher. "What is it, Lisha? I know something troubles you. You seem so alone. But, Lisha, you're not."

Samuel, the shepherd, came up behind Alma, beaming as he tapped Alma's upper arm. Alma turned. "Samuel! Aren't you enjoying the feast?"

"I have something for you." He thrust out a clumsily linen-wrapped package. Alma opened it and handed the linen back to Samuel. A thick, dark blue vest lay in Alma's hands. "I gathered the wool and had Yoseph weave this for you."

Alma looked up, surprised. "Thank you, Samuel. But why the gift?"

Samuel tugged at the collar of his white robes. "For all you've done, Alma."

"We've brought something, too," another voice said. Samuel moved, and Lisha saw Taavi and Rafa, Taavi with a candle scented with lavender and Rafa carrying a delicate wooden flute. These they gave to Lisha. "For the mother of our village."

Emotion rose in Lisha. She flushed, blinking back tears. This she'd never expected. The gifts kept coming. This was not part of the Festival of Trumpets. It was simply an offering of love and gratitude. Lisha's heart swelled, yet at the same time, she felt strangely confused. What was her place here in Helam? Alma was always away, serving and teaching. She had their children to care for and their aging parents. Did she have nothing else?

"Thank you so much," Alma repeated as gifts after gifts were placed before them. When everyone returned to their meals, he turned to Lisha again. "I don't deserve this. All I've done is try to follow the Lord, just like everyone else here. I can't help that he's called me to lead. The Days of Awe are upon us," he continued. "Ten days until the Day of Atonement. The people judge me kindly, but what of the Lord?"

Lisha winked. "If they keep giving you gifts, you'll need humbling for sure."

Alma gave her a warm smile. "See, there's the Lisha I love. I need you."

Lisha needed Alma, too. That's why his absences upset her. Yes, she needed Alma. But maybe she needed something else, too. Something she could only find herself.

CHANNAH, 142 BC, CAMP OF AMULON

*C*Hannah's tears came less frequently. The men seemed very kind when they wanted something, but cross and impatient the rest of the time. Channah scanned their camp. It was so much better than when she had arrived. Shelters were no longer temporary. Baskets had been made to store food that the girls foraged. The men even began to hunt after the girls taught them how to make bows and arrows. Occasionally they brought back meat. Although Channah noted, it was nothing like what the Lamanite hunters would bring back to the village.

Tears blurred her vision as she thought of her village — her mother and father. The tears flowed silently as she scraped flesh from the deerskin stretched out between two trees. Her dress showed the dark spots from tears that fell before she could wipe them away. No matter how hard she tried, as the full moon rose and the sign of her womanhood appeared, she missed her mother. She missed going to the lake. She missed the music and dancing.

The deer hide became thinner and smoother with each pass made by the stone shard in her hand. Channah imagined she was working with the wrinkled old women that knew everything, learning from them as they worked side by side. She was glad her mother had told her to listen while she was young and learn the skills that now were her means of survival. Working one skin at a time, each strung with braided rope between trees around their makeshift village, she scraped and cleaned, applying lard to soften the skins as she worked. Eventually, they would become protective clothing from the season of cold she knew was coming and they were ill-prepared for.

"More tears?" The voice came from behind and startled her.

Channah glanced at her chest and saw the fading evidence of her sorrow. "A few," she said simply.

His hand brushed her shoulder. She flinched, closing her eyes tightly.

"Why do you do that?"

"What?"

"Other women have begged for my attention. Yet, you cringe at my touch."

"I don't wish to be here. You took me from my home; I didn't come to you willingly."

His face darkened. "Maybe if you're hungry, you'll come to me willingly." He turned to walk away. "No food tonight." He paused, then turned, "no food ever again until you come to me and ask for my bed." His face flushed with anger. "I'm Amulon and I'll not be spurned by a Lamanite woman."

Channah's anger rose like bile in her throat, choking out the feelings of love and thoughts of her family. All she could think of was using the shard she held in her hand to end his life. She gripped it too tightly, and it cut her finger. She quickly brought her hand to her lips, sucking off the drops of blood that had formed on the cut. It stung.

Channah stepped into the forest, looking down along the path until she found a plantain leaf. The long, slender, shining leaves were easy to find. Their tall flower spikes and seed heads towered over the woodland plants that competed for sunlight along the pathway. She bent, picked the large leaf, and scrunched it up in her hand. Then she put it in her mouth and chewed it, keeping the herb near the end of her tongue. Then she placed her finger in her mouth, covered the cut with the green poultice, and let it set for a few moments.

A crunching of leaves startled her; she spun around. A wide-eyed, young Lamanite girl approached her. Channah's anger turned to joy as her dearest friend approached with trepidation. Isa scanned the forest edge quickly.

"They can't see you here; the shadows of the trees protect you."

Isa took a deep breath. "My sign has not come for two moons," she said with panic in her voice. "The one who chose me has taken me to his tent many times and now I may have his child within my womb."

The two girls embraced and wept.

After a few moments, Channah gave Isa a final squeeze. "I don't know how to get back to our families, but I'll try to go a little further each day to see if I can find the way to the women's lake. I know I can get home from there."

Isa's eyes grew wide. "If they catch you..."

"I've seen them beat the others that go too far from camp. I know. I'll be careful."

Isa slipped out of the shaded protection of the trees into the open meadow of the camp. She walked slowly back to the task she had been working on, sat down on a long log, and picked up the basket she had been weaving. She glanced back at the shaded place where Channah worked. Their eyes met. Isa managed a weak smile, lowered her head and began the methodical task of bending, tucking, and weaving the flaxen reeds.

Channah walked through the camp. Truly, that's all it really was. Temporary shelters. Not a home by any stretch of the imagination, and certainly not anything like what she had been accustomed to. The shanty structures frequently fell down when the wind blew and rain fell heavy.

Numbly, she walked along the well-worn and muddy path between the tall weeds on one side, and the crude structures that afforded minimal privacy for the occupants on the other.

Most of the Lamanite girls had accepted their fate. Prisoners, slaves, captives. Whatever words they could use to explain their way of living now, they were all too painful to express, so they didn't. They each understood as their eyes met each day, after spending yet another miserable night with these men. The pain and sadness showed in their posture and expressions.

Channah used every skill she had learned in Shemlon under the watchful eye of her mother and the other Lamanite women. She organized the women, so some planted and tended to the crops; others took the small creatures the men caught in their hunting and made meals to share. The furs were used, and bones and guts made into tools. Channah had become a natural leader.

This day in particular was difficult. She felt the need to escape and breathe. She needed to get away from camp. As she walked slowly past the final shanty, she felt a strong hand grip her, spinning her around.

"Where are you going?" Amulon hissed.

"I am looking for bulbs and roots to add to our meals."

"Don't go far. I can see everything you do."

Channah sighed. "Yes, from your little tower, I guess you can see most everything." She turned and pulled away. He grabbed her again, tighter this time.

"You leave when I say you can leave." His grip slowly eased. "You can go now." His glare was as sharp as his putrid breath.

"I'll be back before the evening meal." She began working her way up the hillside, poking a sharp walking stick into the earth, pulling it back to unearth the roots. As she found large tubers, she put them into a sling she had fashioned out of an old piece of woven fabric tied around her waist. Some roots were familiar, others were not. She was determined to find more food to eat, beyond the simple corn cakes and dry meat they consumed on a daily basis. She didn't ask where the corn came from, since they had yet to grow and harvest any in their camp.

"Channah!"

She paused in her methodical march and turned. Several of the girls from camp ran to catch up with her on the path. Channah spread her arms wide to greet each one with a tight embrace.

"We need to walk with you today," Isa whispered.

They each stopped to pick up sticks and replicate what Channah was doing.

Isa looked at Channah with eyes filled with tears. "I would have been able to go to the lake. I wish I could be there with the rest of the women. I'd love a new dress."

Channah stopped, realizing for a moment what Isa was really saying. "I miss my mother too. She would have made you a beautiful dress." She pulled Isa into an embrace. "We must be strong for each other." She looked at each of these girls who were becoming women and learning the family ways without mothers to mentor or teach them. "We will take care of each as their time comes."

Two blushed, glancing down at their expanding midsections. "Let's walk," Channah spoke the words emphatically. "Amulon watches everything I do. We need to find our way home." She stooped down to pick up a recently unearthed root. "Each of us will need to take short walks into the forest, to see if we can find the path the men take. I know they leave. I know they are stealing from someone to get grain. They must leave a trail and we need to find it." The girls all nodded in agreement as they pretended to stab the earth as Channah was doing. "I need to find more food for us to eat and medicinal herbs for the coming winter. If you want to join me, bring your stick to help me dig.

They fanned out, each stabbing the ground to turn up the roots of plants on the hillside. The higher they climbed, the more she could see. Channah gazed out over their little camp, into the valley below. They were quite high up, higher it seemed than the lake where her people had gone - where their lives changed forever. Although Channah had only been there once, she sensed they were much higher. A thin ribbon of smoke wafted up from behind a lower mountain elevation." There are people down there." She whispered to no one in particular.

"I just don't know whose they are."

CHANNAH'S herbal and foraging expeditions had taken her far from the camp, yet she had found no sign of tracks made by other men, only beasts. Tearfully, she returned once again with her basket filled with aromatic leaves and roots but no sign of a trail that would lead back to her people.

As she neared the camp, she followed the well-worn path, which she'd memorized and could follow in her sleep. The tents set up for the girls now sat empty. It was time for the evening meal, and they were all laboring to serve the men. Rarely did they return to their private tents. Most went to the men's tents. It had become easier to just stay than to get dragged out in the middle of the night. Many were with child and had resigned themselves to a life with these men - men who had stolen them away from their families, their lives, and their futures. A tear made its way down her cheek; she flipped it away. She stumbled over a newly fallen branch and grabbed her belly as she caught herself. With her back to a large pine tree, she let herself slide slowly down, rough bark scraping the flesh on her back and stopped on a pile of moss.

The realization hit her, the one she'd refused to accept or believe. She was carrying Amulon's child. She sat; eyes closed, beside the tree that marked her path into the woods. Too much time had passed. She knew Amulon would come looking for her and be angry for having to do it. So many thoughts had marched in and out of her mind. She couldn't figure out how to get out of this situation. Her hopes of finding her family were fading. She winced at the next realization: this is my family now - these men - these girls and women. "NO." She told herself out loud, "I cannot give up," willing the former thoughts to leave her mind.

Channah slowly turned to her knees, breathing deeply, inhaling the scent of cooking meat and corn cakes. The food smelled wonderful, but suddenly, her stomach turned, and she vomited bile, over and over until nothing more came out. The acid burned her nostrils and throat. She weakly dug through the basket of herbs she had just foraged until she found the slender, smooth root of wild ginger. Breaking off a small section, she nibbled on it, wincing at the powerful flavor. She lay back in the leaf litter beneath the trees, leaves crunching beneath her slight frame. She could feel it all: the leaves cushioning her back, twigs poking her shoulder blades, and emerging grasses cooling her skin. The sky was darkening with the setting sun, and a gentle breeze blew strands of her hair, lifting and lowering them across her forehead. Slowly the churning of her stomach eased.

Using the bark of the pine tree to cling to, she pulled herself up and followed her well-worn path back. When she neared the cluster of huts, loud voices captured her attention, and she slipped behind a tree to listen.

Amulon was storming through the camp. "Where is she?"

She peeked around the tree in time to see him swinging an empty basket as he raged. All of the girls froze in their labors, each glancing around with fear in their eyes. One stepped forward.

"I saw Channah foraging this morning. She said she was hungry, unusually hungry."

Channah let out a frustrated sigh and clenched her fists.

Amulon stopped in his storming and walked over to where the girl had been working, crushing corn on a large oval stone. "What do you mean, unusually hungry?"

"She was searching for some herbs to soothe her stomach."

Channah cringed as a tear sprang to her eye.

Even as her eyes blurred, she could see a faint smile cross his lips. "Return to your labors."

Channah held her breath as Amulon walked back to where a group of the men had gathered to watch the exchange. She slipped from around the tree and moved closer without leaving the protection of the forest.

She moved closer to camp, hoping to enter her tent before Amulon found her. The one who had spoken to Amulon, jerked. "Why did you hit me?" She cried.

Channah heard Isa's hoarse whisper, "You told him where she was!" Channah had to bite her tongue to keep from speaking.

"She's always there while we do the work." The girl's eyes darted around. "I thought if he knew…he might not be so angry with her all of the time."

"Channah does more than you know," Isa whispered. "We must trust her if we ever hope to return to our families." Looking around again to see who was nearby, she added, "I trust her."

Several of the girls nodded in agreement.

Amulon's voice echoed from the cluster of men as he called Channah's name, walking toward her. Birds cried out in fear as they fled from their nests, their babies, and their quiet perches in the trees. Amulon stomped about, snapping twigs and stirring up leaves. His voice grew more faint but also more insistent, barking out orders for Channah to return and make herself known.

Channah remained hidden, unable to sneak back into their tent without discovery.

Over time, his voice became louder, then fainter as he circled closer, then further away from the camp. She stayed in place. With eyes closed, she slid silently back to a patch of soft grass and waited.

A small scuffling sound brought her eyelids open, and there he stood. Amulon. His normally angry eyes flashed concern. "Are you unwell?"

Channah sighed. "I was ill and needed to calm my stomach." She turned to her side to push herself up, and Amulon reached down to grasp her arm and help her. "Thank you." She didn't cringe at his touch. He helped her rise and slowly slipped his arm around her to steady her steps.

I can do this…

Channah allowed his arm to stay instead of pushing it away. "Thank you."

"You forgot your basket," He paused. Almost as if wondering if he should pick it up for her or wait to let her pick it up. Their eyes met. He released her to let her walk back and pick up her basket. Channah realized that to him, she would probably always just be a slave girl who bore him children and slept in his tent. She walked behind him as they made their way back to the camp, carrying the basket of herbs.

∼

AMULON SEEMED satisfied with his accomplishment. With pride, he had announced to all of the men that Channah would bear him a child. It seemed to be somewhat of a competition among the men to see who could have the most children born in the camp, which angered Channah greatly. One afternoon, late in summer, when the heat and humidity was making everyone grumpy, a commotion erupted in the center of camp, with two of the men coming to blows. "She's my slave girl; leave her alone."

Channah slid her tent door open to see what was going on.

"No one belongs to anyone!" The one defending himself shouted. "We share them, just like always."

"You know that's not the way it works anymore. You have your girls, I have mine, and you need to stop trying to get mine to come to your tent."

"Mine are not with child yet. Something is wrong with them." His face flushed with anger.

Chuckling loudly, the other sneered, "Maybe it's not your girls, but you."

A fist connected with the man's jaw almost as soon as the words left his lips. He stumbled backward, recovered, and charged back at the one who had hit him, and they both toppled to the ground. Dust flew. Angry words and curses escaped their lips. They were surrounded by onlookers and stunned Lamanite girls. Most of the Lamanites had become women, and most were carrying children. As the scuffle continued, Amulon rushed to the scene. Channah came slowly behind him, now heavily burdened with her child soon to be born.

"What is the cause of this?"

The two bloodied and dirty men stopped fighting and made their way to a standing position as Amulon looked on. The dust stuck to their sweaty faces and turned to mud.

"He was trying to get one of my slave girls to come to his tent."

"Is this true?"

"I wish to have children like the others."

"You selected the two youngest girls." He paused and looked at the faces of the two girls he had chosen as they looked on in surprise. "They might not be women yet." Their faces began to redden, and they stood closer together, hands clasped. Amulon closed the gap between them and stood with hands on his hips. "Well, are you in the way of women?"

All eyes rested on the two. Slowly they both shook their heads. Channah felt their pain and humiliation.

"I have a suggestion." Channah breathed in as deeply as she could. "Let us be married, each to his own." Her expression turned hard as she finished her request. "Each family is its own." She looked into the faces of the women and girls that had become her family. "No more as slaves."

The men, clearly pondering the implication of her words, slowly nodded in agreement.

"Today we wed," Amulon declared. With a flourish of his robed arms, he added, "Bring your women."

CHANNAH WALKED arm in arm with Isa on their ritual morning walk. They wove a path through the tall grasses of the high plateau and through the woods surrounding the camp. As they left the circle of huts and the tall grasses in the meadow, making their way into the outer perimeter, Channah checked to see if they were being watched. Usually, it was Amulon, sitting upon a lookout tower crudely assembled by the unskilled priest's hands. She imagined kicking one leg of the rickety platform and watching it tumble to the ground, man and all. It was a source of immense frustration that he always seemed to know where she was.

"How are you feeling?" Isa asked.

"About the same. The child pushes so hard on my belly. I can almost see its toes." She breathed in the warm morning air. "I have had pains. I know my time is near."

"Are you afraid?" Isa asked breathlessly as she rested her hand on her own expanding belly.

"I wish my mother could be here." Tears sprang to Channah's eyes. "Oh, how I wish I could go home."

Neither could speak for a time, both choked with emotion as their respite walk came to an end. Channah stopped and grasped her belly, unable to speak or walk. "I think it's time," she whispered to her dearest and closest friend. After pausing for a moment to let the pain ease, their pace quickened and they crossed to the middle of the meadow until her next pain came, where they had to stop again.

"Where are your herbs? I'll make the tea," Isa offered.

"In my tent." She paused again as the muscles of her abdomen became taut. "Small basket by the grinding stone," Channah whispered instructions as she walked toward the tent where she realized she would become a mother. A surge of anger coursed through her heart that her own mother would not be there. Tears flowed freely as they walked until a new powerful pain seized her.

"Shall I bring someone else to help? You're the one there for everyone else. Now, who will be there for you?"

"You will." Channah breathed shallow breaths as the pain nearly drove her to her knees.

The pain eased after a few moments and she quickly made her way to the place of women and pulled aside the curtain. Three women were there, awaiting their time. Channah lowered herself to the seat and prepared for the next pain, lifting her skin dress to keep it from getting soiled.

After a few more strong waves, the woven cloth moved aside and Isa stepped in with a steaming cup of tea.

"Drink this."

Channah grasped the clay vessel and sipped the tea, letting its warmth fill her. Another pain came. She took in a breath as four pairs of hands soothed and rubbed her aching back. They knew this was the most difficult moment for a woman in travail. They were becoming better at helping. Hands rubbed her legs, arms, and back like she had done for others in their time.

Before the new day dawned, a cry was heard, first a young woman becoming a mother, then a child being brought into the world and taking his first breath. All of these life-changing events happened in the deepest darkness of a moonless night in the newly named city of Amulon.

DINAH, 142 BC, CITY OF SHILOM

"What is it, Dinah?" Limhi whispered. "Are you not well?"

"I think I did too much today. I felt faint in the heat of the sun as we gathered grain." Dinah dabbed her forehead. The moisture left a dark stain on her sleeve.

"Are you still feeling the heat?" Limhi sat up, pushing the skin blankets from his legs.

Dinah rose up, then paused. "I feel weak."

"Lie down. Rest. I'll get the healer."

Dinah sunk back to her bed of thick wooly sheepskins and kicked away anything that touched her legs as Limhi rushed out of their home.

As soon as the healer stepped over the threshold, he hurried to her side.

"A fever burns her." The healer spoke in whispers as he placed a damp cloth on Dinah's forehead. "I'll gather the herbs and make a tea."

"I'll help," Limhi offered.

"Stay with her. I'll be back soon."

Limhi sat down beside his wife. He placed the back of his hand against her soft cheek and stroked it gently. Dinah smiled weakly as she took his hand, lifting it from her burning face. "That hurts my skin." Limhi pressed a soft kiss on her forehead instead.

"Did that hurt?"

Dinah shook her head slowly, "I'll be fine tomorrow. We have much work to do."

Limhi sighed. "Too much work."

Dinah's voice trembled as she whispered. "Have faith. God…" She paused and licked her lips, "…is aware of our struggles." Her fingers stretched out until she found his hand. "One day, we will be free again."

Limhi's voice wavered with emotion. "Why, though. Why must we be slaves?" He gently placed his hand on Dinah's belly. He felt her breathing, the rise, and fall, but something was different. "Dinah?" he questioned.

Her expression was pure joy. "Yes, my love."

"You're with child?"

A placid smile curled at the corner of her mouth, and she placed her hand over his. "Our child will come when the snow first falls."

Limhi lowered his head to hers, their forehead's touching, eyes closed. "Born in captivity, to a slave king." A tear fell from his eye and ran down Dinah's cheek. "Oh Lord, when will we be free?"

The healer again slipped into their home through the thick tapestry door and set to work preparing the herbal remedy he used with all who became sick with the fevers common to the season. It seemed that as soon as the heat set in and the insects began biting, children and adults alike fell ill. Within a few moments, a fire's glow warmed the room. Steam rose from the clay pot brimming with spring water and herbs, filling the air with a spicy scent. He worked quickly and skillfully, straining the leaves and roots with a woven cloth and pouring the tea into a cup on the table. He took honey from a jar on the shelf and stirred it in.

"Make sure she drinks all of this, tonight if possible. Watch her closely to see if her fever breaks."

Limhi gently lifted Dinah's head from her bed, high enough for her lips to reach the cup. She breathed deeply, sipped some more and closed her eyes. "I'm tired...need to rest."

"I'll leave you and check back in the morning." The healer rose, gathered his things, and slipped into the night -- off to care for another sick one.

As she lay there, skin glistening with moisture and eyes closed, Limhi whispered, "I thank the Lord for her. She's a gift to me every day, especially in this time of trial. Please Lord, bless her. Help her be well again."

SO MANY MORE WERE FALLING ILL. This was far worse than any season that had plagued them in the past. Even some of the Lamanite guards and their families had become feverish.

It took several days for Dinah's fever to break. The healer continued to check in, making a new mixture of herbs each time.

"She's a fighter. She'll recover just fine." The healer spoke softly to Limhi as they stood beside Dinah's bed. Her breathing was easy and deep, with no rattling like some. Those who had the sickness the worst were slow to regain their strength.

"What about the baby? Is he going to be healthy?"

The healer smiled. "A son? You believe she's having a boy?"

Limhi chuckled. "I wouldn't know how to raise a daughter. I didn't have a sister and my nephews are boys. I guess I just thought..."

"God sends children to Mothers and Fathers and each has a role to play. If you have a daughter, Dinah will be a wonderful mother, teaching her to spin, cook, plant, and harvest. You will teach her to work hard, have faith, and be a leader." The healer clapped Limhi on the shoulder. "Son or daughter, the child will be loved, taught well, and raised up unto the Lord."

"Thank you for that wisdom." He reached out and pulled the tapestry aside to let in some fresh air. The healer slipped out and was quickly swallowed up in the crowd of people that had gathered near the temple steps.

"I'd like to take a short walk." Dinah's voice whispered from the dark room.

"You're weak."

"I need to know how our people are doing." She took a deep breath. "And how I can serve them."

"Dinah, you must rest. How can you serve when you're ill and weak?"

"I can pray." She slowly turned to her side and pushed herself up, waiting for the dizziness to subside. "Please take my arm. I want to hear for myself, what the greatest needs are."

"BROTHERS, who is left to harvest grain today?" Limhi asked the small group that gathered on the temple steps as they did each day. "Are there no more that can come?" The worry creased Limhi's brow and he rubbed his forehead in frustration. Dinah was holding his hand, and gave it an extra squeeze.

One merchant stepped forward, speaking in a low voice. "There aren't enough to bring in the entire harvest today."

"The rains will be here soon. Grain must come in today or all will be lost." Many heads turned to look toward the western sky. Clouds were gathering in the distance and they carried the gray darkness of being heavy with moisture. "We won't have enough for the winter to feed our families, and provide the tributes required by the Lamanites," another added.

The grumbling began as whispers then a few angry voices carried above the rumble. "What if we refuse the tribute?" one shouted.

Heads nodded in agreement. "Yes, they do nothing to prepare for the winter. What I gather is for my family and my neighbors. I refuse to gather for the tribute anymore."

Limhi's hand raised in a gesture of calm. "We are slaves. It's not our choice whether to give the tribute."

"Then we fight!"

"No! We will trust in the Lord to deliver us." Limhi let go of Dinah's hand and helped her to sit on the steps. He came down from the temple and placed his hands on the shoulders of one he knew who carried heavy burdens. "Don't lose faith, my brothers." He looked into the weary faces of his friends. "The answer will come. For now, we live as slaves."

"Not for much longer if our food runs out." The merchant kicked at the dirt in obvious frustration. "We will be dead."

"Why can't we fight?" another strong Nephite soldier hissed through gritted teeth. "I'm ready. Now." His cheeks flushed with anger. "If I die, I'd rather die fighting than starving, watching my children starve."

"Do you trust me?" Limhi asked. "Do you trust God?"

"If we perish from hunger, what good is our trust in God?" another called out from the back of the group.

"Do you only trust God if the outcome is what you desire?" Limhi stood tall and squared his shoulders. "Do you only trust God if He does what you want?" He stepped away from the group and up on one of the steps. He swept his hand toward the temple. "Do you trust God when those you love die, or the battle is lost?" He stepped one step higher and placed his right hand on his heart. "I will trust in Him. I will wait on Him."

"Your own wife has been sick. Many of our families are sick. We need the food for them." Angrily the farmer swung his fist in the air. "I plan to fight." Then looking directly at Limhi, he continued. "Who is with me?"

Many fists pumped through the air. All eyes rested on the king.

Before Limhi could answer, an arrow pierced the temple door just above his head. All of the men ducked and spun around to face the attacker.

Two Lamanite guards stood with arrows nocked and ready to end King Limhi's life. The unarmed men placed their hands in the air to surrender.

"You wish to die now?" The larger one asked with a sneer.

Slowly shaking their heads, the farmers, merchants, and soldiers backed away from the threat, forming a protective barrier around their king.

"Harvest the tribute. Get to work."

A third soldier came up behind the others with a leather whip and began snapping it over the men's heads. The Nephite soldier's fists clenched as the tiny end of the whip snapped near his ear. Again, and again the whip licked closer and closer to men's faces, until it got a little too close to a merchant's cheek. The tail of the whip dug into his flesh. He cried out and his hand flew to his face. Drops of blood oozed between his fingers and his teeth gritted in anger.

Two hands gripped the man's shoulders. Limhi spoke calmly to their captors. "We were just leaving for the fields. This is not necessary. Please put your weapons down."

The Lamanite guards grinned. "Move faster. Work harder. We are hungry."

Limhi returned Dinah to their home, then went to work alongside his brothers.

For the remainder of the day, the men toiled, carrying basket after basket of grain to the place of storage. Every other basket went to the Lamanite guards. They carried their begrudged tribute to the entrance of the labyrinth and blew a ram's horn when the day's work was done, the signal for the Lamanites to come and pick up the harvest - food that the Nephites desperately needed.

THE DAYS of harvest blended in one with another with almost no rest. Dinah had to force herself to pause from time to time to have a moment of peace, for herself and her growing child. She stood in the courtyard and gazed at the blazing sunset as if angels were painting the sky with streaks of orange and gold tinged with pink while adding along the lower edges, purple. Limhi and Tamar stepped out of their quarters as if on cue. Together they took in the natural painting that changed before their eyes.

Helam opened the gate into the courtyard and the squeaking hinges brought all eyes to him.

"Hello my friend!" Limhi said with outstretched hands. "Join us as we watch God's handiwork in the sky." All three moved toward Helam.

"Thank you." Helam looked upward and cast his eyes about with amazement. "I walked all the way here and didn't even notice what was happening behind me as the sun set. I was so focused on the memories of this city. Building it up from ruins. Growing up here. My father..." He choked up.

Limhi embraced him.

Tamar and Dinah placed their hands on his shoulders in a show of compassionate support.

Limhi extended his arms to look into Helam's face.

"Is there a problem?"

"Not really."

Tamar, concerned, said "So, yes, there is a problem?"

Helam shook his head. "Can we go for a walk?"

Tamar looked back toward the courtyard, at the open gate, and then at Helam. "Where will we be going?"

"To the spring, if that's alright with you." His eyes were glassy. "I need to be in the place where I feel the Spirit strongly, and I want you to come with me."

Limhi smiled at his friend. "I know you'll take good care of her." Worry creased his forehead. "The soldiers are on edge, so be careful."

Tamar smiled. "I'm happy to go with you and feel perfectly safe with you around."

Helam paused and turned to Limhi. "Do you think it was hard for Jarom, Abinadi, to leave his family and come here to try and teach us, knowing he would likely never see his family again?"

"I think about that often. How hard that must have been, and it breaks my heart, knowing his sons will grow up without their father — Sarai, without a husband," Limhi offered.

"I can only imagine," Helam choked out. A tear fell down his cheek.

Tamar paused to look at Helam. "This is really bothering you."

The sun setting cast flaming light on the trees and on their faces.

"I'm missing that in my life," Helam whispered, looking into each of their faces. "A personal place, a connection - a family." Helam shook his head and stopped. "I have no one to mourn my passing but my friends. I have no children to teach or raise, and no wife to be…mine."

"Let's walk to the spring," Tamar offered, touching his arm gently.

Helam — the warrior and soldier, guard and protector — just nodded his head.

"We won't be gone long," Helam whispered as he took Tamar by the arm and helped her down the hillside to the street, then let go of her arm, casting a quick glance back at Limhi and Dinah, who were smiling at him from the courtyard gate.

Tamar breathed deeply, listening to the water rushing by. The stone slab at the edge of the spring formed a perfect seat for her and Helam to share. She placed her hand on his shoulder. "Tell me what is really causing you pain."

Helam turned to face Tamar. One corner of his mouth turned up, which made Tamar laugh. "You look like my son when he's got mischief on his mind." Her smile grew to her eyes, "Do you have mischief on your mind Helam?" she said in a teasing tone.

A laugh tumbled out of his chest, and he tossed his head back, now fully releasing all the pent-up sorrow but also love that had for so long gone unexpressed. "If that's what you'd call it, I guess I do."

Puzzled, Tamar turned fully on the large stone and faced her long-time friend and protector. "Helam, you're going to have to come out with it and tell me what's going on."

He gathered her hand into his and kissed it, bringing a look of surprise to her face. "I have dedicated my life to protecting you, keeping our city safe, and guarding your family from danger. After Noah's death, I realized my feelings had changed." Helam's eyes met Tamar's. "I would give my life for you, but I realized I wanted to give my life to you as well."

It seemed as though they both stopped breathing for a moment as the realization of his words settled on them both. "My pain is that I have come to love you, deeply, and wasn't sure I could ever tell you."

Tamar turned to gaze at the spring. "I'm glad you brought me here. This is the place where so much changed. Good changes." She looked back at Helam's earnest eyes and met them. "This will change us both, this conversation we are having, if I understand you correctly."

Helam just nodded, then took Tamar's hand and asked, "Will you be my wife?"

Tamar, with joy spilling down her cheeks, said, "Yes."

Helam and Tamar slid from the large boulder they were sitting on, and Helam caught her by the waist in his strong hands. They stood that way for a few moments, eyes locked. "Can I kiss you?" Helam asked shyly.

Again, Tamar responded, "Yes."

Gently, Helam cupped her chin with his large, calloused hand. He moved slowly toward her, then closed his eyes and placed a gentle kiss on her lips. When he pulled back, Tamar saw the slightest quiver in his chin, and a glistening in his eyes. She reached up and touched the tear that fell to his tanned cheek.

"I love you too."

"Shall we go share the news with Limhi and Dinah?" Tamar asked.

Helam responded with a wry smile. "Yes."

THE GATE SQUEAKED as Helam and Tamar slipped through in the darkness, closing the latch behind them.

Soft voices came from the many families living in the old palace, with children getting ready for bed and parents settling in. One set of voices carried over the rest. Helam and Tamar went toward that home.

Limhi opened the tapestry before they could ask for an audience.

Helam bowed his head slightly. "My king."

Tamar smiled. "Son, we have news."

Dinah came to stand behind Limhi with a questioning expression. "News?"

After a moment of the four just looking at each other, Tamar said, "Helam has asked me to be his wife!"

Helam took Tamar by the hand and pulled her close. "I didn't ask when you would like to marry."

Tamar smiled. "Would tomorrow work for you?"

The shock on Helam's face brought a girlish giggle to her lips.

He smiled. "I'm free."

It took mere moments after his response for the courtyard to erupt in joyful congratulations so much that each of the other tapestries pulled back with questioning glances.

"Tomorrow, there will be a wedding!" Tamar shared with a joyful cry. "Helam and I will become husband and wife."

Dinah stepped around Limhi and pulled Tamar into a tight embrace. She whispered, "I wondered when he would ever come around to asking." Tamar pulled back with a questioning gaze. "I've seen how he looks at you." Dinah smiled. "I'm so happy for you. You deserve a good man like him."

Tears fell from Tamar's eyes at the realization. "Yes, I do deserve a good man like him." She pulled Helam's hand toward her, drawing his hand around her waist, bringing their faces closer together. "Thank you," she said with a smile.

"Now, let's let Dinah get back to her rest, and let everyone else get to bed."

Limhi agreed. "Yes, she needs her rest, but she's feeling better. Would you like to arrange to have the priests ready to marry you tomorrow after the harvest is done?"

"That sounds like a great plan." Tamar turned to Helam. "After our work is done."

Helam just nodded in agreement. "Tomorrow."

Before Helam left the compound, Dinah overheard part of their conversation.

"There likely will not be children should you decide you still wish to marry me," Tamar whispered.

"Limhi has always been like a child to me. I have loved him like the son I never had. "

"I know that. Your love for him has been a blessing."

Their voices faded as they walked toward Tamar's home. Limhi took Dinah's hand and led her back into their quarters.

Then a few moments later, the gate squeaked one last time.

LIMHI STOOD in the doorway for a few moments after he and Dinah awoke the following morning. "This day will bring many changes. Especially for Helam and Tamar."

"I'm so happy for your mother. Truly, Helam will be such a blessing for her." Then Dinah added, "She will be a blessing to him."

"Do you want to come with me as we start this blessed day?"

"I do." Dinah linked her arm around Limhi's.

A crowd had gathered at the temple. As Limhi neared the crowd, he watched as some raised their fists with shouts of anger. Voices became louder. With some concern, he made his way toward the group, now better able to hear the exchanges of words.

"I'm tired of giving up half of my food to the Lamanites while my own children are hungry. There won't be enough to last us through the winter." The man hoisted his child into the air with a shout of frustration. "Our children come first."

One of the old priests slowly stepped up toward the temple doors so people could see him. "God is aware of our struggles; He will bless us."

"Why are we slaves if God is aware of us?" one merchant cried. "Why can't He strike down our captors and set us free?"

"Sometimes the struggle is necessary--" an old woman tried to say.

Before she could finish, she was cut off. "We will die struggling then!"

Limhi and Dinah came from behind the group. "What do you suggest we do?" The crowd turned and shifted direction to face them.

"Fight!"

Limhi raised his hands to calm their voices. "The Lamanite guards will come again if you keep shouting. Before we decide to arm our people and risk our lives in battle, we must think of all available options. How are our grain stores today?"

The crowd turned to the group of farmers standing together at the foot of the temple steps. The older, more experienced farmer stepped up to address the people. "With the number of people we have to feed, giving half to the Lamanites has depleted our stores. We will make it through the first snows, but we will run out before the harvest comes again."

"Is there enough to plant if we ration through the winter?" Limhi questioned.

The farmer shook his head.

Again, someone shouted from the crowd, "Let's run the soldiers out, then protect our perimeter."

"We should find the priests who keep stealing from us and take back what is ours," another shouted.

"The priests have taken what little reserve we had. Let's hunt them down first," a merchant shouted from the back of the crowd.

"Then, once we've run the Lamanites out, we will take back the tributes." The young soldier, with all the fire of youth added, "And we will slay any who get in our way."

Helam and Gideon, with swords at their sides, approached the group.

Limhi clapped Helam on the back with a big smile. "Good morning, my friend. How did you sleep last night?"

"I didn't," Helam responded with a boyish grin.

All eyes were now on the two, any arguing having ceased. Clearly, the crowd had missed out on something.

After a moment of silence, Gideon was the first to speak. All eyes rested on Helam and Limhi.

"Out with it," Gideon said with some irritation. "What are you not telling us?"

Helam smiled. "Today, I will become Limhi's father."

The connection seemed to take a moment, but once the crowd

realized what he had said, they sent up cheers of excitement, so much so that the Lamanite guards came rushing from both ends of town. They arrived with spears in hand, but were met with confusion when they arrived.

"Go to work!" one shouted.

Still obviously confused at the joyful mood in the town, the soldiers stood ready for trouble. But the people dispersed and went on their way with smiles and much back-slapping, leaving the soldiers wondering at what had just happened.

Limhi walked Dinah slowly back to their home. She embraced him before he left for the fields and held his face in her hands for a long moment. "Is this all right with you, your mother, and Helam?"

"I couldn't be happier."

THE LABOR of harvesting was done by all, including the king and his mother. Helam even took his turn at carrying baskets when he wasn't on patrol. Each time he came around, he caught the appreciative smiles of the people congratulating him at every opportunity.

When evening came, Dinah still felt strong enough to come to the courtyard and sit to watch the priest as he married two of the most wonderful people she knew. The entire town packed tightly into the palace courtyard to congratulate their beloved Tamar, former queen, to their fierce protector, Helam.

There was joy and rejoicing throughout the evening and that night. Instead of going to his home where he had lived alone for nearly 40 years, Helam joined Tamar in her home, in the humble palace Zeniff had built so many years ago.

DINAH, 142 BC, CITY OF SHILOM

*D*inah slipped out of bed and tiptoed silently to where Limhi rested his hand on the lintel above the fire pit in their home, deep in thought. His eyes were closed. Her touch startled him and his eyes jerked open as he placed a hand over his chest.

"My thoughts were in a battle. I didn't hear you come."

"What battle are you fighting in your mind, oh King?"

"I feel I must allow the voice of the people to be heard. They wish to fight for their freedom, to drive out the Lamanite guards and no longer give the tribute." Concern creased his forehead, "There won't be enough food to get our people through the winter, with the Lamanites taking half of what we harvest."

"Has the Lord given you an answer to your prayers?"

"I plead with Him all the day long, as the Lamanites flick their whips over our heads and lash burdens on our backs. I see my friends smitten, and they suffer it." Limhi looked at his wife with fearful eyes. "They wish for freedom at all cost, and I fear that unless I allow them, they will rebel against me."

His hands fell to the round belly of his wife. "Will our child live forever in slavery, or will the Lord see fit to free our people?"

Limhi took Dinah into his arms and wept, tears falling from his clenched eyes. "Will my people ever choose to be humble and listen to the Lord their God?"

~

IN THE PRE-DAWN HOURS, the Nephites awoke and quietly slipped from their huts. Even the roosters were still asleep. Nothing stirred but the noisy insects that sang incessantly throughout the night. The Lamanite guards were still in their huts as shadowy figures stealthily moved toward the burial mound and the secret stash of weapons hidden inside. Dinah watched her husband vanish into the darkness.

She stood at the courtyard gate and watched the silent shadow of Gideon, now 20 years old, the revered captain in their army of citizen soldiers, slip out of his home.

One after another, farmers and merchants tiptoed into the dark corridor to where their weapons were stored. Dinah silently prayed for each one as they disappeared, then emerged from the darkness with armor, swords, and spears; prepared to fight the Lamanites for their freedom.

She knew she should remain hidden, but she could not. The attack began at the hut of the first Lamanite soldier. The cry of danger from the hut brought out the other soldier from his hut at the other end of town, and he blew the war horn. The Lamanite city of Shemlon would now be alerted to the attack. In the ensuing confusion, the plan to drive out the two guards turned quickly into preparing for an attack from the Lamanite army. Fear gripped the Nephites.

Dinah knew if there was trouble, Limhi would need to view it from the tower. She saw him scramble to the top, straining to see through the darkness. Scanning the catacomb for any advancing soldiers, she heard them before she could see them.

The attack came without any warning. Lamanite warriors flooded into the city from the river, crossing easily through the unseasonably low water and into the city, not risking an entry through the north passage where they'd meet certain death.

Their attack from the back of the Nephite army was swift and deadly. Dinah stepped quickly into the courtyard and latched the gate. Tears flowed as she sobbed, watching her friends being mercilessly slaughtered.

Only when Limhi pled with upraised arms to stop the fighting did the Lamanites cease their work of death.

Through her tears, she could see the Lamanite king stroll up to Limhi, passing bodies strewn across the ground — his soldiers at the ready to begin again. As he passed by the fallen Nephites, using his sandaled foot, he nudged at some to see if they were truly dead. He shook his head. "Foolishness. Slaves don't make good soldiers. You don't have time to train for war when you're harvesting grain for winter. My warriors train each day. Look what we can do when you, our slaves, provide us with all we require to live." He took a spear from one of his nearby soldiers and thrust it at Limhi, poking him in the chest. "We will never allow you to leave, and your men will never beat us in battle. Surrender and admit your defeat."

Dinah could see the faces in the early morning light, men now broken at suffering such a swift loss. The sun crept over the mountain and cast a beam of light like a beacon that illuminated the scenes of bloodshed and death. She knew their names, those that had fallen. They were her friends — her people.

The Lamanite king, seeing the people were beaten, called his soldiers to gather their weapons and follow him. Women emerged from their huts, and cries of sorrow and anguish began to fill the air as they realized those lying unmoving on the ground were dead. They were their husbands and sons, fathers and brothers -- friends. The Lamanite soldiers walked past the women as they filed out of the city, stroking their hair in mocking affection laughing at their pain. They left the way they had come in, across the river.

Limhi's voice rang through the deathly silence. "Oh Lord, my God! When will thy people turn to thee? When will they humble them-selves?" He placed his hand on the still figure of his friend, a man he had worked alongside in the fields day after day. Helam stepped up behind him and placed a hand on the king's shoulder in a show of support.

There would be fewer men to gather the harvest. Fewer men to protect their city. This loss would be felt by all.

"Your God will not save you from my soldiers," the Lamanite king shouted from across the river. "You are our slaves. Your children are our slaves. Your wives are our slaves."

Anger filled the hearts of the remaining men of the city of Nephi, and their desire for revenge consumed them. Thoughts of God, or His protection, utterly vanished, replaced by an all-consuming hatred for the Lamanites.

Over the coming weeks, they went to battle a second and third time. Each time the Lamanites drove them back to their city, suffering great loss. Those who were not slain returned one final time to the city of Nephi: beaten, humbled, and submissive.

"I THINK it's time to choose a different path." Limhi rubbed his hand across his forehead, then massaged his neck with eyes closed.

"What will you say to them this time?" Dinah slipped as close to him as her rounding belly would allow.

"Would you like to come with me? I feel I need your support in this."

"Anything you need me to do. I agree. Something needs to change."

Dinah quickly slipped on a dress, chewed on a mint leaf, and grabbed a sliver of corn cake as Limhi dressed for the day.

Together they knelt and offered a prayer of guidance and pled with God to soften the hearts of the people.

"We need Tamar and Helam," Limhi said before they left the old palace compound. Together they walked to the tapestry door and tapped on the side post.

Helam came and pulled the heavy cloth to the side. After a moment, Tamar came and stood behind him.

"I need your faith today, my friend. The people are consumed with hate and revenge. We must help them see that God is waiting for them to turn to Him."

"We will come, but this is a choice the people must make," Tamar offered.

Together, united, the four walked to the temple steps.

The men gathered as they did each morning. Limhi looked into their tired faces. "What say you, my friends?" Limhi searched their faces. "What will our task be today?"

Silence met his gaze. Each man's hands hung by their sides, expressions blank with resignation.

"Will we fight?" Limhi asked.

Slowly each man shook his head.

"What battle is ours to fight, men?" Limhi demanded.

One took his fist and pounded his chest.

"What battle is God's to fight?" Limhi asked.

A flicker of understanding sparked in a few faces.

Gideon spoke out. "I have fought with my sword for many years. I am ready to let God prevail." He placed his sword at the feet of Limhi.

"Will you let God fight this battle for you? Will you turn yourself, your faces, your trust to Him?" Limhi felt a surge of hope. Were they humble enough for God to hear their cries?

The men seemed to stand a little taller. "Let us pray to God now and all day long. Pray to be humble. Ask God to forgive us for our hatred toward our brethren. Ask for strength to bear our burdens and to trust in the deliverance as our ancestors did in the wilderness. Truly God was with them, and He will be with us if we repent of our pride."

Limhi took his fist as the other man had done and beat his chest. Each man in the small gathering did the same.

A snap of a whip shattered the air. "Get to work," a Lamanite soldier shouted.

Dinah and Tamar linked arms as the men prepared for the labors of the day.

Limhi looked back at his wife as the rest of the women emerged from their homes with their children. Many more families now had widows with children to care for. Life in Shilom was different now;

everyone was needed. The women took their little ones to the fields to work with them each day. The harvest had to come in.

Dinah walked slowly, Tamar supporting her as she stepped cautiously down the steps.

Limhi was giving assignments while Dinah made her way over to stand beside him. Tamar then joined Helam and reached out to clasp his hand. They walked toward the field together to begin work. The air was crisp and most of the laborers carried shawls for warmth.

"Are you sure you want to work today?" Limhi asked as he walked with his wife.

"I must. Everyone is needed."

Another whip cracked behind the group as two soldiers stood with empty baskets, handing them to Nephites. "Fill all of the baskets today, or we keep all of the harvest."

Limhi cringed. "That's going to take most of the day." Anguish twisted his expression as he gazed at his very pregnant wife. "If you can make it today, we can rest tomorrow for the Sabbath." The men and women, one at a time, picked up their baskets and headed to the fields to begin working. "Don't do more than you are able," he whispered to his wife.

Dinah nodded and massaged her belly as she walked toward the stack of baskets. Limhi waited for her to get one before suggesting, "Let's work together today. I don't want you working alone."

"That's probably a good idea," Dinah agreed with a sigh.

Rachel came to walk beside Dinah. "I'll stay by you today as well."

Dinah reached out and squeezed her hand. "Thank you." They walked as a group out to the field.

The roosters called out their good morning as the sun began to warm the night sky, turning the deep blue into shades of pink and purple.

Dinah worked alongside the others, stripping stalks of corn of their ears. They piled the stalks into heaps to be carried to the pasture to feed the sheep and goats. The ears were left to dry in the sun. Men hauled cobs that had already dried and stored them in what had once been the armory. Their secret stash of weapons was gone now, emptied in the summer of fruitless battles with the Lamanites. Now it held food. Squash, beans, and dried herbs lined the walls.

With the corn harvest complete, laborers set aside husks for making new beds for sleeping. The final task of the day would be gathering dry pods of beans. Afterwards, each family would work late into the night by their firesides, to shell the beans.

The group moved slowly through the field that had once been corn into the field that had row after row of bean plants withering and drying as their season ended. Each plant was plucked out of the ground, pods removed, and all remaining stalks fed to the goats. There wasn't enough food for both the people and animals, so nothing was wasted. Every bit of what was grown had to become food for someone or something.

Limhi and Dinah worked their way up and down the rows. Their baskets slowly filled with the dry pods that contained the beans that would help sustain them through what was sure to be a meager winter. Dinah paused as needed while her muscles contracted, then went on with her work.

"Do you think he will come today?" Limhi asked.

"Why do you say "he"?" Dinah responded with a tired smile.

"I think we need a son to carry on the leadership. I can teach him how to be a good king."

"Hmmm. What if we have a girl? Will you teach her how to lead, to be a good queen?"

"Of course--" but his response was cut short as Dinah's face wrinkled up in pain. "Do you need to rest?"

Dinah fell to her knees. Rachel and others started toward Dinah and Limhi. Dinah let out a soft moan. "I need to go home."

DINAH TOOK her time getting home. Walking became more difficult. Limhi held her arm while Tamar and Rachel whispered words of encouragement. Judith had tended the working parents' children in the palace courtyard. She had become quite the teacher and caregiver.

The children raced to the palace each day to see what she had planned for them as their parents went to work in the fields. Her games taught the children to count, and they drew shapes and letters in the sand she carried up from the stream. They had grown and harvested plants in the palace courtyard, and the children were learning to read.

Tamar made sure they had plenty of supplies to learn new skills. She gave them clay to learn to make pottery, yarn to weave, grains to cook, and seeds to plant and grow.

The chatter and activities stopped for a moment as the King and Queen came unexpectedly into the courtyard. Tamar and Rachel followed behind them.

"Is it time?" Judith asked excitedly. "Children, keep working on your letters; I'll be right back."

Judith pulled back the tapestry to Dinah and Limhi's quarters so they could slip through. She held it for the women that followed, who would be there to assist Dinah through the birthing process. Tamar began heating water for tea while Limhi helped Dinah to her bed and Rachel pulled out some clean blankets. "Is there anything I can do?" she asked.

"Can you get some meal and make some cakes for Dinah to eat?" Tamar suggested. "She's been working and will need her strength now."

Judith moved quickly to mix up some meal cakes and started cooking them. She poured a cool drink from the pitcher on the table and took it to Dinah.

"You can do this," she whispered to Dinah, who had become her dearest friend. Judith slipped out after completing her task and went back to the children who had become distracted. They were now playing a game, shouting gleefully, unaware that their queen was descending into the valley of death, to bring forth a new life.

The midwives and the healer arrived shortly after Judith left. Tamar had the tea brewing that would help with the birthing. Limhi arranged her skins into a comfortable bed and the birthing stool was set up, ready for use when the time came.

Dinah's hands shook and her whole body trembled. Limhi's heart pounded as he comforted his wife. Tamar also had a worried crease on her forehead. "Is this normal?" Limhi asked his mother.

"Birth is a difficult and dangerous journey for some. Pray, my son."

Limhi stroked his wife's head and the midwives scurried around. The tea helped to calm and relax Dinah, and the shaking stopped. The pains increased and she focused, with eyes closed. Limhi whispered in her ear as he cradled her head on his shoulder, "go to a place of beauty, to the spring, to the waterfall, to a place of joy where you'll take our little boy one day."

"Our little girl?" she whispered in response.

"Our little boy," Limhi responded with a smile.

Dinah whimpered.

The midwives scurried into action.

"It's time," Tamar said as she helped Dinah to the stool. Surrounded by those she loved and trusted, she went to her place of peace in her mind - the spring where Alma taught and baptized. She hummed the songs of their people, and those around her joined in. They were the songs of faith, of unity and love. There was power in the music that gave Dinah strength.

The cries of joy and pain from a new mother mingled with exhalation and relief from the others there as the little boy cleared out his lungs in a husky cry. Dinah, weak from exhaustion, was carried to her bed and fell into a slumber. The baby was cleaned and cared for as Dinah rested. She slept for some time while the baby boy was cuddled and swaddled. The news spread rapidly as the workers came in from the fields.

Limhi brought the boy to Dinah when she stirred. "Benjamin. How does that sound to you?" Dinah smiled weakly. "Benjamin". She stroked his head while her eyes opened for a moment to take in her son's red face. "My little boy." Still smiling, she said in a whisper, "I'll give you a daughter next time." With that, she was asleep again.

The months following the birth took the family through winter and into spring. The midwives attended to Dinah each day and cared for her and little Benjamin. Food stores ran low, and the winter ran long. The last of the grain was distributed as the sprouts of greenery emerged from the long winter sleep.

Spring had arrived.

They had survived one more year as captive slaves in their beloved city of Shilom.

LISHA, 142 BC, CITY OF HELAM

*W*arm autumn sunlight shone through orange-leafed oaks, crimson maples, bronze sassafras, and cheery silver bells. Nearly thirty women joined Lisha at the east gate leading to the wooded area between the city and the outlying pastureland to the north and farmland to the south. Several children came as well, those too young to be left at home, including Young Alma and Eva, who tottered along, clinging to Lisha's hand. It was the sixth Day of Awe, the sixth day of self-examination and repentance among all the people.

An entire year had passed since the High Holy Days when the people of Helam had showered Alma with gifts, expressions of their loyalty and trust in him. Lisha had come to see their faith in him as a reflection of her own faith that he was a good man, trying to be a better one. Just as she tried to learn and grow, to understand her purposes in life - within her own family and the larger community.

Lisha had set aside a full day for this outing. They'd head south and circle the city, returning before nightfall through the same gate they'd left. A midday meal would be brought to the vineyards southwest of the city, although they'd carry their own water skins and dried fruit for the hike.

The women crowded around her. They entered the shady trails together, humming one of the old songs of hope, perseverance, and faith. Lisha felt a gentle warmth she associated with inspiration or comfort. As they walked, the crowd thinned, with the slower walkers trailing behind, taking their time to enjoy the beauties around them.

As the group spread along the path, the melodies faded into a peaceful quiet, interrupted only by whispered admonitions to unruly children. Lisha led, walking between Yoseph's daughter, Hannah, and Mera, who helped corral Alma and took turns carrying Eva once she tired. Hannah's children wandered to and fro, mostly trailing their oldest sibling, Elizabeth, who had a young child of her own.

Lisha focused on the sensations of the moment, the crackle of twigs as they passed, the soothing coolness of the shade, the gentle heat of the sun when they passed through clearings, and the warm green smell of farmlands. As the path curved toward the south gate, Lisha, now with Eva in her arms, spotted thatched homes peeking over the stone walls, piles of mulch near family gardens, and wild apple trees, heavy with fruit.

"Momma, mamamamama." Eva tugged at Lisha's shirtfront, sliding her small arm inside.

"All right, sweet girl," Lisha said, looking around for a reasonably comfortable resting place. A little farther on, the dirt path expanded into a small, leaf-strewn clearing, open enough to welcome the warm sunlight, yet still sheltered by overhanging branches. If she peered through the woods toward the city, she could see they'd passed many homes and had nearly reached the south gate.

"Let's pause here," she told the others. "We can tend to the little ones, eat a morsel, and reflect on our lives." She disentangled Eva from her blouse and set her down. The small girl didn't cry. Instead, she clung to her mother's skirts.

"Momma, Momma." Eva's upturned gaze was pitiful, her eyes pleading as if she hadn't eaten in days.

"You little urchin," Lisha said. "You'll be happy in a moment. Fat and happy."

She removed her small pack, then settled under a sprawling birch, her back against the papery trunk. She pulled Eva to her breast. Other mothers of small children tended to them as well.

Hannah settled against the same tree as Lisha, resting her head against the trunk. "Be glad Eva's such a sweet child," she said. "Mine were hellions. Now my eldest has a wild thing of her own. Serves her right."

Lisha laughed. Soon the clearing was quiet but for the clamor of the older children, who were growing restless, weary of raisins, cheese, and flatbread. Lisha took a swallow from her water skin, then stroked Eva's round cheek while the toddler nursed. "Fat and happy," she murmured again.

"Shall I take the older ones down the path?" a voice asked. Lisha looked up. It was Sarika, her hand gripping Young Alma, as well as her six-year-old daughter, Shoshannah, by the hand. "They were swinging from trees like possums."

"Speaking of wild things," Hannah said, opening her eyes as her children ambled toward her, the youngest, three-year-old, Zilpah, bouncing with energy. She scooped Zilpah onto her lap and began whispering in her ear.

"Alma!" Lisha leaned around Eva to take his hand from Sarika's. "This was to be a quiet walk, a time for repentance."

"We've been repenting for days," the boy said, wriggling against her grasp.

"I'm happy to run ahead with them," Sarika said again. "We'll circle back and they'll be calmer for the rest of the walk."

"Don't you need time to reflect?" Lisha asked.

"How can I reflect when my girl needs to move?" Sarika said with a laugh. She walked ahead with her daughter, her russet robes swirling around her ankles. "I'll take Shoshannah," she called, "and whoever else would like to come. Perhaps I can grant the rest of you some peace."

Lisha frowned.

"I'll go, too," Hannah said, rising heavily from her resting place. She grasped Zilpah by the hand, reaching for Alma's sticky fingers. "It will be good for them to run and play."

Lisha reluctantly let Alma go. "Be good," she told him.

He nodded enthusiastically, then joined the children flocking to Hannah and Sarika, their fluting voices chattering like birds. Lisha sighed as they scurried up the path.

As the sun rose higher, painting the leaves more brilliant than before, Lisha remembered the scrolls she'd brought to share with the sisters. This would be a proper time to pull them out, to read something they could reflect upon. Lisha suddenly felt shy.

Back in Shilom, she'd kept to herself, ashamed of her husband's behavior. Tamar and Mera had been her only friends, besides her mother, but they were both older, more like mentors. Her sister was long gone to Zarahemla, and her brother, dead. Lisha was mostly alone. Then, when Alma led the believers from the city, she'd been thrown into a new role, one she didn't quite understand, one that made her feel even more separate from the other women. Perhaps that could change.

Eva grunted. She'd fallen asleep, her dark curls plastered against her pink cheeks and one chubby hand clenched in Lisha's shawls. The other had made its way to the girl's mouth; she was sucking on two fingers. Lisha shifted the child in her lap and opened her pack. She cleared her throat. The soft thrum of women's voices stilled. Lisha was surprised to find all eyes on her, as if they assumed she'd take the lead and awaited her guidance. A soft breeze stirred the leaves.

"Lisha," Mera prompted, "could you share some words with us?"

Lisha flushed again. "Of course. I brought some verses." She dug around in her pack and pulled out the parchment. After taking a deep breath, she began reading, "The Lord is my light and my salvation; whom shall I fear?" The women hummed their approval. Lisha continued, her confidence growing, "In time of trouble he shall hide me in his pavilion: in the secret of his tabernacle shall he hide me; he shall set me up upon a rock. Now shall mine head be lifted up above mine enemies. I will sing praises unto the Lord."

She paused for a moment, giving the ladies time to contemplate the message. In truth, she was considering something herself. A strange idea had arisen in her mind—who were her enemies? They were safely away from Noah's oppression. Lamanites hadn't sallied into their region since they'd arrived. Yet, still, she felt on guard. Was her mind inventing enemies among the peaceful people of the community? Was she seeing danger or conflict that was not really there?

"Hear, O Lord," she continued, stumbling over the words, "when I cry with my voice: have mercy upon me, and answer me. Teach me thy way, O Lord, and lead me in a plain path." She paused again.

Mera finished the verse for her, "Wait on the Lord: be of good courage, and he shall strengthen thine heart."

The final words were recited in low voices by many of the women, "Wait, I say, on the Lord."

Lisha leaned back against the birch again, deep in thought.

LAUGHTER DRIFTED DOWN THE PATH. Lisha opened her eyes in time to see Hannah's curly brown hair crest a slight rise. She was red-faced from chasing the children. Sarika, however, looked fresher than before, as if filled with an inner glow. The children seemed drawn to her, darting to show her flowers or snails; from this distance, Lisha couldn't tell which. Sarika giggled and steered them down the trail.

A thought struck Lisha. Did Sarika wish for more children, for a family like hers? Did she long for a different life, one that had been stolen from her? Perhaps Sarika cursed her beauty for the pain it had brought her at the hands of Noah and his priests. She didn't seem bitter, though. How had she moved past her hurt?

Unsettled, Lisha shook the thoughts away. She woke warm, sleepy Eva as she stood and shifted her into a fabric sling around her chest. Eva stirred, blinking wide eyes. Young Alma pounded down the trail and threw his arms around his mother, nearly knocking her back down.

"Alma!" Eva squirmed, trying to reach her brother.

Sarika glided over and gave Eva a stem of pale, purple mallow flowers. "Preeeey!" Eva babbled, patting the blossoms before putting them in her mouth.

"Thank you for watching the children," Lisha finally said.

Sarika nodded. "I sense a rift between us, Lisha. I want to make it right. That's what this season is about, is it not? Not just reflection and repentance, but reconciliation."

Lisha nodded but said nothing. Eventually, Sarika drew back and walked with a more talkative group.

They took their midday meal of braided bread, soft cheese, dried venison, and grape juice near the vineyard, then continued along the open bank of Hope River, past a few girls weaving baskets in the warm water. Some older women, and those with weary children, left the group at the west gate, but the rest pressed on, pausing for prayers and contemplation near the burial mounds, where a few poor souls had found their final rest following a sickness the previous year. The trail wound through thick vegetation edging the northern pasture-land. Eva squealed with glee when they saw fleecy lambs playing on a hillside. All along the way, Lisha thought of her actions of the past year and tried to know the Lord's will for her.

The faith walk neared its close an hour before dusk when the sun was low and the sky full of color. The group made its way across an arched stone bridge over the crystal stream that flowed through the city and into the pastures beyond. Lisha lingered outside the gate, thanking the women for joining her.

Her mother, Avi, was one of the last to amble back down the trail to the City of Helam. She paused beside Lisha, hunched over her hiking staff. "You did a good thing today," Avi said, beaming with motherly pride. "People listen to you."

"Only because I'm married to Alma."

Mera was several paces ahead of them, leaning on Naomi. She tilted her head toward her friend, whispered something, then turned back.

"Alma," Naomi called, beckoning to the active boy. "Come with Grandma. We'll stop by my home and bake some sweet bread for dinner."

Thank you, Lisha mouthed to her mother-in-law. She felt a slight lift in her mood as she watched Young Alma gamboling beside the older woman, in and out of the brush like a playful kitten.

Mera waited for Lisha and Avi to reach her on the path. "What you said is not true, Lisha. Look at what's happened today. You brought unity and hope to all the women who came with us. They admire you."

Lisha twisted her hand in her skirts. Not everyone admired her. "I've done nothing."

"Do you remember, back in Shilom, when Alma mistreated you?"

Lisha went very still. "Of course, I remember. I wish I didn't."

Mera laid a hand on Lisha's arm. "You showed great courage during that time. You gained strength through your persistence with Alma, your faith in him, and your faith in God."

Where did that strength go? Where did that faith go? Lisha didn't voice her doubts, but knew they must be written on her face because her mother wrapped her in a hug. Eva gurgled and tugged at her grandmother's hair.

"You were stoic when Alma defied King Noah and fled into hiding, even though you were with child. Everyone remembers that," Mera said. "It was you, as much as Alma, that gave the rest of us the faith to follow him into the wilderness. If you could do that, after all you'd been through, and even being with child, we could manage as well. Remember singing that hymn with Queen Tamar, the one that signaled hope and gathering? You have the same power, Lisha. You have the power to love and unite. Don't let your fears overshadow your strengths."

THE DAY of Atonement had been long. Twenty-five hours of fasting, five sermons, and more prayers than Lisha could remember. Really, she only remembered one.

The words Sarika had spoken during the faith walk would also not leave her mind: *That's what this season is about, isn't it? Not just reflection and repentance, but reconciliation.* Mera's comments followed that memory, as if they were linked somehow. *You gained strength through your persistence with Alma, your faith in him, and your faith in God.* Once again, Lisha wondered where her strength had gone and whether she'd spent it in loneliness and fear.

There had been many prayers that day. Communal prayers during services in both the sanctuary and the gathering place, prayers with the family around their dinner table when they finally broke their fast. Many of the community had come together for a feast, but Lisha had refused. In this, the holiest day of the year, she needed to be alone with her family. Alma relented and stayed home with her. For this, she was grateful.

The dinner prayer was not the one that stuck with her.

No, it was another, more private prayer, offered in the night, after her family had fallen asleep.

Earlier in the day, she'd sought out Mera and found her in the potter's studio, shaping clay into platters and bowls. Naomi was the head potter here, despite Mera's greater experience. She didn't mind cleaning up so Mera and Lisha could talk. As they left, Lisha wondered whether Naomi wished she'd confide in her. As her mother-in-law, she must have precious insights. But Lisha couldn't do it. No, it was Mera she needed.

From the potter's stall, they skirted the edge of the gathering place, where people thronged together, singing around the bonfire. Lisha saw Sarika dancing with Rafa, his eyes glinting in admiration. Sarika smiled at her, and Lisha returned her smile. She and Mera continued their walk, passing the produce and grain stores, their doors shut in deference to the ritual fast. They passed the linen and fur shops, smiling and greeting others along the way. "A good final sealing," they said again and again. They soon moved beyond the gathering place, through a series of homes and sleepy gardens, and outside the city wall, to their favorite place, the crystal stream.

A group of stumps clustered together under the tree line, close enough to the brook for people to sit and enjoy its burbling sound and the way the evening light sparked off its surface. Lisha and Mera paused there and sat for a while.

"I know you are feeling confused and alone," Mera said with her usual candor and insight.

Lisha hesitated. "I like this place," she said. "It reminds me of the Waters of Mormon."

"Yes, the light is much the same. But much is different as well."

Lisha nodded. "When we pledged to follow the Lord, into the waters of baptism, then into the wilderness, that was a special time." She paused. "Frightening. Dangerous. But the joy and peace were real."

"Transformation isn't an event, Lisha, but a process. After the energy and newness wears off, we must choose patience and persistence. That's when miracles happen. And when pain and fear rear their heads, patience and persistence triumph with the Lord."

They talked some more, then resumed their walk home.

"A good final sealing," Mera said at her cottage doorway, bidding Lisha goodnight.

"A good final sealing," Lisha responded. She hoped Mera was right, that with the Lord's help she could seal away her anger and resentment, not hide or suppress it, but give it to Him. And by so doing, that she'd be forgiven for carrying it so long. Wasn't that what atonement was about? A fresh start? This was her prayer, the one that really mattered.

LISHA, 142 BC, CITY OF HELAM

*L*isha strode to the gathering place, her heart pounding like thunder. She tugged Eva along while Young Alma trailed behind them, dragging a stick through fallen leaves.

"I caught one, Momma!" he held the stick over his head, triumphant. A crisp brown leaf quivered on its end, dropping fragments to the soft earth as they passed.

"Good job, Alma," Lisha muttered, trying to be supportive, but her thoughts were elsewhere.

"It's a fish, Momma!" Alma persisted, now waving the twig in front of his mother. It snagged in her skirt, crushing the leaf and breaking the tip of the stick.

"Mommy broke Alma's fish!" Eva said, her lower lip trembling.

Lisha paused. She gave Alma a stern look while disentangling the slim branch from her clothes. "Didn't you hear the horns, son? This is not a time for making merry."

Young Alma groaned. "Are we going to the sanctuary? How long do we have to sit and listen this time?"

The corner of Lisha's mouth twitched. Hadn't they all felt like that at one time or another? She straightened her son's collar and sighed. "Not this time, Alma. Those horns warn of danger. We must hurry and find out what's happened." A ribbon of fear coiled in Lisha's chest. "Come on."

She led her children through the west gate, into the city, passing thatched homes and the potters' shed. The walkways were strangely empty. Oh, why had she chosen today of all days to take her children across the mud flats to play at the river's edge? She tugged Eva along and twisted her other hand into her own skirts, not caring if the fabric wrinkled.

As she and the children neared the gathering place, a rush of voices assaulted her ears. She picked up her pace. What had happened? An attack from the Lamanites? Had Noah's priests found them? But no, the horns had not warned of attack. She remembered the sequence she'd often heard back in Shilom before rushing to the caves to hide. They'd never had need of that here and never would. Noah was long dead and his priests scattered. And they had no dealings with the Lamanites.

So why was that ribbon of fear billowing in her heart?

A large crowd jostled against each other at the gathering place, huddled together, focused on something near the cold, ashy fire pit. Lisha rose to her tiptoes but couldn't see past those in front of her. As she pushed her way through, someone caught her arm. She looked up and saw Mera, her lined face tight.

The older woman shook her head. She tried to pull Lisha away. "Don't look."

"What is it, Mera? What is it?"

"Alma's been gored by a deer."

Lisha felt colder than the empty fire. She thrust Eva's hand into Mera's. "Take her for me, and Young Alma, too. No one keeps me from my husband."

Mera caught the two children and gazed at Lisha with a mixture of admiration and worry. "You never could hold back, could you?"

"No, I can't." Lisha squared her shoulders and pressed through the crowd. She found Alma lain out on the packed earth beside the hearth. His skin looked papery and gray but Lisha was relieved to see him moving, even if it was to flinch in pain. He was alive.

She rushed toward him then stopped short, leaving room for the healer to do his work. The healer knelt beside him, dusting bloody wounds in his thighs with a yellow powder. Lisha recognized it as yarrow she'd helped pick the autumn before.

"Lisha," Alma croaked, curling his hands at his hips.

The crowd made way as she hurried around him and knelt at his side, opposite the healer. She took his hand into her smaller, yet still strong one. A slight pressure came from his fingers as she gazed into his pained eyes.

Oh please, Lord, please don't take him now, not after all we've been through.

She felt a comforting hand on her shoulder and turned.

It was Asher. "He'll pull through this." He sounded like he was convincing himself.

"How did this happen?" Lisha demanded. "I thought this was a morning hike, not a hunt?"

"It *was* a hike. Thank the Lord several of us were with Alma when the buck attacked. It barreled out of the woods and knocked him down, then raked his legs with its antlers." He shook his head. "I've never seen the like."

"But deer are skittish; they don't attack," Lisha argued, knowing she was being obtuse because obviously, it had.

"There must have been something wrong with it. Rafa said it had an injured leg. But I didn't see. I was trying to chase it off." He looked helpless. "We didn't even have real weapons, only a few daggers."

"It's dead now? It won't hurt someone else?"

Asher nodded.

Alma groaned and Lisha's attention snapped back to him. The healer had finished cleaning and dusting his wounds and moved on to more painful ministrations involving bone needles and sinew. On impulse, Lisha reached to push the healer aside.

Asher caught her hands. "We've given him drink to dull the pain."

She gave him an incredulous look. "He is still in pain."

"If she can't control herself," the healer said to Asher, "take her away. I can't have her cause trouble while I sew Alma up."

Lisha went very still, ignoring the concerned looks of Asher, Hannah, Sarika, and others in the crowd.

"Come with me," Hannah said, moving next to Lisha.

"I'm not leaving Alma." Lisha's gaze remained steadfast on her husband's dark, intense eyes. He needed her and that was that.

"This isn't a place for the tender hearts of women," Asher said. "A wife shouldn't have to bear seeing her husband…"

"Leave her be," Sarika snapped. "You have no idea what women can or cannot handle. I've seen this woman bear the unbearable." She gave Lisha a curt nod. "She can bear this."

ALMA MOANED, then shifted in the furs on their bed. One of his legs slipped off the piled wool blankets, and he gave a muffled cry.

"Daddy!" Eva cried, abandoning her dolls and bounding across the one-room cottage.

Lisha dropped her beadwork and caught the girl before she flung herself onto her father's lap. "You can't climb on Daddy right now, remember?" she said in a hushed voice.

"But he needs kisses." Eva's hazel eyes were huge and serious.

Lisha huffed out something between a laugh and a cry, then pressed a kiss to their daughter's dark curls.

"It's all right," Alma said in a hoarse voice. "I need my Eva. Bring her closer."

Lisha pulled up a stool beside her husband and settled onto it, keeping a close grip on their little girl.

Alma reached out to stroke Eva's round cheek. She promptly turned her face and plastered her father's hand with kisses.

"That's a good girl," Alma said. Eva beamed. A moment later, he dropped his arm back to the bed, and dug his elbow into the furs, trying to shift again.

"Here," Lisha said, "Let me help you. Eva, honey, do you want to play with your dolls some more?"

The girl nodded and ambled back to her play corner.

Lisha slid her slim hands under Alma's bandaged legs and adjusted the pile of wool blankets under his knees. As she did so, his face went tight, the color draining from it before returning in a flush of red. Sweat beaded across his brow.

"I'm so sorry," Lisha said, "I know it hurts."

Alma gave her a weary half-smile. "*I* am sorry, Lisha. Now I've doubled your work and you're stuck taking care of a grumpy old man."

Lisha snorted. "You're not grumpy. You're not old either, because that would make me old, too. And I am much too young to be old."

Alma laughed, then winced. "Speaking of young, where's our son?"

"I sent him to Ruth and Daren's cottage so he could play with Levi." She sighed. "I can't have him under my feet all the time, tormenting Eva while I'm trying to take care of you."

"Understandable," Alma said with a wry look. "There's nothing wrong with letting our son play with friends. Stop worrying yourself."

Lisha sighed. "It's just that every time I start to feel safe, something happens to upend our lives. I find myself fearful about the simplest things."

Alma patted her hand. "The Lord will take care of us. He always does."

Lisha bit her lip. "Like how he took care of Abinadi?" Fire and screams rose in her mind. She stood abruptly and brushed off her skirts. "I have work to do."

"Lisha—"Alma called as she stalked to the table and began cutting vegetables for their evening stew. "Lisha, you know it's not that simple."

She lined carrots up and chopped with great vigor, reducing them to a pile of orange shavings. The knife clattered to the tabletop. "I just know that answers are not easy to come by. I've lived a life of faith, Alma. I'll continue living in faith. I build my life on faith and hope. I've made that choice. So why doesn't God take my fears away?"

SUNLIGHT STREAMED through the reeds covering Lisha's windows. She rolled over in her blankets, taking care not to jostle her husband. Alma had suffered injuries before, as had most of the inhabitants of Helam, to one degree or another. Carving a life out of the wilderness was hard on the body. But this time, his healing seemed slower than usual. Heat radiated from him, and the blankets were soaked with his sweat.

Lisha crawled out from under the covers and checked on their sleeping children. Young Alma looked so peaceful in sleep, so like his father, so unlike the frenetic, chaotic boy who took up so much of his mother's time and energy. Eva curled beside him; her fingers coiled in his hair.

Best get a few chores done before they woke. Lisha stirred the kitchen coals back to life, feeding them with a little bark and twigs. Then she drew a heavy knitted shawl around her shoulders, grabbed an earthenware pitcher from a shelf in the cooking corner, and slipped out the reed door. A clay rain jug stood near the corner of the cottage. She pushed aside the lid and peered inside. It was still half full. *Hmmm.* The water looked a little more brackish than she liked. Using a thin sheet of cloth and a ladle, she strained some water into the pitcher and then brought it inside to boil.

Soon she had the fire going and water bubbling merrily. She set some aside to cool for drinking water and stirred the rest into corn-meal mush.

Alma groaned from their pallet. Young Alma stirred, and little Eva poked her head out of their blankets, rubbing her eyes. "You hungry, Daddy?"

Alma just groaned again. Lisha paused in her stirring, giving him an appraising gaze. Alma looked pale as if his very essence were washed away, his dark hair stuck to the sides of his face by sweat. She set the ladle aside.

"Let me check your wounds."

Alma blinked at her, his gaze bleary and unfocused.

"Alma?" Lisha hurried over and touched his forehead. "Oh, but you're burning up. Worse even than an hour ago." She wrung her hands as she thought about what to do. Check the wounds. That was the first order of business, every morning. But the fever? He needed cool clothes. She rose and strode to the table. The water she'd set aside to cool was still quite hot.

"Son. Alma, my son, wake up." She shook his shoulder. "I need you to fetch some water from the rain jug. We need wet clothes for your father. He isn't well."

Young Alma snored into his arm.

"Son! Wake up! I must tend to your father's wounds. Please get the water."

Young Alma grunted and rolled over. "I can't move the lid, Mother. Last time I broke it."

Lisha sighed. The boy was right. It was too much to expect a five-year-old to shift the heavy clay lid without knocking it to the ground. "All right," she said. "Come to the table then. I need you awake and ready to help."

"Yes, Mother," Alma said, slowly kicking his blankets back.

"Eva help!" her piping voice, though sweet, was more of a distraction to Lisha at the moment.

"Keep an eye on Eva for me. I'll be right back."

Young Alma nodded, his bright gaze following Lisha as she snatched some cloth from her sewing basket and strode outside. She sighed again when she saw the brackish water but dipped the clothes into it anyway. It wouldn't matter that it wasn't as clean as she liked. It was just for cooling Alma down.

She returned to her husband's bedside and draped the cloths over his forehead, sponging them down his chest. Alma groaned again. When she removed his bandages, Lisha gasped. His wounds were red and angry, leaking yellow fluid and a terrible smell.

"Alma," she said, her voice hushed. "I need you to run and get the healer, and Asher, as fast as you can."

Her son rose to his feet, looking shocked. "I'll hurry Mother. I'll run like a deer, faster than a deer. I'll…"

"Just get going, son."

It seemed like time stood still while Lisha waited for help. Her husband's breathing was slow and labored, his eyes closed, except for the occasional bleary blink. Even Eva remained quiet, sensing Lisha's somber mood.

The door flew open and Young Alma rushed inside, followed by Asher and the healer, who immediately set to work.

"Bring me hot clothes and a bowl," he told Lisha. "We must drain the sickness from his injuries."

"Here," she said, thrusting the supplies into his hands. She stood back while he cut Alma's stitches. When he pressed the knife to Alma's flesh, she looked away. Young Alma's hand found its way into hers. Eva clutched her skirts. Lisha flinched at her husband's cries while the healer cleaned his wounds. She looked to Asher, who was helping hold Alma still.

Finally, it was over. Alma's legs were bandaged once more, and he lay very still among his blankets, his face pinched and gray.

"He needs water," the healer said. "Even if you have to drip it into his mouth from a cloth. The more he can take, the better."

Lisha nodded to her son, who scurried to bring clean drinking water. Then she turned to Asher. "Will you give him a blessing?"

"Of course."

Lisha scooped Eva into her arms and went to stand by her husband's bedside. Young Alma bowed his head, his eyes huge and worried. Asher and the healer rested their hands on the elder Alma's head.

Then Asher began to pray.

A prayer filled Lisha's heart as well. A prayer of pleading, of faith, of hope. *Please heal Alma. Help him be all right. Please. We need him.*

"I bless you with faith, courage, and strength," Asher continued. "I command this sickness to leave your body. I bless your family to be comforted, for their fears to be relieved."

Lisha felt a rush of hope and the sweet calm of peace.

The prayer ended.

Over the next several weeks, Lisha treasured up the blessing in her heart. When concerns threatened to overwhelm her, she reminded herself of Asher's words, of the promises that came through him from the Lord. Alma would be healed. Her fears would be relieved. She clung with absolute faith to these blessings, and in so doing, felt her fears lose their power. Not just her worries for Alma's health, but the fears that plagued her day-to-day life.

Alma slowly regained his strength. The swelling went down, the redness faded, and his wounds knit closed. He soon could walk across the village without limping or losing his breath. As he returned to his work, ministering to the people, Lisha felt a new sense of purpose and calm. It was time for her to set aside her fears and share her hope and her strength with those around her.

CHANNAH, 139 BC, CITY OF AMULON

"

No, move left! Not my left, YOUR left!" The beam fell to the ground with a thud. "Didn't you listen?" Amulon shouted. "Are you deaf to my words, or is your thick skull not letting them in?"

"You build it yourself. I'll no longer help while you yell at me." Zoar kicked at a small stump, cursing as he hopped, then spun and limped away. "And don't ask for my help again!"

"How will we build then, with no artisans? We aren't in Shilom, are we?" Amulon waved his hands around in obvious frustration. Then, muttering to himself, he continued the rant, "I'm a priest, not a craftsman." He turned to Channah. "Why do you look at me like that?"

"I was just listening. I didn't mean to..." She shook her head and bent over to pick up Lemish. He was nearly three, but she felt he would be safer further from his angry father. "Can you take this to feed to the chickens?" She handed him a dry cob with some kernels of corn barely hanging on.

"Can I play with Adir?" He asked with a smile.

"Not now. Just sit over by the tree and call the chickens so I can still see you."

Kicking up a cloud of dust as he shuffled his moccasins, he looked back, eyes locked with his mother. She shook her head. "Ok, Momma."

She turned her attention to her husband as their son went off to feed his chickens. "Your work is better than it used to be," she said softly so no one else could hear. "Don't be angry at everyone for their learning mistakes. You'll never win their love with anger."

Amulon paused and looked at his young wife. "For someone so inexperienced with life, you seem to think you know how it all works."

She breathed deeply, clenching her fists and biting her tongue. *Don't speak, just ignore it.* She told herself.

Houses were built as fast as children were born, but that was too slow for Amulon. There were no artisans or craftsmen to do the work. The once elite priests of King Noah now had to do all of it themselves.

Amulon paused in his labor to remove some splinters from his calloused hands. Channah walked over to where Lemish was teasing the chickens with the few remaining kernels of corn. He was occupied and having fun. Channah, having taken a moment to cool off, returned to where Amulon was struggling with the ridge beam.

"Can I help?" Channah asked as she moved from the shelter of the trees to where her new home would be. "I have a suggestion of how to do this if you'd like."

Amulon's eyes closed in obvious frustration. "Do you ever stop telling me how to do things?"

"To get this done by the time the snow falls, you might need my help," she offered humbly.

He paused, looked at her expanding belly, then gave in. "Can you pick up this other end of the beam and hold it while I get the pin in it?"

Channah called to Lemish, "Can you come and be a helper for your father?" Lemish tossed the remainder of the corn cob to the chickens and ran to her. "I need you to stay right there while I help your father. Our new house is almost done! Can you hold the pins till your father needs them?" The young child looked at his mother, picked up some smooth round pegs, and sat down on a stump beside his father. "That's a good boy."

"I just need you to steady that end; it's heavy, but once my end is up, it won't be as hard to hold it in place." Amulon lifted his end to the highest ridge and placed it securely over the outside framework. "Can you climb up here and just hold it in place so it doesn't fall off again? I'll lift the lower end and secure them both."

Channah carefully climbed the ladder to where the beam rested and laced her fingers around it as tightly as she could, using her weight to keep it from falling off again. Amulon, eyeing the beam, lifted the other end and began moving it toward the outer edge of the structure. The roof was the last part of the project but also the trickiest. In Shilom, the craftsmen who built the palace and opulent structures made the process look so simple.

"I wish I'd paid more attention to how this was all done," Amulon complained out loud.

"You've almost got it. I'm holding my end."

The beam began to slip a little.

"Hold it tighter, or it will fall!" he shouted.

The weight was too much for Amulon to hold, and gravity took over. Channah was in the path of the falling beam. "Move!" he spat.

She couldn't. The slipping log teetered on the edge, then, with one fell swoop, knocked her off the ladder, hit her square in the abdomen as she fell backward to the ground. Because he was holding the other end, the teetering motion launched Amulon off his feet momentarily.

When everything settled, the ringing in Channah's head was louder than the voices in the distance. She felt like she was in a cave with faint voices rumbling in and out of her fuzzy mind. She could see the blurry face of Amulon, but the darkness kept closing in. A wailing sound, which she couldn't decide if was her or Lemish, made her squint, closing out any remaining faces. Only voices floated in and out of her mind.

"Help!" she heard Amulon cry. She tried to move her head toward his voice, but things just became darker. "Help!" She heard him again in the far distance.

Voices swirled around her; she wanted to open her eyes to see but her lids were so heavy.

"I wish we had a healer," she heard Amulon shout above the others and felt he must be close, but she couldn't feel anything but the pounding in her head. "Don't die. Please, don't die."

She wanted to assure him she was just fine. She wanted to tell him that *she* was the healer and had the skills necessary to remedy the situation. She, however, could not move. Nor could she do more than moan.

A sound from the echoing bleak cave of her mind kindled the desire to wake up. A child wailing for his mother!

"Momma," he cried.

For a moment, keenly aware of his touch on her forehead, she heard him whisper. "Momma, wake up."

CHANNAH'S HEAD WAS POUNDING, the tent was dark. Faces began to appear above her, but they were blurry, and the throbbing in her head was too much. She closed her eyes.

"Channah, can you hear me?"

A loud ringing in her ears mingled with voices echoing in the distance.

"She's not waking up. What more can we do?" she heard Amulon say with more concern than she'd ever heard before.

She wanted to thank him, compliment him on his tenderness. She couldn't.

She heard other voices and tried hard to open her eyes. In the faint glow of the open door, she saw Isa and heard her speaking to Amulon.

"There are some herbs she uses when we don't feel well," Isa whispered, "I can try and use them on her."

Amulon reached for a basket to help make tea. Channah tried to stop him, but her arms wouldn't move.

"Oh, not that one!" Isa said, "That will make her..." Isa lowered her eyes. "It would be bad for her."

"What would it do?"

Channah's eyes opened a sliver as she took in the exchange. Isa's expression was troubled. "I don't want to say."

Amulon now focused more on what Channah's closest friend was saying than how his wife was doing. "Tell me. Now!"

Isa's eyes connected with Channah's. She glanced away and Channah gave in, closing her eyes tightly, listening to hear if her dearest friend would reveal the secret. "If one wishes to not carry a child, this tea will make the woman not conceive."

Channah grimaced. Amulon would be angry.

"Has she used this? Is this why it took many years for her to conceive? Have any of the rest of the women used this?"

Fuming, Amulon took the basket of herbs and threw it out the tent door.

"You will bear us children," he raged.

Channah, now trying very hard to focus and wake up, felt her lips, dry and rough, her throat constricted. Her hand obeyed and touched her face and then brushed down her chest to her belly, expecting the round bump of her growing child. There wasn't one.

Now alarmed, Channah attempted to speak to the women waiting outside the open flap door of her dwelling.

She heard Isa's voice. "When will you tell Channah about her child?"

An angry Amulon's voice responded. "When she wakes."

That would not be necessary—she already knew.

CHANNAH'S RECOVERY from the accident had gone well, but occasionally she still heard the ringing in her ears. To remedy it, she would stop, pause, breathe, and close her eyes to relax. It usually went away.

Amulon sent the message to gather early in the morning. Everyone was to attend this meeting. The time would be noonday in the village, which was finally starting to take shape. The main assembly place was a basic pole structure with a roof and gave them a covered area to have meetings. They also cultivated a small patch of ground near the woods with corn and grains they had foraged or stolen from the Nephite city. Channah guessed the priests had found the way to get back to Shilom and Shemlon, but they always went at night when no one could watch the direction they traveled. She knew it was to keep the women from finding their way home.

As the people gathered, her hands smoothed over her flat abdomen. Her child would have been born by now. She would have been holding her in her arms. She silently mourned the little girl she never got to hold but knew she had been laid to rest in a tiny blanket at the edge of their small city. All of that took place while Channah lay semi-conscious in her hut, with no recollection of even giving birth.

The City of Amulon had a small burial mound. Some of the young mothers had died in childbirth, and their bodies just not able to take the stress. They had been laid to rest with their babies. This would be their final home. They would never again see their families.

Home. A word with so many meanings now. She cast her eyes around and viewed the city, which was currently the place she was forced to call home. It would never hold the reverence of her true home, Shemlon, where she had family, parents!

An area along the hillside had the beginning signs of wine production. Grapes were twining their way up trellised structures. The men had insisted on that project even before homes were constructed. Skins were always in different stages of tanning, and looms were built for the women to weave cloth.

The time had arrived, women's work was done, children had been cared for, and meals all prepared. Each member of the village looked up with anticipation at the tower where Amulon held a large skin, tanned almost to a translucent thickness.

"We know where the land of Shilom and Shemlon are located. We have been scouting out all of the areas around the rivers and believe this one leads through the land. We will begin a new expedition soon."

They've known for a long time. Channah felt the anger welling in her chest. She had suspected for some time, but now she knew. *If they mapped the way back, we can find it too.* Then the realization hit her. Tears welled up in her eyes. If they went back, they would be shunned. They had born children to these men who were hated— no, despised —by her people. She and the others now had children they loved, but they too would also be outcasts from her people. Neither city would welcome them back - Nephite or Lamanite. They no longer had a true home, except this one. The thought both angered and saddened her.

Tears escaped the corners of her eyes with the realization that as much as the women hated their captors, they were all they had besides their children. This was their new reality, and they could never go back.

Amulon continued speaking, "Some of you may have been using the herb that keeps you from carrying a child. This will no longer be allowed. My vision of our city is one of growth and wealth. Our sons and daughters will live as we once did. We will trade and grow in prosperity. Our children will have only the finest things."

Channah glanced around at the ramshackle hovels they lived in. The partially completed structures mocked his words. "Who will build this grand city?" she said just loud enough for those around her to hear. Somehow, her voice carried to Amulon on the tower. He heard. She knew if he was closer, he would have struck her. Amulon's eyes did what his hands could not, warning her with an angry glare.

"We will take what is rightfully ours from the Nephite city, and the rest from the Lamanite city. We helped build Shilom." His fists were clenched, and spittle flew from his lips as he spoke.

"Is that why you seek the location?" Channah asked. "Instead of building proper structures here?" She continued, "You've been taking things for some time, though. How long have you known the way back?"

He chuckled. "Yes, we have found things we needed that they would never miss." His smile turned to a grimace. "We took things that belonged to us. The Nephites have no right to keep the city we built with our cunning and leadership. We will retake it and make the Nephites our slaves." The look Amulon gave Channah warned her not to say anything else. "The expedition leaves in the morning. Those who remain will complete the homes we have started here."

He curled the map carefully and tucked it beneath his arm. He walked over to Channah and took her firmly by the wrist. They walked briskly back to where their son was happily playing. He stacked rocks and tipped the stack over, laughing as he did. "Mommy, see me!" He began carefully stacking again, with his little tongue tucked outside the corner of his mouth in concentration.

"Good boy!" Channah crooned as Amulon practically dragged her into the hut.

He didn't even wait for their eyes to adjust to the darkness to launch into a tirade.

"Don't ever question me in front of the others. Ever."

"Why must you take what belongs to others?" As the words escaped her lips, she knew she had chosen them sloppily, and Amulon's hand struck her across the face.

She had been in this position before, hands on her knees, bent over. Channah breathed deeply to stop the spinning in her head and slowly stood to face Amulon. She used to be a Lamanite princess, the daughter of the King, with all the privileges and protections that came with her position. Now she groveled just to survive.

"What I meant to say is that with your leadership and vision, could you not build a city like Noah did? You're much more cunning and smart than he." She continued to breathe deeply, willing the spinning echo in her head to stop. She reached to brush her hand across her cheek - now hot and painful. She could feel the welt rising like the anger in her heart. She shifted her weight to her feet and slowly stood to face him.

Amulon smiled. "My vision is more refined than Noah's. One day my city will be better and will be built by Nephite hands. If we take the city back, I plan to build it grander and change the name."

"This is your city, the city of Amulon." Channah looked around. "We've worked so hard to build this." Her eyes rested on the face of this very confusing man. "Is this not enough?"

He laughed. "This?" Waving his arms to each side, "This village is nothing like what I envisioned my city to be. We need craftsmen to make my visions reality." He spat on the dirt floor. "We will retake the city that rightfully belongs to us, the priests."

"Will you continue to build this city - Amulon? What about our homes? We need fire pits to cook in--"

Before she could finish, Amulon cut her off. "We will live here until our forces are sufficiently strong."

"Will you wait till our sons are grown?"

Amulon laughed. "I have a better plan." He took the map from where he had tucked it beneath his arm. "This is my chance to be king."

Channah watched him walk out of the hut, carrying the key to her escape. An idea began to form in her mind.

DINAH, 138 BC, CITY OF SHILOM

*T*he people endured four more winters, barely scraping together enough food to stave off starvation. Families were beginning to grow again, with children gradually adding to the number of people living in Shilom.

Tensions were growing as the murmuring voices whispered again about the need to fight for freedom. The angry gatherings had become more frequent and usually resulted in trouble with the Lamanite guards when the assemblies were discovered. The men were becoming restless as their families slowly gained strength and recovered from recurring seasonal illnesses. Many more were now able to work. And to fight. The harvests had come in each year, but there was never enough food for the winter. Springtime was both a time of anxiety and hope. The question inevitably came up whether to eat or to plant.

"Have faith. A seed, when planted in good ground, becomes something much more than it was." Limhi encouraged his people, "Planting a seed requires us to have faith and hope for a better outcome." He held a seed up for all to see. "If we consume the meager grains we have left, instead of planting, we eat once and then starve. Or, we endure some hunger for a short time and harvest an abundance." He fisted the grain. "Choose faith, my people. Faith in the Lord and in His bounty."

Tamar stood. "Come. Let us venture yet again to see what the Lord has provided with the spring plants." She waved her hand, encouraging all to follow her. "Bring your baskets, for we will find food for today." The people followed, encouraged.

Except for Dinah!

She languished. Limhi spent more and more time with her and less time advocating for peace. Their son, now almost four years old, was going to become a big brother. He helped care for his mother and was wise beyond his age. He seemed to know how to do so many things and was so good and kind in caring for Dinah. He even knew which greens to pick that were good for food.

"HOW ARE YOU FEELING TODAY?" Limhi asked as he stepped into their home. "Can I start some tea for you?"

"I'm ready to get out and see something more than these four walls. Could you carry me to my garden?" She sat up weakly. "I miss working in the soil."

"If you would like to go outside, I'll carry you."

Limhi gently scooped up Dinah's thin frame, and she laid her head on his shoulder. "Thank you, my love." She whispered in his ear.

He carefully placed her on the grass near where she had cared for herbs that were been part of the garden started by his grandmother, Mera, and tended to by Tamar and Dinah. The patch was full of weeds.

A tear fell from her eye onto a blade of grass. Her hand caught the next one before it watered the soil. Limhi knelt down beside her and began pulling the weeds.

"I should have been doing this for you."

"No, there's much unrest. You have enough to do."

"This little garden means a lot to you. I shouldn't have neglected it."

Dinah's small hand brushed across his cheek. "You cared for me. That was most important."

"You and our little one." He smiled, looking at her belly, the fabric of her dress pulled taught.

"Yes, you've cared for us well, our soon-to-be family of four." She leaned over and kissed him gently. "Thank you."

He fiddled with some of the weeds he had pulled. Stripping their leaves, twisting the spines into rope. "The people want to fight, yet again." His fingers turned green as he gnarled the stems. "I ask them to trust in the Lord, but now I'm not even sure anymore what that really means." Their eyes met. "Do you think we should fight?"

"What does your mother say?"

"She is confident God will deliver us. She pleads with the people each day to have faith, to take care of each other, and to not be angry or hateful.

"I agree with her." Dinah's soft voice whispered. "I've had dreams of being free. In my dream, we aren't old. Our children are young, and your hair is not gray." She reached up to run her fingers through his curly locks. "I think my dreams need to be fulfilled soon though, because I am seeing a few gray hairs on your head these days." She continued to finger his curls and smooth them out, stroking his head with her hands, gazing with adoration at her husband.

DINAH'S STRENGTH RETURNED SLOWLY. Each day she was up for longer than the previous, and she started making short visits to the widows in the town with Benjamin in tow. Often Tamar would come when she was finished with the planting.

"My heart aches for so many who have lost husbands and sons." Dinah spoke the words reverently. She looked up at Limhi to gauge his readiness to hear her thoughts. She continued wrapping some freshly baked corncakes. "Is there nothing more we can do?"

"You're doing what is needful. They are hungry; we have enough and can share." Limhi took Dinah by her shoulders and tilted her chin so he looked directly into her eyes. "Encourage them to pray. To have faith and plead for deliverance."

Dinah nodded, tears welling in her eyes. "I will." She brushed the tears away, slipped out, and walked slowly down the road toward the old temple.

"How are you doing today?" she asked as she drew the tapestry aside and stepped into one of the nearest homes.

The woman sat in tears, in the corner of the room, holding her sleeping child — quietly weeping.

Dinah went to her. "What is wrong?" she asked.

"I miss him."

Tears sprang to Dinah's eyes. "Oh, Elah, I'm so sorry."

"He wanted a child so badly, and now he's gone. I don't want to do this alone. I don't want to die a slave. I don't want to starve." Her tears now flowed freely amidst hiccups and sobs. "I don't…want my baby to starve." Gaining some composure, she continued. "Please, my queen, is there nothing that can be done to free us?" Sobbing again, "If he had not been on patrol that day and been attacked by the Lamanites, he would be here."

Dinah held her as she wept, feeling the pressure on her own unborn child as she embraced Elah and her sleeping child.

"Let me see what I can do."

"Limhi, you must understand the utter despair some feel, especially the widows, as they see the food supply dwindling. They have no way to provide for their needs. No one to hunt for food." Dinah lowered herself to the pile of skins and let out a slow breath. "The attacks from Lamanite soldiers come more frequently, and there are so few men left to protect our city." Dinah's eyes filled with tears. "I understand their fears. I would feel the same if you had been killed in battle."

"Would you wish others to meet her same fate? Would you want other families to lose father or brother?" Limhi knelt to sit beside her and took her hand in his. "The widows in the city outnumber those who still have husbands, and we can't risk losing any more of our men." Limhi let go of her hand and rested his head in his hands for a few moments. "What is keeping the people from focusing on faith instead of fear?"

"The people feel helpless if they aren't doing something to free our city," Dinah begged. "Anything is better than dying a slave."

"No, there are worse things than dying," Limhi whispered. "Do *you* wish for us to fight the Lamanites?" He added soberly.

"It might be time to fight, to try again to win our freedom so we can find our brothers who went with Alma." Dinah looked into his eyes. "I don't wish for others to die; I just don't know what else to do."

"Waiting on the Lord is not doing nothing," Limhi spoke with confidence. "It is exercising faith and working until the Lord shows His mighty arm. I trust in the Lord."

DINAH, 137 BC, CITY OF SHILOM

*D*inah knelt beside her garden, shaded by the sycamore tree in the courtyard. Little Benjamin slept on a skin in the soft shaded grass. "Your herbs are coming up well. It looks like they have set flowers," Limhi said, startling her.

She turned her head with a quick intake. "It's you, my king." She smiled demurely.

Limhi smiled in return. "My queen, it is I." He bent and took her hand, dirty fingernails and all. He turned and kissed the back. Dinah smiled.

"To your comment, yes, flowers have set," she turned and pointed to some closed buds and open blossoms. "I'm pleased. I'll gather the seeds and grow more next season, so many can benefit from these blessed plants during the season of fevers."

Limhi sat down on the grass.

Dinah looked intently at Limhi. "You have something on your mind. Do you plan to tell me?" Dinah placed her hand on his knee and made sure their eyes connected. "What is it?"

"I don't want war. I'm tired of the bloodshed. I have one more thing to try before consenting to battle. I know the Lord led Alma and those who followed him away from here. I don't know if they made it to Zarahemla. I have the records from my grandfather that describe the journey from Zarahemla to the Land Nephi." He paused and inhaled deeply. "I plan to send some men to retrace that journey and look for Zarahemla and for Alma." Limhi paused, then added, "We can ask for their help! If they come in force, maybe the Lamanites will allow us to leave without bloodshed."

Limhi closed his eyes and rubbed his forehead like he did when he was perplexed. "The Lord has told me we will be free. I just don't know how." He turned to face Dinah. "This thought came to me in a dream last night so I feel it is guidance from the Lord." He looked into Dinah's eyes. "I fear though, what the Lamanites will do to those that remain, when they find some of our men have escaped."

Limhi took his wife into his arms and held her tight. The baby in her womb gave a firm kick. Limhi chuckled. "I guess that was a bit too tight. She's a fighter."

"She?" Dinah questioned him.

"I saw her in a dream this past night. A little dark-haired girl came and sat upon my lap." Limhi smiled broadly. "You did promise at Benjamin's birth that the next would be a daughter."

Dinah teasingly added, "God gives us children and not in the order we request."

"I'll take whatever He gives us. I'm just grateful." Limhi placed a small kiss on Dinah's forehead and brushed some dirt from her dress. "Maybe the Lord will bless her with a freedom we don't yet enjoy." With a more serious tone, he added, "We need to focus on faith. Far too many are looking to their own strength and wish for one final battle. The Lord has shown he will fight for us if we but have faith in Him." Limhi held his wife away for a moment to look into her eyes. "Do you trust that all will be well?"

Dinah's eyes dropped for a moment as she looked at her hands, covered in soil. Dirt caked under her fingernails; smudges of brown colored her dress where she'd inadvertently wiped her hands. "I'm quite the queen with my dirty hands and filthy dress." She was silent for a moment, "Lacking faith." Tears filled her eyes. "Pray for me that my faith can be as strong as yours. I see your strength, and it gives me courage."

"You're wonderful, dirt and all, and I love you," Limhi whispered as he leaned over to pull her into an embrace. "Together, we are stronger than we are apart."

"What of the widows? They have no one."

"They have us. They have others in this city. We will make sure none are unprotected, and none go hungry."

"That feels right and good." Dinah smiled at his conviction.

"Tomorrow, we will organize once the men have escaped."

Limhi turned at the sound of the gate scraping across the stones of the courtyard. "For now, though, I need to talk with these two."

Helam and Gideon walked through the gate into the courtyard. Limhi stood, and they joined him in the shade of the tree.

"Gideon, I need you to bring six of your strongest soldiers and meet me at the temple after dark tonight."

Gideon nodded.

"Be prepared for a journey of several weeks. If discovered, you must say you are hunting," Limhi cautioned.

Helam spoke, "I can go, my king. If you need me to."

"No, you're needed here." Limhi clapped Helam on the shoulder. "I wish I had three or four of you, my friend."

Gideon took Limhi by the hand and placed another on his shoulder. "I'm at your service. I'll ready a team."

"I will remain by your side to protect you should anything happen," Helam offered.

The two men slipped out of the courtyard without a backward glance.

Limhi stooped to pick up his son, who occupied himself practicing building fire stacks with twigs. His other arm reached over to help Dinah stand. In silence, they walked back to their quarters in the old palace.

The children scuffled in the city street. Chickens clucked outside the courtyard. Merchants traded their goods as they did every other day. Tomorrow things would be different.

~

THE NIGHT WAS FOGGY. The river babbling past roots and boulders covered the sounds of men coming from each corner of the city. Limhi slipped out of bed while Dinah and Benjamin slept.

Dinah whispered to him, sensing him leave. "I'm coming." She lifted carefully away from Benjamin's sleeping form.

"You should be asleep."

Seeing she was determined, he helped her move around their son without waking him. She pulled on a shawl and took his hand.

They walked silently to the courtyard gate. Knowing it would make a noise that could possibly wake the sleeping guards, they waited. Stealthy figures moved toward Limhi and Dinah until the expedition group stood just outside the gate.

Darkness cloaked the gathering. Limhi pulled a rolled scroll from beneath his tunic.

A silver moon cast dim light on the gathering, and Limhi spread a map on the stones so all could see. Helam stood guard at the gate, watching for any trouble.

"This is the journey Zeniff took from Zarahemla to here. It's rough and has few details, but it's all we have. Gideon, take your men and try to find Zarahemla. If you find the city, and our brethren are alive, bring them here to free us from captivity." Limhi looked into the faces of the men he loved as brothers, trusted with his life, and warmly called friends. "God has told me that we will be free. I don't know how it will come about. The Lord expects us to reason things out and act, so I feel we must proceed in faith and not wait."

They stood and Gideon spoke. "I know that I speak for all who are here. Watch over our families and we will go as quickly as we can. Men, bring your provisions and weapons as if we are hunting. If the Lamanites find us escaping, we will tell them we *are* hunting. Just not tell them what we are hunting for."

All nodded in agreement.

"Go with God," Limhi breathed as he grasped their hands, one at a time, through the metal bars. His eyes met Gideon's. "You are a true friend."

Without a sound, Limhi and Helam returned to their homes as a small group of their most beloved and trusted friends disappeared into the night.

~

A NEW DAY DAWNED.

The Lamanites discovered that several of the men in the city were missing. Shouting guards alerted Limhi that there was trouble. He rose from his bed. "Dinah, please remain indoors for now."

Ten soldiers stood apart from the courtyard but close enough to be visible to Limhi as he emerged from his home. "Is there a problem?"

Despite her condition, Dinah also poked her head out to hear what was happening.

The largest Lamanite guard stepped forward. "Men are missing. We tracked their footprints to the river and beyond. They left down-river in canoes." Sweat dripped from his forehead. "Why did the men leave? You are still slaves to us."

Limhi raised both hands as he approached the gathering. "They left on a hunting expedition." They will come back.

"When will they return?"

"When they find what they seek," Limhi spoke in complete honesty and didn't give any additional details.

That seemed to pacify the guards.

"All food must still be gathered. Women will work in their place." With that declaration, the guards returned to their positions around the city, armed with whips and spears.

Limhi breathed a deep sigh. They wouldn't pursue the expedition party. He closed his eyes and said a silent prayer of gratitude.

~

ALL WERE ASKED to come to the temple steps.

Limhi aided Dinah in her walk to the temple steps. She scanned the crowd, realizing for the first time how few men there were.

Limhi stood and climbed to the platform to speak. "My friends, my people, thank you for gathering today. With those that have gone for the hunting expedition, our numbers are fewer. The work to be done will not decrease but will need to be done by those who are left behind. God expects us to care for one another, as Alma taught by the Waters of Mormon. Bearing one another's burdens comes in many ways. Widows and children have needs. You are becoming very good at this." His face became sober. "We must not hate our brothers, even those who are our captors." A ripple of murmurs rose, and many heads turned to whisper to those nearby.

"Love our enemies is the commandment." Limhi pointed to the Lamanite guards who stood far back, armed in case of trouble from the gathering. "We must not hate."

The crowd seemed to ease. "Unity is what we need. In caring for the widows and fatherless, those who have should share with those who have not." He paused to survey the crowd. "Who is a widow? Raise your hands."

Slowly, hands crept up. There were more than just a few. Hands kept rising. "Those who are able to meet their own needs, please join up with a widowed family." The people looked at him, confused. "Move over to stand beside a widow family. Make groups." There was a small movement, then more, then the whole gathering began to mingle. Once the movement ceased, he began again. "Are there any widows remaining that have not been connected to another family?" A few more hands raised. "Who can take on more?"

Helam raised a hand. Tamar smiled, and he put his arm around her and volunteered to help yet another family.

A few more hands went up. "Please take these women and their children into your care." Once all hands were down, Limhi began to speak again.

"You're families now. Women, watch out for each other. Help care for one another in every way. Men, you are to make sure none go hungry. Love the children of these families who have suffered so much. Care for them. Find out what their needs are and together, we will work to meet those needs. All must labor in the fields from now on. Planting, harvesting, and storing food all need to be done and children can help in the work."

Limhi smiled as he saw the clusters of new families. "Now, let us get on with the day."

～

IT HAD BEEN A FULL MONTH. The men had not returned. Fall heat and lack of rain caused the fields to wither and turn golden. The intense sun beat down on the people working in the fields. Tempers flared. Lamanite soldiers were weary of standing in the heat watching their captors work.

"Work faster. Finish," the guard shouted, flicking his whip above the heads of the men. He began snapping the whip above the heads of the women and children — not carefully. A woman cried out in pain and grabbed her shoulder where the lash landed. Those around rushed to her aid. It didn't take long for a chaotic scene to erupt. Men took their hoes and shovels and rushed to the guard who had caused the injury. A scuffle ensued, and the shouting caused the other guards and men from the city to come to render aid. A cloud of dust grew as men fought their captors in defense of those who they'd been asked to protect and care for.

When the dust settled, the guard was dead. So was one of the Nephite men. A loss of life would bring consequences. Everyone stood back, waiting to see what was going to happen. A Lamanite solder took off toward the catacomb that led to their city. Limhi knew the response would be swift.

"Arm yourselves," Helam advised.

"Men, escort the women and children home," Limhi ordered. "Then, take both bodies to the shade of the river. They will be washed and buried."

～

THE CONSEQUENCES DID COME. Following the burial, twice as many guards returned. New Lamanite families moved into the city, and small widowed families were again displaced. Limhi called for the people to gather again. Guards stood closer this time.

Limhi spoke loud enough for the guards to hear. "There will be no more attacks on women or children. We will defend ourselves. Let me be clear that if we are attacked, we will fight back." The soldiers raised their spears.

"You are our slaves," a soldier shouted.

"Dead slaves do no labor," Helam responded.

THE NEXT FEW days passed without incident. In the following week, the guards again became aggressive, spitting on men, shouting at the women, and threatening to whip the people who were not working as fast. Their whips snapped above the heads of those toiling in the fields.

It was not until a few weeks after the first attack that one guard took his abuse too far, and his whip grazed the ear of one of the older children. The child cried out, and immediately, another battle ensued.

Helam shouted, "Arm yourselves!"

Each person with a tool turned it into a weapon for defense. Crops that had been so carefully tended to, and were needed for their very survival, disappeared, trampled by those who were now engaged in a full-scale battle.

The fighting raged on throughout the day and moved up the hillside above the city and into the woods. Bodies littered the hillside. More Nephites perished and the wailing of new widows filled the air.

Dinah witnessed the destruction with tears streaming down her face. Her time of giving birth drew near, but she rushed to the center of town anyway. Survivors carried the bodies of the deceased to the river. Her knees buckled as the mourning cries grew louder – children discovering they had lost their fathers and women learning they had lost their husbands. She fell to the ground and wept into her hands. "Why would God let this happen over and over? There is too much death and sorrow here." A hand rested on her shoulder. She turned to see one of the widows who had lost her husband years before.

Elah choked out the words, "We will get through this together." She reached out a hand to Dinah, lifting her up. They embraced, and both wept tears of sorrow for the pain of remembering all who had gone before and for those now lost.

Tamar came and took Dinah, leading her away from the work of caring for the dead, and finished the job while Dinah began to sing. There would be a period of mourning, but music seemed to soothe her troubled heart, so she let the sorrow leave her heart in the form of a hymn. Others joined in, and soon, their music carried through the trees. Songs that had been sung by their people before Alma's escape were remembered as they joined in sorrow to bury their dead.

The dead of the Lamanites were taken to the catacomb and left, where they would be found and returned to their city.

Tamar and Dinah began the visits to the homes of those who had lost so much already. Their hearts were broken, but their faith was building.

THERE WERE new widows to be cared for. New groups formed, and the few remaining men in the city were now caring for multiple families. Dinah moved through the crowd, gently touching, embracing, and comforting those she loved and hurt for.

"People of Nephi," Limhi called as they gathered together to mourn their dead. "We have been warned. Abinadi said we would be driven and smitten. Truly his words have come to pass, and we are captives of our brothers the Lamanites who, by definition, are indeed our enemies but don't deserve our hate. We must not canker our souls with hate. My people, let us covenant with the Lord to keep His commandments. Let us follow the commandment to turn the other cheek." Limhi took a deep breath, looking into the faces of those stricken with grief and pain.

"We will not fight. We will ask for the Lord to deliver us." Limhi raised his arms to the sky, "Pray mightily in your hearts and homes for strength. Plead for patience to endure this trial until the Lord sees fit to deliver us." Limhi let the words sink in while he looked from one friend to another. "As we care for one another, humble ourselves, and plead for relief, we will put our trust in the Lord and exercise faith in His timing."

Dinah moved to stand beside Limhi as he bowed his head. She took his hand in hers while her other held Benjamin's small, wiggly fingers. "Dear Lord, we entrust our lives into Thy hands. We have been hard-hearted and prideful. We have fought our own battles and now, unified, ask for thy help. Please, Lord, be our guide, our guardian, and our strength. Lord, bless us with the will not to fight, not to speak out, not to anger, and not to hate our brethren, the Lamanites. Bless us, Father, to be one. We pray for deliverance and, until Thou seest fit to free us from slavery, please let us have peace in our hearts, knowing that Thou, oh Lord, are aware of us and watching over us."

Limhi ended the prayer over his people. Dinah smiled and squeezed his hand. She looked out over the sorrowing faces and saw resolve, and also a softening. They were ready to be taught.

Limhi added, "We will continue to care for the widows, fatherless, and those who cannot care for themselves. The sick and weary should be fed and nurtured."

As the final word fell from his lips, there came a cry of joy from the shadows of the river. The shouts startled everyone and the focus shifted to what was happening.

Six men emerged from the shadows, immediately engulfed by the crowd. The expedition had returned.

"We followed the map the best we could. Through our travels, we saw signs people had once inhabited the land. Trees had been cut down and hewn into temporary structures. We began to see remnants of a great civilization as we journeyed on." He paused to take a drink from a cup that someone handed to him. "To our great sorrow, the cities that may have been our people, our friends, and those we knew once are no more. There will be no help for our deliverance." Despair engulfed the crowd as the words they spoke settled in.

Dinah blurted out, "So, we still don't know if Alma and his people ever found Zarahemla?"

Limhi cast his eyes toward heaven. "Lord, if those we love have indeed perished, we pray for their souls. They were faithful and good. Please watch over us. Guide us. Help us learn thy ways, for we long to make a covenant as Alma did and enter into the waters of baptism."

The people all fell to their knees, some sorrowing to tears, others sorrowing for their past sins, and the remainder sorrowing for their plight.

Limhi continued, "We are not alone. Nor should we lose hope. The Lord has promised that we would be delivered. My friends, let us not despair, but instead, have faith." Limhi walked among his people. "Dust off your clothes. Rise. Let us hear more of what our returning brothers can tell us."

Limhi waved his hand at the six, indicating that the temple steps were theirs. They took turns describing in detail the great land they found.

Gideon took a turn with the narrative. "The people had experienced great death and destruction, for their bones lay upon the ground in heaps without proper burials. Their cities had crumbled but not entirely, and the evidence spoke of a great civilization." He passed a wrapped bundle to the king. "We found this amongst the ruins, oh King, and it is one of the few things we took from that place."

The king carefully folded the cloth back to reveal plates made of metal. "We cannot read the writings," Gideon added.

Dinah peeked over Limhi's shoulder and reached to touch the plates. They were cold. The wrinkled metal gave slightly with her touch. "What is the language?" she asked.

Limhi let his finger trace the engravings. "These look similar to plates kept by the kings of our people, but I cannot read the writings. I will keep them with our records and, one day, maybe God will send another Prophet who can teach us what is contained in this record."

Gideon, and the others who had embarked on this important journey, returned to their families, who embraced them warmly.

"I knew God would bring you back to me," Rachel proclaimed through her grateful tears as her son embraced her and held her tight.

Limhi raised his arms and said, "Let us all return to our homes. Tomorrow will dawn a new day. There is much to be done."

IT WAS WELL after midnight when Dinah cried out in pain. The waters that held her child safe and warm flowed from her, and the midwife was called. As the rays of the coming day cast a pink glow across the sky, a tiny baby was placed into a mother's loving arms. Dinah had become a mother to a tiny dark-haired girl.

There was rejoicing in the city of Nephi the next day. Flowers that bloomed on the hillside were picked and strewn along the path to Limhi and Dinah's home.

Dinah was much stronger this time. She held her baby girl with a beaming smile. "We will call her Miriam." She kissed her little brown curls and breathed in the scent of a new life.

LISHA, 137 BC, CITY OF HELAM

*L*isha huddled in the sanctuary with the rest of the City of Helam, one arm around Eva and the other around her own swollen belly. Beside her, Young Alma was spinning twigs he'd carried inside in his pockets. Across the broad room, her husband slipped through the frightened community members, summoning Asher, Samuel, Rafa, and Taavi for a private discussion near the roaring hearth. Outside, the wind howled, rattling the bolted shutters of the stone building. The thick wooden planks overhead kept the rain out but did nothing to hide the sharp sounds of hail pelting the city.

Not again, Lisha thought. She wiped sweat from her brow. So many storms had blown through in the past few years, but this was the worst. Sweltering summer heat was scorching the crops, bit by bit. When clouds rolled in, and rain began to fall, they'd all rejoiced. But then the sky turned ugly. They'd rushed to the chapel for safety.

The whimpers of small children echoed through the chamber. Lisha felt a stab of pride that her children remained calm, then felt a flash of shame. *I should help.* She said a quick prayer for courage, then threw her arm around Eva and took ten-year-old Alma's hand.

"Don't, Mother," he said, tugging against her grip. "Let me play with Grandma Naomi."

Lisha hesitated. Alma could be difficult to manage.

Naomi reached for him. "Let me take him. You go do some good among the women. This sweet boy will be comfort and distraction enough for me."

Alma glared at his mother. Ever busy, he twirled a twig up and down his fingers.

Lisha sighed. It *would* be easier without him. Seven-year-old Eva, on the other hand, would cheer everyone with her dimpled smiles, her big hazel eyes, and her insistence on wearing flowers in her curly hair. She'd climb into laps and give hugs to anyone who'd let her. But if Lisha gave her older child that freedom, Alma would slip away into all sorts of trouble, even while confined to the sanctuary with the entire community watching. "All right," she said. "But stay with Grandma and obey her. If you don't, you'll have chores all day tomorrow."

"I'll have chores all day tomorrow anyway, with this storm," said Alma, glancing at the shuddering boards barring the windows, an unusually serious expression on his face.

"Well then, you really better obey Grandma. We need your help."

Alma smirked. He darted forward and tugged Eva's hair, then dashed out of reach behind Naomi, peering past her rounded side with gleaming, mischievous eyes.

Lisha sighed again.

"He'll be fine," Naomi said. "There are plenty of us here to help."

Lisha glanced around and saw Mera, Yoseph, and Hannah nodding their willingness to help corral the active boy. "He can play with Zilpah," Hannah offered.

"Thank you." Lisha added with an undertone, "And keep an eye on my mother, too, if you don't mind. She's been confused lately."

"Of course," Mera said, moving closer to the bent form of Avi, who sat hunched on a stone bench. The old woman stared off to nowhere as if her mind had taken a journey or she were seeing things none of the rest of them could.

Lisha brushed a kiss against her mom's wrinkled cheek.

"Goodbye, my dear," Avi said, raising a gnarled hand to the place Lisha had kissed.

Lisha gave her a wistful smile, then squeezed Mera's arm. "Thank you." With that, she pressed through the crowd toward the sounds of crying children.

~

"Hush," Sarika murmured. She bounced a toddler on her hip, soothing her with soft whispers. Her daughter, Shoshannah, rocked a baby on her shoulder, singing softly in her sweet, child's voice. They made an adorable pair.

Lisha brushed past them with barely a glance. They obviously had Belen and her children well in hand. The weary woman was tending the other of her twin babies, stealing occasional glances at her husband, Asher, as he conferred with Alma across the room. No, Lisha wasn't needed here.

Eva waved at Belen's toddler, but Lisha moved on. Belen would understand. She didn't need Lisha right now. She had Sarika's help. Sarika buried her face in the toddler's neck, kissing her until she giggled. But Lisha didn't really notice this. She didn't really notice how happy Sarika looked, her cheeks pink and eyes aglow despite the pounding storm. Instead, Lisha focused on Ophir, who was struggling with her fretful five-year-old, Rebekah.

"But Momma, I'm scared," Rebekah said. Her hands twisted in her skirt. Her lips were pink from constantly worrying them with her teeth. She shivered. "That's why I want Meggie."

"Poor thing," Lisha said, gathering Rebekah against her. "Don't worry, girl, we'll be just fine. Won't we, Eva?" Eva giggled and reached for Rebekah.

"But my kitty is out in the storm," Rebekah said. "She'll be hurt or lost!"

Eva knelt before the worried girl. "Animals know to hide when there are storms. She'll find a hollowed tree or a cave. Don't worry."

She patted the other girl's knee with her slim hand, her hazel eyes wide and serious.

"Could you help me and Eva visit some of the other women?" Lisha asked.

Rebekah bobbed her head and looped her arm with Eva's, who promptly started playing with Rebekah's long, caramel-colored braids.

"Your hair is so pretty," Eva said, glowing. Rebekah couldn't help but smile back.

"Thank you," Ophir whispered. "I'll see what I can do to help as well." She headed off toward a cluster of weary mothers.

As Lisha made her rounds with Rebekah and Eva in tow, she offered encouragement, but it was really Eva who buoyed people's spirits. Small children played with her. She batted her dark lashes at tired parents, making them smile. She sang, she giggled, she hugged, then she returned to Rebekah, who glowed at her newfound responsibility of cheering up the group with Eva.

Lisha felt the tightness in her chest unfurl just a bit.

A clattering noise drew her attention to the door of the sanctuary. A hunched figure tugged the doors open, despite the roaring storm. A fierce wind blew in. The torches guttered in their brackets, smearing soot on the stone walls. Lisha pulled Rebekah and Eva close, sheltering them from the biting blast. What was going on? She rose on her tiptoes to see a commotion at the entryway. Someone was struggling to go outside. Others tried to force the doors shut against the wind.

A man was pulling the hunched figure back, trying to prevent the person from leaving. But why would anyone in their right mind try to go out in the storm? A child, maybe, who didn't understand, but not a full-grown adult. Not...Lisha cocked her head to the side. The hunched figure turned slightly, throwing off her head scarf.

Lisha gasped.

It was Avi, her mother.

As Lisha pushed through the crowd between her and the door, voices drifted back to her.

"You can't go out there," Mera shouted over the storm.

"But Eli, my Eli, I saw him." Avi pulled out of Yoseph's grasp.

"Who's Eli?" Yoseph shouted to Mera.

"Her husband, but he's been dead twenty years!"

Avi slipped out the door.

Lisha was almost there now, close enough to see Young Alma break away from Naomi and run out after his older, frail grandmother. Yoseph grabbed him and hauled him back inside, kicking and screaming. Mera and Hannah rushed out after Avi. There was a crashing sound. Lightning lit the sky. Lisha saw their silhouettes, and, beyond them, an uprooted tree tearing through the gathering place, headed straight toward them. The two women turned and fled into the sanctuary, slamming the doors behind them with the help of several others.

Something pounded against the chapel. Dust and grit showered from the stone walls. Slim branches forced their way through cracks in the wooden doors. Everyone near the entry stood back and fell quiet. Except Lisha. For the moment, she forgot Alma and Eva. She forgot the storm. She threw herself against the door, screaming for her mother.

THE HOURS until the storm blew out were bitter for Lisha. She held her arms around herself and wept. Despite her pleading, no one would let her leave the sanctuary and search for Avi. Her husband and Asher tried once. They pushed through a mountain of limbs, only to be forced back inside by hurtling debris and fist-sized hail. A few balls rolled past the shattered tree blocking the doorway. Lisha picked one up, the cold wrinkling her fingers and seeping into her bones. She wouldn't let it go, even when Mera tried to gently pry it from her grasp. Some distant part of her knew it made no sense, but the part that was in charge just now insisted that the cold and pain were her one link to her mother, lost out in the storm.

She felt a hand on her shoulder. Alma.

"Your pain does not bring her relief, Lisha."

"I—I need to do *something.*"

He pulled her into his arms, and she let the hailstone drop to the ground, clinging to him instead. They bowed their heads together and prayed.

It was barely morning when the storm ended. Most of the city slept, too worn out to want to see the wreckage in the watery light of dawn. Lisha, however, would not wait. Hannah and Mera took Eva and Young Alma while Lisha climbed over the branches, cloth, and tent poles clogging the sanctuary doorway. Alma, Asher, Rafa, and Taavi came right behind her to search for Avi.

The tangled mess in front of the chapel snagged at Lisha's skirts, making her progress slow and unsteady. Twice her feet caught, and she tumbled to the side, only to be prevented from falling by Alma's strong, quick hands. Once clear of the debris pile, she ran through the gathering place toward their home near the forest edge. She skirted broken vases cluttered around broken benches. She dodged upturned water troughs and collapsed wood-and-thatch homes. She turned her head aside when she saw a dead and bloody ram, apparently dropped near the bakery by the storm. The bakery was still standing. It almost looked untouched.

"Lisha, wait!" Alma called, but she didn't slow down. "Each of you, search a quarter of the city," he told his companions. More men had spilled from the sanctuary, ready to help. "I'll catch up to Lisha and cover our section."

Alma's voice sounded distant, but Lisha felt glad she wouldn't be the only one searching. "Mother!" she shouted over and over, her voice growing more and more hoarse. She shoved aside a broken table, tilted half on its side, but Avi was not beneath it. She pushed through the underbrush at the edge of the gathering place, calling and searching, but Avi was not there. Her foot sank into a hole. Lisha fell. Pain shot up her leg, but it was nothing to what she felt when she landed, spread-eagle against a chaotic pile of logs.

"Lisha!" Alma reached her moments after she cried out. He helped her onto her side, pulling her foot from the sodden ground. "Is it broken?"

Lisha bit her lip, her breaths coming painful and short. "Just sprained, I think. But…" She flinched and wrapped a protective arm around her midsection.

"The baby?"

"I need to lie down,"—hot tears filled Lisha's eyes—"but my mom," —she tried to stand, but her ankle gave out—"I have to find my mom."

Alma slipped an arm under Lisha's knees and another around her back, then lifted her from the ground. "I'm taking you back to the sanctuary. You need a healer, and you need rest. Asher and the others are searching for your mother. They'll find her. Don't worry."

Lisha rested her head against Alma's chest. His strength and warmth were as reassuring as his words. But a persistent, cold fear squeezed Lisha's heart. They'd find her mother, but what would they find? How could anyone survive such a storm?

Tight pain rippled over Lisha's belly, and she suddenly felt a different, more immediate fear.

LISHA LAY on a pallet of dry blankets and furs, shared by those who'd thought to bring them into the sanctuary when they fled the storm. Devorah, the midwife, rubbed Lisha's hands and feet and gave her warm chamomile tea to help relax her and—they hoped—stop her labor pains. The comfort of Devorah's touch did little to ease her worry for her mother. The search had gone on longer than it should have. Alma had wanted to stay by Lisha's side, but she'd told him to go, to find Avi and bring her home safe.

It wasn't a fair request, but Lisha couldn't help herself.

Dear Lord, bring mother home safe and alive.

She'd prayed more times than she remembered and felt nothing but her own hollow fear. Now another prayer added to the first, like another voice joining a pleading choir. *Save my baby. Save my mom.*

Eva's small fingers wove their way through Lisha's hair, stroking and petting her. "You'll be ok, Momma, you be ok, and Grandma will, too." She looked at Lisha with wide, hopeful eyes, then snuggled against Lisha's side. Lisha wrapped her arm around her girl. The warmth and sweetness of her daughter soothed her more than anything. *Save my baby. Save my mom.*

Pain rippled over Lisha's belly again. Devorah noted it, marked it on a parchment scrap, then stepped to the now unshuttered window to judge from the sun how much time had passed. "It's almost midday," she said. "I believe your pains are slowing."

Lisha nodded, blinking. *Save my baby. Save my mom.*

Eva snored softly, shifted a little, and burrowed closer to her mother.

The sanctuary door creaked open, spilling a shaft of weak sunlight over the pallet. Alma stepped inside, his head low. The door hung open after him, people coming and going, carrying what could be salvaged into the sanctuary for the good of all. No one met Lisha's gaze.

She tightened her grip on Eva and shook her head. "No, Alma. Tell me it's not true. She can't be gone. Not like that."

Alma's face tightened. He knelt beside her. His voice choked, "Asher found her in the shade of a thick spruce. She looked like she was sleeping. She looked peaceful, Lisha." Lisha shook her head again. She felt warmth streak down her face, but didn't brush the tears away. Alma stroked her hair, her cheeks, her brow. "I'm sorry, Lisha."

Lisha swallowed a sob. "She shouldn't have been out there. If I'd stayed with her...she shouldn't have died like that, alone in the storm. I prayed, Alma! I prayed and prayed."

"I know, Lisha. I know." He took a deep breath. "They say she saw Eli." He cast a sidelong glance at Lisha, gauging her reaction.

Lisha set her jaw. "I heard her. I know she thought she saw my father..."

"Maybe it was her time, Lisha," Alma said. His voice was gentle, like the voice he'd use when speaking to a spooked animal.

"She was alone, Alma, alone and afraid." Lisha tried to swallow her bitterness but couldn't.

"She wasn't alone, Lisha. Eli was with her. For all we know, angels were with her."

"That's a happy thought," Lisha said. "But how can I know it's true? There's suffering in this world, Alma. You heard the prophet's cries when he burned in Noah's fire. Why didn't the Lord take away his pain? Why would He comfort my mom in the storm, as she lay dying, and not comfort the prophet? And what about Shadrach and Meshach in the fiery furnace? Why did they not burn, but Abinadi did?"

"I don't pretend to know all the ways of the Lord," Alma said quietly. "But I know He loves us and makes things right."

Lisha was silent for a long time. "Does our son know?" she finally asked.

"He's with Mera. She blames herself. She said she was supposed to look after Avi."

Lisha sighed a shuddering breath. "She and Yoseph tried to stop her. They did their best."

Tightness spread over Lisha's middle again. She hunched around her belly. Eva mumbled and buried her warm face in Lisha's neck.

"You're still having pains?" Alma asked. New worry lines etched themselves on his brow.

Lisha nodded. "They're not as bad as they were, though."

He nodded, almost to himself. "That's something, then. I'll send my mother to tend to you. Devorah needs to check her home."

Lisha nodded again. She felt so, so tired. The night of fear, the morning of searching, labor pains, and terrible loss weighed upon her like a blanket heavier than those draped around her. And though the door hung open, letting in the feeble light, and people streamed in and out of the chapel, Lisha slept.

MUGGY HEAT HUNG over the City of Helam like a sickness. Lisha woke on her pallet in the sanctuary, feeling a strange coolness at her side.

"You're awake," said a brisk voice. It was Naomi, Alma's mother. She brought a cup of warm broth to Lisha.

Feeling disoriented, Lisha squinted up at her, then pushed up on her elbows and accepted the drink. She still felt like something was missing, something out of place. What was that sense of loss?

"No more pains?"

Lisha shook her head. She swallowed a sip of broth. The salty liquid slipped down her throat, warming her and waking her just a little more.

Naomi settled into a pallet beside Lisha. "Well, it's about time you woke. It's nearly dinnertime." She glanced toward the open door. "Thank the Lord your labor stopped. Alma's been worried sick."

"Where—"

"He's at your cottage, what's left of it anyway, trying to rebuild enough for you to come home. He knew you'd rather sit shiva there."

The feeling of loss deepened. Sit shiva? Lisha's heart pounded. Sit shiva. Her mother had died. They would sit shiva for the next week. Her mother was gone. She wrapped her arms around herself and became aware of the other absence she'd noted, the coolness at her side where warmth had been before. "Where's Eva?"

Naomi looked up. "Eva? She wasn't here when Alma sent me. You don't know where she is?"

"She was here when I fell asleep." She moved to stand, but Naomi forestalled her.

"I'll fetch Alma. She's probably with Hannah or...or someone." She ran her fingers through her graying hair, then strode toward the door. Before she reached it, she froze, gazing straight ahead. Her hand rose to cover her mouth.

Alma entered the sanctuary. A small, sodden form lay in his arms. He looked to Lisha, his face a study of pain.

Lisha stared, but all she saw were dark lashes pressed against dimpled cheeks and broken flowers trailing from curly, matted hair.

LISHA, 137 - 136 BC, CITY OF HELAM

hiva was over. Seven days of prayer and grief. Seven days of visitors bearing boiled eggs, lentils, and bagels. Seven days of other mothers watching Young Alma or cleaning Lisha's home, trying not to show their relief that her loss hadn't been theirs. Seven days of sympathy for the sorrow they couldn't possibly comprehend. Seven days filled with so many people—Mera, Naomi, Hannah, and countless others—yet still so alone. Lisha had never dreamed she'd sit shiva for her mother and daughter at the same time. How could this be? How could the Lord let this happen?

With trembling hands, she picked up a dirty dish from the table and took it to the wash basin. Her thoughts were torture and didn't bring back her mother or her little girl.

"Careful, Lisha, you'll tire yourself." Alma rose from his seat by the unlit hearth, all kindness and concern. He plucked the plate from her hand and began wiping it himself.

"I can't keep still, Alma. My mind runs. I have to move or I'll...I don't know what I'll do."

Alma set the clean dish atop a small stack of clay plates on the battered shelves in the corner.

Not much remained of the finery that had once graced their cottage. Naomi had washed the mud and filth from their bedding and clothes, but the stains lingered, stubborn and unyielding.

"You need rest," Alma repeated. He ran a gentle hand down Lisha's back and across her middle. "I can't lose you."

She tensed. Was he thinking of her or the baby? Lisha tried to take comfort that she hadn't lost the baby, too. There was comfort in that. There was. So why did she feel like it didn't matter? Why did she feel like it wouldn't matter if she were gone herself?

Alma guided her to the bed, helped her in, and tucked the blankets under her chin. It was too warm for heavy furs, but Lisha shivered anyway and burrowed under the woven wool, relishing its weight on her body. It only seemed right that her blankets should weigh her down. She pulled them over her face, blocking the afternoon light streaming through the open window. She never wanted to see sunlight again.

"I'm going to walk to Mera's and pick up Young Alma," he said. "You'll be all right by yourself for a while?"

Lisha nodded under her shroud of wool. For a moment, she felt a soft pressure on her head, the touch of Alma's hand, then the cottage door creaked shut, and she was alone. She rolled over to face the wooden slats of the 0wall. She shoved her fingers through cracks that hadn't been there before the storm.

How long she lay there, seeing nothing, feeling nothing, she did not know. She may have slept but wasn't sure. Her cheeks were wet, and her eyes crusty. A sharp jab from her belly roused her enough to shift her position, turning toward the empty room. She didn't croon to the baby inside her like she used to whenever it moved. She didn't have the heart to do it. This baby would never be carried by a dimpling, laughing elder sister. This baby would never know what it had lost.

Outside, birds chirped, children laughed amid the sounds of community effort, rebuilding what the storm had destroyed. Lisha pulled her blanket tighter. No amount of rebuilding would bring back what the storm had stolen from her. The cottage air was warm, tight, and silent. Lisha couldn't decide what was worse, being surrounded by well-meaning people with pitying eyes or being alone with her thoughts.

A tap sounded at the door, soft enough that Lisha dismissed it. The tap came again. Lisha tightened her lips. Did she want company? The comfort of Mera or Naomi? Alma wouldn't knock; he'd just come in. The tapping increased, insistent, determined. Most people would have left by now. Most people would know what the silence in the cottage meant. Not that it was empty, but that Lisha was alone and couldn't bear anything else. The tapping continued. Lisha sat up, still unsure whether she longed for a friend or for solitude in her grief.

The door creaked open, and her question was answered.

Solitude. That was what she needed.

Absolute seclusion with her thoughts and God. Not friends, not sisters, and definitely not Sarika.

Sarika swept in without invitation or apology and set a fragrant loaf of herbed bread on Lisha's table. She pulled a three-legged stool alongside the bed and seated herself with a rustle of skirts, graceful as ever.

"Shiva is over," Lisha said. Her voice sounded as broken as she felt.

"I know."

"I can cook my own bread, Sarika. Alma will not go hungry."

"I am not here for Alma."

Lisha stared at her. "You shouldn't have come."

Sarika took a deep breath as if steeling herself to say something important.

Lisha didn't think she could bear it, not now. She couldn't bear more suffering, not even the heartache that had hung between them all these years, long enough to become a familiar, almost comforting presence. But to speak of it now would be no comfort at all. She sat up, the blankets settling around her hips like an undertow. "Sarika..."

Sarika's face set with quiet determination.

Lisha sighed and waited. She didn't have the strength for anything else. But it was kind of heartless, she thought, for Sarika to confront her now when she was drowning in sorrow. *Drowning.* Her breath hitched in her chest. She'd never think of that phrase again without anguish.

When Sarika finally spoke, she didn't say what Lisha had expected. She didn't mention Alma, King Noah, or the palace. She didn't mention Lisha's cold glances or their strained attempts to tolerate each other. It was as if, for Sarika, the pain that hung between them didn't even exist. She spoke, instead, of her childhood.

"When I was young, I ambled all over Shilom, up and down the green hills, teasing the sheep or climbing trees. I knew to stay within the city walls and well away from the river."

Lisha furrowed her brow. What was Sarika doing? Did she think to distract Lisha from her grief with stories of Shilom? Or was she leading up to the moment when Noah and his wicked priests had first noticed her? Lisha didn't want to hear about that. She didn't want to know. Still, she found herself leaning forward, rapt and silent.

"One day, I found a stray kitten, a fluffy black and white thing with eyes the color of corn silk. I followed it all through town, behind the temple, around the potter's stall, over the bridge, and into the pastures. That's when it climbed a tree. It was an old maple with sprawling branches that arched over the river." Sarika clasped her hands in her lap, gazing into the distance. "It was such a pitiful thing, scrawny and hungry, mewling and afraid. If I could just catch it, I knew could help it. I'd tame the starving thing, brush out its tangles, and feed it up fat and happy."

"What is this to do with..."

"The cat scrambled out on the limb, almost slipped off into the rushing water." Sarika glanced over to Lisha as if suddenly remembering she was there. "You'd think that would've been a warning to me." Her voice grew small. "I've always wished I'd heeded that warning. Everything would've been different. Everything." She took a deep breath, then released a shaking, drawn-out sigh. "But all I could see was the helpless kitten, scared and trembling, barely clinging to the tree. I could save it. I knew I could. I climbed out on the branch."

Lisha pulled back.

"When the branch creaked, I ignored it. After all, seven-year-olds are invincible. The wood splintered. The branch broke. When I fell into the water, I didn't feel worried, not at first."

"Stop." Lisha didn't want to hear this.

"There'd been a storm. The river ran brown and strong, rushing across the land. It tossed me like a leaf. That's when I began to feel fear."

"*Stop.*" Lisha turned her face to the wall.

"My father was away fighting the Lamanites. I knew he couldn't help me. I fought the water, but I wasn't strong enough. My head went under. I stayed under so long I thought I'd never breathe again. Then my mother's hand grabbed mine. She had dived in to save me. But the river tore us apart."

"Why are you telling me this?"

"You couldn't have saved Eva. This is not your fault."

Lisha made an incoherent noise.

"The first time I felt the Spirit was in that rushing water," Sarika said. "A sense of calm came over me. In that moment, I knew the Lord would care for me, whatever happened, whether I lived or died. I no longer felt afraid." Sarika scooted the stool closer and took Lisha's hand in hers. "He is caring for Eva. He will care for you, too, Lisha, I know He will."

Lisha swallowed a sob. Sarika squeezed her hand, as if willing her hope and faith to enter Lisha. A small kindness, but somehow the gesture broke Lisha's reserves. She buried her face in the blankets and cried, her shoulders shaking while Sarika's strong, slim hand stroked her hair, rubbed her back, the way a mother would, the way Avi would have, had she been there to share Lisha's grief.

In the quiet sorrow of the cottage, Sarika began to sing. Softly, sweetly, her lilting voice drifted into the shadowed places of Lisha's heart. She sang of hidden things, deep sorrows, and hushed hope. While she sang, Lisha's sobbing slowed. The afternoon sunlight shifted to a deep, evening gold.

Finally, Lisha lifted her tear-stained face to Sarika, whose eyes glowed with a strange brightness.

"Why are you being kind to me?"

"I know what it is to experience loss, Lisha. You're not alone."

Lisha eyed her, wondering what losses Sarika had felt that could possibly compare to losing your child and your mother the same day. Sarika patted her hand and stood.

"Wait," said Lisha, "you never said what happened, how you got out of the river."

A flicker of sadness crossed Sarika's face. "Somehow the water threw me ashore." She dropped her voice. "The Lord saved me. I don't know why."

Long after Sarika's skirts had swished away through the damaged door frame, questions lingered in Lisha's mind. *What had Sarika lost? And if the Lord had helped her, why hadn't he saved Eva?*

"I saw Sarika leaving the cottage." Alma sat by their table, whittling a small chunk of wood by candlelight. Their son slept on his pallet in the corner, curled up with Eva's favorite toy - a tatty cat their grandmother, Avi, had knitted for her the year before.

Lisha nodded, her fingers busy carding wool. Back. Forth. Back. Forth. Pulling the strands straight. With the fibers aligned together, the spun thread would be much stronger. "She brought us bread." She didn't know why she didn't—couldn't—tell Alma more.

"I don't know if you've seen Rafa watching her. I noticed on the Day of Atonement. They'd be a good match. Rafa has a history of his own. He'd not judge Sarika."

Lisha's brow creased. The candlelight flickered, sending dancing shadows along the walls and ceiling of their small cottage. Much of it was still in shambles, but everywhere she looked were evidences of the care and love of a strong, dedicated family. She saw it in the toys Alma carved for his children, the determination on Young Alma's face even as he slept, the woven rugs from Mera and Yoseph, and the clay bowls from Naomi. For the first time, she wondered—where was Sarika's family? What had happened to her mother that day? Had her father returned from battle to find Sarika alone? Had he returned at all?

Everything would've been different. Everything.

Sarika's regret burned in Lisha's memory. Lisha knew pain like that, pain over actions that ended in sorrow. Apparently, Sarika felt it, too. She'd said everything would've been different. If what? If her mother hadn't died and her father had come home from war? Lisha shook her head, the enormity of it settling like a weight on her heart. Sarika must've lost them both in the span of days. What must it have been like to be alone in the world, with no one to defend her virtue from the likes of King Noah, no one to turn to when Noah and his priests were done?

Yet Sarika still managed to find peace. She still managed to bring others comfort. Lisha's hands grew still. Something in her heart shifted, something akin to harsh noon light, deepening to gold.

THE RIVER MOVED SLUGGISHLY; its edges crusted with ice. Lisha walked along the shore, the ice splintering with her every step. It was brittle, fragile, like the cracks in her heart. Each full moon, she returned to this cove east of the sanctuary, the place where Eva's small body had been found. Alma begged her not to go. He told her that fifteen months of mourning were enough. Perhaps he was right. She raised her chin. A breeze blew up behind her, whipping tendrils of her hair out of her scarf and into her face.

Young Kaleb stirred in his swaddling against her chest. He was growing too old to be carried this way. Lisha's back constantly ached, but she wanted him close, not toddling around. She needed his warmth against her. And she would never let him be harmed.

"Momma?" Kaleb stirred again. He opened his wide, dark eyes and blinked up at her. His curls were stuck against his cheek by sweat caused by their shared body heat.

Lisha stroked his round cheek and began to sing. It was the same song Sarika had sung to her in the early days *after*. Lisha had mentally divided her life. *Before*, she had a mother to lean on, a charismatic—if distracted—husband, a rambunctious five-year-old, and a sweet girl who smiled like sunshine and wore flowers in her hair. *After* was much different!

Of course, she had Kaleb now. She drew her thumb across his forehead. He was a study of black and white under the gray light of the moon. He snuggled his head into her chest, humming along as she sang. Lisha felt a tear drop from her chin. Her voice wavered, her breath coming in hushed puffs of white. Alma thought it strange she'd come here, of all places, to honor the memory of Eva. But this was where her girl took her last breaths, where God carried her soul away. Lisha liked to imagine Him wrapping Eva in His arms. She liked to imagine Eva hadn't felt afraid. Sarika's experience had planted that idea in Lisha's mind. For that, she would always be grateful. Her words that day, and her hopeful song, had become the light Lisha clung to in those first dark, lonely weeks. She clung to them even now.

Lisha shivered. Her voice had grown thin, the wind whipping words from her lips. Sometimes she dreamed of Eva. Sometimes she thought she saw a hint of her in the fog rising from the river. On warmer nights, when she stayed at the riverside, she thought she glimpsed Eva in the morning haze as the sun crept above the horizon. The beams of light reached through the forest, warming her spirit, the same way Eva warmed every life she touched.

One more time, Lisha thought, *I'll sing it one more time.* Halfway through, someone's fingers slipped into her right hand. Lisha gasped, but the singing continued. Another voice had joined hers. She turned. It was Sarika. She stood on the shore beside Lisha. They met eyes, then gazed across the river, their voices twining in mingled grief and hope. When the song ended, Sarika wrapped her arm around Lisha.

"Come," she said. "You can warm by my fire. My home is much closer than yours."

Lisha nodded and let the other woman lead her from the river. "How did you know to come?"

Sarika gave her a look. "It's a full moon. I knew you'd be here. The bitter cold couldn't keep you away."

～

INSIDE SARIKA'S SMALL COTTAGE, her daughter, Shoshannah, slept soundly, curled in a ball in a bed of heather and furs, her dark hair escaping its long braid.

"I set some tea boiling before I left to find you," Sarika said. She gestured for Lisha to take a chair by the fireside. Smoke curled up to escape through a small gap in the cottage ceiling. While Lisha pulled off her shoes and stretched her toes toward the warmth of the fire, Sarika poured mint tea into earthenware mugs. "I'm out of honey," she apologized.

Lisha gave her a wan smile. "You are kind, Sarika. More than I realized."

Sarika flushed and glanced away. "You can lay Kaleb on my bed if you like. I know your back must ache."

Lisha tightened her arms around her son.

Sarika nodded, understanding.

"Does everyone know I go to the river at full moon?"

Sarika shook her head. "I've heard you singing. My home is close to the river and, well, I know that song. It's not one we share at gatherings. I knew it was you." She paused and sat on her bed. It was tucked in a corner, but the cottage was so small that she was still close enough for Lisha to hear her easily. "I asked Alma about it. He said to let you grieve. But it has gone on too long, Lisha."

Lisha looked away.

"I don't mean that you should forget her," Sarika hurried on. "And I don't mean that you shouldn't grieve or feel sad, but you're losing yourself. Kaleb needs you. Young Alma needs you. So does your husband." Sarika sighed. She picked up a braided leather bracelet from her bedside stand, running it through her callused fingers. "For a long time, I wondered if I would always be alone. How could any man accept me after...after what was done to me? Would any woman want

150

to be my friend?" Her voice choked. "It's why I left Shilom." She waved a hand. "I believed Abinadi and I saw how the truth changed Alma. I wanted that. I wanted peace in my life."

Lisha gestured at the bracelet. "From Rafa?"

Sarika nodded and gave a shy smile.

Rafa had good reason to admire her, Lisha thought. Sarika was beautiful. But it was more than how she looked. She was beautiful inside. "He's a good man."

"So is Alma," Sarika said. "The way he's grown and changed since he chose to follow the Lord—he's a different person now. He's shown us how the Lord can transform us."

Sarika hesitated, but Lisha knew what she'd almost said — it was time Lisha grew and changed, too. But Lisha didn't know if she had it in her. She had so many hurts tucked carefully inside. How could she let them go? And if she did, what would be left?

"You know," Sarika said, "the atonement is not only for forgiveness. It's also for comfort and healing, especially when you feel you can't possibly be healed." She rotated Rafa's bracelet in her hand, then set it on her rough blanket.

Lisha nodded, turning these ideas in her mind. "Sarika," she said, her voice wavering as it had at the river. She paused, remembering the strength of their two voices twining together. "Thank you for being there for me."

"I've learned that the only way through loneliness and pain is to lift others. If I can find meaning, life is bearable. Sometimes it's even beautiful." Sarika's eyes glistened with unshed tears.

A flower of hope unfurled within Lisha, hope for herself, hope for Sarika, and hope for the people of Helam. Sarika was right—the Lord was there for them, to heal, to comfort, and to help them be there for each other. Lisha leaned forward, and Kaleb let out a sleepy grunt. "What of Rafa? You'll give him a chance?"

Sarika picked up the bracelet again, an odd expression on her face. "I've never been courted before," she said. "I don't know what to make of it."

"I can help you with that." Lisha grinned. A strange feeling bubbled up inside her, a sensation she hadn't felt in more than a year. She laughed. After months and months of sorrow, she felt a spark of joy.

CHANNAH, 137 BC, CITY OF AMULON

Channah stood in the cool of the summer morning. Mountain air swept the tendrils of her long hair in dancing patterns across her closed eyes. *Two winters. So many young mothers and newborn children have died. Why God? What was their purpose in life? What is my purpose in life?* She glanced around to make sure she was not being watched by Amulon. *Will I have another child? Will others still die before we can find our people again?*

She felt a tug on her tunic. "Mother?"

Lemish, now five years old, looked at her in concern. "Are you sad?"

Channah hid her pain again, pushing it deeper into her broken heart so it wouldn't show in her eyes - the eyes that took in her precious son. "What is that you have in your hand?"

"I caught him," Lemish said with a big smile. He held up a squirrel by its fluffy tail.

"Let's fix this one for dinner. He's big enough to feed two families," Channah said with encouragement and enthusiasm.

"Not really, Momma. I know he's not that big."

"Well, he's the biggest one I've seen in some time. He'll make a fine meal." Channah smoothed the boy's curly hair, drawing her slender fingers through the tangles. She plucked out a few pine needles and twigs. "You had to really work to get this one, didn't you?"

"Not really. I caught him in a trap."

"Tell me, Lemish, how did you do that?"

"I watched him. He had a nest high in the big tree by our hut. I watched what he did each day and saw that he picked up the acorns from the ground under the climbing tree. He would carry them up to his nest. So, I piled some acorns up for him and set one of your baskets over the nuts with a stick to hold it up. I made a string to tie to the stick and waited. I had to wait a long time, but when he discovered the nuts, he came right in. I pulled the rope and there he was. Caught."

"My son, you are bright and clever beyond your years." She drew him close and took his chin in her hands, drawing his gaze upward. "I love you. I always will."

He gave her middle a squeeze and smiled. "I'll always love you too."

"Why don't I teach you how to skin and clean this squirrel, and you can help me fix dinner."

"Yes, Momma." He went to the cooking area and took an obsidian knife from the table, carefully turning it over in his hands. "Am I big enough to use a knife by myself?"

Channah's stomach clenched, realizing that such a knife could be used for good or evil. Once he learned to use the tool, she must teach him to respect its power. "Yes, son, today you will learn to properly use that knife."

Still holding the squirrel by the tail, he held it up to his mother. "What is first, Momma?'

"First we thank the Gods for the life of the creature."

She held the tail up and chanted a thankful prayer to the nature God. "The creature received life from the Gods, and we take that life for food. We become part of nature when we consume it. That's what my mother taught me."

Channah began carefully removing the fur, using the tail to hold on to the creature. Her hands worked quickly as she explained each step.

"Tell me about your mother."

Her hands froze. She choked on the words that swelled in her throat. She looked at her son, realizing she had never shared with him the history of his grandparents; their teachings, their love for her. He would never know them and the pain was like a spear in her heart. The only way he could know them was through her. That time at home seemed so long ago. She began with her first recollections as a child. Their work preparing the squirrel for dinner became a time of tearful remembrance of the times her father and mother taught her the very same skills.

"Your grandfather would be proud of how you caught this squirrel. You were very observant, my son. I'm proud of you."

Amulon stepped out of the hut as Channah and Lemish carefully adjusted the kindling and logs to make just enough fire to cook the meal but not so much that it created smoke that would blow into the door of their hut. "I have the last of the stones for the fire pit. You won't have to cook outside like this much longer," Amulon said as he turned to walk away.

Channah could tell he was weary. "Thank you."

He sat down on a log bench outside their hut. "Who caught the squirrel?"

"I did," Lemish said proudly. "Just like my grandpa would have. He's clever like me." He proceeded to share the details of his catch.

Amulon sat forward as Lemish finished his story with that of his grandfather. "What have you been filling his head with?" Anger seared his words with a warning glare.

Lemish continued, "Mother taught me all about the Gods and how the creatures we eat become part of us."

Channah realized that this wasn't going to end well. "Son, let's give Amulon time to rest and not use so many words right now."

With cold calculation, Amulon spoke. "Your mother is confused." He took Lemish by the hand. "Remember when she hit her head and didn't wake up? She doesn't remember her family. She's making it all up. There are no Gods." With a look of satisfaction at Lemish's new puzzled expression, he finished with, "You're not clever, either — not if you believe in Gods."

Lemish looked from his father to his mother. He dropped Amulon's hand and stood between them, his eyes searching for which truth to hold on to. Channah's eyes, full of love, took his in and held them. They said what words could not. The little boy breathed a sigh of relief. "Alright, father," he said as he slid closer to his mother and grasped her hand.

Angrily, Amulon stormed into the hut. "I'll be working on the fire pit if you need me."

CHANNAH no longer had to cook outdoors. She adjusted the stones carefully around her very own fire pit. Lemish watched her intently.

"How large must it be, mother?"

"Only enough for a small fire, for cooking one meal." She continued to fit the stones into a perfect puzzle.

"Will our home fill with smoke?"

"No, look at the very top, the peak. This is built like the tents of my people…" she paused to let her voice recover from the wavering that always accompanied memories of her home.

"Tell me more about your people, mother?" Lemish reached down to help move stones closer to his mother's hands. While scooting them, she touched his hand and held it for a moment till he looked at her.

She held out her arm next to his. "My skin is a different color than yours. Father has pale skin so your skin is darker than his and lighter than mine. Your father's people and my people are different. My people have dark skin and live in separate cities than those who have light skin."

"Why?" he asked. "Can't you live together?"

Channah realized he was no longer a child, innocent and unaware. She was stepping into new territory in this discussion with her son.

"We came from different parents who didn't get along. One

brother believed the other had treated him unfairly. They had many children and their children were not friends. We fought with them, often. Many died."

"Why don't they say sorry and be brothers again?"

Channah paused. This had never occurred to her before, that they could make amends and be brothers again.

"I don't know." Her brow wrinkled. "It would solve many problems, but I don't think they want to be friends."

"You tell me to be friends and share with others. Could we tell the big men to share also?"

Channah smiled. "We could try."

"Why did you leave your people and live with light skin people if the people of the brothers don't get along? Did you say sorry?"

A tear sprung to her eye and she quickly brushed it away with a lock of hair that had fallen from behind her ear. She continued to work. She didn't answer him.

"Momma, why?"

Channah knew if she told the truth, there would be trouble. *What could I ever tell my children? What about the other children in the camp?*

Carefully, she chose her words. "The men, your father and the other fathers of your friends found us at the mountain lake, away from our village, and wanted us to come stay with them. They were lonely. They wanted families too."

"Why weren't they with their people?"

Channah shook her head slowly, knowing any more information would surely come from her dear child's lips at the wrong time and incur the wrath of Amulon.

"I need to finish this so I can prepare our first meal in our new home. Can you go get some small sticks for me?"

Excited to have a way to help, Lemish ran off to accomplish the task he had been given."

Channah buried her face in her hands and wept.

∽

ANGRILY, Amulon stormed into their hut, nearly tearing off the hide that covered the door. "This is getting out of hand."

"What?" Channah asked, startled.

"For weeks now our son has gone around holding his arm next to everyone else and saying something about brothers. What did you tell him?" Amulon stood at least a head taller than Channah, but she had risen to her full height and faced him squarely.

"I said nothing wrong. I'll not lie to him. He asked intelligent questions. I answered in a way that was truthful."

"Lie! Do whatever you have to, but I don't want any more of this nonsense about being friends and saying sorry." Without waiting for a response, he stormed out again as quickly as he had come in.

Then, completely catching her off guard, he came back in. "Are you using those herbs for yourself? The ones that keep you from being in the way of women? Are you with child yet?"

She could feel her knees shaking. "No. I have not used those herbs. Since the accident and the loss of that child, I have not carried another." Her eyes fell.

"I don't believe you." He took all of her carefully dried herbs; each layered between woven mats in a basket. "You'll not do this anymore. No more herbs. Nothing."

In shock, Channah questioned. "What about when you've been ill? Do you really want this?"

"Nothing, I said. Ever again. Now, I want another child and you'll not be able to do anything about it. His dark eyes burned into hers as he held them. All the while emptying her basket of precious herbs on the floor, crushing them with his feet."

Tears welled up in her eyes, turning her vision to a blurry mess. With clenched fists, she gritted her teeth and stared at his back as he left their hut. He had the map of their lands, that key to any possible escape, tucked into his tunic. But, in his anger and haste, it had fallen to the ground. He never left it in their hut, or even allowed her to see it when he was working on it. There it lay, on the floor.

Channah looked out the doorway as he stormed through the village street and waited until he was out of sight. She quickly unrolled the map, fingers trembling, and memorized as much of it as she could. As a child, she had often wandered off and become lost, but, over the years, she had trained herself to look at landmarks in her foraging for herbs. She knew the area around the city of Amulon very well. As she studied the map, engrossed in the details, she neglected to hear the footsteps of her husband returning.

"That's why I keep it with me."

Channah spun around to see Amulon's form filling the doorway. His eyes blazed, but he didn't strike her. "Give it to me."

No longer the quivering child, her gaze met his, and she slowly rolled it up and passed it to him. He grabbed it out of her hand, never letting his eyes leave hers.

"Now that you've seen where your home is. Do you think you could ever make it there alone? His eyes bored into hers with such contempt and anger that it made her blood run cold. "I have a solution, though. Lemish will stay with me at all times." His expression took on a look of victory. "Would you leave your son?"

The realization hit her like a falling branch. No, she would never leave.

THE SEASONS HAD TURNED cold too quickly and caught them all off guard. Children's noses ran and there seemed to be a general feeling of sickness about the camp. Channah held her cramping stomach and kept Lemish wrapped up beside her, by the small cooking fire. No one got out much when the weather was wet and cold, so she'd not seen anyone else for the past week.

Snow was falling, and that made the men irritated. They'd been so focused on finishing huts, and getting out of tents, that they hadn't been able to do their hunting.

Amulon slipped inside the hut to warm his hands by the fire. "We need to hunt at least one or two more times to have enough food for winter. We are late this year."

"I appreciate this home, its sturdiness and warmth," Channah said slowly. "It will be an easier winter for us all."

Her eyes clenched at another pain.

"What's wrong?" he questioned.

She shook her head as Lemish leaned over.

"Momma?" her son said with concern. "Are you alright?"

Darkness crowded around Amulon's face and Channah felt as if she were sitting in the back of a cave peering out through the opening. That opening became smaller, the ringing in her ears overtaking the voices of her concerned son and husband. A fuzzy warmth spread through her entire body until sleep overcame her.

THE HAND STROKING her head was tiny and warm. Gently, the fingers smoothed over her hair, trailing down her shoulder and tickling her back. Voices were muffled, and she was so very sleepy. Sinking back into sleep, her visions returned.

They were lost, but not afraid. Warriors of her people mingled amongst them. They were traveling somewhere. The men who were now their husbands appeared friendly to the warriors of her people, which confused her. She felt herself being touched and voices echoed in her mind, which made the vision difficult to continue. She ignored the voices. Her vision opened again, and a city unfolded to her view. Nephite men worked in the field alongside Nephite women. All were fair-skinned. As they came near, fear filled the eyes of the people. They fled. Amulon and the Lamanite warriors cheered; the cheering became so loud that Channah squinted and put her hands to her ears.

"Please stop shouting," she whispered in a hoarse voice, "I'm trying to sleep."

Isa brushed the hair from off her cheeks and tucked the tendrils behind her ear. "She's back!"

"I've not been gone. What do you mean?" Channah mouthed slowly, lips sticking to her tongue and teeth. "I need a drink." Her eyes fluttered open, and six pair of eyes studied her intently.

"Momma!" Lemish placed his head on her chest ever so gently. "I knew you'd wake up."

Once again, Channah had to work to regain her strength. The other women in the camp kept her company, played with her only son, and kept her nourished. Their supplies of food became scarce, and everyone's meals were more simple and sparse. There were moments when Channah wondered if they had been abandoned. Amulon and the others were gone for so many days she lost count. Then, one day when the snow fell heavy, and none of the families left their huts; the men came back. Each carried deer and other small animals that would be used for meat and skins. They would all survive one more winter.

CHANNAH WAS able to do much more on her own, but the long winter had sapped her of her usual vigor and strength. She longed to forage for herbs, gather flowers, plant seeds, and watch them grow. Her energy melted like the hoar frost and she craved the sunshine.

She pulled back the heavy skin that served as a door to their home and breathed in. The air was crisp but carried a hint of spring. With eyes closed, she remembered the days of her youth, running through the new tender blades of grass to catch fish in the stream that flowed beside their city. The same stream that ran through the Nephite city and brought food and water to them. One stream. Two cities – worlds apart. They would laugh that if they caught all of the fish, the Nephites would run out of food and leave their lands. Channah knew better now. Nothing would make them go back to their old country. She had heard the stories of the old king coming from the north and taking over the ruins of what had once been a Nephite city. There had been a time of peace but it never lasted long. All her life she had been told to hate the Nephites. So, she did. Now she was married to one.

She closed her eyes in what had become a ritual. The map. She had memorized each tiny detail, and she let it come alive in her mind's eye. She moved from landmark to landmark, seeing each twist and turn that led back to the city of her childhood. Even though she knew there was no way to return on her own. She could not leave Lemish or the other women. They were her family, and she could not abandon them. She wandered those roads in her mind until they were as real as if she had walked them. When she completed the journey, she allowed herself to return to her present reality, as painful as it was.

Others were out and about, gathering fallen branches for fires, spreading boughs along muddy paths to keep children and moccasins clean, and searching for any signs of tender green shoots of winter grain. She stepped out, her own feet feeling the crunch of old snow and the melting ice. She pulled her skin blanket tighter around her chin, just in time to shield herself from a shower of ice crystals falling from the pine tree next to their hut.

"Sorry!" Lemish shouted. "I didn't know you were coming out." Her young son was barely visible in the darkness of the evergreen's branches, but his eyes, wide with excitement, danced in the shadows. "I made it all the way up here!" he said as he stood on one branch and held to another, bending and stretching to ride the dipping, swaying branch. "This is so fun!" Additional ice crystals sprinkled down with his laughter.

"Be careful, son," Channah called as she stepped out from under the dancing branch. One by one, skin flaps opened to let out children with their chattering voices, along with the women who were their mothers. Girls who were growing up and becoming women, sons who were on their way to becoming men, mothers, and friends chatted pleasantly as Lemish continued to laugh in delight at his new-found game.

The women of the city of Amulon were drawn to Channah like moths to a flame, and they gathered around her as she walked through the mountain city.

DINAH, 130 BC, CITY OF SHILOM

*B*enjamin stood at attention as his father read from the scrolls. Limhi took every opportunity to teach the people from the words of Abinadi about power and authority. Benjamin's eyes showed such admiration for his father. Dinah smiled at the blessings she saw before her. He was nearly as tall as his father and was a head taller than her — but he was still her little boy.

Miriam wiggled as she sat on the large boulder at the spring, her feet swinging in an alternating rhythm, one poking out as the other disappeared beneath the ledge of the stone. The constant sound of falling water provided an ideal setting for disguising their voices from any wandering Lamanites. The spring wasn't far from Shilom, and the soldiers knew they left to worship one day a week, allowing it when they were in pleasant moods. Today was one of those days, and the people were grateful for the respite.

This was their place of peace, the only place they were truly free. Dinah watched Limhi with love as the people, rapt with attention, seemed to soak in his every word. She closed her eyes and thought back over the years and pondered in amazement at the peace they had begun to enjoy, in spite of their captivity.

After the sermon, Limhi and Benjamin came to sit by Dinah as the people began singing the songs they knew from memory. Some sang when they were joyful, and others they sang when they were mournful. It united them. Their melodies floated up through the green leaves that shaded the spring, over the sounds of the waterfall. Dinah truly felt as if God himself was listening. She thought if she could close her eyes and reach out, she might grasp his cloak.

Lost in her thoughts for a moment, she felt carried away. She saw her family in a different place. She saw Lisha and Alma, Helam, Limhi, and her children. Helam was standing alone. He was keeping guard next to Alma. She felt joy. She felt free, but there was a tiny prick of sorrow. Such happiness overwhelmed her, but the thread of sorrow wove its way into her heart and came out as a tear. She opened her eyes.

Everyone was here. Tamar was right where she should be, beaming, in the arms of her love, leaning back on his chest and gazing up into the clear blue sky. No room for sorrow; all was right. She wiped the tear and smiled at the blessings she saw all around her.

Gideon came to talk privately to Limhi. They spoke in whispers for some time till Rachel came and slipped her arm through Gideon's.

"What's all this serious talk about?" Rachel said with a smile as she laid her head on Gideon's strong arm.

"Let's head back to the city, Mother." Gideon nodded to Limhi and held her arm tightly as they walked the much-worn and familiar path back to Shilom.

Before leaving, Dinah saw the look pass between Limhi and Gideon.

As more people filed past the king and queen, they greeted and shook hands with each one, simply enjoying the time away from the city in their place of refuge.

Tamar came and sat down beside Dinah but didn't let go of Helam's hand. "Would it be wrong to try and make a match between two good people?" She looked quickly up at Helam, who immediately smiled in return. "It has been the greatest blessing to me to have Helam, and I wish maybe we had found one another sooner." Tamar's cheeks flushed slightly. "I would have liked to have given Helam a child."

Dinah squeezed Tamar's free hand. "You've given him much more. He is happy. I've never known him to, well, glow." Tamar and Helam's eyes met, and they both beamed. Dinah chuckled, "You two."

"We have our moments of disagreement, like any marriage, but this is so much more than I ever dreamed of having." Tamar rose to her feet. "We should get back. It feels like rain is coming."

"I suppose we must." They all slid from their stone slab seats onto the smooth path. "Until next time," Dinah breathed in the fresh cool air, then turned her face toward home.

As the ruling family, they walked last in the line and wove their way along the well-worn path, touching trees that were smooth from years of travelers holding on to them for support. Well out of earshot, Dinah whispered to Limhi. "What were you and Gideon speaking of?"

"He wonders if he will ever have a chance to take a wife."

"Why has he not chosen one to ask?"

"He is afraid Rachel will not approve."

"Is there one he wishes to marry?"

"Yes."

"Can you tell me who?"

"No, he wishes to speak with her first to see if she would consider him a worthy companion."

Dinah chuckled, "He's definitely that. He's brave and loyal. His heart is trustworthy and strong. He is faithful."

"That is part of the problem, though. Rachel sees him as the finest of men, which is wonderful, but she has told him he must wait until we are free and in Zarahemla to find a worthy wife."

Dinah stopped. "She wishes him to be single and alone till we are freed?"

Limhi's brow furrowed. "Yes. She loves him dearly, but I would have to disagree with her on that point. I believe there are good women here in Shilom, widows even, that would make a good match for Gideon."

They began walking again, then she stopped and pulled Limhi

closer, looking intently into his eyes. "Would she have approved of me?" Neither moved. They just looked at each other.

"I don't know, honestly, but if she didn't, she would have been so very wrong."

Limhi took his wife into his arms and they embraced for a long moment. As Dinah pulled back, she kissed him tenderly. "Thank you. Thank you for loving me. Thank you for saving me from a truly terrible path. Thank you for leading me down *this* path." She smiled and, for the second time that afternoon, wiped tears from her eyes.

"Let's get back to Shilom and see if we can remedy this lonely man's situation."

"Should I talk with Rachel?" Dinah asked.

"Yes, I think that would be a good idea."

DINAH SLIPPED OUT of the palace grounds as Benjamin and Miriam busied themselves, making new wrapped string balls for their games. They worked hard to strip the long flax stalks into fine threads that would easily wrap. Then they took the shorter strands of yarn from the women's weaving projects and knotted the pieces together to do a final wrap that wouldn't be as rough on their hands. The final product would be bright, colorful, and soft.

As she walked toward the home of Rachel and Gideon, Dinah relived the many years she had known them and felt such a love for both of them. She steadied herself and took a deep breath before knocking on their doorpost.

Rachel's gray head poked out of the tapestry, and her face lit up. "Come in, my queen!" she exclaimed as she pulled the tapestry door aside to let Dinah enter.

"Thank you."

"What brings you to our home?" Rachel pointed to a stool cut from a log, worn smooth from use. "Please sit."

"Is Gideon here?"

"No, did you need to see him or me?" Rachel's expression turned puzzled.

"Oh, I came to see you but wanted to talk privately."

Now Rachel truly wore a confused and concerned face. "Is there a problem, my queen?"

Dinah, unsure of how to gently approach the topic, decided to jump right in, even if it made ripples or messy splashes. "Do you wish for Gideon to marry?"

"Oh yes," joy radiated on Rachel's face. "There will be wonderful, suitable women in Zarahemla! Soon we will be free, and then my son can find a wife."

"Yes, he is one of the finest men in our city. That is true," Dinah proceeded slowly. "Do you wish him to wait for some future time to find his purpose and joy in a mate, or do you think maybe he can find that happiness now?" Dinah unconsciously held her breath.

Rachel appeared confused. "Marry someone from Shilom?"

"There are some wonderful widowed women here that would make Gideon a fine wife."

"Yes, there are good women, but none I see as good enough for my son," Rachel said indignantly.

"Have you asked Gideon what he would want in a wife?"

"No, but I know my son. He needs someone pure and undefiled."

Dinah had to pause and take a deep breath. The thoughts were tumbling about, and she needed to sort them out before speaking.

"Do you remember the days when Alma was one of King Noah's priests?"

"Yes, I do recall. That was very long ago, and Alma has truly changed." She grimaced as a level of recognition hit her.

"Do you love and admire Alma?"

"He is a man of God." Her eyes fell, and she was silent for a time before looking up.

"I have been wrong, haven't I?" A tear fell from her eye. "I have asked my son to wait, to be lonely and not look for a wife here." She wiped the tear as it rolled down her plump and wrinkled cheek. "He has been honorable and good to me, caring for me, guarding our city, and doing all that was asked of him. He could have had a wife to bring him comfort and joy, and I stood in his way." Rachel began to weep in earnest. Dinah slid from her chair and knelt beside her, stroking her wrinkled hands.

"The Lord is blessing us, and I know He will see fit to free us when the time is right. Gideon can take a wife of the women in Shilom, and, together, they will help our city prepare for the miracle of freedom when that time comes."

Rachel, still weepy, just nodded her head.

Gideon stepped in as Dinah stood.

"Mother, what is wrong?" he asked with concern.

Rachel wiped her tears and stood. She looked at him for a long moment, then stepped toward him with arms outstretched. "Forgive me, son. I have been wrong in asking you to wait to take a wife. God will lead you to one who will make your heart whole. You have my blessing. I will love whomever you choose."

A smile crept across Gideon's face, and he picked up his mother and pulled her into a tight embrace. She giggled and said, "Son, put me down!"

"I loved you first, mother." With a new light in his eyes, he added, "I will always cherish you."

He winked at Dinah, and, before exiting, called out, "I may need your help with something."

Dinah and Rachel smiled at each other, quite surprised at his rapid departure. Dinah returned home after leaving Rachel with a reassuring hug.

DINAH CALLED from her window as Elah stepped into the courtyard, glancing about as if she was expecting someone. "I'll be there soon. I need to finish something."

Elah knelt on the ground and tugged at a few bits of weeds and grass that had crept into the garden over the past week. There was so much work to be done in harvesting and providing an acceptable tribute to the Lamanites that there wasn't much time left for tending to their personal garden.

She must not have heard the approaching footsteps because she was humming one of the songs of her people. A hand touched her on the shoulder.

"I'm sorry to interrupt your work and your song," the masculine voice said.

Elah spun her head and rocked back on her feet, landing squarely on her backside in the grass. "Gideon!"

He reached down to offer a hand, so she could get up. She accepted, and, in a mere second, she was standing, although a little too close, next to him.

"I'm waiting for Dinah to come and tend to the garden. Were you looking for her?"

"She's been detained, so I offered to take her place."

Dinah made sure she stayed busy as the two of them worked in the garden. She kept her tapestry open to listen in on their conversation.

"You're going to weed the garden with me?" Elah asked with surprise.

"Yes, my mother taught me well. She was a master potter but made sure I knew how to find and pull weeds."

Before the sun set, the garden was weeded and both had dirty hands. Gideon had learned more about her son, Aaron, and her life before she became a widow. She shared how she came to be in Shilom, brought by her father, who traded goods with Noah and decided to stay. Her father was one of many killed in the early battles with the laminates, and Elah had grown up on her own since that day. With no mother to teach her, she had learned from Dinah and Tamar the things she missed out on.

"Let's walk to the stream to clean up," Gideon offered.

"Normally, I don't leave the courtyard after dark, but I think I'm safe with you," Elah offered shyly.

They stood at the gate of the courtyard, looking toward the stream. "I promised Dinah I'd help her, but she still has not come out. Should I wait for her?"

Dinah pulled the tapestry aside and poked her head out. "Would you two like to go for a walk?" she said with a broad grin. "I'll listen for Aaron. He can come to our home." She again beamed. "You two just enjoy your walk."

Elah looked at Gideon with a puzzled expression. "Yes, that would be wonderful, thank you."

Gideon spoke up, "We weeded the garden and will go wash up at the stream." He took Elah's dirty hand and smiled.

"THAT IS the border of our freedom," Gideon mused as he pointed to the stream with his soil-covered finger, releasing Elah's hand. "This stream is our prison wall," he added, pointing with both hands. "If we could but cross this, we might find our escape."

"Or we can decide to find our happiness inside and live, not waiting for something better. I have learned that I can be content, even if my situation isn't what I always dreamed of."

Gideon nodded. "You're wise," then added, "What are your dreams?"

Elah chuckled. "Well, I can promise you my dreams did not include being a slave, a widow, and raising my son alone." Then, in a more serious tone, she continued, "I dreamed of the places my father talked of from his days as a merchant trader. When I was young, he would come home and have stories of far-off places and people. He talked of finding ore, shells, and yarns spun out of the softest wool, and I dreamed of going with him one day. After my mother died, I went with him a few times before Noah convinced him to stay here. I believe Noah wished for me to stay to join his wives." Elah blushed. "I'm glad I was spared that fate."

Gideon nodded. "I am, too." Their eyes met. "I would like to court you."

"I would like that," Elah whispered. "I'd have liked it if you'd asked me years ago, actually."

"Truly?" Gideon gasped.

"Yes, I would have loved for my son to have a father to teach him. I've watched how kind you are to all of the young ones, teaching the boys the art of the bow and preparing them to protect our city and our people."

"Would you wish to marry again?"

"Yes, I would."

"Would you be my wife, Elah?

Elah looked up into his earnest face. "Yes, I would."

Gideon took both of her dirty hands in his and smiled. Then he kissed each one gently.

He took Elah in his arms and pulled her close to his heart, the heart that was now beating wildly.

"Let's tell Limhi and Dinah."

"First, we wash," Elah proclaimed.

"THAT WAS SOME QUICK HAND WASHING," Dinah quipped with a huge smile as Limhi took her hand and pulled the tapestry aside, tugging her out into the courtyard. Their eyes glanced at the clasped hands and the smiling faces of Gideon and Elah.

"We will be wed," Gideon announced.

Dinah pulled Elah into an embrace and Limhi clapped Gideon on the shoulder. "It's about time," the king exclaimed.

"When?" Dinah asked.

Gideon glanced down at Elah. "On the morrow?"

"After our labors," Elah added.

"Wonderful!" The queen gushed. "I'll prepare the celebration."

"Now to tell my mother," Gideon added hesitantly.

"She will welcome the news," Dinah added.

THE MARRIAGE of Gideon and Elah was celebrated by all, including Rachel. She joyfully welcomed the news of a new daughter, and even the unexpected blessing of adding a grandson to their small family. Aaron was now eight-years-old and quite useful in the palace court-yard keeping rabbits away from the family gardens.

Their days as a new family were spent working together and spending time with Rachel. She seemed to come alive again, teaching the skill of pottery to her grandson. Aaron found any excuse to go visit his new grandmother, and together they would go explore the old pottery studio.

Elah visited Tamar and Dinah often, since they all lived in the old palace compound together. Their children played as the women worked and honed their cooking, spinning, and sewing skills after their long days in the fields planting and tilling the ground. Spring had come and gone; summer days were long and hot, and the children found every excuse to play in the stream.

After a particularly long and hot day, all the families came to find relief from the heat in the stream. The Lamanite guards never spoke to the Nephites, but it seemed their wives suffered from loneliness. And their children would watch the Nephite children play but never join in, until that day.

One boy, about the age of Aaron, stood in the shadows upstream. Everyone noticed him but made no effort to communicate with him or include him, except Aaron. He kept moving upstream and came closer until they stood across from each other.

Dinah moved away from their group with Elah to stand a little closer to Aaron in case there was trouble of any kind. They silently observed the two boys.

Aaron held out a small bowl he had made with Rachel, which contained some tadpoles. Both boys smiled as they watched the tiny creatures wiggle and swim in the dish. The Lamanite boy held out a small arrowhead he had been lashing to a stick. Aaron took it in his hands, turning it about and admiring the way the stone flecks were chipped away. They both smiled.

It was as if time had stopped. Now everyone watched these two boys just being boys. They were children, and that was all that mattered to them.

The women all looked at one another, and it was as if they all had the same idea at the same time. "Do you think maybe it's time we meet the women who have lived here for so long, separated from their people?" Dinah asked the others.

"The soldiers are still on the bluff. Should we go now?" Dinah suggested.

"There's no better time when a thought to do something kind enters the heart." Tamar added.

Together the women made their way up the street to the hut at the very end and did something they'd never done before.

They rapped lightly on the doorpost of the Lamanite hut.

The Lamanite woman's expression held fear, until they each handed her a small handful of flowers and flowering herbs. When the women had given their small gift over with a smile, they nodded and walked away.

Nothing more was said about the encounter, but the expression on the women's faces spoke volumes.

The following day, by the gate of the palace courtyard, they found a small woven cloth with several warm cakes inside. Dinah saw it first and brought it to the others. This became a ritual of sorts. Every couple of days, someone would take an offering to the Lamanite women, and the next day, there would be a gift by the gate.

Guards still shouted orders, whips cracked over their heads, but something was disappearing from the hearts of the people. Hate.

THE DAYS WERE WANING, and crisp fall mornings became more common. Tamar loved to walk to the stream with Helam in the morning when steam rose from the surface and created a layer of fog. It was beautiful and heavenly.

Helam took her hand as they walked. "I love our life. Do you wish we had married sooner?"

Tamar's eyes lit up with her smile. "I used to say that, but something wonderful has happened. I wanted to give you a child. I thought my time had passed." She stopped and took Helam's hand and pressed it to her belly. "Your child grows in my womb."

Helam's expression revealed a tumbled mixture of emotions. "A child...is that possible? Are you sure?"

"Yes, I'm sure!" Tamar laughed an almost girlish giggle. "I can't believe it. I'm a grandmother, and I'm going to be a mother again!"

"How do you feel?"

"Tired, but good overall."

Helam grabbed her by the waist and twirled her around, giving a whoop as he did.

"Hey, that's a bit loud for the morning, you two," a voice called from the palace courtyard. Gideon and Elah emerged from the squeaky gate, hand in hand.

"What's all the excitement about?"

Helam released Tamar gently and kissed her on the forehead. "Should we tell them?" he whispered with the kiss.

"Yes," Tamar gushed.

Gideon led Elah down the slope to the road where Helam and Tamar stood.

"We have news," Tamar said, beaming.

Elah's eyes quickly flicked to Tamar's midsection where Tamar's free hand rested, and she exclaimed, "A child?"

"Yes! We are having a child!"

Elah embraced Tamar and gave her a squeeze.

"Well, if we are sharing news, I guess we can too...I'm carrying Gideon's child."

Gideon and Helam embraced and clapped one another on the back with words of congratulation.

The news spread quickly of the blessings coming to the families in the old palace. There was such excitement for the former queen and the new family that she would have with Helam.

Fall gave way to winter, and the snow came early, signaling the time of hunger the people had experienced year after year. Only, this time, the gifts of fresh cakes came to more families and although there was no work to be done, no harvesting to complete, the tribute of hunted animals was gladly shared. And it seemed as though the Lamanite soldiers were less concerned with who went hunting and for how long. The people felt almost free.

"The healer and midwives are here. I'll let them in so they can get warm," Helam said as he put some water on the fire to make tea.

"I don't understand why my tunics don't fit. I seem to have grown so fast, and I know my time has not come."

"How are you feeling, Tamar?" the midwife asked as she entered and walked to the fire to warm herself. "Come sit over by the fire and let me take a look."

Tamar scooted off her pile of skins, and Helam gave her a hand to stand. She walked slowly over to where the midwife waited. "Is the healer coming too?" she asked.

"Yes, he is finishing up with Elah, checking her health."

"Is she well?"

"Yes, and Aaron has already carved some toys for the new child. He is as excited about a new brother or sister as his parents are."

Tamar chuckled. "Look at what Helam has made." She pointed to the corner where a beautifully crafted cradle stood. "He is so happy to be a father."

The healer poked his head through the tapestry, pulled it aside, and stepped in quickly.

"Your home is warm, and that's good. It's going to be a long and cold winter." He rubbed his hands together by the fire.

The midwife placed her hands on each side of Tamar's round belly. She pressed gently one side, then the other. "Tamar, I need you to lie down. Her expression showed concern.

"What is it?" Tamar asked.

Helam stepped closer, "Is there something wrong?"

Tamar moved to her skin bed and lay down.

"Does it feel like there is always movement?" The midwife asked.

Helam chuckled, "Like a battle raging at times."

The midwife pressed in different places all around Tamar's belly and as she did so, little bumps rose and fell and pushed so hard that Tamar could nearly see an entire footprint pressing outward. "There are too many elbows and knees for just one child," she said, then paused, "I believe you will have to carve another cradle. There are two."

The healer came over to her bedside. "There is danger in having two, especially at your age." He wore a grave expression. "We will need to be very watchful when your time comes." To Helam, he said, "And pray."

THE DAY CAME for Elah first. Tamar was confined to her bed, unable to rise, but she heard the welcome news. A son. She longed to be at Elah's bedside and help her through her travail and recovery, but she was so full and heavy she could only rise once or twice each day without pains beginning.

Later that day, Gideon brought his newborn son over to the home of Helam and Tamar. He beamed with such pride and love as he gazed down at his son, wrapped in cloth woven by the women in Shilom. "Isaac will be his name."

"He is fair like Elah, but has a head of hair like yours, Gideon." Tamar stroked the little boy's fine, soft hair. "Such a handsome little boy," she beamed with a tired smile. "Give your wife my love and let her know I'll be joining her soon. These two make quite a commotion when they start stretching. I can't wait to hold them."

"Soon enough," Helam soothed. "Not so soon that they won't be healthy in this cold." He passed a hand over Tamar's very swollen belly.

"I don't want Isaac to be out or away from Elah long. I think the midwives should be done cleaning. This birthing is quite..." Gideon didn't finish, he just shook his head. "I don't know how our women do this."

Helam clapped Gideon on the shoulder. "They are strong, stronger than you and I!" They both smiled.

Elah was up and around in a few days and came to be with Tamar. They talked of children, of dreams, and hopes for freedom.

"Maybe when spring comes the Lord will see fit to free us," Tamar whispered. "I long to be truly free."

IT WAS DEEPLY cold and winter refused to release its icy grip on Shilom. Food was rationed and the snow lay heavy on the ground, making caring for the sheep and goats difficult for the shepherds. In spite of the snow and cold, the ewes inevitably gave birth on the coldest of days. The blessing of twins from every herd did not go unnoticed. None of the winter squash rotted and it seemed as though the corn meal went further than expected, although the supply of grain dwindled. None went hungry. Limhi likened it to the miracles of the Children of Israel when they left Egypt. Truly the Lord blessed them.

Dinah visited Tamar often with Limhi, ministered to her needs, helped her to get up when needed, and made her meals each day.

"Son," Tamar whispered one day. "What does the Lord tell you about our freedom?"

Limhi came to sit by her side. "I just know we will be free." He rubbed his forehead for a moment. "There is no timeline; He has shown me the day. We will be together with Alma's people once again. We will be in Zarahemla together."

"I feel it will be soon," Tamar whispered. "The Lord has heard my prayer to be free." She smiled a weak smile. "When God shows me, I am holding my son, and the day is glorious and bright. It is beautiful and green." She closed her eyes. "It is warm." She shivered. "I long to be warm. I am chilled to the bone."

A pain coursed through her, and she gasped. Her breathing increased, then slowed as she relaxed. Again, a pain took over, and she whimpered.

"Mother, is it time?"

Tamar nodded.

Limhi called to Helam, who was carrying wood to all of the homes in the palace compound for their fires. He dropped the wood and came to the tapestry door where Limhi stood. "Call for the midwives."

The healer and midwives came quickly. The concern on their faces, evident.

Tamar focused on breathing as hands caressed her back, arms, and shoulders. All was in readiness. The first child came quickly, a daughter. Dinah cleaned and wrapped the child in blankets and skins and took her to the fireplace to warm.

"Bring her to me," Tamar whispered between pains, "I need to see her." Dinah brought the girl, the image of her mother, with dark hair and fine features. She leaned over to place a soft kiss on her head. Another series of pains took her attention and she cried out. Dinah kept the baby warm as everyone focused on Tamar and the final child to be born.

The healer and midwives tended to Tamar. "The child is breach and stuck," the healer finally stated. "We must move things along or we will lose them both."

The color drained from Helam's face. "I can't lose her, or the child." He fell to his knees beside Tamar and prayed silently.

Limhi took his mother's hand into his and looked into her pained face. "Don't give up, mother. Please." His concerned expression revealed his fear.

It was long into the night when the second child was finally born. A son. His body, blue and limp, never gained strength enough to take a breath. Tamar held him and wept bitterly. "His name," she paused and looked into the face of the man she loved more than life, "is Helam the younger." She curled the blankets around his perfect face and kissed it tenderly.

Time stood still for just a moment as the family surrounded their mother, wife, and former queen. They mourned with her. Dinah held the little girl, brought her close to Tamar so she could see both of her children together one last time.

Pale and weak, Tamar pulled Dinah close and whispered in her ear. Tears fell from Dinah's eyes. The tiny girl began to cry. Dinah put the baby to Tamar's breast so she could suckle and took little Helam, gently moving him from Tamar and placing the child in his father's arms. Helam took the boy and cradled him and wept openly, mourning the son he would never know in this life.

THE FUNERAL PROCESSION wound through the snow to the top of the burial mound. The tallest tree belonged to Zeniff, and they knew the landmark well. Slowly the stone hoes worked their way through the frozen ground to make a burial place for this tiny boy. Helam, surrounded by citizens of Shilom, mourned the loss. As the procession wound back down the hill, several people stood near the bottom, off to one side near a copse of trees. As the family and friends neared them, the Lamanite women handed a small parcel to Helam, then waited for the Nephite mourners to pass by.

Dinah and Limhi passed first and smiled. They were closely followed by Helam and Gideon. Dinah made eye contact with the women, one at a time, and placed her hand over her heart, dipping her head toward each one.

They all went immediately to Tamar, where she was still being tended to by the midwives. Tamar was not reviving, and there was grave concern for her health. Elah stayed by her side with her new baby, taking turns with Dinah to keep her company.

Tamar motioned for Helam to come to her. She pulled him close, and he knelt by her bedside, placing his cheek next to hers. His tears fell on the pillow beneath her head as she whispered in his ear.

"I feel my soul trying to go to a place beyond. It's as if those I loved and lost are calling me." She paused for a moment. "Our daughter doesn't yet have a name. What will you call her?"

Helam's shoulders shuddered. He whispered a shaky response. "She is the image of you, my love. The only name she could have is Tamar!"

Tamar smiled weakly. "Zeniff and Jarom are here. I see a handsome young man that looks much like you." She took his hand. "Ask Elah to care for our little girl, please. She needs a mother's milk."

Her strength gone, Tamar fell into a deep sleep and slipped between heaven and earth for a time until her spirit left altogether.

The little parcel from the Lamanite women sat on the table next to the bed, two sets of beautifully beaded newborn moccasins.

There was too much heartache to bear. The much beloved Tamar was gone. They buried her next to her child, Helam the younger, Zeniff, and Jarom, to rest until the resurrection day when all would be made whole again.

Helam's heart would not, could not, be whole.

LISHA, 130 BC, CITY OF HELAM

lute music drifted through Lisha's cottage window. She looked up from the necklace she'd been stringing with colorful beads and exchanged grins with Alma and Sarika.

She no longer saw Sarika as a rival but as a friend, one who'd reminded her that life was worth living, even amid loss. Six years had passed since that night by the river. In that time, Lisha slowly awoke, emerging from the clawing abyss where time stood still and all she could do was grieve. The hurt was still there. So were her questions. But she'd rejoined the living, frequently gathering the women of Helam for songs and laughter, helping Sarika gain the courage to give Rafa a chance. Lisha no longer felt lonely. She filled the hours when Alma was away with other people and other things. It was enough.

"Is it time?" Sarika's daughter, Shoshannah, bounced with excitement, breaking Lisha from her reverie. Lisha set aside her work and hugged her.

"I'd say it's time," Alma said, throwing his hands up. "Who courts a girl for six years before marrying?"

"Alma," Lisha chided, feeling heat rush to her cheeks. "Sarika wasn't ready."

Sarika flushed a pretty pink and smoothed the lace veil over her hair. "I'm ready now."

"Indeed, you are," Alma said, "and unless my son has suddenly mastered the flute, I'd say Rafa's ready, too."

Shoshannah hurried to the window. She pulled aside the curtain, took a deep breath, then turned back with all the gravity of a young woman with life-changing news. "It's time."

Sarika flushed. She rose from her stool at the smooth maple-wood table, fluttered her hands, and sat back down.

Alma and Lisha opened the door. Outside, Rafa waited in his best deerskins, swaying slightly as he tried to control his nerves. His dark hair clung to his brow. Behind him, chickens milled about, pecking at the ground. The sky was eggshell blue, clear of any clouds. A perfect day for a betrothal. "I come to thy house to ask thee for Sarika to wife. Let me find favor in your eyes," he said.

Lisha leaned against the doorframe, her husband hovering at her back. Their son, Kaleb, sat in a willow chair under a tree, his brow furrowed as he whittled a bone flute. Alma the Younger stood beside him, watching with open curiosity, dangling a twig from his fingers. It wouldn't be long, Lisha mused, before he'd be declaring his intentions, perhaps to Zilpah, Hannah's daughter. The two spent all their free time together, tromping through the forest. Nothing would make Lisha happier than to join their families, even if Zilpah was still a handful. Lisha remembered her and Young Alma swinging from the trees at village picnics as recent as a year or two past.

"I would be honored to stand for Sarika's father," Alma said. He moved past Lisha to clasp Rafa's hand. Rafa looked supremely relieved. Alma gave a sly grin. "Assuming the bride has agreed?"

"Of course, she agreed!" Lisha said with a smile. Young Alma fidgeted with his twig.

A giggle came from inside.

"Quiet!" Sarika whispered, but her voice carried.

Rafa tried to peer around Lisha. She shifted to fill the doorframe.

"And Shoshannah?" Alma asked. "Would you like Rafa for a father?"

"As if I need a father at my age," a high voice called. Shoshannah pushed her way around Lisha, her long braid swinging. She flashed a mischievous grin at Rafa and went to stand beside him, her face aglow.

Sarika waited in the small kitchen, her hands folded in her lap. Lisha caught her eye and nodded toward the door. Sarika leaped from the stool, her blue skirts flying as she hurried to join Rafa and her daughter. They would make a sweet little family and were obviously deeply in love. Lisha could tell from the way Rafa gazed at Sarika, like she was his world, and ruffled Shoshannah's hair. They walked away, talking and laughing.

Alma watched them with satisfaction, then patted his vest pocket. "I think I left my knife at Asher's place." He strode off without another word. Kaleb didn't seem to notice their father had left. Alma the Younger threw his twig down and strode away as well.

Lisha smoothed her skirts with a sigh. "Time for some chores."

Kaleb looked up, realizing he was the only one left to help.

"I'll go get Alma," he offered.

Lisha shook her head, her gaze lingering on Young Alma's distant silhouette blending with the trees.

"It's all right, Kaleb. Come inside."

A frown creased Kaleb's face. "Why's he so grumpy?"

Lisha shook off a sinking feeling. Happiness would have to wait. She had bread to bake and a wedding to plan.

THE PROCESSION STARTED at the western gates of Helam amid fluting music, trembling lyre strings, and graceful song. Alma led Rafa and Sarika past clusters of thatched homes, between the potter's and woodworker's shops to the communal gathering place in front of the temple. Lisha walked one step behind the pair, alongside Shoshannah, who wore a simple yellow dress with a sheepskin cloak and a garland of winter heather in her hair.

A fine layer of snow dusted the ground, glittering in the sunlight like a blessing from heaven. Everything had come together. The women of Helam had outdone themselves, weaving cloth for the couple's home, decorating the temple with dried flowers and winter berries, braiding breads, and baking meat pies. Lisha was exhausted from directing it all but felt the pride of a mother, or older sister, perhaps, when she looked at Sarika's glowing face.

She knew Sarika had often longed for her mother, had needed her protection and wished for her guiding hand. Much as Alma the Younger and Kaleb needed Lisha. Sarika often said Alma needed Lisha, although Lisha couldn't see it herself. He strode ahead of the crowd, a bounce in his step and straightness to his back that seemed wholly unrelated to her. Did he need her at all? Lisha cast aside these thoughts, preferring to focus on the joy of the moment. Dark thoughts were intruders, not welcome in a day like this. *Please, Lord,* she thought, *bless this sweet family and bring them peace.* She hesitated, then added, *and bring me peace, too.*

Due to the icy weather, the couple had forgone the tradition of bathing in the spring on the morning of the ceremony. Instead, a heated pot of water stood outside the temple doors, with clouds of steam spiraling upward like a prayer. The people of Helam crowded around Sarika and Rafa. They dipped their hands in the steaming water, symbolically washing away the past and signifying their new future together. Lisha held out a soft cloth for them to dry off.

Alma opened the sanctuary door and led them inside to a wedding canopy at the far end of the hall, where Alma usually preached. Reed torches burned in bundles spaced along the walls. Sarika looked radiant in woven layers of cream and white, topped with snowy sheepskin still bearing its wool.

Once everyone was seated, the couple took hands before Alma and covenanted to join their hearts and home. "I am my beloved's," Rafa said.

Sarika finished, "And my beloved is mine."

Rafa slid a copper ring stamped with flowers onto Sarika's finger, then pressed her hand to his lips. Her eyes sparkled in the winter sunlight as she gave him a ring stamped with eagles. They shared a cup of wine to seal their vows. When the ceremony finished, Sarika and Rafa embraced, then received the well-wishers that crowded around them. Shoshannah clung to her mother's side, beaming like morning light.

Lisha moved among the people, guiding the men who moved tables into the sanctuary since the weather was far too cold for dinner outdoors. She and Mera scattered crimson berries and deep green cedar boughs across the table tops, setting candles carefully among them so as not to set the cedar ablaze. They worked quickly while Sarika and Rafa received congratulations. Naomi trailed behind them with a thin, creamy taper, careful not to drip wax as she lit the remaining candles. Across the room, Hannah and Zilpah performed similar tasks. Several others followed behind, setting out food and plates. It was a carefully orchestrated dance, designed to finish quickly so there would be a little wait.

"It was a beautiful ceremony," Mera said to Lisha. "You should be proud."

Lisha flushed, surprised at the praise. "It's no different from other winter weddings."

A faint smile lingered on Mera's lips. "You've done well, Lisha. Accept our gratitude."

Lisha nodded, her cheeks burning. She moved along the table, straightening stray needles.

People began settling themselves. Lisha smiled, noticing Alma the Younger had managed to wedge himself in with Zilpah's family.

"It's high time we had *another* ceremony," a gruff voice said. It was Asher, speaking to his wife, Belen, as they corralled their squirming twins and older children. "Crowning Alma king," Asher continued. "He already is in every way but the title."

Lisha blinked then focused on the tables, her mind running. *King?* It was true, Alma led the people. They loved him. But what would it mean for Lisha if he became king? How would that affect their family? If he were king, he'd have advisors and priests to help him.

Lisha's breath caught. Would she see more of Alma?

Mera had been queen. Lisha's sister, Sarai, would've been queen, too, had Noah not usurped the throne back in Shilom. The idea wasn't foreign to her. She'd just never thought it would apply to *her*.

But maybe it could. Maybe it should.

~

LISHA PACED BACK and forth in Mera's small cottage, her skirts swirling around her ankles. Yoseph and Alma the Younger chatted while six-year-old Kaleb played in the corner, entertained with balls of wool yarn. They seemed too occupied to pay any mind to what she was saying, but Lisha pitched her voice low nonetheless. She paused by the chair where Mera rocked, her hands folded in her lap.

"I hardly know Alma anymore. He's so absorbed in his work, and it takes so much time to care for everyone." Lisha hated to complain, especially when she knew Alma was doing such good. But if anyone could understand her pain, it was Mera. She forged on, opening her heart to the older woman. "I can't admire him from afar, like everyone else, following him through Helam, like a beggar for scraps. He's my husband."

Mera opened her mouth, but Lisha pressed on. Combine with next

"I know he's on God's errand. Maybe I'm selfish. But shouldn't he be there for me? For our family?"

"Alma loses himself in service," Mera said. Her lined face showed years of hardship, but the light in her eyes showed something else, a quiet, burning faith that guided her life.

"He avoids his pain! He's never shared it with me. He's buried Eva so deep in his soul that it's like she never existed!"

"You know that's not true, Lisha."

Lisha sank into a chair beside Mera, dropping her face to her hands. "I'm so weary."

Mera reached out and stroked Lisha's back. "What has brought this on?"

Lisha raised a tear-stained face to Mera. "I know I'm not alone. You've always loved me like a daughter. And Sarika, we've become good friends. And Naomi, of course. She's a wonderful grandmother to the boys. But I need my husband. I thought maybe if he saw how hard I worked for Sarika and Rafa's wedding, he would notice me again and remember the excitement we felt when we first courted. But he's in another world. And I can't pull him from it, no matter what I do."

Mera nodded, chewing her lip as she thought.

"You must've gone through this with Zeniff?" Lisha asked. "When he was king?"

Mera cast a quick glance at Yoseph in the corner with the boys. As if he felt the weight of her gaze, he turned toward her, his wrinkled face lifting into a grin. Young Alma raised his head as well.

"Life is simpler now," Mera said. "Yoseph and I have not had to share the pressures of leading a kingdom." She tapped her chin. "Still, Zeniff had more help than Alma does. Alma is like a king without advisors or other assistants."

Alma is like a king. There it was, twice in one week. *Alma is like a king.* If he were king, he could arrange things differently. He'd be able to be home with her, Young Alma, and Kaleb. And Lisha would know exactly where she belonged—at Alma's side, as Queen. "I think it would be easier if Alma were king. He would have help. And my voice would matter."

"Your voice matters now, child."

"Don't call me that. I've buried a child of my own. I am not a child anymore."

"Then stop acting like one," Mera snapped.

Lisha took in a sharp breath.

Mera sighed. "I'm sorry, Lisha. I don't mean that. But you must not brood over your trials. That will destroy you."

"I can't continue as I am, Mera. I can't live like this."

Mera nodded. "Then you must find a new way to live."

Lisha's face tightened. What did Mera mean?

"You must change your heart, Lisha. But you cannot do it alone. Only the Lord can soften your heart and help you find your way."

But Lisha wasn't listening. Her hands clenched in her skirts. "I will see to it that Alma becomes king. Asher and Samuel can advise him.

We will divide the work of ruling these people. Alma will see that his place is with his own family."

Mera opened her mouth. "That's not—"

"It's the only way."

With a growing sense of rightness, Lisha strode through the gathering place, the winter sun warm on her back. She bypassed the cold remains of the bonfire, nodding at Elizabeth, Hannah's daughter, who lumbered toward the butcher's shop, three small children in tow. Lisha stopped and sighed, then turned back and scooped up one of Elizabeth's stragglers.

"Oh! Thank you, Lisha," the heavy woman said, wiping her shining face. "I would have carried him, but I can hardly manage my own self."

Lisha smiled and chatted with Elizabeth until they reached the shop, then resumed her original course. She had left Kaleb with Grandma Naomi for the day, a choice that thrilled him almost as much as grandmother. By now, they were probably up to their elbows in clay. Lisha sighed. More lopsided bowls for her cooking area. Of course, lopsided bowls were a good start. After a few years, Naomi would have Kaleb crafting intricate goblets and ewers if he took the time to learn. But for now, they dabbled in clay.

Alma was once like them, puttering about the potter's studio, crafting clay flowers, and stringing them on leather for a necklace for Lisha. That had been years ago, in the early days of their courtship. He'd been a bit like a lopsided bowl back then, prone to cave under the pressure of Noah and his priests. A biting wind chafed at Lisha, pulling her hair from beneath her scarf. She tucked it back in and shook her head, continuing toward Asher's house. Alma was different now. Strong, resilient, and clear-sighted in his purpose. And the people loved him for it.

Alma the Younger, though, was a different story. More like a half-hardened clay ball that rolled and stopped at unexpected moments. Where was that boy anyway? She'd meant for him to spend the day with Naomi as well. But he must have had plans of his own. She sighed, pausing outside Asher and Belen's home.

The wood structure gleamed in the sunlight. Ice glazed the long vertical wood of the cottage like frosting on a cake and hung from the thatched roof like daggers. The green-painted shutters were closed against the cold. They looked like frothy water churned up in a stream. Lisha scraped her nail against the wood. The ice came away in a soft, white ball, which melted quickly in her hand. She rapped her knuckles on the door, the sound muffled by the layers of cloth she'd wrapped around her hands for warmth.

Belen opened the door, her face flushing as she grabbed the collar of one of her twins, who'd just made a bid to escape.

"Oh my, Amos!" Lisha hugged the small boy. "And where do you think you're going?"

"I wanna play in the snow." Amos squirmed in her grasp, kicking his stocking-covered feet against her cloak.

"Come on in," Belen said, opening the door wider.

The small cottage was packed with visitors.

Samuel sat on a three-legged stool near the fireplace. "Hannah's gone to help Elizabeth with the children," he said by way of apology.

Asher was in a corner with several others, including Rafa, Sarika, Yoseph, and Mera. Ira, the painter, hovered near a window, his slim shoulders bowed as he inspected the peeling paint. He raised his head to greet Lisha, his dark eyes serious. Several others crowded in the shadowy corner, their heads bent in conversation.

"Here," Belen said, guiding Lisha to a wide maple wood chair woven with strips of buffalo hide. It was tanned with the fur still on and was arguably the most comfortable seat in the cottage. Belen reached for Amos, who wriggled into her arms. She deposited him on a pile of furs with his older sister, who was already entertaining his twin. Then she turned expectantly to Lisha.

Lisha felt her own cheeks pink. She wasn't sure where to begin.

But Asher spoke up, taking some pressure off. "Belen and I are honored you chose our home for this gathering."

Lisha nodded, feeling yet more self-conscious. The certainty she'd felt on her walk to their house was wavering. But she forged ahead, knowing she'd feel more confident once the conversation got going. "I chose you because of your love and loyalty for Alma."

"I'd give my life for him," Asher said simply.

"In a way, that's what I'm asking," Lisha said without thinking. "Well, not exactly, not really." She was messing this all up. Her face burned. Who did she think she was to call a meeting like this and discuss the future of their people? Yet everyone in the cottage waited for her to continue. She chose her next words carefully. "Alma needs help. He leaves home in the early hours and returns after nightfall, often too tired to eat dinner. His sons barely know him. He is exhausted, and to be honest, so am I."

Samuel nodded from his place by the fire. Ira folded his arms. "Why isn't Alma here?" he asked.

Asher shook his head. "You know, Alma. He'll ask you to help your neighbor, but he'll never ask for help himself."

The others nodded.

"What is it you suggest?" Rafa asked. "We'd do anything for Alma."

"And for you," Sarika added. "Do you need help with the children? Or repairs on your home?"

Lisha looked to Asher and Belen, who had settled next to him on a colorful rag rug. "I'm thinking of something that will help not just Alma but all of Helam." Asher cocked his head to the side, his eyes bright. "I got the idea from Asher, actually. And from Mera." She nodded to the corner. "Asher, I overheard, but Mera, I spoke with directly." Asher's brow furrowed, and Yoseph looked bewildered. Mera, however, looked thoughtful, considering.

Lisha took a deep breath. "It's time our people had a king."

Her pronouncement was met with a stunned silence, then murmuring broke out in the room, like the whispering of spring wind through the pines calling for warmer days. Samuel nodded in deep conversation with Yoseph. Ira leaned against the wall; his eyes gleaming. Several others huddled together, talking animatedly. Only Mera remained quiet, her gaze distant, lost, perhaps in the past.

Asher stood, running his hands down his deerskin vest. "I have long thought Alma should be king. It would put to rest any grumbling and give Alma clear authority to make decisions for our people."

Grumbling? Who had been undermining Alma? Lisha wondered. She pushed the thought aside. "As king, Alma will need advisors to share the burden of ruling."

Several men nodded.

Sarika beamed. "Then he can spend more time with you."

Lisha's mouth curved into a small smile. "I hope so," she said. "I really do."

"We will spread the word," Rafa said eagerly. "We'll each host meetings so that when the time comes to crown Alma, everyone will know and we'll be ready to shout down his modesty. We had a king in Shilom, in Lehi-Nephi, and, if the rumors are true, in Zarahemla. We need a king in Helam. Without a king, our city is nothing more than a bunch of people living in the same place. We need a king to protect our people, to negotiate treaties. We need a king."

Lisha caught Mera's gaze then. "We'll need your counsel, mother. You've been queen before. You're the only one in Helam who knows the ways of the court." Mera's eyes glittered. "In the meantime," Lisha continued, "I will convince Alma."

"I can help with that," a deep voice said.

Lisha blinked as the last person she'd expected to see emerged from the group in the corner—Alma the Younger.

LISHA, 130 BC, CITY OF HELAM

"Absolutely not," Alma said. He turned away from Lisha, staring at the bluffs towering over the sluggish, ice-fringed river. She had brought him here, outside the city, to the place where Helam had begun. In the distance, she could see the winding path that led up the hills beyond the city, the spot where she'd stood and gazed down at their future home. It was a fitting place, she thought, for Alma to accept his role as leader of this people.

She shivered in the frigid winter air and pulled her shawls tight around her neck. "It's the only way, Alma. The people love you. They hunger for a leader."

"I already am a leader. I do not need the title of king nor the absolute power that comes with it."

"But why?" Lisha pressed. "What can it hurt to be king?"

They'd had this conversation before, with Alma the Younger joining in on the discussion. He seemed focused and determined like never before as if a fire were lit inside him. Instead of battling Lisha at every turn over unimportant things like chores or childish behavior, he had finally gained a purpose outside himself. He understood, Lisha thought. Young Alma understood that the people needed a king and how their lives would change if Alma embraced his true role.

Alma's face darkened. "You saw what that power did to Noah. It corrupted him."

Lisha frowned. "Noah was corrupt before he became king. He stole the kingdom and destroyed it. You're not like Noah. You are above that." She drew closer to him, resting her mitten-covered hands on his chest. In the distance, she heard the faint sounds of sheep bleating, sheltered in the tree-lined pastures south of the city. "Let's climb the hill, Alma, and see what we have built."

Alma took a deep breath, but he let Lisha lead him over a small bridge and up the winding path. Once they reached the summit, they turned. The rolling landscape looked quite different from how it had looked fifteen years before. It had been summer when they'd arrived, the grass green and gleaming, the rivers crystal in the sunlight, and the wind warm in the trees. It was still beautiful, despite the starkness of winter. Now smoke rose from thatched cottages. Winter crops grew in tilled fields. Vineyards sprawled along the riverbed. The gathering place hosted regular singing, and the chapel stood tall, a place of safety, warmth, and hope.

Lisha wound her arm around Alma's waist. "You have done a good thing here. Helam is a flourishing city. The people are happy. But without a strong, good king, things will fall apart. Who will decide conflicts among neighbors?"

"I already do that," Alma said.

"Yes," Lisha nodded, "and the people allow it because they love you. But that may not always be the case. Already some grumble against you. Who will decide conflicts with them?"

Alma waved off the thought. "If the people don't want me to lead them, that is their choice."

"But that's just it, Alma," Lisha said, leaning her head back to look up at him. "They do want you. They need you. The city needs you. Who is to negotiate treaties if another people come? Who is to settle differences? We need you, Alma, and we need you to be king."

A line formed between Alma's brows.

"I've already spoken to Asher, Samuel, and Rafa. There are others, too. They're all behind you."

"Lisha," Alma's reply was quiet. "I didn't agree to that."

"You didn't need to," she said. "They were already talking. I just brought them together."

Alma took another deep breath.

"They've agreed to be advisors, Alma. They can carry some of the burden of caring for these people. You need their help as much as we all need you. Maybe more. And I need you. Your family needs you. We need you to have this help."

Alma ran a hand through his dark, wavy hair, then settled his arm around Lisha's shoulders, squeezing her tight. She leaned up and kissed his cheek, feeling a warmth and closeness between them that had been missing for a very long time.

TWO WEEKS LATER, all of Helam gathered in the sanctuary. It was a bright Sunday morning. Lisha trembled with anticipation. She had worn her best dress, a pale wool embroidered in gold thread. Alma had been up all night and had dark circles under his eyes. But his gaze was steady, determined.

Usually, he spoke first, but this time Asher stood in front of the fireplace and altar to address the group crammed into the broad wooden structure. The benches were packed, and many families sat on the floor or leaned against the sanctuary walls, careful to avoid bumping the reed torches that lit the room. Lisha knew Alma had tried to speak with him before the gathering, but Asher had bustled away, mindful of his role in today's proceedings.

Kaleb sat quietly between Naomi and Mera, his face solemn. When Lisha caught Alma the Younger's eye, then he beamed with pride—his father would soon be king. She'd sewn him a fine, fur-lined cloak for the occasion. His constant pushback against Lisha and Alma worried her. Maybe she and Alma had taught him all they could, and now life and God would teach him the rest.

She glanced over at her husband and gave herself a mental shake. Parents' roles changed when their children were grown; there was no doubt of that. But if she'd learned anything from her closeness with Mera, it was that she still needed a mother, even as an adult. Lisha hoped that being king might have a positive effect on Young Alma. He seemed to feel such pride and purpose in that. Surely it would solidify his role in Helam and give him direction.

She squeezed her husband's hand, an expression of faith in him and hope for their family's future. Alma smiled vaguely and withdrew his hand from hers. "I really must speak with Asher," he said, rising from their bench at the front.

But Asher had already stood. "Welcome!" he cried. "Welcome to the greatest day in the history of Helam."

Bright beams of sunshine slanted through gaps in the shutters, casting light in dazzling patterns along the sanctuary floor. Alma strode toward Asher, passing through the streams of light. Dust motes whirled in the air moved by his passing, a symphony of disarray.

What is he doing? Lisha wondered. *He shouldn't be interrupting Asher. He's getting everything wrong.*

Alma, however, did not seem at all concerned about the proper order of things. He stepped up beside Asher and whispered in his ear. Whatever he said must have been a shock, because the blood drained from Asher's face, leaving him pale as winter frost. He spoke to Alma in an urgent undertone. But Alma remained steadfast; Lisha could see it in his face. She leaned forward, straining to hear.

"I thought Lisha had convinced you," Asher said, "to at least do it for her and your son Alma." He didn't seem to notice he was wringing his hands.

"She had," Alma said, "until I took it to the Lord."

Lisha felt as if a snow bank had fallen on her, cold and suffocating.

Alma turned to face the people. "You have come here," he said, "expecting to crown me king. But this is not to be. I have sought the will of the Lord, and it is this—that we have no king! The Lord commands that we esteem not one person above another. Nor should one man think himself above others. Therefore, it is not expedient that we have a king."

"But we need a king," Rafa cried from the back of the room. "We want a king. We need you!"

There were murmurs of assent, followed by chanting, "We need Alma. We need a king." Alma the Younger's voice rang out among them, and he pounded his foot on the hardwood floor. His face shone with a fervor Lisha had rarely seen.

Alma blinked, caught by surprise, and shared a bemused look that Lisha could not return. "Please, listen to me. Remember the wickedness of King Noah?" The chanting faltered. Alma started slow pacing. "If it were possible to always have a just, righteous king, that would be good. It would be right. But kings are not always righteous. They're often corrupted by power."

"You would never be corrupted by power," Ira argued. His wife, Ophir nodded sharply. So did many others. But, as Lisha glanced around, she noted Mera's strained expression and Sarika looking grim.

"I *was* corrupted by power, ensnared by Noah's power and his lies." Alma's voice shook and his hands trembled. "I did many things"—his voice broke—"many things which were abominable in the sight of the Lord, which caused me sore repentance." His voice grew stronger now. "I went through great tribulation. And I did not suffer alone." His gaze lingered on Lisha. Hot tears spilled down her face. As much as she sometimes resented Alma's past, she never meant for him to face these things in front of everyone. He didn't deserve that.

"Nevertheless," he continued, "the Lord did hear our cries and answer our prayers. Now I am an instrument in bringing you to the knowledge of his truth. This is enough. More than enough. We do not need a king."

Lisha shook—out of sorrow, relief? She didn't know. When she looked to the crowd again, she saw Young Alma, his face a dark, angry cloud.

"King Noah oppressed us. He enslaved us. He brought iniquity among us and taught us to love evil." Alma's voice was urgent now, his movements strong and bold. "The Lord delivered us from King Noah. He delivered us from iniquity. We cannot repay Him by subjecting ourselves again to a king! Stand fast in the liberty wherewith God has made you free." He paused and took a great breath. "Trust no man to be a king over you."

Alma the Younger rose, threw aside his cloak, and stormed out of the sanctuary.

BACK HOME IN THEIR COTTAGE, Kaleb slipped into a fitful sleep amid a welter of furs near the fireplace. Lisha was tidying up the cottage with an energy unwarranted for the task. Alma was bent over a scroll, reading. How could he sit there so calmly after what he had done this night? Not only had he refused to be king, but he had also shamed their family in front of everyone. He wasn't considering their needs at all. Especially their son's. Hadn't he seen the growing sense of purpose and direction in Alma the Younger? She turned to face Alma, her fury boiling over. "How could you? You promised me. You promised *us* you would be king!"

Alma set aside the scroll. "I never promised, Lisha, and I have to follow the Lord. I have to. That's what I do. That's who I am."

Lisha looked away. She wrapped her arms around her homespun nightgown. "This isn't the Lord's will, Alma. It isn't."

He crossed the room, took her hand, and led her to their small bed. They sat together, holding hands across the distance between them. He gazed at her, patient, waiting.

"It wasn't wrong for Zeniff to be king," she said. "He was a good man, a good leader. And Mera told me his advisors helped him. You need help, Alma." She paused. "I, well, I miss having you around." Her eyes pooled and she wiped them against her arm.

"Zeniff was a good man," Alma said. "But his son, Noah, was not. If Jarom had become king instead of Noah, everything would have been different." He tipped his head to the side. "Or maybe not. Noah would have killed Jarom for the throne."

"He killed him either way," Lisha whispered.

Alma nodded, his face bleak. "This is why we must never have a king. The power destroys families and corrupts nations. It isn't right."

Young Alma shouldered his way into the cottage. Snowflakes clung to his hair and had melted on his shoulders. Clearly, he'd been wandering through the woods, oblivious to the cold. "Mother is right," he said. He stood just inside the doorway, his arms crossed and his jaw set. An icy breeze blew a dusting of snow in behind him. "We can't trust you."

Lisha gasped. "That's not...I never..."

Alma stood. "Son, you cannot continue pitting us against each other, undermining the love and the trust in our home. I will follow the Lord's will in this. I hope you can both come to understand His will as well."

Lisha's lips tightened.

Young Alma took another tack. "You said you fear a wicked king, that he brings evil to the people."

Alma nodded.

"But what if the king is good? Would you limit your influence? Is that the Lord's will?'

Alma smiled. "Perhaps He trusts me to influence them in other ways."

Young Alma wore a troubled expression.

Alma opened his mouth, but Lisha interrupted him. "How can I feel it's right when you feel it's wrong? How can the Lord work that way?" Alma sighed and leaned back against the wall. Their son listened closely, still looking conflicted. "Is it ever right to have a king?"

Alma rubbed his forehead. "I don't know. And I don't know why our answers are different, Lisha. Revelation is not a simple process. We can only receive what we are ready for."

Lisha bristled at this. "Maybe you're the one who's not ready. Maybe you need more courage."

"Lisha!" Alma said reproachfully. Young Alma furrowed his brow. Alma took a deep, steadying breath. "We don't always have the same knowledge or information. You didn't see the things I saw in Noah's court, Lisha; thank heaven for that."

"I can't continue the way things are, Alma; I just can't." Lisha sank into the chair Alma had vacated. "I am so weary and always, always alone."

He took her hand again. "You are never alone, Lisha. Nor are you, son."

Young Alma said nothing.

There was a light tap at the door, and Mera poked her head in. "Oh good," she said with a mischievous grin, "you're up. I thought you might need to talk."

Lisha nodded.

Mera set her terracotta oil lamp on the table, then shuffled to the low-slung bed. She paused. "I think if I sit there, I might never climb back out." She pulled a stool over beside them instead. She took Lisha's hands in her wrinkled ones. "These hands have seen a lifetime, a lifetime of suffering and a lifetime of joy." She examined Lisha's and her own. "Don't add to your suffering, Lisha. What is done is done, whether we like or understand it or not. There are other ways to find peace and solve your problems without Alma being king."

Young Alma gazed at her appraisingly. "It won't be the same," he said.

"No," Mera said calmly, "it won't. But maybe that's for the best."

"I never see my husband," Lisha said, feeling an unexpected surge of bitterness. "I hardly know him anymore. I hardly know myself."

"We will find answers," Mera said. "In the meantime, Alma still leads us."

"As a spiritual leader," Alma clarified, "as the Lord directs. And Lisha, He has a role for you, too, one you've already begun to explore. And you, son. We all have callings to fulfill, service that only we can do for the Lord."

Lisha blinked. "I'm not a leader." She felt Mera's hand tighten on hers.

"You are, despite yourself," Mera said. "You lift all you meet. You comfort the people; you're a spiritual leader among the women, especially. As you embrace this role, you will find great depths of strength and compassion."

"How can I be a spiritual leader when I've suffered such loss? My mother is dead. My baby girl is dead. My sister is gone to Zarahemla. I'll never see her again."

Mera leveled a gaze at Lisha. "You think leaders don't suffer?" Mera's voice was soft and low. "You think everything must be right in your life in order to serve? That you must take care of your own problems before you can see to others? That is never true."

A small line formed between Alma the Younger's brows, and Lisha realized he'd suffered all the same things she had. But he'd been a child. How much of his anger and defiance was a result of hidden pain? She felt a sudden longing to help him resolve the hurts he'd concealed deep inside. But how?

Her husband moved to a little table he'd made for study, with cubbies and a small shelf. Lisha watched with wary eyes. Had she upset him? What was he thinking? He returned with several rolls of unmarked parchment and handed them to Lisha.

"Write your feelings, Lisha. Write your thoughts."

"But parchment, it's so valuable." Lisha thrust it back toward him, but Alma shook his head.

"We can scrape it clean if we need it. For now, use this to hold your questions and your thoughts, to note your inspiration. When I was hiding from Noah, I recorded Abinadi's words on parchment like this. But I also wrote my own dreams and words I received from the Lord. My own writing brought me much peace."

Lisha studied the rolled-up ivory-colored skins, stretched thin, and prepared for precious writing. She pressed them to her chest and nodded. Maybe she and her son could both find peace this way.

CHANNAH, 128 BC, CITY OF AMULON

Channah knelt on the soft mossy ground where the earliest spring flowers were emerging from their long sleep of winter. She carefully dug them up with the sharp stone spade and added the tender bulbs encased in dark soil to the basket she carried.

"Mother," Lemish called out. He came running toward her. "I found more, over in the high clearing. Would you like me to gather them for you?" He stood nearly as tall as her, with dark curly hair that hung well past his shoulders. At fourteen, he was as tall as Amulon but looked more like Channah's father each day.

"Let's go together; show me where you found them."

"If I show you, promise not to be angry at me."

She took his arm. "Why would you say that?"

He looked over sheepishly as they walked comfortably. "It's where we found the lizards."

"Lizards?"

"The ones in the baskets . . . When the girls were weaving."

Channah burst out laughing. "That was you?" She pulled her son closer so no one could hear. "I wondered if you were behind it."

"Not just me, but I was the best at catching them, so, I guess it was mostly my fault."

"Son, your actions were mischievous but not unkind. I think the girls actually liked the attention." Channah caught his eye and added, "Mariah seems to have forgiven you."

Lemish took her hand, face flushed, and began walking faster. "I'm glad you're not mad. I'm not sure what you mean about Mariah, though."

"It's alright if you like her. Just be kind. Remember to be gentle. A woman appreciates that more than you know."

Lemish stopped. "Father is not kind to you. I'll never treat the woman I love like that. You've taught me well, mother."

"Show me those beautiful flowers you found, son."

"You'll love these larger yellow ones. Come!"

Together they walked past one hut after another, each being expanded or added on to. Lemish was among the oldest children in the city. With many of the priests having two wives, the population growth was just the kind of problem Amulon wanted. Dozens of children of all ages played in the streets enjoying being outside after yet another long winter. Lemish dodged a wad of fabric kicked about by some younger boys and tugged Channah through the city, weaving through the crowds filling the street.

The busy thoroughfare was lined with huts and the beginnings of a merchant district. Wine produced in abundance was traded for tanned hides, and dried fruits were traded for dry meats. The warmer weather brought everyone out and it was happy chaos.

A hand grabbed Channah just as she and Lemish were breaking free of the crowd. As Channah stopped abruptly, so did her son. Both turned to face the one person they were hoping to avoid: Amulon.

"Where are you going?"

She held the basket out so he could see. "Gathering flowers for the burial mound."

"I found some yellow ones up along the bluff," Lemish pointed to the shaded outcropping of rock. "Just right up there. We will be right back."

Channah met his gaze. "Yes, we will be right back. Then we will plant them at the base of the burial mound for my little girl."

"I'll be waiting." Amulon turned and walked toward his makeshift tower in the center of the city.

"Why does he always watch you, mother?"

"He thinks I will leave and go back to my people."

"Would you?"

"I don't know where they are. I'd never find my way." Channah paused in thought, knowing she was not being completely truthful. "I wanted to, so many times, but I could never leave you behind. Maybe, one day, you will meet my family. You must never speak of them though. Never say you want to see them or meet them unless you wish to see your father very angry."

"Yes, mother," he replied in a serious and understanding tone.

"It's for the best." Channah focused on walking, her chest, heavy with pain, had seized up and refused to even let her breathe normally.

As they walked through the final stretch of the busy merchant district, Aliza, one of the older women in the community and wife to Zoar, approached Channah. "Can I speak with you in private?" she asked. Lemish looked at his mother and then at Aliza.

"I'll go trade for some jerky. Just come get me when you're ready to go get the other flowers." He trotted off to talk with his friends. Everyone was at the market, trading, buying, and selling. The warmth had brought most families out.

"What is it?" Channah asked. Without responding, Aliza hooked Channah's arm and began walking. When they were out of the crowd, closer to the wooded perimeter, she began speaking.

"We can't talk for long." She looked around as if she were afraid to be seen talking to Channah. "I overheard the priests talking. Zoar is planning an expedition to capture Nephites to come here as slaves to finish building the city. They are tired of doing the work. Amulon wishes to be king over the whole land, Nephite and Lamanite."

"What about our people?" A sick feeling grew in Channah's belly as she asked the rest of her question. "My father is the king. What would happen to him?"

"All I know is that Amulon talks of taking all of the people into captivity. I believe he speaks of the Lamanites too.

Channah saw a movement in the corner of her eye. Amulon.

"You two appear to be talking about something very important." He took Channah's arm. "What would be more important than picking flower bulbs to plant for your daughter?" Aliza dropped away to rejoin the milling crowd.

"Oh, we were just talking about the growth of our fine city and how many new babies have been born. The women are healthy and strong, and so are the children."

Amulon's chest rose. "Indeed, our city grows larger by the day. Our children can now marry and have children. Think of how many there will be!"

Channah gasped. The thought of her son...marrying the daughters of her closest friends had never even crossed her mind. With new eyes, she scanned the city, taking in the faces of those she loved, Lemish, Isa... Mariah and the other beautiful young ladies that churned around them–it was true. Before long, there would be a new generation. The realization sank like a stone in her chest, settling in her stomach as she walked to her son, now a young man.

She took his hand. "Come, son – Let's find those flowers now.

IT WAS early spring when the expedition arrived back at the high hill country and the city of Amulon. Their yearly explorations added more details to Amulon's map as Channah watched him with his quill pen scratching on the piece of thin leather he kept with him at all times. He thought she was asleep.

The families had anxiously greeted the weary travelers. Some carried young sheep and goats. Others were leading pack animals laden with baskets of grain and salted meats.

Channah eyed the young animals suspiciously, recalling the large herds that were kept by the Nephites near her childhood home. More than anything, she wanted to confront the men and ask where these domesticated animals had come from. There were women and children milling about the group, relieving the pack animals of their burdens and welcoming the travelers home. Sheep and goats were placed on the grass in the courtyard and immediately began grazing, not running. Clearly, these were animals from someone else's herd, not wild as the men claimed.

Aliza made her way over to where the meat was being distributed. "They could not have dried this in the short time they've been gone," she whispered in Channah's ear. "Those young kids and lambs are tame, not wild."

"I know. I thought the same. They've been to the Nephite city," Channah whispered back.

"It appears so." Aliza reached up to receive her share from Zoar who was proudly handing out food.

"See how we provide for our people," he said loudly. "You have food even after a long winter, thanks to your leader Amulon."

Amulon beamed proudly. "Yes, our city grows, and we faithfully care for all of you."

The other priests nodded in agreement, shouting accolades to their leader Amulon.

"Tonight, we feast on fresh lambs! Start the fire!" Amulon waved his hand as he gave the order. Several of the priests shuffled off toward the center of the city, where a large fire pit had been constructed. Lemish walked over to where the lambs had been released into a holding pen. They scampered about playfully, obviously unaware of their fate. Each one bleated a unique call, searching for its mother in these new surroundings.

Much of the winter storage of firewood had been depleted, and the men began taking the small stacks the women had gathered daily and stored at each hut. This would mean the women or children would have to go gather more wood, much further out, for the morning fires.

"Find more wood for the fire, young men. Go quickly," Amulon shouted. "Lemish, you stay and help me prepare the lambs." He motioned for the men to stop robbing the small personal stacks. "Let the younger men do that."

The celebration had become loud, and the bleating of sheep and goats even louder. Channah watched Amulon and Lemish leave the melee. They walked to their hut. Channah followed quickly and made herself busy tending to their wood pile as she listened through the skin covering.

"Father, those appear to be healthy young lambs. They almost seem tame." Lemish had spent much time learning about breeding and raising animals from the women who were given the task of caring for the flocks. "Do you think these escaped from the Nephite flocks?"

"No, these were caught wild, son. We found a whole herd in the valley. Nowhere near the Nephites."

"Do you know where the Nephites live?"

"Yes, of course, we do."

"Do these belong to them?" Lemish asked.

"Who they once belonged to doesn't matter. What's in the Nephite city also belongs to us. If we take what is rightfully ours, there's no harm in that, now is there?" Amulon paused for a moment. "I've decided to take you with me next time. We need help to build the finest structure in our city: The Palace. We will bring Nephite workers back. They will be our slaves to build the rest of our city."

Channah could imagine his face beaming with self-importance.

"Why should they do that for you?" Lemish sounded confused.

"Why not?" Amulon questioned. "We shouldn't have to do all the work."

"It's not their city; it's yours." Lemish stated.

"True, it is my city. Someday, I'll be king, and it won't matter where people came from, Nephite or Lamanite. I'll be king over all the land." She heard a loud clapping sound as if Amulon was slapping Lemish on the back. "Finally, I will have the finest of everything, just like I deserve."

Channah quickly moved to the back side of the hut and headed into the woods where all of the other women had gone to gather more firewood.

~

"THE CITY WOULD BE NEARLY complete if you weren't always taking the men on expeditions," Channah spoke boldly. "If your goal is to build a city, then build it."

Amulon raised his hand, but stopped. Lemish was nearby and had a habit of stepping in whenever Channah cried out. He was now larger than his father in height, and his strong build reflected the work he did around the city.

"I'm the king, and you can't speak to me that way."

"The king of who?" Channah countered.

Color crept up Amulon's neck. His cheeks began to flame. "The land. This whole land will be mine. Just wait."

"Is that why you're always gone, taking the map with you? Taking the men who should be finishing our homes and hunting for food?"

"You're observant. The map still interests you." His hot breath came close to her face as he breathed out the next words. "You'll never see it. You'll never leave here. You'll never return to your people. I'll kill your father, and I will be king."

The sting of being struck always faded, but this blow hit Channah to the core. She fell to her knees. "No. Please don't. I'll do whatever you want, but please don't hurt my father or mother."

Amulon's sneer disfigured his weathered face. "That's more like it. Beg for mercy."

He left her like that, brokenhearted, sobbing. "We leave in the morning, and I'm taking Lemish this time."

As if right on cue, Lemish came through the doorway of their hut. Concern was evident in his eyes.

"Prepare to leave in the morning," Amulon ordered.

When he had gone, Lemish knelt down beside her. "Mother," He spoke softly. "Are you hurt?"

"Not in a way that you can see." She placed her hand over her heart, clutching her chest, and wept. "My heart aches to see my people, my father, and mother."

Lemish leaned over his mother and took her into his arms. "I'll protect you and if I have the chance, I'll protect them."

"You'd go against your father?"

Without skipping a breath, he replied, "Yes."

"I couldn't bear it if anything happened to you, son." Channah looked up into his face. "Promise me you'll never cross him."

Slowly Lemish shook his face. "If the day comes, I'll do whatever is necessary to protect you." His voice was a hoarse whisper, "Don't ask me to make that promise."

"Please be wise, then."

"Yes, Mother, I will." He pulled away and a smile overcame his frown. "I have news."

Channa's breath caught in her chest. "Good news?"

He nodded.

"Mariah?" Channah questioned.

He nodded again.

"Son! I'm so happy for you!"

"I've not told father yet, and he wishes to leave in the morning."

"Go with him and when you return, there will be a wedding. I will help prepare while you are away. Maybe this will be a shorter expedition."

Lemish shook his head. "I believe he wishes to bring Nephite artisans and craftsmen back as slaves to finish the city."

"Are you sure?"

"Some time ago, he told me his plan. I believe he wishes to take a small army down with all of the young men and the priests and take them captive."

"He knows where the cities are?" Channah asked breathlessly.

"He's known for some time, yes."

"Appease him for now. There is nothing more we can do until we have sufficient strength to strike out on our own." Her words came out in a whisper. It seemed as if Amulon was always close enough to hear anything that escaped her lips.

The next morning came all too quickly.

Before she knew it, she was alone. Like many of the women in the city of Amulon, their sons, now men, were gone.

~

THE EXPEDITION HAD ONLY BEEN GONE a few days - much shorter than they had been in the past. Amulon was fuming. "They must have been expecting us. There were new guard stations around the city, with Nephite soldiers, not Lamanites."

Channah was puzzled. "Aren't the Lamanites still guarding the city?"

"Of course. The Nephites are their slaves."

"Why are the Nephites standing guard?"

"To watch for us."

"So, you *have* been taking from the Nephites."

"What did you expect? Those things rightfully belong to us. We are the priests. The people are there to serve us. We have a right to anything in the city. They can't keep it from us." He was pacing, shouting, kicking up dust.

Channah busied herself preparing him dinner so there would be one less thing to be angry about.

Lemish entered, tossing his cloak on the table. "That was further than I've ever been from our city." He slipped off his moccasins and sat down on his pile of skins on the floor. "The river bottom country is so beautiful."

"You saw the Lamanite lands?" Channah said, now completely focused on her son.

"I did. We stayed on the high bluff, but I could see both cities."

Tears filled her eyes. "Did you see the people? My people?"

Amulon interrupted her questioning. "Don't get any ideas. He doesn't know how to get there without the map." He slid the rolled-up skin from its sheath. "Every time we go out, I add more information to the map." He waved it in front of her. "You'll never see it."

Lemish gave a slight nod to his mother. "Father, you're weary. I'll get you some wine so you can rest."

"Now that's more like it. Son, bring some for yourself too." Lemish nodded and slipped out into the night.

"Did he share his news with you?" Channah asked as Amulon reclined on the pile of skins.

"Mariah?"

Channah smiled. "Yes, he wishes to marry. He loves her very much."

"Love. Nonsense. She's beautiful. If I were just a little younger, I'd..." He caught Channah's warning glance. "I have the right to take any woman I wish, and don't think you can stop me. I won't take her because Lemish should have his pick for the first of his wives."

Puzzled, Channah asked, "First of his wives?"

"Of course. Our son should have as many wives as he wishes." Amulon paused as if wondering if he should add anything else. "I plan to bring some young Nephite girls for our son and the other priest's sons. We will also bring Nephite men to finish our city."

Channah refused to look at Amulon. She had known for some time about his plan for the workers. The girls were a different matter. Her mind reeled at the memory, flashbacks of being taken from her family, from her home, into the night by strangers. Breath caught in her throat as it constricted, threatening to collapse into her chest and smother her heart. Her whole soul was empty and crumbling to dust inside of her.

She wanted to cry out. To somehow explain how painful it would be for those girls to be taken from their mothers. Nothing would come out - no sounds, no tears, no words. She felt her world begin to spin. Darkness closed in, and she heard her son's voice as she fell.

"Mother!"

When she awoke, she was in his arms with the night sky overhead. A gentle breeze bathed her hot skin.

"Are you alright, mother?" Lemish asked as he bent to set her feet gently on the ground.

"I'll be fine. Steady me first, son." Channah breathed deeply and took in the cool night air. "You will marry Mariah tomorrow. It's all arranged. Please remember what I've taught you. One wife."

"Of course, mother." Then almost as an afterthought, he added, "Why would you question me on this?"

"Your father wishes to bring you a Nephite girl as a second wife. This must not be. Do whatever it takes to keep this from happening."

Channah began breathing shallow breaths again. "Don't let them do what they did to us."

Understanding registered. "I'll never allow that. Ever."

THE DAY dawned bright and clear. Lemish became a husband. Channah wept as he took his new bride to the place where the spring flowers bloomed thick along the bluff. His favorite cave. A light from their campfire glowed in the distance, high on the bluff. After a few days, they returned to the hut of his parents, where a lean-to had been constructed for him and his new wife. Lemish would begin building a hut for his family with help from his friends. A new generation had begun.

It wasn't long before Mariah announced, with joy in her eyes, that she carried Lemish's child.

LISHA, 127 BC, CITY OF HELAM

*L*isha chose a scroll from the many bundles in her small wooden chest beside her bed and tucked it into her deerskin satchel. The chest contained a record, not scripture or the record of a people, but of Lisha's thoughts, struggles, hopes, and transformation over the past ten years. It meant the world to her. Though not as much as her growing family. She strode across the room and woke young Eviana from her afternoon nap.

"Time to go, sweet girl," Lisha said, her heart swelling as it always did when she found Eviana nestled in her furs, blinking sleep out of her large, green eyes. They weren't quite the same hazel as Eva, her namesake, and Eviana's hair shone a straight, rich black instead of falling in nut brown waves, but she carried herself with the same sparkle, the same zest for life and love of people. The two sisters would have been best friends, Lisha felt sure. She picked the two-year-old up, holding her close. *In the next life,* she thought, *they'll love each other.* A warm thought occurred to her—maybe they already did. Maybe they'd mingled as spirits and grieved together when she'd suffered after Eva's death. Maybe Eviana had promised Eva she'd cheer their mother up. Maybe God had sent Eviana to let Lisha know she wasn't alone. She'd thought she might be beyond child-bearing, but then Eviana came along, a final gift from a loving God.

Of course, she already knew that. She had Alma, Young Alma, Kaleb, Mera, and her friends. But more and more, her thoughts turned to the Lord in this way, wondering how much a hand He took in her life and thanking Him for all the good.

"Are you and Kaleb almost ready?" she asked Young Alma. He was helping Kaleb practice writing on thin slabs of slate. Kaleb watched Alma with great intent, copying the way he held his bit of chalk limestone.

"I'm not going," Alma said.

"Me neither," Kaleb said.

Lisha slung Eviana onto her hip and moved toward the boys. Chalky sketches of warriors marched across the slate. Lisha cocked her head. At least, she thought they were warriors. It might be bears or a forest! It was hard to tell. "You're not even writing, she chided.

"Drawing is important, too, Mother," Alma said. "Don't squash the life out of him."

Lisha sighed. "Put the writing things away. Visiting Mera is important, too."

Kaleb hesitated, his chalk hand in the air as he glanced between his elder brother and his mother. Alma shrugged, then dropped the chalk to his slate and shoved it into a cubby in the little table in the corner. Kaleb did the same, albeit more quietly.

"Thanks for practicing with him, Alma. In a few years, Kaleb will be practicing with your little Helaman."

Alma grunted. "You think you could teach my boy to write, Kaleb?" He gave his brother a playful cuff to the head.

Kaleb grinned. "You think Grandma Mera will have cookies for us?" he asked Lisha.

Lisha smiled. "Perhaps, but remember, we are there to help Grandma."

"We never have to pull weeds for Grandma Naomi," Kaleb said. He grabbed a wool hat and jammed it on his head. His dark curls peeked out from under the floppy brim. He'd look angelic if it weren't for his expression.

Alma looked amused.

"Well, she's not quite as old as Grandma Mera." Lisha thought for a moment. They probably *should* be doing more for Naomi.

"And she doesn't keep a garden," Kaleb piped up.

Lisha laughed. "That's true, but we could find other ways to help her."

Kaleb groaned. "That's all we ever do."

"Put your shoes on. The others will be waiting."

"I'll meet you later," Alma said. "Zilpah will be needing me."

LISHA LED Kaleb on a meandering path through Helam, pointing out purple and yellow flowers growing in sunny spots, and keeping him from tumbling into wild hawthorn bushes full of creamy white blossoms and wicked thorns. She couldn't help but think the bushes were a perfect symbol of the human condition - goodness and danger rolled up in one.

We all have to choose, Lisha thought, *pluck the blossoms or trim away the thorns. Either way, you get your hands cut. If you take the blossoms, only the thorns remain. If you trim away the thorns, you're left with a lovely plant and blossoms that fade over time as nature intended. But what would protect the thornless bush from marauding animals? Maybe the analogy isn't quite right,* Lisha thought. *Then again, maybe a few thorns are necessary if you know when to use them.*

She heard a rumble of young voices as they neared the gathering place. Eviana squirmed, so Lisha set her down, allowing her to toddle on ahead. Kaleb took off, passing her in his eagerness to see his friends. Lisha followed, rounding the corner by the tanner's shop in time to hear a voice cry out, "Lisha!"

It was Sarika, carrying her own toddler, Talya. "I think we're all here."

Lisha glanced around. The gathering place was full of mothers and children. The women turned to her expectantly.

"How is Mera?" Ophir asked. Her youngest grandson, ever timid, peeked from behind her skirts.

"She keeps her spirits up," Lisha said, "but she is growing weak."

"Of course, she is, at her age," Ophir said, "and with Yoseph gone."

Behind Ophir, Hannah blinked hard. Her father had passed a year ago, but the pain was still fresh for Hannah. Lisha knew what that was like. She reached out and squeezed her friend's shoulder. Thank the Lord she had a grandson of her own to distract her now.

"How are Zilpah and little Helaman? I know they break bread with you most mornings."

Hannah nodded, brightening. "Isn't he the best? I hope you don't mind me taking up so much of their time. He's your grandson, too."

Lisha smiled and hugged Hannah. "It brings me joy to see you happy. Alma brings him around to see me, too." She said to the group, "We should head to Mera's. We'll pull weeds and visit awhile. You brought the honey rolls?" she asked Devorah, the heavy woman who served as a midwife to the women of Helam.

"We used the last of our honey, but it's worth it for Mera."

"No, it's not," said a small wisp of a child standing beside her.

"Yes, it is, Rachel," said another girl, who was clearly her older sister. They had the same round cheeks and haphazard braids. "Now, hold your tongue."

Lisha knelt before the small girl. "Thank you, Rachel, for sharing your honey."

Rachel flushed and bobbed her head.

"Come, it's not far to Mera's."

The group left the clearing, moving past the weaver's shop—Hannah's eldest son had taken it over after Yoseph's passing—and headed to the small cottage on the other side. Mera already leaned against the open door, waiting.

"I take it you heard us coming?" Lisha asked with a wry grin.

In response, Mera held out her arms. Before Lisha could embrace her surrogate mother, Kaleb and Eviana rushed in for their own hugs.

"Did you make us cookies?" Kaleb demanded.

"Kaleb!" Lisha chided, but Mera smiled.

"Might have," she said, glancing around at the large group of children rambling through her derelict gardens. "Might make a few more while I'm at it. Come on, Evi; you can help me." She squeezed Lisha's hand. "Thank you, my daughter." She glanced around at all the warm, waiting faces. "For all of this."

Soon the weeds were pulled and bellies filled with cookies and honey rolls. Most of the women had gone, leaving behind Hannah, Sarika, Lisha, and Mera.

"You can go play now, Kaleb." Lisha ruffled his hair, smiling as he rushed outside.

Eviana cuddled with Mera, playing with the beads in her braids.

Lisha cast Sarika a concerned look. "You and Rafa still having trouble?"

Sarika sighed. "I've managed life on my own for a long time now. It's hard to adjust to Rafa. Don't get me wrong, I love him, and I'm glad we married. He's just so protective. It's suffocating."

Lisha withdrew the scroll she'd been carrying in her satchel and passed it to Sarika, who took it with surprise. "What's this?"

"It's one of the first scrolls I wrote when Alma refused to be king. We see many things differently, and I had to find a way to make peace with our differences."

Sarika unrolled the parchment, scanning the words inked on the page in curling brown letters. She shook her head. "It's never easy, is it, being married?"

Mera chuckled. "No, but if you work at it, it's worth it." She refilled Sarika's mug with mint tea.

"I heard some strange things last week in the gathering place," Hannah said. "Daren was talking to a crowd outside the smithy. He claimed that when a husband and wife are unhappy together, they should look elsewhere. You were there, Sarika. Do you think he's right?"

"Sounds like she burned his dinner one time too many," Sarika said. "He should be more patient."

Hannah shrugged. "Maybe she's tired of hearing him complain."

Mera looked to Lisha with knowing eyes. "It's never that simple, is it?"

Lisha looked down at her hands. Folded in her lap, her fingers wove together to create a single whole. If she didn't look closely, it might be easy to lose track of which fingers belonged with which hand. Yet they could completely separate, and if she weren't careful, they might even hurt each other. "All I know is that the more purposeful I am in loving Alma, the stronger our marriage is, and the more he loves me in return." When Sarika started to interrupt, Lisha raised her hand. "I'm not saying we never need to ask each other to change. But the important thing is that we work through problems together."

Sarika sighed again. "Rafa doesn't want Talya to play outside at all, even though I'm right beside her. I told him about when I almost drowned, and"—she cast a nervous look to Lisha—"he remembers what happened to Eva." Lisha nodded, her gaze steady. "I know he's worried, but I can't live like this."

Lisha nodded. "I was like that with Kaleb at first after Eva died. I never let him out of my sight. But a child can't live that way, especially as they grow. And neither could I. Talk with Rafa, contend with him, work it out together," Lisha said. Mera nodded. "But remember, the point of the discussion is not to win. The whole point is to understand each other and find a way forward that you both can work with. This way, your disagreements strengthen your marriage instead of destroying it."

Hannah bit her lip. "Daren's ideas are making people doubt themselves and those they should love most."

A soft knock sounded at Mera's door. Rafa poked his head inside, his worried face breaking into a grin when he saw Sarika. "Speak of the devil," she murmured.

Rafa's gaze darted around the room, then sharpened on Sarika. "Where's Talya? Why isn't she with you?"

Sarika's mouth tightened and she took a deep, calming breath. "Shoshannah has her. Talya's with several of the older children."

Rafa's hands tightened to fists. "Well, that's the problem, isn't it? With all the children around, she's bound to lose track of Talya."

"Give her some credit, Rafa," Sarika snapped. "She's been watching over younger children since she was six. She's twenty-one. She knows to keep a close eye on Talya."

Rafa's expression darkened. "Let's go. It's time to take care of your *family*."

A deep flush rose in Sarika's cheeks, but she stood and followed Rafa. At the cottage door, she glanced back. "I'm starting to believe Daren. Some things just aren't right. Some things a wife shouldn't have to deal with." She straightened her shoulders and marched outside.

Lisha frowned. "Daren's not the only one preaching selfishness disguised as dignity. He's just the loudest. It's causing contention and confusion. I'll speak to Alma. Maybe he can help sort this out."

"Shouldn't we defend ourselves when we're mistreated?" Mera asked, her eyes glinting.

"Of course," Lisha said. "You know that's not what I mean."

Mera nodded, suddenly serious. "That's why these teachings are so damaging. Daren's taking a true principle and distorting it to support a false one. Sometimes we *should* sacrifice for the good of others. We cannot only think of ourselves."

LATE THAT NIGHT, long after the children fell asleep curled in warm furs and skins, Lisha waited up for Alma. The golden light of the candle gilded her brow as she wrote in her journal. She'd grown accustomed to his long hours, though she missed him and worried he'd wear himself out. The cottage door pushed open, and Lisha looked up from her work.

"Hello, dear," Alma said. He trudged inside, pausing to kiss her on the forehead before sinking into a chair by the low fire.

"You look exhausted," she said, carefully wiping the end of her turkey-feather quill so it wouldn't drip ink. "Are you hungry?"

He waved away her concern. "I ate at Asher's. There wasn't time to stop home." He gave an apologetic smile. "There's been some unrest in town. Several couples needed counsel. And the widow Amaranth wanted a blessing. She has a brutal cough."

"Rafa and Sarika?"

Alma shook his head. "I didn't see them. Why?"

Lisha half shrugged. "She seemed unsettled today. We spent the afternoon together with Mera. She really loves when we come by."

"By *we*, I assume you mean half the women and children of Helam?"

Lisha nodded. "She needed help with her yard work."

Alma ran his hand over his face. He looked older these days, more timeworn, definitely more weary. "Ah, you're a good woman, Lisha."

She opened her mouth to speak but hesitated. Alma was so tired she hated to burden him with yet one more thing. Instead, she rolled up her scroll and tucked it away in her chest.

"What is it?" Alma asked. He leaned forward, resting his elbows on his knees. The movement rounded the muscles in his back and shoulders, reminding Lisha that the hard work he did all day was much more than simple teaching. He ministered with his hands and, sometimes, a hammer.

"It's nothing," Lisha said. She pulled back the covers on their bed. "You need rest."

A faint smile curved Alma's lips, wrinkling the corners of his eyes. "If my years married to you have taught me nothing else, it's that I can't spend myself on the people of Helam and leave nothing for my sweet wife. Please, tell me what's on your mind."

Lisha settled onto the heather mattress. "I may know the source of the conflict among the young couples. Some of the older ones too." She told him about Daren and the others teaching hardheartedness instead of cooperation, sacrifice, and forgiveness. "They make it sound like it's a good thing to demand your way instead of trying to work together."

Alma rubbed his brow. "I've heard some of this but hadn't realized these ideas had grown so prevalent, or those teaching them so bold. Thank you for bringing it to my attention."

"I know this is nothing compared to the trials back in Shilom: Noah's oppression, the wicked priests seeding doubt, indulgence, and greed among the people. And enforcing their wicked ways with the sword--" Lisha said, lost in thought. "I often wonder how Limhi and Dinah are doing. And what of Tamar and Helam? Have they helped the people turn their hearts back to the Lord? I miss them. Tamar especially! She never got to meet Eva, and now it's too late."

Alma gathered Lisha's hand in his. "And now you're troubled by the discord among our people."

She nodded.

"Those who most need to hear my message aren't listening." Alma frowned. "They aren't even coming for worship."

"Then we must reach them in the streets," Lisha said. "We must reach them through words, service, and song."

Alma nodded. "You can lead that. This is one of your gifts."

"And once I've gathered the people, you must speak from your heart."

Alma knelt and looked to Lisha, who still sat on the edge of the bed. "I'll be up for a while. Do you mind if I keep the candle burning?"

Lisha shook her head. She leaned down and kissed Alma. "I miss you, you know. All the time."

He took her hand and pressed it to his lips, then bent his head in prayer.

Lisha crawled under the blankets and said some prayers of her own.

Lord, guide us, protect us. Help us find ways to protect these, thy people. I fear for Alma, that he will work and serve until there's is nothing left of him, nothing left for me or for our children. Are these thoughts wrong, Lord? Am I thinking more of myself and my own needs than of others and of Thy will? I know it is not Thy will that we sacrifice until we harm ourselves or those we love. But where is the balance? What are the answers? What is Thy will?

∾

A MONTH HAD PASSED since Lisha's desperate prayer. She spent that time serving others, sharing small kindnesses, and building connection, finding ways to include those often forgotten. She filled the streets of Helam with song, as she had done back in Shilom. This time the songs were not a warning to escape but a call to gather, to unite in faith and hope, to rebuild community, courage, and strength. Many joined with her, and the music spread like sunshine, touching even the darkest heart.

Alma spent so many nights on his knees that circles lingered beneath his eyes like smudges of soot. Even now, in the sanctuary, with decisions made and the way forward planned, he looked exhausted and apprehensive beneath his hopeful countenance and determined faith.

The night before, he'd told her his thoughts as they lay side by side, staring up at the stars gleaming through a patch in the roof where a spring storm had blown away the thatch. Alma hadn't had time to repair it yet, and Lisha certainly couldn't, not with three children to keep track of.

"You know," he said, "I could still have advisors of sorts. I could call Asher and Samuel and others to teach and minister to help settle concerns. I wouldn't have to be a king to do that."

A slow warmth seeped down Lisha's face. She didn't brush the tears away because she didn't want Alma to know. *Finally, he would accept some help.*

"It's like with Moses," Alma continued. "When Jethro advised him to have judges help him govern the people. I'm not ruling the people, but I am guiding them and leading them in the ways of the Lord. I need help with that. I don't know why I didn't see it before."

"But what about Daren and the others?"

"This will help with that, too. I'll call good, just men as priests and teachers. They will have the authority to lead the people and help them follow the Lord."

Lisha felt a wellspring of hope. The Lord was making a way to bring strength to their people and also bring Alma home. He would still work, they would still sacrifice, but they would do it together a little bit more.

Now, Alma stood at the head of the sanctuary, a fire crackling in the altar behind him and incense smoke swirling up to the rafters. The building was packed, the benches filled, with people leaning against the walls, crowded into open areas, and thronging the open doorway. Asher had done his job well, spreading the news that changes would be announced. When Alma raised his arms in welcome, the multitude hushed. He offered a prayer, then began speaking.

On one side of Lisha, Alma the Younger sat with his small family, gazing up at his father, expectant. Kaleb played with a loose string on his shirt front, and Eviana curled in Lisha's lap, sucking her thumb. Mera reached for Lisha's free hand, giving her a slight squeeze. The pressure felt frail and cool but reassuring nonetheless.

"Over the last few years," Alma began, his voice booming to reach those in the back, "Helam has grown. We have grown as a people. We have struggled through hardship and tamed our little neck of the wilderness. We have created a thriving and prosperous city. We have kept the commandments and followed the Lord. He blesses us at every turn and lifts our burdens when trials fall upon us." His eyes lingered on Lisha, and she straightened, encouraging him with her gaze.

He clasped his hands. "We are not a perfect people. We aren't the City of Enoch. We must always repent and strive to follow God's ways a little better every day." His face grew serious. "The Lord has commanded me to call priests and teachers that they may preach and minister unto you by the authority of God."

Murmurs rumbled through the room like storms in the distance. Lisha glanced around. Most people looked approving. Some smiled, and some nodded. But others looked wary, particularly those who'd been teaching their own ways. Daren narrowed his brows and whispered something to his wife. Her expression hardened.

"Asher, Samuel, Rafa, please come forward," Alma said. He called several others forward as well. Then, one by one, he placed his hands on their heads and consecrated some to be priests and others teachers, commanding them to lead, minister, and teach in the ways of the Lord.

As he finished, Daren's face darkened like a thundercloud. Young Alma watched him closely, his brow furrowed.

"We must be led by men of God," Alma proclaimed, "or we will become like Noah, who destroyed Shilom. When we trust teachers and ministers who walk in the ways of the Lord, this brings us safety and peace."

DINAH, 122 BC, CITY OF SHILOM

"

She truly is a miracle." Limhi stroked the tiny baby's soft, thick hair. "How are you feeling?" With all the tenderness of his touch on the baby's head, he stroked Dinah's hair, tucking her long hair behind her ear so he could look into her eyes. "Are you improving?"

"Oh yes, tired but better each hour."

A small knock on the doorpost interrupted their conversation. A small hand parted the tapestry. "Can I come in?"

Elah poked her head in before hearing a response. A second head poked in next to hers, hiding behind her tunic. "I couldn't stay away," Elah gushed. "You've been so good to me I had to bring you some of your own tea." She stepped fully inside, followed by a young girl with flowing black hair, large eyes, and a warm smile. They both slipped quickly to Dinah's bedside and offered a steaming cup. "I just made it. It'll help the pains."

Little Tamar smiled shyly and handed her some cakes. "Elah taught me how to make these. They were my mom's favorite like the Lamanite women make."

"Thank you. I was just wondering how I was going to get some tea, and here you are." Dinah turned her tiny baby toward Elah and Tamar so they could see her.

"Oh, she's beautiful. Such a miracle."

"I was just saying the same thing," Limhi whispered. "She's doing well, but I'm sure your visit will boost her spirits. She's tired."

Limhi lifted his little sister into his arms and gave her a big hug. "I love you."

"Why do you have tears?" Tamar asked. "Did I squeeze you too much?"

Placing her back on the floor, Limhi knelt on one knee to look her in the eyes. "No, they are happy tears, remembering our mother."

Tamar hugged him back, then wiped his tears. "It's Ok. I see Momma in my dreams. She tells me stories. I have a big brother; he's big like you."

Limhi just stared at her. "You never told me this before."

Tamar smiled, "Momma says my dreams are just for me." She turned to see the new baby. "She's just the sweetest. Momma gave her extra hugs and kisses before she came to you."

Stunned, Dinah and every other person in the room gaped at Tamar. "You saw your mother, and my little one, together?"

Tamar, looking confused, asked, "Don't you see Momma too?"

"No, that's a special gift, just for you. It's true, little Tamar, those dreams are gifts, and they are for you." Limhi gave her a squeeze. "Next time you see our Momma, let her know I love her. And I miss her."

Dinah yawned but tried to hide it. "It's been a very long night, and I can't wait to eat those cakes. I like them too, just like your Momma did."

Limhi seemed to hover with a worried expression. Elah put a gentle hand on his shoulder. "She will be fine. She's strong, and everything went as it should. She will recover."

Sensing his concern, Dinah added, "Oh Limhi, every woman is tired after birthing a child. I'll be up and around tomorrow."

"You rest. No need to rush anything," Elah said. I'll make an extra portion of meal cake tonight. I soaked some venison for a stew and will bring that to you before nightfall. I better get back, or there will be trouble in our quarters." She began to leave, then stepped back and embraced Dinah, taking little Tamar's hand in the process. "You're like a sister to me. I love you. Thank you," she whispered to Dinah. She then slipped quietly out the doorway, guiding young Tamar behind her, and was gone.

Benjamin, now a strapping young man of seventeen, filled the doorway. "Have you seen Miriam?"

"Not since the baby was born hours ago. Why?" Limhi questioned. "I think she went to pick some flowers."

"Oh, some of the shepherds were looking for someone to show them how to make a braid of wool. I thought she could show them."

Puzzled, Dinah questioned him, "What do they wish to braid?"

"I'm not sure. Braiding, weaving. One of those - anyway, it's Miriam's skill, and they asked if she would come and show them. Is there anything I can do? Mother?" He looked from Limhi to Dinah.

Miriam tucked her head in and saw the full room. "My, what a gathering," she said as she pulled the rest of herself through the tapestry door to stand behind the crowd at the bedside of her mother and baby sister. She put her flowers into a tall pitcher on the table. "Can I use this for flowers, mother?"

Laughing a little, Dinah said, "It looks like you just did." With a tired smile, she added, "Thank you, those are lovely."

"Son, you asked what you could do to help; please bring in enough wood for a couple of days and keep the fire going while I tend to your mother." Limhi turned to Miriam and added, "Can you get a clean pitcher of water and a cup for your mother to keep beside her bed?"

Benjamin brought in enough wood for several days, then picked up a large piece of birch and began whittling.

"What should we name her?" Dinah mused

"Miracle! That's the first thing that came to my heart as she entered this world." Limhi stroked her dark hair, "Should we call her Nasya, our miracle?"

"I like it. I'll always remember this feeling as I say her name," Dinah said while stifling another yawn.

"You need your rest; let's make things quiet in here so you and Nasya can sleep." Everyone left rather quickly. Benjamin continued whittling and talking in low whispers to Miriam.

ELAH CAME BACK LATER in the evening after Dinah had napped for several hours with the promised stew and a meal cake for their dinner.

"You are a blessing to us," Limhi said as Elah placed the food on the table beside the bed.

"No, you are that for me." She looked at Dinah. "Do you recall the day you came to my home?"

"I do."

"Those were dark days. I had lost hope. I didn't want to go on." A tear escaped her gentle, dark eyes. "I don't know what I would have done without you that day." She gently embraced Dinah. "Truly, you saved me from my time of despair, and I'll never be able to repay you for your kindness. It changed my life, my future."

Limhi watched the two embrace each other. "Thank you so much for this," he said.

"I'll leave you to enjoy that sweet baby now. Rest and be well." And with that, she was gone.

"I think I'm beginning to understand something. The Lord commands us to be one, but the way to becoming one is by serving, reaching out to others in their times of need, and allowing others to serve us. I could have prepared a meal this evening but permitting her to do that service blessed her as much as it did us." Dinah said, stifling a yawn.

"I see that, too."

MIRIAM AND BENJAMIN followed Limhi out the following morning so Dinah could have some rest. Limhi called the merchants and farmers together to plan the crops for the next year and to take an accounting of the winter stores. Gideon and Elah were given the task of keeping records of what remained in store.

"Elah, can you report the numbers from your scroll?" Limhi asked.

"Six dozen pumpkins or squash, four baskets of wheat for the meal, and two for seed, three baskets of dry meat, one basket of beans, thirty lambs born this past month alone, with four being stolen by the priests."

Once again, the people had made it through the winter with an excess of stored food. Families were growing, but none went hungry.

"My good people, do you realize how richly we have been blessed? Our herds have doubled in number, and our crops have sustained us through another winter with a bounty still on hand. Sheep bore twins and triplets; goats all seemed to bear multiple kids. New life abounded, and the grain stores grew in unexplained ways. The Lord truly sees to our needs."

"I know the Lord watches over us in our captivity. I have seen this people change and I believe this is God's way of letting us know He is pleased. Let us begin the new year with gratitude."

SPRING GRASSES GREW; baby sheep and goats played in the fields and filled the air with their happy bleating. The people sang as they labored. Even though their loads were heavier, their hearts were lighter.

The Lamanites had to take additional trips to deliver tributes to their king because of the increased harvest.

When baby Nasya was several weeks old, Dinah wrapped the baby in her swaddling clothes and tied her to her back. She and Miriam walked through the town and witnessed the visible difference. People *were* happier. Even in the worst of circumstances, they hummed while they worked. As they ventured to the fields where harvest was taking place, the sound of voices singing echoed through the valley. In unison, they picked, shucked, packed, and carried the bushels of corn to be taken into town. The voices were laced with joy. She stepped over to where Limhi worked beside some of the older children, teaching them how to quickly remove the silk and husks from the corn and how each part of the corn would get used. "You see, nothing is wasted this way, and now it's ready to dry."

Limhi stood as Dinah approached. "You should still be resting."

"Miriam reminds me of the same thing. She's my constant companion, always making sure I'm careful and resting." Miriam blushed at the attention. Dinah gave her a squeeze.

"Besides, I need to get some sunshine. Little Nasya is sleeping soundly, and a walk about town does me good." Dinah looked around at the women and children working in the fields. "The Lord has made our people equal to their burdens."

"I've seen it too," Limhi smiled. "The women do the work of men. There are so few men left to labor; it has been necessary."

Benjamin loped over, taking a quick break. He placed a kiss on his baby sister. "I love how soft her hair is, and she smells so...well, so much like a baby." That brought a chuckle to the group.

"We better get back to work, son." Limhi placed a quick kiss on his daughter's soft hair as well and one on Dinah's cheek. "And you go home to rest."

"I'll make sure she does," Miriam nodded.

"Oh, Limhi," Dinah called back. "Has Gideon found how the sheep have been escaping?"

Limhi's eyes flashed anger for a moment. "They aren't escaping."

Then recognition hit her. "The priests of Noah are at it again?"

"Yes." Limhi pointed to some of the young men; the oldest ones available were heading toward the field's perimeter. "At the end of the day, we now post guards and hope to keep them from taking any more."

"Do they steal from the Lamanites too?"

"I'm not sure, but I wouldn't be surprised."

Limhi waved an arm toward the field and shouted, "Let's plant the last baskets and head back to the city." He wrapped an arm around his wife and child and began walking back home.

A Lamanite guard sneered as they walked past, and he spat on Limhi.

Limhi simply ignored him, wiping away the insult with his sleeve.

DINAH BEGAN GOING with Limhi to the fields each morning and tried to help where she could. Miriam and Judith cared for the youngest children, who were not much help in the field. Sometimes she kept Nasya so Dinah could be of assistance. Most days, she came back early, before lunch. Together they would prepare a mid-day meal, feed the children, and take food to those working.

Most of the inhabitants of the city were working in the fields during the day, but Limhi would go out early and meet those who had been out all night long, thanking them for guarding the flocks and offering them a corn cake to eat on their way home.

Dinah watched as Limhi made his way through the far field to where the youngest guard was stationed and saw movement beyond the young boy on the hillside above them. She ran to the gate and shouted to get Limhi's attention. He stopped and strained at her words, then spun around to look in the direction Dinah was waving. The young boy also turned to see what had captured the king's attention so suddenly.

"Gideon, bring your men!"

Gideon ran toward the king.

"Go back to the city; tell the people to stay inside the walls until we return."

Gideon had reached him, and four other men followed close in his footsteps.

"Dinah! Stay inside the courtyard. Keep Miriam there too!" Limhi shouted.

She turned and began walking quickly toward the city gate. The Lamanite guards had not yet arrived so Limhi, Gideon, and the group of soldiers made their way to where Limhi had first seen something in the trees.

Limhi's voice echoed through the still air. "Listen. If what I saw were some of the Priests of Noah, they would be armed and possibly planning an attack on the city. Go search for them. I'll prepare the people in case there is trouble."

Dinah waited until he was able to come speak with her. Benjamin was now up and ready for the day, and stood beside his mother.

"What did you find?" she asked breathlessly.

"Possibly some of Noah's priests. Gideon is going with his men."

The people knew all about Noah's priests and their decades' long practice of stealing their food and animals. To have them strike during the day was unusual. Their practice was to come on moonless nights, when they'd not be seen, and carry away sheep, goats, grain, and supplies.

It wasn't long before a cry was heard to open the gates. "We caught them! They're up in prison on the hill. We've secured them for now, but we need to know what you'd like us to do with them."

"I'll call the leaders together. We will decide their fate."

"I'd rather just kill them now," Gideon offered. "I can take care of that easily if you'd permit me to."

"I would like to question them. If they have the daughters of the Lamanites, I want to know where they are. Maybe there is a way we can trade them for our freedom."

THE PEOPLE WAITED for the king's orders. Their anxious faces looked up to Limhi as he stood on the temple steps. Dinah held little Nasya, and she, too, awaited his command. Benjamin stood beside his father, becoming somewhat of a protective shadow: not actively participating as a guard but observing and learning.

"Bring the captives to me now. Being in prison for two days should loosen their tongues."

All of the citizens of Shilom watched for the return of the soldiers from the hillside prison once used for Abinadi. It had been decided that if the prisoners would not reveal the location of the rest of the priests, and the daughters of the Lamanites, they would be put to death. A search party would then be sent to track their path and find those who had been stolen many years ago, and thus buy freedom for the Nephites.

Gideon returned with the men. They had long beards and were disheveled and dirty from the cramped prison they'd been forced to stay in. As they passed by the crowds of people, many turned their noses and fanned their faces. They smelled as if they'd not bathed in some time. They fell down before the king.

Dinah soothed Nasya to keep her asleep, and Miriam stood beside her, clutching her arm.

"Why were you so bold to come near the city when I was outside the gate? Are you priests of the former king Noah?" Limhi questioned. "Choose your words carefully. Had I not needed information on the missing Lamanite daughters, I would have had my guards put you to death."

The largest of the men lifted his eyes and, in obvious confusion, asked, "I'm thankful to God that we were spared our lives, and we can speak to you. However, we know nothing of King Noah."

"Are you not high priests?" Limhi questioned.

"We are not. I am Ammon, a descendant of Zarahemla seeking the people of Zeniff who left the land of Zarahmela long ago. Are you the king of this people, and do you know of Zeniff's people?" the man asked.

There was an audible gasp from the crowd. Dinah moved closer to hear their exchange clearly. Instantly the mood of the room changed.

"Our brothers in Zarahemla are yet alive!" Limhi said as he leaped from his throne. "How do you know of my grandfather Zeniff?" Limhi now knelt beside the man, grasping his shoulders.

Gideon stepped forward, clutching his sword still. "We sought the land of Zarahemla and found only the ruins of a great city and dead men's bones strewn across the ground."

The people began to move closer, filling the temple steps. The king raised his hand and stood. "We need to hear what these men have to say." As the murmuring voices ceased, Limhi said, "Rise, you may speak."

"We have recently come from Zarahemla at the request of King Mosiah. And I assure you that the city is thriving and the people that live there are very much alive. The prophet Abinadi, who was born Jarom, a son of Zeniff, came back to preach to the wicked king Noah, who was his brother. We seek to know of his whereabouts."

Limhi sat down upon his throne again. "Please bring these men something to eat. Let them clean themselves, and then let us resume our conversation. There is much we need to discuss."

"Thank you, King--"

Limhi answered the question before Ammon finished asking it. "Limhi, grandson of Zeniff, son of the wicked king Noah." He reached out his hand. "Thank you for coming, Ammon. Please accept my apologies for the harsh treatment you received at my hand. You'll be given a proper meal, a place to rest, and will stay in the palace with my wife and me." He motioned to Gideon to come, "Please gather the people together again after these men have had a good meal. I would like for all to hear what they have to say."

Ammon took Limhi by the hand, covering it with both of his. "Thank you, King Limhi. We are thankful for your kindness."

"Keeping you locked in prison, with no food or water, was not kind." Limhi bowed his head. "I'm sorry to have treated you that way. We thought you were an enemy."

"We understand," Ammon said with a quick bow of his head.

The men cleaned up in the river, trimmed their beards, and were given fresh clothing. By the time they returned to the gathering, they had a much different appearance. Out of intense curiosity, the people had come, setting aside whatever their tasks were, to hear from these men who had so unexpectedly arrived in their city.

"Tell us of Zarahemla. You said that Jarom made it back there and returned here as Abinadi. What was it like to see him change from Jarom to Abinadi?" Limhi asked.

The men glanced at one another, and Ammon spoke. "We all knew him as Jarom. When he first arrived, he told us of your city. He and his family were very happy in Zarahemla. The children grew. Jarom was a merchant and had a successful trade. He often traveled to bring goods to the city. He returned one day and told of a vision from God, instructing him to return to the land of Nephi to his brethren. He said the Lord had given him a new name, Abinadi, and he didn't know when or if he would return. That is all we know."

Limhi turned to Dinah and then to Gideon. "You don't know what happened to Abinadi?"

Scanning the faces around him, Ammon asked, "Did he return? Is he still here?" He searched the faces of those around him.

Limhi proceeded to give a detailed account of the inspired message of Abinadi, of Noah's angry response, and of the eventual execution of Abinadi. Ammon and his brothers wept bitter tears at hearing the fate of the one they had called a friend and brother. The manner of death of Noah was also shocking to hear. Stories of the struggles with the wicked priests only added to the men's sorrow. Limhi shared the records he had kept that gave the accounts of their wars, losses of so many men, women, and children in battles with the Lamanites. He talked of Alma's miraculous escape and the circumstances that led to their current state of captivity to the Lamanites.

There was joyful and sorrowful weeping when the story of Alma was shared. Remembering those who left with Alma reminded many of the painful separation they felt from family and friends.

"We would be baptized if there was one who had authority," Limhi said. "We have entered into a covenant with God to serve Him and keep His commandments. Can you baptize us?"

Ammon shook his head. "I am an unworthy servant."

"Then, we will await the day of our baptism and join ourselves with the Church of God," Limhi said with a touch of disappointment.

"Are these all of the records?" Ammon asked.

"There is one more, but we cannot read the writings," Gideon offered. "We found it on our expedition to find Zarahemla."

"Bring it, and I'll see if I can interpret them," Ammon suggested.

Gideon slipped inside the temple doors and came back bearing the plates of ore. "Do you know this language?" he asked.

Ammon and the others turned the pages, looking intently at each one. "Some characters look familiar, but there is only one that can read the writings. King Mosiah has a gift from God to interpret such engravings."

"Then we must take them to him!"

Limhi shook his head. "We are in bondage to the Lamanites. We cannot leave."

DINAH, 121 BC, CITY OF SHILOM

*D*inah rocked and cuddled her little one as Limhi reviewed with her what he had been discussing with the Nephite explorers and their own soldiers.

Speaking in a low voice, Limhi replayed the meeting to Dinah. "We have talked of various ways to escape captivity, but each plan ends with many of our people likely being killed." Limhi rubbed his forehead and closed his eyes. "This has never worked for us, so the Lord must have a better way. I have not received any direction yet, so I asked Ammon to come and meet with me here this evening."

"Father," Benjamin said as he stood and walked over to where his parents sat. "I would like to be trained as an archer."

"The Laminate guards don't allow any training, son."

"I can practice in the courtyard in the early morning before we go to the fields. Will you teach me?" Before Limhi could respond, Benjamin pulled out a hand-carved bow and a fistful of arrows from behind his bed.

"It appears you've made quite an effort to prepare. Your uncle, Jarom-- Abinadi-- was quite an archer. He taught me as a young boy. I will teach you what I know."

Benjamin, obviously pleased with his father's answer, tucked the weapons behind his bed and resumed carving what looked like a small toy.

"Can I stay and listen in on your meeting?" Dinah asked with sincerity. "I might have some ideas too."

"Of course," Limhi said as they heard the squeak of a gate from the courtyard.

Ammon tapped on the doorway of Limhi's home. "Is this still a good time to talk for a few minutes?"

Limhi parted the tapestry and pulled it open wide. "Please come in."

Miriam rose quickly and went to the table to pour some fresh spring water into the cups she had prepared. "Would you like a drink?" she asked, with a slight blush heating her cheeks.

"Yes, thank you," Ammon replied with a smile. "I have a son about your age. Maybe when we all get back to Zarahemla, he can introduce you to the many young women and young men in the city. You'll make many friends there."

Miriam nodded her head vigorously, "I would love to meet them, all of them!" Looking around the room, she added, "There are not many of my age in Shilom."

Ammon turned to Limhi. "I need to ask some important questions. King Mosiah taught us that when faced with a difficult task or question that we should both fast and pray." He paused, "Limhi, have you made this a matter of fasting and prayer?"

"No. Please teach me what that means." Limhi added, "The Lord told me in a dream that we would one day be free. We have fought many battles and lost many good people, so that approach did not work. We humbled ourselves to the dust and have been blessed. I don't believe we are to fight to be free. I believe the Lord has a plan and will reveal it when we are ready to receive it."

"The time is now, Limhi." Ammon stood and looked into the faces of those who were in the room. "Ask the people to fast and pray for an answer. I believe the Lord will show us the way."

The meeting was short and the family discussed what they had learned and felt till late into the night.

LIMHI INVITED the people to gather at the temple following their labors of the day. The Lamanites had lost interest in beating them and were already in their huts with their families when the clouds in the sky began to turn dark and take on the shadows of night.

"My people, the Lord is aware of us. He has sent Ammon and his brethren to help us." Keeping his voice low so as not to share any information with the Lamanite guards, he continued. "Will you fast and pray this night and tomorrow so that the way can be made clear to us, how we can gain our freedom without bloodshed?"

The excitement was palpable. Nodding and quiet whispers of agreement were all Limhi needed. Dinah stood beside him with her hand in his. "Tomorrow the way will be revealed. I know it. I feel it."

Dinah whispered loud enough for only Limhi to hear. "I feel it too."

IT WAS hard to sleep but Dinah knew, deep down, that she would need every ounce of strength. She fed little Nasya and fell into a deep sleep. *Her dreams were vivid. Some parts were frightening and others, beautiful. Lamanite soldiers were in the very act of beating Nephite people. She thought she saw Alma and Lisha in danger. Next to them stood angels, protecting them from blows. Burdens placed on their backs were carried by the angels. Then she saw her own people in the wilderness protected on all sides by angels.* Dinah awakened with a peaceful calm she had never before felt. "Limhi, the Lord is with us. He will protect us." She paused, then, with conviction, added, "Whatever danger Alma and his people are in, they are being watched over too." She reached out to embrace Limhi, holding him tight. "We will be alright."

Limhi and Dinah made their way in and through the city, speaking with as many as they could, assessing their feelings and listening to their fears. Dinah shared her conviction that the Lord was aware of them and would answer their prayers.

As they moved through the fields, they worked alongside Ammon and his brethren. Limhi continued to receive advice from Ammon. Dinah carried a small basket to do what she could to help.

Gideon darted around workers and ran straight to Limhi. He clapped the king on the back. "I have the answer. As I made my perimeter check last night and took the Lamanites their tribute of wine, the way came into my mind. We will take an additional tribute of wine to the Lamanites as they watch the back pass. They will be drunken with the excess. If the people are ready, we can leave tonight, go around the land of Shemlon, and let Ammon lead us back to Zarahemla.

The men exchanged glances, smiles, and clapped each other's shoulders, sending puffs of dust dancing through the air. "The Lord has provided the answer." Ammon announced.

"We must spread the word," Dinah whispered. "We will gather our flocks, herds, provisions, and those things that are precious." Soon the information had passed to each family.

Limhi gathered all of the records, including the plates of ore. Dinah selected the seeds that she had collected and placed a couple of the most useful plants into woven baskets to take on the journey in case of sickness. Little Tamar helped dig up the roots of the herbs she had learned to tend that had been so vital to their health and healing. She tucked them, along with the four little beaded slippers, carefully wrapped in woven cloth, that had been a gift from the Lamanite women at the birth of her and her twin brother. Benjamin packed his bow and arrows, Miriam, her wool for spinning and braiding. The community hummed with an energy of faith in action.

"Are you afraid at all?" Dinah asked Limhi as they each packed the few things they would take on their journey.

"I trust that the Lord has and will open the way for our escape. I'm filled with the excitement of a new day: a new future for us and for our people."

GIDEON TOOK the tribute of wine. Then another, and another. The Lamanite guards drank every drop. When they fell to the ground, asleep under the influence of the prepared wine, the signal came to begin driving the flocks and herds into the wilderness.

Limhi and Dinah watched until every family had slipped through the secret passageway. Dinah had little Nasya strapped to her chest; Benjamin and Miriam each carried a pack with bedding and items they would need as a family. They fashioned litters to carry the bulk of their needs and the tamest of their sheep dragged them behind their twitching tails.

As the ruling family made their way through the dark night, looking one last time at the only place they had ever called home, Dinah's eyes were drawn to the top of the burial mound and saw a lone figure: a man kneeling at the base of a small tree. Tears blurred her vision as she watched Helam rise and quickly make his way down the mound to where his young daughter waited. They were the last to leave the city of Shilom. He carried his young daughter, Tamar, on his back.

Tomorrow they would greet the new day as a free people.

CHANNAH, 121 BC, CITY OF AMULON

They named her Anat. A little dark-haired girl entered the world on a moonless star-filled night. Her cries mingled with those of her mother as Mariah labored to bear her first-born child. Thankfully the village was filled with women who had much experience and compassion. Channah was there with her herbs; others brought warm clothes to sooth her aching back. Mariah held her little girl and wept tears of joy. Lemish could not be kept from her. His tender expressions revealed the depth of his love for both of them.

"She's a beautiful gift from the Gods," Mariah whispered.

Lemish, choked with emotion, simply nodded and embraced his very weary wife.

"Rest; I'll bring food in the morning," Channah said before she slipped through the tapestry door into the muggy heat of the summer.

"Mariah has given birth to a baby girl. Both are doing well," Channah whispered to Amulon.

"Our city will grow even faster than I had planned." In the moonlight, the thirst for power gleamed in his eyes.

"So, is this part of a plan, or just the way things happened?" Channah half expected to be struck for saying that, so she cringed for a moment, then opened her eyes to see Amulon staring at her.

"Are you afraid of me?" he asked.

"Honestly, yes."

"Do you trust me?"

"If you wish me to be honest, the answer is no."

"Do you love me?"

"In a way, I do. In other ways, no."

"Given the chance, would you leave?"

"I cannot answer that."

Amulon moved closer to her and stroked her face. "I do love you. In every way, but I have always seen you as a child, a wild child that needed to be tethered." He looked intently, cocked his head, and added, "You're not a child. You are a woman of strength, and your child has born a child. You're a good mother. I've been wrong."

Channah bowed her head, but the pit in her stomach remained. "Thank you."

THE DAYS WERE hot and the air, heavy. Puffy, lazy clouds changed from one shape to another on their journey across the heavens. Lemish took a moment away from his wife and child to walk with Channah.

"Mother, are you happy?"

"I have you, and Mariah, and your little Anat to bring me great happiness."

"You're avoiding my question." Lemish gently reached out to take her arm, turning her toward his face.

"Are you happy?"

Channah sighed, looking into his eyes. "I long to see my parents if they are still alive. I want to see my home and live the way I want to, free of fear. I have been captive for so long I have forgotten what it is like to be free. I do long for it, though."

"Would you leave Amulon if you had the chance?"

"That is a difficult question." Channah thought hard. "I've considered what choice I would make if I ever had the chance."

"What would your choice be, mother?"

"I would never leave you behind," Channah responded with fervor. "Never."

Lemish embraced her. They stood for some time in the shadows of the forest that was the perimeter of Channah's world.

The day was like any other, crops were gathered, corn was laid in the hot sun to dry, and children played games around the huts that lined the growing city. Chickens clucked, and sheep called to their lambs.

The first indication of trouble was the shrieking of a young girl gathering chicken eggs laid in the forest leaf litter. She was screaming at the top of her lungs. Men from all directions ran, grabbing tools and hunting weapons as they came. As they neared the girl, they stopped. Everyone in the village was riveted to the shadows.

The men retreated toward the open courtyard of the city. One scared young girl was in the arms of a dark-skinned warrior who was armed with both spear and sword. Others came after him, spilling out of the darkness like ants from a disturbed mound.

The people of Amulon moved away from the incoming strangers.

Channah looked intently at the soldiers.

Amulon slowly made his way to the front of the crowd, facing the unexpected visitors.

"We seek the people of Limhi," the leader barked. "They are our slaves, and they escaped after the sun set by giving our guards wine to make them sleep. Have you seen them?"

"The people of the city Nephi are gone?" Amulon spat the words in a high-pitched, unnatural voice.

"Yes, gone, escaped," the Lamanite barked.

"Did they take their flocks and herds?" Amulon squeaked.

"Everyone!"

"Their grain and supplies?" These words came almost as a whisper. "All."

Amulon turned and faced his people, looking from side to side as if evaluating them. He spun back around to face the stranger. "There are no more Nephites in the land?"

"Do you know where they have gone?" the soldier shouted. "Tell me, or you die now. You are Nephites; we can tell by your skin." The Lamanite soldiers whispered one to another. An older soldier came up and whispered to the leader. The leader's face reddened and his fingers clutched his spear tighter.

Amulon backed away. "We don't know where the people of Limhi have gone, but if we saw them, we would capture them and return them to you as your rightful slaves." His face flushed. "Or we would kill them for you immediately." He spoke the words with frightening fervor without turning his back on the soldiers.

The Lamanite leader scanned the people that stood before him. He pointed his spear at Amulon.

"You are Noah's priests." His spear pushed at Amulon's chest. "You took the daughter of the King of the Lamanites many moons ago."

Amulon stepped back until he ran into someone behind him. He felt for who it was, obviously afraid to turn around. He pulled at the clothing of the person and realized it was Channah. He thrust her in front of him. "Here she is: the daughter of the king. Take her. Spare our lives."

The soldier lowered his spear and knelt at the feet of Channah. "Your parents grieved each moon for you."

"Are they yet alive?" Channah choked out, with emotion that had been buried for so long. "Do my mother and father live?' She fell to the ground, where he knelt and grasped his cloak. "Tell me!"

"Your father lives. Your mother has gone to the next world. She watched for you at the fields each day, hoping you'd find your way home." The soldier gently touched Channah's shoulder. "She was buried in that spot where she stood waiting for your return."

A cry that Channah didn't recognize as hers came from deep within her soul, weeping for the mother she would never see again. Tears fell freely as she mourned in that moment in front of all who knew her. Lemish wrapped his arms around her as she wept.

The priests of Noah all retreated behind their women and children.

"Are these the ones you took from the lake that day?" the soldier demanded. "I want to see them all."

One by one, the women stood forth. In a single line, they faced the Lamanite army.

"Bring the king," the soldier barked the order to his next in command. "Tell him we have found his daughter and the others."

A single Lamanite runner vanished into the woods with just the sound of his swift feet crunching the dry leaves and twigs. Frightened women with tear-stained cheeks stood between the Priests and the Lamanite soldiers.

The soldiers all moved to where they could get a better look at the women. After a few moments, with exclamations of surprise and joy, different soldiers rushed forward, identifying the faces of the ones they knew as sisters, friends, and relatives. Tears fell. They embraced, speaking in their native tongue. The Priests of Noah cowered behind the women and children that formed a temporary protective barrier. Mothers introduced their children, some dark-skinned, some fair-skinned, but all a mixture of Nephite and Lamanite blood. It was a joyous reunion.

After a few moments, the army formed their ranks again, spears raised as if poised for battle. The women, realizing the gravity of the situation, stepped forward. Their husbands, the Priests of Noah, stepped back.

Channah acted as their voice. "We don't wish to have blood spilled this day. Nor do we wish to see our men killed for their crimes. They are the fathers of our children and are our people now. Have mercy on us." She looked at the ground, head bowed, focused on the feet of the soldiers.

Her words fell on the hearts of the soldiers, and they lowered their weapons.

The leader of the army knelt at the feet of Channah. "You are the rightful queen."

Amulon, apparently sensing a loss of power on his side and an increase of authority on his wife's side interjected.

"I have a map," Amulon offered. "I can take you to the Nephite lands."

The Soldier turned his attention to Amulon. "We will spare your lives if you will lead us to Limhi's people."

Amulon ordered, trying to sound as if he was in charge, "Men, we leave today. Bring your weapons and provisions. We will help these good soldiers find their rightful property. Those Nephites took what belonged to us and to these honorable Lamanite people. They must pay. Who will help?"

The men, catching on quickly to Amulon's ploy, raised their weapons with a shout of support. Find them, punish them, capture them, came the shouts from the crowd.

"My men will join you in capturing the Nephites," Amulon gushed.

The Lamanite soldier, still wary and not ready to trust Amulon, suggested they all eat and wait for the king to arrive. It would be his decision to make.

The women, eager to welcome their own people, prepared the best they had to offer. The feast was in readiness when a new contingent of Lamanites arrived.

Amulon pulled Channah aside and whispered into her ear. "If you value the life of your son, your little Anat, and Lemish's wife, you'll do all I ask." Channah pulled away to see the warning in his eyes. "I will be king, even if I have to kill your father to do it." Amulon grasped her arm tighter and pulled her close to his hot breath again. "Everyone you love will die if I don't get what I want. Do you understand me?" Channah nodded slowly.

She watched the forest for hours as she worked, waiting for any sign of her father. When the commotion sounded, she placed her preparations on the ground and ran into the darkness. She found him as he stood in a shaft of moonlight, his white hair flowing down his shoulders. With arms outstretched, Channah ran to him and buried her face in his chest, sobbing the words in a language she was never permitted to speak. She spoke of her love, her pain, and the sorrow she had felt for so long. "I have one child who lives, a son. He looks just like you." The king's expression was tinged with sorrow for what Channah hadn't said.

"I've lived long enough to see you and will see your child soon. It is enough for me." Looking straight into Channah's eyes, the king sadly added, "There will be a new king soon. I have lived my life and will not walk in these moccasins much longer."

Channah embraced him and wept. "Please, father, stay a while longer." She wiped her tears. "Come meet my son and the place we have made our home."

The king's anger grew. His expression hardened. "I'll kill those men with my own hands."

Channah took a deep breath. "There is a better way, without shedding blood." She stepped back so he could see her seriousness. "See what their plan is. I believe we can have peace. We have become the wives of these men and have born them children." A flash of anger crossed his face as she spoke. "Please, father."

Channah and the king entered the city of Amulon as royalty. Everyone bowed to them. Amulon stood. Then he, too, bowed.

"Let us feast," Amulon said in his most powerful voice.

Following the feast, when the wine had been distributed in abundance, Amulon presented to the King of the Lamanites his plan. He pulled out his prized map. "This, oh king, is a map to where the Nephite cities are. They have escaped and must be captured. They will become our slaves-- I mean, your slaves. We will use them to build up our cities."

With the wine to warm him, the king agreed to Amulon's plan. Channah felt at peace. She had her father back. For now, she would hold on to that gift.

"LEMISH, you are in charge of the city. Watch over the women and children." Amulon ordered. Then almost as an afterthought or a veiled threat, he added, "I have the map with me, which no one else has seen. You don't know where the Lamanite lands are, so don't try to leave or allow anyone else to leave." He glanced back at Channah, who stood behind him. "I'll return to finish what I've begun. I expect to find you here when I get back."

LISHA, 121 BC, CITY OF HELAM

*Y*ears of peace and plenty. Trust. Community. Hard work and hope. The people of Helam had found ways to work together, to be there for each other in times of need, to lend strength, to build and not tear down. Lisha's heart swelled with gladness, thinking back over the years of struggle, along with the persistence and faith that had built this people.

When they had fled the city of Shilom, led by Alma, that had been a supreme act of faith. Lisha had done her part, too, of course. And Mera had been a grandmother to them all. Lisha still missed her. But she knew that change and loss were part of life. Much as she had fought against that truth in her youth, she accepted it now. In a way, she embraced it. With so many years behind her and new aches in her body every day, it was high time she made peace with her own mortality.

She shifted the water skin on her hip as she walked. It was heavy, and her hip pained her, but Kaleb would be thirsty. "Come along, Eviana." Lisha glanced over her shoulder. Evi had grown tall, almost as tall as her mother. She carried a woven basket packed with challah bread, goat cheese, a small crock of honey, and dandelion greens.

"Momma," Evi groaned, trudging up beside her mother. "I'm tired. This is too far."

Lisha laughed. "You go farther than this when you're out running through the woods with your friends."

"Yes, but that's for fun, and we can pretend we're being chased by Lamanites. This is boring."

Lisha smiled, grateful Evi could run through the woods, pretending to flee Lamanites. "I went on a very long journey once," she told her daughter. "We walked for eight days when we left Shilom."

Evi's eyes flew wide. "Eight whole days? Why did you go so far? Why not just stay in Shilom?"

"King Noah was chasing us. He would've killed us if he could."

"But he died, right?" Evi asked. "And you had friends there, didn't you?

Lisha nodded, remembering Tamar, Helam, Limhi, and others.

"Why didn't you go back?" Evi caught her foot in a tangle of roots in the path and nearly went sprawling.

Lisha grabbed her shoulder and steadied her. "Careful, my daughter."

Evi rolled her eyes and shook off her hand. "I'm fine. I'm big now."

"Of course." She glanced up at the fleecy sky, noting the sun's height.

Evi mimicked her. "We need to hurry, Momma, or we'll get there after lunchtime."

Lisha suppressed a smile.

Evi picked her way daintily through some clover and violets. "But you still didn't tell me."

"I would've gone back," Lisha said. "For many years, I longed to and believed we someday could. But Rafa came and told us about the Lamanites enslaving our friends back in Shilom. That's when I knew we could never go back, that I'd never see Tamar and the others again." Her voice caught as she remembered the love and support Tamar gave her while Alma was one of the priests of Noah and was finding his way back to her and, again, later, when he'd stood up to the wicked king and became a fugitive.

"There's been more refugees from Shilom, haven't there, Mother?"

"Not in the last few years. All I know is that a few years ago, my friends still lived, but the Lamanites are cruel and exact heavy tributes. Anyone who tries to escape is killed."

She couldn't imagine the horrors the people of Shilom must be enduring. Even now, she still thought of Tamar as she had been nearly twenty-five years ago when they sought a safe place to worship and live according to the truths in their hearts. Lisha remembered Tamar's steely determination and the spark of light in her beautiful dark eyes.

She sighed, sending a silent prayer that the Lord would protect her friends and ease their heavy burdens. The two continued in relative silence; each lost in their own thoughts. They passed through the tree cover surrounding the city.

As they neared the farmland on the outskirts of Helam, Evi regained the spring in her step. She darted ahead, turning in every direction, trying to spy her older brother before her mother did. Lisha smiled. These two were like a pair of squirrels when they were together, despite the six-year age difference. The best of friends and constantly in mischief, though there was kindness in them both, a kindness that her older son, Alma, sometimes seemed to be missing.

They crested a small rise, and Lisha saw Kaleb in the distance. His homespun clothes, in varying shades of brown, made him blend with the field he was tilling ahead of planting time. Kaleb's face lit up when he saw them. Lisha did not often bring lunch to him out in the fields. But this was a special day. Kaleb was turning sixteen, and judging by how much time he spent with Devorah's daughter, the two would soon be betrothed. Lisha's heart leaped at the thought.

Kaleb set down his obsidian spade and wiped his hands on his pant legs, depositing little streaks of earth. He grinned at them, sunny as ever, and mopped sweat from his brow with a rag from his pocket. "You brought me lunch, did you?" He ruffled Evi's dark hair.

She beamed at him, not bothering to straighten the ties in her braids. Then, remembering her important duties, she puffed out her chest, set the basket down, and said with great solemnity, "It's not every day you come of age, Kaleb." Then she made a skeptical face. "Of course, you'll probably never grow up, no matter how old you get."

"You little bunny!" Kaleb said, grabbing for her again.

She darted out of reach, giggling.

Lisha shook her head, opened the basket, and spread its contents on a grassy patch near the edge of the field. "All right, you two, time for our meal."

Moments later, they were seated together, sharing the bounty. Other men lunched a distance away, casting longing looks at Kaleb's spread and his company.

"I brought you something for your birthday," Evi said.

Kaleb grinned through a mouthful of bread. "Was it something you made?"

She cocked her head to the side in mock indignation. "Of course, it was something I made."

Kaleb laughed. "All right, all right. Let me see."

She pulled a small twine-wrapped package out of the picnic basket and handed it to her brother. Kaleb untied the string and pulled away the thin outer cloth. Inside, a warm yellow kerchief was folded into a neat square.

"I wove it myself," Evi said smugly, "and dyed it with chamomile."

"It's beautiful," Kaleb said, tying it around his neck. "And much better than this old thing." He tossed his old rag into the basket.

"What about you, Momma?" Evi asked. "What did you bring for Kaleb?"

Lisha smiled. "Your father and I will give him a gift at dinner tonight. But I'm going to go ahead with our family tradition and say one thing I love about Kaleb." She turned to him. "Son, you have such a willing heart; you are obedient to the Lord, even when you wrestle with questions." She forestalled his interruption with a raised hand. "I know you wrestle questions, Kaleb. Most everyone does at some point. But the important thing is, what do you do during the wrestle? And you, Kaleb? You live in faith, even while you sort through issues in your heart and mind. That makes all the difference. And I love your happy heart."

"That's not fair. That's more than one! Now I don't have anything to say." She cast a mischievous glance to Kaleb.

"Only one good thing, hey? That's all you can think of for me, and Mother already took it?" He shook his head, obviously trying—and failing—to look devastated.

They all laughed. It was a golden moment, the sunlight streaming over the three of them, happiness in their hearts, and sunny Kaleb wearing Evi's yellow bandana. It was a priceless moment, the kind Lisha would treasure up in her heart and revisit again and again, long after the moment was gone and life irrevocably changed.

This moment was broken by the sound of the shofar horn, a long, drawn-out warning. For Lisha, it was a terrible echo from her past. She rose unsteadily to her feet, feeling the blood drain from her face. "Lamanites."

WAVE AFTER WAVE of men crested the hill, flooding toward the village. They were on Lisha, Eviana, and Kaleb before they could so much as look up in horror. Kaleb grabbed for his spade. He squared his shoulders and stepped in front of his mother and sister.

"No!" Lisha cried.

But it was too late. A Lamanite warrior thrust a knife into Kaleb's chest, knocking him to the ground as he and the other Lamanites stampede past. Kaleb curled in on himself, blood frothing from his lips.

Lisha knelt beside him. "No, no, no." She slipped her arms under him, cradling her son against her body. He stared up at her, then over to Evi, who was frozen in shock. He tried to speak but subsided in a bubbling fit of coughs. "It's all right," Lisha said, "save your strength."

His fingers gripped her sleeves. His message was clear. He knew he wasn't long for this world. And he wanted his mother. He wanted her to tell him it would be all right, that she loved him, that she would watch over Eviana and give his love to his father and brother, and maybe even his future betrothed. Now that his future was gone.

Lisha nodded, hot tears pouring down her cheeks. Warriors still streamed past her and her children. It was like they were in a bubble, or maybe they were an eddy in a river, and the water flowed around them while they stood impossibly still, for the moment unnoticed. Evi dropped to her knees beside Lisha, sobbing and shaking. Kaleb's grip loosened, and his body went still.

Evi's fingers went to his bandana, now tinged red. She untied it and wrapped it around her wrist. All Lisha could see was ruined gold.

A rushing Lamanite jostled against her. He turned back, leering at Lisha. "We'll be back for you later when we celebrate. Don't be going anywhere." His gaze drifted to Eviana and sharpened. "Oh yes, we will definitely be back." Then he ran on toward the village.

Lisha felt a dawning horror. Fury rose within her, and she knew she would rather die than allow these men to violate her daughter. She also knew she couldn't stay here with Kaleb, no matter how it pained her to leave him so still and alone in the field. She crossed his hands on his chest, then turned to Eviana. The little girl's cheeks were wet, her face pale and haunted.

"We have to go," Lisha said in a hushed voice. Evi nodded. "We'll circle around to the river and come in through Helam by the river and find your father."

LISHA MADE her way through the city gates, past the woodshed and the pottery shed, pressing through the crowd of men packed into the place of gathering. It looked to be a tense standoff. Not a place where Lisha should be. But Alma needed to know what had happened.

Lamanite warriors filled half the space, only a short distance from her people. They clogged the paths through the village, hefting atlatls and spears. Alma stood in the center of a huddle of men, consulting with Aaron and Rafa. He looked up as Lisha approached.

"Lisha! What are you doing here? Women and children should be in the caves."

"I left Evi there with Hannah and Sarika." She felt strung tight, stripped bare. "Alma--"

He grew pale at the tone of her voice.

"Lisha, what's happened?" From anyone else, the question would've been absurd. A huge army of Lamanites had invaded. Enslavement was all but certain. But Alma must've seen what was written on Lisha's face. His eyes gave a quick search of the men in the vicinity, then turned his gaze back to Lisha. "Where's Kaleb?"

She swallowed, feeling weak, but knew she must be strong. "He's dead." Her voice was glassy – like ice atop a spring stream, thin and fragile, about to be broken. "We were in the fields." She shook her head as if this were somehow her fault. "We brought a picnic. He… he…they might've let him live, but he tried to protect Evi and me. He tried to protect us." She felt herself shaking and wrapped her arms around her chest.

Alma stumbled back, bumping into their eldest son, who, seeing their interaction, had strode over.

"What is this?" Alma the Younger demanded.

Lisha just looked at him.

"It's Kaleb," Alma said, his voice breaking. "They've killed him."

Fury rose in Alma the Younger's face, and Lisha felt a stab of terrible fear. She couldn't lose him, too. "Alma, no," she hissed. "Zilpah needs you. Your children need you."

"What good am I if I can't avenge my family?" Alma spat.

"What good are you to them if you're dead?" Lisha said, feeling heartless, but determined to talk her son down.

Rafa and Aaron exchanged glances and braced to grab Young Alma if he should try to break ranks and attack the Lamanite warriors, bringing destruction upon them all.

"Son," Alma said heavily.

"These people have no mercy," Lisha said with a sob. "They cut Kaleb down right in front of me.

Alma tensed with his expression tight.

"We cannot fight them," Aaron said. "There are too many."

"They'll kill us and take our land no matter what we do," said Darius.

"No, they'll enslave us," said Rafa. "Taavi and I saw it back in Shilom. They'll laze around while we break our backs serving them."

"What do we do, Alma?"

Alma shut his eyes for a moment and took a deep breath. Lisha knew he was offering up a silent prayer, pleading for guidance, courage, and strength. She offered a prayer for the same, pleading for comfort as well.

"Be not afraid," Alma said to the crowd around him. "I know this looks terrible. It is terrible. And we've already suffered losses."

Alma the Younger made a disgusted sound in the back of his throat.

Alma caught his son's eye and shook his head. "We must remember the Lord."

"Why hasn't the Lord prevented this?" Young Alma demanded.

Lisha flinched. Her husband's mouth thinned.

"Quiet your fear and your fury, son," Alma said.

"I'm not afraid."

"Well, I am," said Asher. "We all are."

Alma nodded toward his friend. "We must quiet our fears, all of us. The Lord will deliver us. Pray that He will soften the Lamanites' hearts, that this standoff does not turn to violence, that they will spare us, our wives, and our children."

Asher and Darius nodded; their expressions grieved as they joined in silent prayer.

"After all we've been through and all we've built, we have to negotiate with murderers? With people like this?" Alma the Younger gestured toward the waiting Lamanites, who stood lazily glowering at them as if the people of Helam were no threat.

"My son's right," Lisha said, prompting shocked stares from both Almas. "It isn't fair that we have to deal with this. And I don't know why the Lord doesn't intervene right now. He could swallow the Lamanites in the earth or sweep them away with strong wind. I don't know why He doesn't step in and take over whenever we are in danger or hurting or afraid. But I do know He is there for us. I do know He lifts our burdens and grants us strength." She gathered her courage. "We are a good people. We're dedicated to the Lord, happy to help those in need, and faithful in times of plenty and times of heartache. We will be faithful now. I can't control how you feel or what you choose. I certainly can't control the Lamanites. But, as for me, I will call on the Lord. And in His own time, He will deliver us."

Lisha felt a hand on her shoulder. It was Rafa, tears sparkling in his eyes. Murmured prayers rose around them. Her son, Alma, held her gaze, then looked down, his brow heavy with grief.

"What are we waiting for?" asked a boy about Kaleb's age. "Why is everyone just standing around?

"We are waiting for their general. Apparently, he leads from the back." Alma's tone did not hide his disgust.

At that moment, the Lamanite army stirred, parting to allow their leader to step forward. To Lisha's surprise, he was a fair-skinned man, unlike most of the Lamanites. He bore a twisted expression on an all-too-familiar face. Lisha's stomach clenched.

"No," she breathed and shared a look of horror with her husband. "How can it be?"

Amulon, leader of Noah's high priests. The man who had incited Noah to burn the prophet Abinadi to death, then to pursue and attempt to destroy Alma and all the believers. How could he be here? And with a Lamanite army?

"I thought he was dead," she whispered.

Amulon called out, "I would speak with your king."

Alma squeezed Lisha's hand and stepped forward, his shoulders square and his head held tall. He reminded her so much of Kaleb in his last moments. A hot tear streaked down her cheek.

"We have no king," Alma said, "but I lead these people."

Amulon's eyes widened and he barked out a humorless laugh. "Why, it's Alma!" His tone was incredulous. "You lead these people? Oh, this is too good." He prodded Alma's chest. "You betrayed Noah; you destroyed the people's faith in him. Look what it's brought you."

He gestured at the army surrounding them. "Now you'll get exactly what you deserve."

Lisha's prayers grew more fervent. All around her, the people cried out to the Lord, in soft murmurs or in silence.

Amulon sighed, then laughed again. "You will cede the city to us. What do you call this place anyway?"

"We called it after one of the most noble of men I have ever known." Alma breathed in deeply. "This is the land of Helam."

A flicker of mirth chased across Amulon's face. He waved his hand carelessly and nodded toward the fields. "Well, Alma, you and your people in the land of Helam are now our subjects. Bury your dead, and we'll finalize terms tomorrow. No need for the stench of putrid bodies smelling up my new home."

Lisha's restraint cracked. She tore towards Amulon, but too many hands held her back.

Evil humor danced in Amulon's eyes. They lit with recognition when they rested on Lisha. "I remember you," he said. There was a familiarity to his tone that made Lisha shiver with disgust. "You always were a wild one." He moved toward her. She refused to flinch away as he lifted her chin, then let his finger drift down her neck toward her chest.

"Don't touch my wife," Alma said with quiet resolve.

Amulon laughed, incredulous again. "You never minded sharing women when we were priests back in Shilom."

A flash of anger spread across Alma's face. "I am not the same man."

Beside him, Alma the Younger stood rigid, his expression black.

"Enough," a sharp voice said—one of the Lamanite warriors.

As Lisha gazed at the man, she saw he bore himself differently. He carried himself with the confidence of a great leader, trusted by his men. The king. And suddenly, she understood, Amulon was not the general of this army or king of this people. He was merely an underling who had somehow pleased the Lamanite king.

She felt a rush of relief, followed with persistent fear.

The Lamanite king frowned in distaste. "Enough of this squabbling. I tire of it. I'll stay in there this night." He pointed his ornate spear toward the sanctuary. "See that it's warm and comfortable," he said to the warrior beside him, who nodded crisply and left to fulfill his request. Then he turned back to Amulon. "Bring me food and wine."

Lisha flinched.

"Quarter the men throughout this city," he continued to Amulon. "Use their huts and set up tents as needed. We reconvene at first light to clarify our future arrangements."

LISHA, 121 BC, CITY OF HELAM

The burials the night before had been difficult for everyone, especially the families who suffered losses. There would be no time for sitting Shiva now, not with the Lamanite army in their borders, and even in their homes. No community circled around to support those in mourning, no meals brought, no quietly sitting together, to share strength.

Still, Lisha knew there were many who needed the courage and comfort that shiva typically brought. Despite her own grief, and their tenuous situation, she reached out to others in the community, giving a hug to widowed mothers and a bit of crystallized honey to their fatherless children as she made her way through Helam to her son's home, Eviana in tow.

Alma the Younger wasn't staying in his home anymore. His small family sheltered in a nearby tent while his cottage was overrun with Lamanite warriors. He opened the tent flap and welcomed his mother in, his eyes seething with fury. "Mother," he said, wrapping his arms around her. "Come, Evi, Helaman and Yael have been asking for you."

Lisha nodded to Evi, who scurried outside to join Helaman and Yael where they were playing under a shade tree, apparently digging for worms. Yael's dirt-smeared face lit when she saw her aunt. The three were so close in age they acted more like cousins.

Zilpah rose heavily from a stump Alma had dragged in as a seat for her, little Shiblon clinging to her skirts. "How are you holding up, Mother?"

"Well enough," Lisha said. "Please, sit back down. How are you feeling?" She scooped her two-year old grandson into her arms and settled carefully into a pile of old furs. At the last moment, her legs gave out and the two fell the final inches, causing Shiblon to burst into a peal of giggles. Lisha gave him a kiss. "This is all they let you have from your home?" She looked around at the sparse furnishings and tools.

Alma's expression darkened. "We'll get our things back. Where's Father?"

"Peace talks in the sanctuary," Lisha said, "with Amulon and King Laman."

"More like terms of enslavement," Alma said.

"I told your father we'd meet him there."

Alma the Younger nodded. "Evi can stay and help Zilpah with the children. She and Helaman will keep track of Yael and Shiblon, all right?"

Zilpah nodded. "We'll be fine. You should both be there for any important decisions." She waved them away.

Mother and son strode through their fallen city, oblivious to the spring sounds of birds, crickets, and bleating lambs. A few minutes later, they joined the restless crowds in the gathering place. Nephite men huddled together, some sitting on the split log benches, others standing, poised to defend themselves against the Lamanite warriors standing guard throughout the city. A high concentration of Lamanites prowled along the gathering place. They looked wary, frightening, and somehow self-satisfied. It turned her stomach.

She was one of few women who had come. Most stayed away, sheltering their families from the predatory gaze of these strange men. Lisha still felt gutted by Kaleb's loss and the horrible prospect of Lamanite oppression, but trust in the Lord gave her a wellspring of strength in the depths of her soul, a calm courage, and determination.

Beside her, Alma the Younger paced, murmuring to the other waiting men. Agitation poured off him, and it was contagious.

"Alma." Lisha rested her hand on his arm, but he shook it off.

After what seemed to be hours, the sanctuary door opened and Alma stepped out with Rafa and Asher, his closest advisors, letting the heavy door swing shut behind them. They strode to Lisha's and Alma the Younger's side. The crowd surged forward, surrounding them.

"What is it, Father?" Young Alma asked, "What are their demands?"

Alma's face was drawn, but his eyes bore a glimmer of hope. He exchanged glances with Rafa and Asher. "The Lamanites King wants us to take him to the land of Nephi. I tried to convince them that we didn't know the way. But they don't believe us. They know refugees have flooded here. Amulon recognized Rafa. Somehow the Lamanite army that went searching for Limhi's people got lost."

"How did Amulon end up with the Lamanites?" Lisha asked. "How did he end up in a position of power at all?"

"Apparently, the army searching for Limhi's people stumbled upon Amulon and his men," said Alma. "He has a whole city full of people now, named after himself."

"You're not going to believe this," Rafa said. "Amulon and the other priests stole young girls from the Lamanites years ago. Then, when the Lamanite army found them, it was like some kind of reunion. One of the girls was King Laman's daughter. She and the others pled for the lives of their husbands and families. Amulon convinced the king he could help them. Showed them what he built in his city and how he had cared for their women."

"Somehow, I doubt he provided much care and compassion," Alma said drily. "But you know how slippery he is. He can convince anyone of just about anything. He promised to lead the Lamanite army back to the Land of Nephi, so they could return to their homes in Shemlon."

"What do we know about Limhi's people? Did they find them?" Lisha asked, her voice spiked with anxiety.

Alma nodded. "They escaped."

"That's why the king and Amulon are so edgy. They want to find them and bring them back. Apparently, life was pretty good for the Lamanites when the Nephites were their slaves."

"So Amulon got lost, too, then?" Alma the Younger said. "Bumbling about in the woods?"

"Yes. They found game trails and happened upon us." Alma sighed. "But, if we show them the way to the Land of Nephi, the king of the Lamanites has promised they will grant us our lives and set us free. If we don't show them, they'll stay here. This will become their land, and if it comes to blood, so be it."

"Why does Amulon care about getting back to the land of Nephi, to Shemlon and Shilom?" Lisha asked.

Alma took a deep breath. "He's always wanted to be king. I believe, now that the city is empty, he plans to take over and make it his own."

The group sat in silence for a moment, contemplating his words.

"Will they truly leave us in peace if you show them the way? Or will they take our families," Asher asked, "and kill all our men?"

Lisha took in a sharp breath. "Alma, we can't let that happen. We can't let them destroy us."

Murmurs of agreement rose from the men gathered around them.

Alma sighed again. "They've promised to give us our lives and our freedom if we do as they ask. So, we have a choice before us."

"You believe them?" Alma the Younger asked. "Do these men have any integrity at all?"

"I don't know if I believe their promise," Alma said. "They're despicable. They wrecked the sanctuary and toppled the altar. Amulon was using it as a footstool." He cast a wary glance toward Lisha. "The king has reined in his other men's lust thus far, but the longer the Lamanite Army stays here without their families, the more danger our women and daughters are in." Alma winced at the thought.

"I don't know that we have any reasonable alternatives," Asher said.

"So, show them the way to Nephi," Darius said from the crowd. "People we love are no longer there. They can have it."

Alma nodded, deep in thought.

"Then it's agreed," Asher said. "We'll show them the way to the Land of Nephi and hope against hope they keep their word."

IN THE END, Alma, Alma the younger, Rafa led a party of Lamanites back to the Land of Nephi. Asher stayed behind to see to their people and prevent abuse by the Lamanite soldiers. It was a tense situation, with little clarity about roles and protections. Most Lamanite warriors remained behind in Helam, security against any temptation to escape.

The day dawned bright and warm when the signal came that King Laman and the search party had returned.

"Call the people together," the King ordered wearily. "Ammon, step forward."

"You will remain here," King Laman said, "as king of Helam, subject to my will. Keep as many men as you need. They can bring their families to Helam from Shilom."

"You lied," Lisha said to King Laman. "You lied to us all along. Why do you need Helam when you have the entire city of Shilom to use?"

"We need tributes to support our expanding civilization," the king said. "The power of the Lamanites will fill this land."

Alma, the younger, struggled against Rafa's and his father's hands.

"Yes." The Lamanite King eyed Alma, Rafa, Alma the Younger, and Lisha. "Yes, I lied. And I'd do it again."

"You see, Alma?" said Amulon. "King Laman, the true king of all of this land, the land you've tried to steal from the Lamanites, has made *me* ruler." He beat his fist over his chest. "I'm in charge now. We can live peaceably together, right?" Amulon's proud chest and girth expanded as he puffed up with his pride over becoming the Lamanite King's representative. "I can do as I wish, as long as I don't go contrary to the wishes of King Laman. Expanding his reach and control over Nephites in the land, and ensuring they pay tribute to him is all he requires."

His eyes narrowed to menacing slits as he added, "That won't be a problem, will it Alma?"

DINAH, 121 BC, JOURNEYING

*T*he night of their escape, they had all fasted and prayed. Sheep didn't wake the sleeping guards. Children crying and wanting to go back to bed didn't cause even a stir. Nor did the noise of people brushing the branches of trees with the packs on their backs or the crunching rocks beneath their feet disturb their deep slumber.

Dinah watched them all pass by the still forms of the guards. At every loud noise, she cringed, yet was amazed that they didn't move. Not one bit.

BEING SUMMER, the nights were pleasant, the herbs plentiful, and edible plants provided sustenance along the way. Wild berries grew abundantly along the waterways, and although the briars were sharp, the sweet juices were a treat. She had taught her people well, and little bumps and scrapes were treated quickly with soft leaves of herbs they found along the trails. Animals had worn the paths to and from water sources, so they always knew where to find a cool drink at a spring. The springs seemed to be plentiful and flowed from caves and over rock formations along bluffs.

"Do you think the guards are awake yet?" Dinah asked Limhi as they walked together near the rear of the company. "Should we be worried that they might be pursuing us?"

"I believe the Lord will protect us and keep us from harm. We have been diligent in our journey and are moving as fast as we are able. I don't doubt that they will seek for us, but in spite of the tracks we have left, I don't think the Lord will allow them to find us."

"I wish I knew how the Lord worked miracles."

"I do too. For now, I just trust that we are in His hands."

Limhi put his arm around Dinah. "Would you like for me to carry Nasya?"

"I feel I need to rest soon. I'll feed her then and let you carry her while she sleeps. Nasya stirred and stretched, scrunching up her face as she yawned. Her eyes squinted closed at the brightness of the sun coming up.

"I'll ask Ammon if we can stop for a rest since we've been walking most of the night." Limhi ran ahead, patting people on the back and shouting encouragement as he passed them along the way.

Dinah could see that, up ahead, they were likely coming to a river. The trees were thick. The fields of grass, growing tall in the open, gave way to small shrubs and a thick carpet of green covering the forest floor. Limhi appeared through the crowd, running back toward her.

"We will stop here." He paused to catch his breath. "There is a point where we can cross with the animals, but the rivers become larger, and we will have to make some rafts for the animals to go across."

"I'm not looking forward to that part," Dinah said with a touch of apprehension in her voice. "How deep are the waters?"

"Ammon said they get pretty deep, but we will cross where they are wide and slow. They have explored these rivers and know where it is safe. We will be fine."

The rest was welcome. Most of the company fell asleep on the thick layer of moss and leaves. Sheep munched on the vegetation, and children napped, safely tucked beside a parent or two. The widows were added to groups of families, with each of the men Ammon had brought with him leading one of those groups.

Dinah woke rested and hungry. "Would you get some dry meat for me to eat?" She asked Limhi.

"Yes, and I'll go fill your skin with fresh water. I'll be right back."

Miriam came to where Dinah and Nasya rested on a skin blanket spread out under the shade of a giant oak tree. "Should we gather food for our meals as we go? There are plenty of acorns here."

"I think it would be wise to take some, but I heard Ammon speak of the bounty of food we would find along the way. The men will probably hunt in a couple of days and give us fresh meat when our dry meat is gone."

"What will it be like in Zarahemla?"

"I don't know. I just know that there is a Prophet of the Lord there, and we will find peace."

"What will they think of us?" Miriam seemed nervous. "I mean, what will they think of those who were wives of Noah and his priests or kept in the palace?"

"I hope they will welcome us in as their friends."

Limhi came just as Miriam was leaving. "Water for you both." He sat down on the grass. "What a beautiful place. If Zarahemla is anything like this, I'll think myself blessed. We're only two days journey from Nephi, and already I'm seeing land I've never seen before."

"Have the scouts seen any sign of the Lamanites?"

"Not at all. They did at first when they retraced our steps, and the soldiers were following our tracks, but the further they came, the more scattered our tracks became. They think the soldiers turned back."

"That's a relief. I was worried our large group was going too slow. I can relax some."

WHEN THE PEOPLE of Limhi came to the point where the river was wide and not especially deep, they determined it was time to cross. Trees were cut down and made into large rafts. Fences were fashioned around one raft to keep animals from jumping off the edges, and men ferried them across the river in small groups. Truly the river was wide, but never over a man's head. The sheep didn't appreciate being out on the water, and the shepherds tended to them to keep them calm, but a few were determined to get off the raft and ended up swimming the last few yards of their journey. All went well, and everyone made it across safely.

Ammon addressed the group once they had all crossed over. "The rest of our journey will be on this side of the river. Your flocks can graze on the grasses that feed the buffalo as they migrate along this same path. We may see some, and if we can, we will hunt them for food." Ammon pointed to the north. "We will follow this river until we reach Zarahemla. There is a bounty of food along the way. Fish in the rivers, deer, and squirrels in the forests, and, if we are lucky to find bees, we will have sweet honey."

"What a bounty of food for our journey!" Dinah exclaimed. "Truly, the Lord is providing for our needs."

Dinah watched Limhi as he moved from group to group, checking to make sure everyone was managing their resources and supplies. They traveled in the same way they lived in Nephi. A father with his own family, caring for several widows and their families.

Helam rotated from the front to the rear of the group, armed with a sword and spear, on the lookout for any pursuing Lamanites. The guards all wore breastplates of brass and copper that had been found with the twenty-four gold plates. They were aged but perfectly sound. Helam had fashioned new hilts and cleaned the rust from the swords they found in the land. These were their only weapons since the Lamanites had confiscated everything else in Shilom.

Gideon chuckled at his wife. "The chickens have a mind of their own!" She was darting side to side with children giggling along with her as she tried to herd the chickens.

"Children, come get some cracked corn!" Dinah shouted. "Hold it in your hands and give the chickens a nibble now and then. They'll follow you."

Gideon walked over to his breathless wife and took her hand. "Let's walk in the shade of the trees for a moment."

Dinah observed as Limhi stopped and spoke with individuals along the path. He called each one by name and gave words of encouragement, thanking those who were doing so much to render aid to their neighbors. Dinah hugged little Nasya a little bit tighter. "You my sweet, have the best father in the world." With a smile on her lips, she greeted Alma.

"What?" he asked. "What's that look for?"

"I'm just enjoying watching you shepherding your flock out here in the wilderness."

"Wilderness?" Limhi spread his arms out wide. "This is a bountiful land!"

Dinah smiled. "Yes, it is! It's all just so new and different to me."

"We are free!" he exclaimed. "The Lord has opened the way for our freedom and our return to Zarahemla." He embraced Dinah and pulled her close as they walked. "Benjamin has natural skill with the bow." Limhi shared. "He's already brought in several rabbits and is hoping to land a deer. He's quite a ways ahead of the group, so we will likely not see him till nightfall."

"Miriam has been such a blessing, carrying babies for some of the mothers and playing with the children to keep them occupied." Dinah beamed. "She comes back every so often to even check on me."

Limhi nodded in agreement. "We have been blessed with wonderful children."

"We have." Dinah breathed.

Ammon led the way through fertile valleys along the river teeming with fish. They feasted nightly on the catch and plucked berries and fruits throughout each day. Early one morning he called the camp leaders together. "We will arrive today!"

Cheers erupted from the group.

Ammon continued, "There is likely no danger from the Lamanites at this point, but still keep your children close. Zarahemla is a big city. We don't want anyone to get lost."

~

BENJAMIN WAS with the advance party and stood near the outskirts of Zarahamla when Limhi, and Dinah saw him on that final day of their journey. "We made it!" he exclaimed. Dinah took him into a tight embrace.

"We did." She whispered through her tears. Limhi joined them and pulled Miriam into their circle. They stood together surveying the city. The weary travelers then fell to their knees in gratitude and prayer. One by one, the families who came up the road joined Limhi's family in grateful praise. King Mosiah and his guards made their way through the throng of people and animals.

"Welcome home, Ammon." King Mosiah bellowed. He pulled Ammon into a warm embrace. "Were you successful? Are these the people of Zeniff?

Limhi stepped forward. "I am the grandson of Zeniff."

"Welcome to Zarahemla," Mosiah announced. "We have long since wondered what happened to your people. We have Jarom's, family here in our city and look forward to learning more of your history."

At the mention of Abinadi, a hush fell over the group.

"Will we be blamed for his death?" Dinah whispered to Limhi.

"We will tell the truth." Limhi stepped forward. "Oh King, we are subject unto you. If you wish us to be your slaves, we would gladly do so. We have no land or possessions and are willing to work to make this our home. What would you have us do?"

The people, hearing Limhi's words, awaited King Mosiah's decree.

"You are free. You will not be slaves to anyone."

The people cheered and hugged one another.

"You will be given a place to rest, and tomorrow, we will give you land for your inheritance. Your flocks and herds will graze with ours." King Mosian offered.

"Will you take us to Jarom's family?" Limhi asked.

"They await your arrival. Sarai has been watching for your company to arrive."

King Mosiah raised his arms, and the crowd became silent. "We have prepared a feast and will provide homes for you to rest and sleep. Come to the palace this evening and we will celebrate."

WHEN EVENING CAME and all had arrived at the palace, the king waved his hands at a table laden with more food than they'd seen in quite some time. "Sit, please have something to eat and drink. You're weary and we are not."

Limhi remained standing. "With gratitude and humility, we express our love and appreciation to you for sending Ammon to find us. Truly the Lord has blessed us as we were slaves to the Lamanites and in bondage which we could not be freed from."

Ammon sat silent and let Limhi tell the sad tale of Abinadi's tragic end. Sarai wept silently and was comforted by her sons.

"I knew he was gone," Sarai admitted. "He had come to me in a dream. I just needed to hear for sure. I have already mourned him, but now I know. He died nobly and never wavered in his faith."

Limhi joined in. "The Lord called him to preach to his family to save us from our sinful ways, and he willingly went. He loved us. He blessed our lives, and for that, we will always remember Uncle Jarom, the Prophet Abinadi." There was silence for a few moments.

"Alma, one of Noah's priests, felt the truth of his message." All eyes were on Limhi now as he told of Alma and his conversion and their miraculous escape.

"Where are they now?" King Mosiah asked.

"We don't know. We had hoped we would find them here," Limhi offered.

"They are in God's hands." King Mosiah said quietly. "Did you keep a record of your people, Limhi?"

"We have two. The record of our people, which I have kept, and the record we found when my men were searching for Zarahemla.

They found a land covered in human bones. Once a great civilization, it had been destroyed and was completely barren. They found this record." Limhi handed the twenty-four sheets of gold, covered in tiny characters, to the king.

"I'd like to keep both and interpret the writings on these plates."

"Can you read the writing?" Limhi questioned.

"Through the power of God, I can."

King Mosiah announced, "Let's thank the Lord for this bounty and enjoy the feast."

After they had eaten their fill, small groups formed to visit. Sarai made her way over to Limhi and Dinah. "Would you like to stay in our home? After all, we are family."

Limhi nodded at his aunt with a smile. "We would be most grateful. Please take Dinah and our children, and I'll make sure the rest of my people are settled. Then I'll come for some much-needed rest."

Dinah, Benjamin, Miriam, and a fussy baby followed after Sarai and her sons to begin their new life in Zarahemla as free people once again.

CHANNAH, 121 BC, JOURNEYING

hannah's heart sank as she climbed to the top of the cliff beside her mountain home and saw the Lamanite soldiers, minus Amulon and the rest of the Nephite priests. She and the other women were left without food, had suffered hunger, and resorted to catching squirrels and rabbits for sustenance. The men – in their haste to leave – had taken all of the dry meat and stored food.

The soldiers entered camp later that afternoon and gave the order to pack up. They would each carry their own burdens and would be permitted to stop in Shemlon to see their families. Channah braced herself for the moment she would pass by the last place she ever saw her mother.

As she packed, she practiced the words she wanted to say in her native tongue. "Mother, I would have come back. I tried to come back." She looked about the city. The ramshackle huts, rickety platform, and disorganized farming operations, all spoke to what these men lacked. She couldn't help but feel angry. This was not the life she wanted. She had tried to make it a home for her family, and once again, Amulon's vanity and laziness would uproot her and force her to make her home in another strange place.

Lemish and Mariah prepared their packs, and the city, a hive of activity, quickly prepared to leave, likely never to return.

Channah carefully wrapped the herbs in bunches, tucking them into a skin pouch she could carry on her waist. There was nothing else she wanted to keep from this place except a flower from her daughter's grave. She quickly scrambled to the place her little girl had been laid to rest — a daughter she never got to see. She fell to the ground and let her tears fall as she plucked a flower, placed it in the pouch with the herbs, and bade farewell to her child and the difficult life she had led in this mountain home. At last, she would return one last time to the home of her childhood.

The path was familiar; she knew many of the ways through the woods but always got stuck at the bluffs. There never seemed to be a way off the cliffs. No matter which path she took, it ended with a steep drop-off. The women and families followed the Lamanite soldiers to an unfamiliar copse of trees that hid a ravine lined with large boulders. Mentally, Channah created the map in her mind of where they were and where they had gone.

The Lamanite soldiers began climbing down the massive slide of boulders, dropping six feet at a time in some places.

Channah watched with pride as Lemish held his wife's arm, making sure she didn't stumble or slip. He went ahead if the way was difficult and helped Mariah cautiously slide down the slabs of stone, careful to make sure the baby was always safe and protected.

As they reached the bottom and stepped into the valley, it all became familiar and clear. The high mountain lake, the bluff above them — freedom had been just beyond her reach. That must have been how the Priests found them, watching from high on the bluff. Then, sneaking down when most of the women had left. Channah shuddered at the memory.

She knew the way back now. It was a well-worn path. She wondered how often, in the last twenty years, the men had watched her people, the women, bathe at the lake. The thought made her want to retch. She couldn't dwell on it. She focused on her son, Lemish, and the good man he had become. Many of the children of the priests saw them for what they were.

It had changed some, but she knew where the fields of corn were, where her friends had lived, and the home she had been born in. She paused by the marker where her mother had been laid to rest. She took the flower from her pouch and laid it at the base. Channah spoke the words she had practiced, and they flowed with her tears. She recalled the tender words her father had whispered to her before he left with Amulon. "Your mother longed to see you again." It brought more tears. She was a grown woman now, and her father, an aging king.

Briskly, the soldiers gathered their own families from Shemlon and bid farewell. The caravan turned their backs to the city of their birth and the mountain city of their captivity.

LISHA, 121 BC, CITY OF HELAM

$\mathcal{M}$ost of the army was gone. Lisha felt that was a blessing, fewer warriors tromping through the city looking for a fight. Although King Laman had left behind more than enough men to secure the city of Helam. Even the wives and families of the Lamanite guards had moved into the city, some taking over existing homes, and a few building their own.

Amulon strutted about town, reminding everyone that he was now king of Helam. It made Lisha sick especially when she saw his little cruelties. As soon as he claimed their city, he had taken over Alma's home and tasked Alma and the other men with building huts for themselves.

Lisha lived in a tent for now, with Eviana and her husband, not far from Young Alma and Zilpah's tent. Winter was fast approaching, frost already dusting the ground in the mornings, but Amulon clearly did not care for the potential cold and want of the people he conquered. Instead of pitching in or ordering the guards to help build, he left the task to the Nephites while depriving them of the assistance of their young men. These he sent to the far reaches of the farmland, along with all children above eight years of age, demanding they build stone walls, a useless task, particularly considering how sorely every hand was needed in Helam to prepare for winter.

The women carved clay bricks out of the land bordering the riverbed, laying them out to dry in the afternoon sun. These Amulon used to build a smokehouse for curing meat. Lisha was part of this labor crew. Her back grew weary from the daily strain of cutting and hauling bricks, but she did not complain. All were suffering, and her strength and courage was needed. She still grieved Kaleb, just as many others grieved their own lost family. But, in the depths of her heart, she knew she would see him again. She would see Mera, Eva, and her mother.

Now she sang as she worked, encouraging Hannah, Sarika, and the others. And, when Eviana returned home tired from the fields, Lisha did not curse Amulon or the tragic nature of life. She wrapped her arms around her daughter and told her she was strong, to keep praying, and that God would see her through this and would eventually deliver them all.

One afternoon, after a particularly exhausting day, Lisha hauled a small heap of clay bricks over to her former home. She had seen Amulon's wife at a distance several times over the prior weeks but did not relish meeting her up close. The woman was bound to be as cruel as her husband.

If she was, there was nothing Lisha could do about it. She couldn't control this woman, much less the Lamanite men. And she refused to return evil for evil. Instead, she squared her shoulders, lifted her chin, and pasted a determined smile on her face.

As she neared the cottage, children were playing outside, a young man, in the same wicker chair where Kaleb had often sat, whittling a stick into a flute. He looked to be about twenty, an age her son would never reach. A woman lounged beside him, a little younger than he was; perhaps his wife? She rocked a little one in her arms. Lisha's heart pounded, and she felt a flash of anger. But she pushed it away. None of this was their fault. She couldn't blame them for the sins of Amulon. And endless fury would only harm her, not bring Kaleb back.

The cottage door opened, and a Lamanite woman stepped out. Her skin and hair were a dark, nut brown. Her eyes were darker still, although they glowed as if reflecting the sun. Lisha stumbled over some toys in the yard. The bricks tumbled out of her cart. She caught herself against a rough adobe structure, the beginning of the smoke-house. Lisha flinched, ducking her head, expecting to be shouted at, or maybe even slapped.

Instead, Amulon's wife hurried forward, looking concerned. "Are you alright?" She clasped Lisha's upper arm.

"Yes, I'm fine." Confused, Lisha kept her eyes downcast.

"Here, let me help you." The woman started picking up the bricks and stacking them in a pile with those waiting to be used. A few had chipped at the edges from the fall. Lisha froze when she saw the woman noticing them. But the Lamanite woman shifted some of the other, more pristine bricks aside, then stacked the scuffed ones on the bottom.

"There! That should do it." She dusted off her hands. "My name is Channah." She waited, expectant.

"I'm Lisha."

Channah's face lit with recognition and her mouth formed a round *oh*. Pink rose in her cheeks. "This was your home, wasn't it? I am so sorry."

Lisha looked away. The children had stopped tossing their rag ball around and were staring at the two women.

"Come inside and have something to drink and a bite to eat," Channah said.

Lisha didn't know how to feel being invited into her own home. Amulon's wife was not at all what she'd expected.

THAT EVENING, Lisha baked bread in her favorite glazed pot. Mera had crafted it for her years ago. It was one of her few treasured items, one she thought she'd lost forever. Beside her, in a woven basket, were several of her other treasures. Lisha swallowed a lump in her throat, remembering how they'd come to be in her possession again. She rose from a low stump and lifted the lid to check the bread's progress.

"Mother!" Alma the Younger called. He walked up, carrying a pot of his own. Zilpah, Helaman, Yael, and Shiblon ambled up to the cookfire as well. Zilpah, being great with the child, did not toil at the riverside with the other women. Lisha gave her a hug and gestured to her seat. Zilpah sank onto it gratefully, and Shiblon crowded against her, trying to get into her nonexistent lap.

"We brought a pot of stew," Zilpah said, nodding to Alma, her husband.

"Wonderful," said Lisha. She shifted some of the coals to make space, and her son tucked it in close to the bread. His eyes lingered on the pot, narrowing for a moment.

"You should rest, mother." Motioning to Helaman, he called, "Drag a log over from the forest for your grandmother to sit on. Evi can help you; she's hunting mushrooms."

While the boy darted away, Yael scurried after him. "Keep your sister close!" Zilpah called.

Alma the Elder trudged in from his day's work building huts and shepherding his people. He grabbed Helaman and Yael in for a quick hug as they hurried past.

"Hello, father," Alma the Younger said stiffly. The space between them always seemed strained of late. Lisha wasn't even sure at this point what issue they were grappling with.

The elder Alma nodded at his son, then turned to Lisha, dropping a kiss on her forehead. "You need help with dinner?" He gave an exploratory sniff toward the fire. "Smells wonderful." He cocked his head to the side. "That pot...how did you get Mera's pot?"

Lisha looked up at her husband, emotion welling within her. "That's not all." With a heart tender for Channah, she opened the basket the Lamanite woman had given her. Lisha's journals lay inside, the parchment scrolls carefully stacked one atop another. Beside them was a roll of cloth tied with a ribbon.

"Oh!" Lisha reached for it and unrolled the cloth. It was a small stack of embroidered napkins sewn after a fashion foreign to her. Tears rose in her eyes.

"What is it, sweetheart?" Alma asked, running a weary hand across Lisha's back.

"My journals, all of them," Lisha said, "and now this, too. She must've tucked them in when I wasn't looking."

Zilpah peered inside. "Those are beautiful," she said. "I've never seen any like them. Where did you get them?"

Lisha swallowed again. "From Amulon's wife. Her name is Channah, and she's not how I thought she'd be. She's nothing like him. She's kind, gentle, compassionate."

Alma the Younger's eyes sharpened. "Don't run away with yourself, mother. You're grateful because she gave you your journals and a few napkins. Fine. But she stole your entire home."

Lisha paused, taking a deep breath. "She was kind, and she didn't have to be. She's not like Amulon. She even seemed sad, as if she had no choice in the matter. Which, of course, she doesn't." Lisha looked up. "I think...I think maybe we could be friends. Perhaps we could be answers to each other's prayers."

Alma the Younger scoffed. "Like she prays. She's a Lamanite, mother. She knows nothing of our ways or of our God. And even if she somehow did, why would the Lord listen to her prayers? We are the ones who are enslaved."

"Alma," his father said in a quiet, thought-carrying voice. "The Lord hears all His children. And the more we pray, the more we become closer to one another and grow to understand each other, our different lives, and our different ways. I pray that we can find peace and understanding someday."

Young Alma huffed out his breath. "At this point, I'd settle for freedom."

"I don't understand it," Zilpah said. "I know we're not perfect, but we're a good people. We've tried so hard to serve the Lord. Why would He let us be enslaved? We are suffering so much."

"The Lord chastens even the righteous. He tries our patience and our faith, that we may grow," Alma the Elder said.

"Of course," said Alma the Younger. "But surely God would not abandon us to slavery just so we could learn a lesson."

Alma the Elder's face tightened. "You know that's not what I meant."

"I think," Lisha said with a small hesitation, "God allows us free will, the freedom to choose and direct our lives."

"We can't direct our lives if we're enslaved," Young Alma said.

"Well, that's where you're wrong," Lisha said. "We can always choose how to think, how to feel, and how to respond. We can choose to share with our neighbors, to offer prayers and words of kindness and comfort. Even if other choices are taken from us."

Alma the Younger rubbed his forehead and sighed.

"But with free will," Lisha continued, "also comes oppression and suffering because some force their will on others."

Her son caught her eye. "Free will must matter a lot to God if He allows these terrible things to happen. I saw Amulon beating a woman today because some water from her jug slopped onto his sandals. It isn't right."

"The Lord will deliver us," Alma the Elder maintained. "Just hold faithful and continue in prayer. The Lord will inspire us on what we should do. Sometimes that may mean we take up arms and fight, other times, we wait, and, as we have seen in times past, we escape. Until we know the answer and find a path forward, we continue in hope, faith, and prayer." He reached over and checked the heavy pot of stew, which was starting a sluggish bubble.

"Shift the bread out of the fire, Alma, would you?" Lisha asked, looking around as Helaman returned, dragging a log with Eviana, who carried a mushroom bag looped over her wrist. They propped the log against some stones, creating a makeshift seat for Lisha. "Thank you," she said, then sank down on the log. Shiblon left his mother's side and climbed into Lisha's lap.

"Come, sweet boy," Lisha murmured. "Grandma will tell you a story."

THINGS ONLY GREW WORSE for the people of Helam. Amulon was crazed with envy at what Alma had built and the respect his people gave him. He gave the people more and more pointless tasks, setting Lamanite warriors over them as taskmasters, forcing them to haul stone, construct buildings, and spend countless hours carving the new buildings' walls, whether made of wood or stone. He expected the women to keep the cobbled lanes swept spotless, no matter that dirt constantly blew in from the fields. The children were forced to weave linens and rugs until their fingers were red and raw.

All the while, Lisha, Alma, and the others cried out to God. In her free moments, Lisha whispered words of comfort to the other Nephites, sharing small loaves, charred fish, or whatever scant bounty she was able to obtain. She knew Amulon watched her as he watched all the people of Helam, growing angrier as they continued to thrive.

Once, when she and Sarika broke bread together at midday, at the edge of the riverside where they were still crafting mud bricks, Channah and the girl from her cottage appeared, darting unexpectedly from the woods that lined the city walls. "My husband doesn't know I am here," Channah confided. She opened a small bag and pulled out a tiny crock of wild strawberry jam. "I thought we might share this. This is Mariah, my son's wife. You've met Lemish?"

Lisha nodded, recalling a conversation she'd had with Channah's son the last time she'd hauled bricks to her former home. He'd asked why the Nephite men bowed their heads over their midday meal. He'd also noticed Lisha doing the same when she'd left their cottage that first time, pouring out a silent, heartfelt prayer of gratitude for Channah's kindness. He asked her what it meant. She'd felt hesitant to explain at all. Wasn't she courting danger to tell the son of Amulon about prayer and faith? But he seemed so earnest, so sincere. He listened, too, though she wasn't sure what he thought or if he felt anything at all.

"Hello, Mariah," she said to Lemish's wife. The girl blushed but stared openly at Lisha. "This is my friend, Sarika."

Sarika smiled her usual welcome. Then the women set out their small meal. Sarika and Lisha caught each other's gaze. Lisha hesitated, wanting to pray, but felt self-conscious and unsure, as if she were treading dangerous waters.

Channah smiled at her. "Isn't it your custom to bow your heads over your meal?" she asked. "Don't let our presence stop you."

Lisha smiled, feeling an upwelling of relief. Yet again, Channah shared kindness and understanding. Lisha started to pray, feeling her new friends' eyes on her, and as she said the words blessing the meal, she offered a silent expression of hope as well.

"What is going on here?" A male voice boomed, drowning out her reverent tones. It was Amulon. He stalked toward them, followed by lesser priests, and grabbed Channah by the arm, hauling her to her feet. "I've told you not to associate with these women," he said, his voice thick with contempt. "I'll not have their shallow beliefs and simple ways contaminate my family. Come." He directed the last word to Mariah, who flushed and rose to her feet. "If I hear of you consorting with the people of Helam again…" His voice lowered, and Lisha couldn't catch the end of his threat.

Channah and Mariah both looked shaken. Lisha gazed at them, willing her own hope, strength, and courage to somehow enter the pair. When Channah glanced back to her, Lisha was surprised to see a quiet strength reflected in her eyes.

"And you," Amulon snapped, whirling around to face Lisha and Sarika. He kicked their small meal aside. "Back to work."

Then he grabbed his wife and daughter-in-law and dragged them away.

DINAH, 121 BC, CITY OF ZARAHEMLA

A gasp came from the crowd rising above the murmurs of curious people gathered at the Temple steps. Two men walking beside an elderly woman made their way to the palace steps, where King Mosiah stood with Ammon and Limhi. She was regal with her snowy white hair, but her face, although wrinkled with age, was unmistakable.

"Sarai," Limhi whispered, looking from one man to the other, "Jair? Neria?"

Limhi reached out and pulled both men into a tearful embrace. His head was bowed in front of Sarai.

Sarai reached out and touched Limhi's face. "Where is your mother?"

Limhi brought his head up slowly as his shoulders shook. Tears were streaming down his cheeks, and the pain in his eyes told her what she had asked. Helam came to stand behind him, as did Dinah and Gideon. Limhi took a deep, shaky breath and whispered, "We lost her before our journey. There's much to tell, so very much." He nodded to his wife. "Dinah, my wife, and these are our children."

In the midst of their tearful reunion, Mosiah announced, "We must have a feast in celebration of the newcomers' arrival. We will call the people together tomorrow to read their records. First, our friends must eat and rest. They are weary travelers."

Limhi pulled a skin bag from his pack that contained a number of scrolls and plates, which held the records of his people in Shilom, and the thin plates of gold the explorers had found. "Oh King, my men uncovered these plates in a land once populated by a great civilization, now desolate with the bones of men and beast left moldering on the ground. We cannot read the writings." He handed the plates to the king. "Can you translate them?"

The king nodded. "I have the seer stones and the gift from God to translate."

Limhi handed him the remaining scrolls. "These are the words of Abinadi, the records of our people, and the record Zeniff kept in his journeys." Mosiah nodded his head, gratefully accepting the scrolls and plates.

"We need homes for these families, a place for their animals," Mosiah announced. People stepped forward, one after another, offering to help. "Once everyone has a home, let us begin preparation for a feast."

The reunions were sweet, introductions made and friendships rekindled. Tears were shed at the understanding they would not see some dear ones again in this life. The food was abundant and the feast ensured no one went to bed hungry. The lost people of Zeniff were home.

When King Mosiah came to the temple steps the following day, the merchants closed their shops and word spread quickly that the king was ready to read the records that Limhi had brought.

Each family gathered to hear, prepared to stay as long as was needed. King Mosiah read first the record of Zeniff from the time that they left Zarahemla. Then he read from scrolls that contained Abinadi's teachings. The final entry was that they had returned once again to Zarahemla. The reading of Zeniff's words took the people of Zarahemla back in time to when he left with families from the city and took his journey south to the land Nephi-Lehi. There were gasps, tears, and expressions of joy at different parts of the account. The story of King Noah brought sadness at the realization that a wicked king could do so much damage to a people.

Sarai was surrounded by family, and friends moved closer to comfort her as the words of Abinadi were read, and the account reached the tragic end of his mortal life. Jair and Neriah were comforted by their wives and children as they wept after hearing how their father met his death.

Mosiah held up the plates of pure gold. "I have spent the whole of the night interpreting these records, and they are of a people, like the Nephites, brought to this land by the hand of the Lord. They were called the Jaredites." He unfolded the story of a people more numerous than the hosts of Israel. The gold plates contained the entire account of their life and their turn to the wickedness that ended tragically. The people, stunned at how such a great civilization could fall and be completely destroyed, wept with sorrow.

As Mosiah read from Zeniff and Limhi's plates, there were joyful acclamations expressed at the miraculous escape of Alma and Limhi's people.

"Where is Alma?" One individual shouted from the crowd.

Limhi stood. "It was our desire to find his people or the land of Zarahemla. I sent fifty-three men to find them to help free us from the Lamanites. My men came back thinking the Jaredite land was what remained of Zarahemla. We mourned, thinking we were left as the last remaining Nephites among the numerous hosts of Lamanites. You can imagine our joy when Ammon and his men came to us. We still do not know where Alma and his people are, but we believe the Lord also watches over them and preserves them as He has us."

The people were spent after the emotions of the day, and a second feast was held to give the people time to contemplate and ponder the events that had impacted so many lives, for good and for bad. Tears were shed, and friends comforted one another in an effort to begin healing.

Their new life in Zarahemla had begun.

LISHA, 121 BC, CITY OF HELAM

*L*isha drove her stone trowel into the cold ground, loosening the hard soil, careful not to damage the small, misshapen root she was trying to remove. Women and children knelt in the field around her, on their knees, digging, digging, digging.

"My fingers ache," Eviana said, rubbing her hands. They were rough and pale from the chill air.

"I know," Lisha said, "but we need food."

Eviana's small face looked more angular than it had months ago before Amulon and the Laminate army had invaded. Now, there was far too much work, much of it frivolous, and far too little food to go around.

Several children, younger than Evi, huddled near their mothers, crying softly as if they knew that grumbles and groans were no use but couldn't stop their tears all the same.

"Go cheer up little Malachi and his sisters," Lisha said, "then we'll sing a song."

Music was one of the few things Lisha felt was still her own, one of the few things that couldn't be taken from her. That and prayer. The scrawny root she was tugging on finally came free, dusting her with a shower of dirt. She placed it in the basket beside her and sighed. They'd need quite a lot more if they were to make it through winter.

She rose, moving to an area where more frost-damaged tufts of green poked above the earth. As she moved, she felt the eyes of the Lamanite guards on her and sped up her pace. The last thing she wanted was a cuff on the back. They were gentler with the children, but not by much. Sarika and Shoshannah knelt around a broad swath of leaves, digging and tugging, their baskets as sparse as her own. She knelt beside them and joined the work. "Where's Talya?"

"I left her with Zilpah and some of the others, to help tend to the younger children so their mothers can work."

Lisha nodded. "Good idea. We need all the help we can get."

Shoshannah freed a root pocked with rot and tossed it aside with a grunt of disgust. She wiped her hands on her apron and glanced around at the guards. "I don't see why Amulon thinks we need guarding. We're as hungry as they are. They should be helping."

"Perhaps he fears we'll keep the roots for ourselves," Sarika said. "It's what he would do."

Lisha didn't contradict her; her words, however bitter, were true. "We need to lift our spirits," she said. "Sarika, could you start a song for us?"

Shoshannah looked startled by the sudden change in conversation, but Sarika nodded.

"You're right," she said. "Let's sing. But you lead us. We'll join in."

Lisha's voice, gentle, but strong, drifted across the field, a seed of hope carried by the wind. The other women lifted their heads and straightened their shoulders. After a moment, their voices twined with Lisha's. As they sang, hope swelled within them, their tasks seemed just a bit lighter, and they found themselves able to dig or pull a bit harder.

The guards shifted and looked at each other, unsure about this new development. One of them shrugged. "They're still working," he said. The others nodded and looked away.

Morning passed, and the piles of roots grew from tiny to small. The afternoon sun lent warmth to their bodies, and Lisha felt looser, less stiff. She smiled across the field at Hannah, who was working with several grandchildren, their voices still raised in song. Sometimes they sang rounds or echoing songs, so the music continued without wearing them all out.

Suddenly the music hushed. One of the younger women shot to her feet. "The men are coming!"

The guards stiffened, alert for trouble.

The baker's wife heaved herself from the ground.

Lisha peered into the distance. It looked like the hunting party had returned, guarded by Lamanites, of course. She prayed they'd found meat and that no one was hurt during the hunt.

"Back to work!" a guard barked, and the women resumed toiling. There was no singing now, only a palpable tension as they continued digging and tugging, with occasional hopeful glances toward their men.

As the group neared, Lisha saw her husband in the center, leading them. Several men carried a deer. It hung upside down, its feet strapped to a stout branch. Alma the Younger had a brace of rabbits hanging from his belt. One man carried a coon by the tail. A wash of relief swept over the women. The men were safe, and there would be meat for dinner.

"You," the lead guard commanded Asher and the other men carrying the deer. "Take that kill to Amulon." He nodded for several other guards to accompany them. Lisha noticed their belts bore far more rabbits than did the Nephite men, not, she was certain because they'd gotten the rabbits themselves. She sighed. At least they would have some meat to share among their families.

"The rest of you clean up and come with me. We need you to haul stone for Amulon's temple."

Several of the children broke away from their mothers and ran to their fathers' arms.

Lisha stood. "Surely they can take a moment to greet their families."

The guard snorted. "You have five minutes." He and the other guards strode away, talking amongst themselves while Asher and the other men lumbered away with the deer.

Alma the Younger watched them go, his expression dark.

"Father," he said, "Why don't we leave? Limhi was brave enough to lead his people away. You left the Land of Nephi all those years ago. Why don't you leave now?"

"This is our home," Alma said. "We built this place from nothing. Where would we go? To another valley to rebuild and be enslaved again?"

"Zarahemla," Alma the Younger said. "You've spoken of it before. Abinadi spoke of it. Perhaps Limhi's people are there now. We'd be safe there."

"Abinadi is dead," said Rafa. "We saw him burn. Who's to say if Zarahemla still stands? Or if there's a prophet there or if we'd even be welcome?"

"This is a different situation from when we fled Shilom. Amulon hates me and would love an excuse to hurt me, and that could mean he'd do it by harming those I love. The guards watch our every move here. Until I hear differently from the Lord, we stay," Alma said. "I'm not having our families slaughtered by angry Lamanites."

"Are you afraid of losing power if we flee to Zarahemla?" Alma the Younger accused.

"Son," Lisha said reproachfully, "You know that's not true."

"I refused to be king many years ago," Alma the Elder reminded him.

"Alma," Lisha said softly to her son, "you may not remember this, but when we left Shilom, it was because the Lord warned us. He commanded us to flee."

Alma the Younger shook his head, glancing around at the families clinging to one another. "I don't know how much longer we can take this."

Lisha looked and witnessed what her son saw as well - frail bodies, clinging hands, despairing glances. "We must continue to pray for deliverance," she said. "The Lord will guide us."

Alma the Elder nodded. "Let's pray together now." The group

huddled closer together, folding arms and bowing heads. Even the children squeezed their eyes shut. "O Lord," Alma said in a hushed voice so as not to provoke the guards. "Please grant us strength and courage in this difficult time. Please see us through this; bless us to have enough food, and enough warmth to survive the winter. Lord, if it be Thy will, deliver us from the terrible bonds of slavery. Thy people love thee. We pledge our hearts to Thee even now. We know of Thy loving kindness. Please deliver us, according to Thy will. We lift up our hearts in praise and hope..."

"What is this?" a sharp voice demanded.

Amulon strode up to Alma and shoved him in the shoulders. Alma stumbled, his head snapped back, and the prayer died on his lips. A crowd of Lamanite warriors stood alongside Amulon, who had arrived while Alma and the others were talking. Lisha wondered what they'd overheard. If they'd heard her son, she feared what they'd do to him.

Amulon's wife, Channah, stood with their son, Lemish, and several of the other Lamanitish women and their older children, apparently out for an afternoon stroll to warm themselves with activity.

Alma said nothing, just returned Amulon's florid fury with calm, stony restraint.

"You were supposed to return to Helam, not dally with your wives and stir up rebellion," Amulon said. He stepped toward Alma, who did not move away. "There will be no more gathering without close supervision." He cast a withering glare at the guards who stood some distance away, looking sheepish. Then he poked Alma in the chest. "And there will be no more prayer on penalty of death. I'll not have you fomenting discontent among my people."

"Your people?" Alma the Younger breathed.

Lisha tensed.

Alma placed his hand on his son's chest. "Enough, my boy," he said, ignoring Alma the Younger's infuriated exasperation.

Amulon snorted. "Ten stripes," he said, "for the *boy's* impertinence."

Lamanite guards grabbed Alma the Younger by the arms, tearing his shirt over his head.

"Wait!" Channah cried. The women with her looked as stricken as Lisha felt. "Please, Amulon." She knelt before him, her hands on his robes. "He's young, barely older than our Lemish. Young men can't always keep their counsel, can they?" Lemish shifted uncomfortably but met his father's gaze. "Please, just a warning this time."

Amulon's frown deepened. He placed his hand beneath Channah's jaw and tipped her head upward, his fingers lingering on the soft, vulnerable flesh of her neck. Then he sighed. "Very well. For you, my dear. Let's be off. I grow weary of this Nephite nonsense."

But Lisha didn't miss the evil look he shared with his head guard, and her fear did not abate.

As the Lamanite party strode away, Amulon said in a deliberately careless, offhand way, "Oh, good hunting, Alma. On the way here, I passed your men carrying a deer. My family and my warriors certainly appreciate it. By the way, we need your women to weave thick woolen blankets for us. It's growing very cold." He nodded to a guard. "And grab some furs from their camps. These Nephites are accustomed to cold and privation; they'll not need them."

Lisha couldn't help glancing at Channah. She looked sick. Her son's gaze was at his feet. From his profile, he looked disgusted as well.

As soon as the Lamanite group was out of earshot, Alma the Younger wheeled on his father. "Now we can't even pray!"

"Son, even if we cannot raise our voices to the Lord, we can pour out our hearts to Him. We do that anyways, all day long," Lisha said.

"The Lord will hear our cries, even if they are silent," Alma the Elder said. "He knows the thoughts of our hearts. And He has promised to strengthen us so that we might bear our burdens."

"When I was praying this morning," Lisha said, "I felt a great sense of calm and comfort, a certainty that the Lord will hear us, that He will deliver us."

"I felt much the same," said Sarika. "We have been through great trials over the course of our lives. I lost my parents. Noah and his priests caused great harm among us. We barely survived with our lives. Through all of that, the Lord has been there for us."

"This blessing I lay upon us all, by the will of the Lord," Alma said, "He will deliver us. Until He does, we must lift up our hearts and be of good cheer. He knows we are faithful to Him. He knows we have covenanted to follow Him, no matter the cost, to build our lives upon Him and to fill our lives with the truths of the gospel. We must continue faithful. He will continue faithful to us." Alma raised his gaze to the heavens. "This very morning, the Lord's voice came unto me. His heart is with us. He promised that He will deliver us from bondage."

"But when?"

Alma looked pained. "I don't know."

"Lift up your heads and be of good comfort, for I know of the covenant which ye have made unto me; and I will covenant with my people and deliver them out of bondage. And I will also ease the burdens which are put upon your shoulders, that even you cannot feel them upon your backs, even while you are in bondage; and this will I do that ye may stand as witnesses for me hereafter, and that ye may know of a surety that I, the Lord God, do visit my people in their afflictions."

The voice of the Lord had come to the Nephites many times over the past several weeks as they poured out their hearts in anguish. Lisha clung to these words, even when Amulon's men beat her son only a day after Amulon had promised his wife he wouldn't. The only thing Lisha and all the people of Helam had was their faith. They clung to it, lifting their thoughts in prayer. It was so clear, in the hope in their eyes and the radiance in their expressions, despite their oppression and abuse. Amulon and his men breathed out threatenings and tormented them at every turn, short of killing them. He wouldn't allow it unless he or his men heard them pray. The fact was, Amulon needed them to support his life of ease.

Channah saw all this, no matter how he tried to hide it. Lisha noticed her, and several of the other Lamanites women and their adult children watching them. Lisha had had enough experience with

Channah and her kindness that she knew something else was happening.

When, in the week after Alma the Younger's beating, Channah and several other women brought him linen poultices made of onion and herbs that her husband would have rather eaten, Lisha and Zilpah accepted them with gratitude. They welcomed the women into their tents and shared what little bread they had.

"How are you happy?" Channah asked Lisha one morning while they changed Alma's bandages. "You're enslaved. You're abused. Yet you and your people still manage to find hope and peace. I don't understand it."

"You've been through much the same, Channah," Lisha said. "How did you survive it?"

Channah's brow creased. "I suppose I remembered the things my mother taught me, to be strong, to be kind. And I reminded my friends, who were in the same situation as me. We taught our children what we knew." She winced, looking at Alma's raw back. "I know this hurts, but it will heal."

Lisha did not ask how Channah had gained this knowledge of plants. She felt a flood of compassion, coupled with gratitude, as she watched Channah's expert care. "You *are* kind. You've been kind to me from the moment you arrived. Thank you."

Channah's eyes glistened. "I am so sorry for what my husband does. If he were a better man, more like your Alma, none of this would happen. And maybe we would all be happy and find peace. Is that the difference? Is that why your people can find hope and peace? Because you have good men?"

Lisha thought for a moment. There was a certain truth in that. But she had more truth to share. She took Channah's hand. Zilpah listened from the corner, nursing her new baby. "It's true," she said. "There are many good men among us. They care for us, love us, and protect us to the best of their ability."

A tear rolled down Channah's cheek, and she lowered her gaze.

"But, Channah, that is not all."

Channah looked up, hope and confusion mingling on her face.

"Channah, we believe that there is a God, that He will send His son to atone for our sins, to make all wrongs right. We believe He strengthens us, guides us, helps us grow. He cares for us, Channah. He cares for our pain. He cares for *you*."

Channah blinked away more tears. "For me? Why would he care for me? I'm not a Nephite. I'm not one of His chosen. I know my ancestors did not believe these things. Why should the God of the Nephites care about *me*?"

"Because He's not only the God of the Nephites. He's the God of us all. And any who follow Him will find hope, comfort, and strength."

"But you're slaves, and you're still faithful," Channah said. "Why doesn't He free you?"

Lisha offered a brief silent plea for help, then continued. "We may not understand the Lord's timing in our lives. We may not know when relief will come. Much as we wish we could, we cannot control Amulon or his Lamanite warriors. But we can choose how to lead our own lives. We choose faith over fear, happiness over misery, hope over despair, and gratitude over bitterness."

Channah nodded.

"The Lord has promised to ease our burdens," Zilpah said from the corner, her voice small, but sure, "that we cannot even feel them upon our backs. And He will ultimately deliver us."

LISHA'S WORDS of hope spread among the Lamanite women. They returned in ones and twos to meet with her and Zilpah, eager to learn. Others met discreetly with Sarika, Hannah, or Shoshannah, bringing them what food they could spare, and the occasional blankets that would not be noticed going missing.

Meanwhile, Alma the Younger's recovery continued. Channah's son, Lemish, took his spot among the men, carrying stone. This enraged Amulon. More than once, Lemish arrived to labor, bearing bruises that did not come from the work. But he refused to stop coming. Two other Lamanite men his age joined as well. Even when

Alma the Younger rejoined the work crew, his movements slow and ginger, Lemish continued hauling stone.

Amulon threatened to make them slaves. But so far, he had not. It seemed he hoped to persuade his son to follow his ways. He forced Lemish to witness beatings, clearly hoping to either intimidate him or to remind him of Lamanite superiority, forgetting that he, himself, was of Nephite descent. When Lemish reminded him, he earned another bruise on his cheek.

"Lemish says Amulon claims that how you live makes you Nephite," Alma the Elder explained to Lisha one night. "He says we live as animals, that none but the simple-minded would believe in a God they can't even see, and that if He existed, He would have freed us long ago."

"He has eased our burdens," Lisha said. "Did you tell Lemish that?"

Alma smiled. "I didn't need to. Lemish told me himself. I think he is growing to believe. He's seen the hope we have and the strength it gives us. He's experienced his burdens lifting as his faith has grown. He's been oppressed all his life, his mother enslaved. Now the fear, anger, and resentment are lifting from them. At first, he couldn't understand it. How could he not feel angry, hurt, and afraid when his father is the way he is?"

"He's abusive and cruel," Lisha said. "He takes pleasure in it."

Alma took her hand. "I'm sorry you have to know of these things."

Lisha lifted her chin. "I would rather know the truth. What did you tell Lemish?"

"I told him that God heals our hearts, even when others are doing wrong."

Lisha nodded. "He and his mother are sharing the Lord's message of happiness." She smiled. "I never dreamed good could come out of Amulon and the Lamanite army enslaving us. But it is. It really is."

LISHA AND CHANNAH, 120 BC, CITY OF HELAM

ime passed. Amulon's cruelty never abated. Lisha and Channah joined together in the quiet work of lifting souls. Lisha sang with Sarika, Hannah, and the other enslaved women. And, when Amulon forbade them to sing, they carried a song in their hearts, whispering to one another so they still shared the song. Their fingers grew tough and stiff from digging clay in the daytime and spinning or weaving cloth by firelight late into the night. Their bodies grew lean, but their spirits were not weak.

That night, when the men returned from their labors building Amulon's temple, ragged and worn but bright-eyed nonetheless, Alma took Lisha by the hands. She was cutting limp carrots and potatoes for a stew, but he pulled her from her task. "The voice of the Lord has come to me," he said, his face aglow. "I've already told most of the men. Asher and Rafa and our son spread the word while we worked."

"What is it, Alma? What's happening?" Nighttime sounds seemed loud in that moment: the shush-shush sway of branches, bereft of their leaves, the clatter of cooking from nearby camps. Lisha felt a lift in her heart. She clutched Alma's tattered shirtfront. "Alma?"

He smiled down at her. "Always so eager. That's my girl." Then he grew serious. "The Lord has told us to be of good comfort."

"Yes?"

"And that He will deliver us out of bondage."

"Praise Him," Lisha said, pulling Alma closer. "But when? How much longer? Amulon grows restless. Channah fears he will kill someone. She fears it will be her or Lemish."

Alma nodded. "On the morrow. Tomorrow we will be free. You must tell Channah. Find some excuse to see her. Bring her something. Will she be able to tell the others?"

Lisha nodded. "She will find a way."

Alma added. "Those who want to come must bring what they can and meet us before the sun rises."

LISHA WASN'T sure Amulon believed her excuse. The napkins she brought to Channah were her own, the ones Channah had given her soon after Amulon first took over her home. But she'd wrapped a meager loaf in them and pretended it was to honor the wife of the king of Helam.

"Thank you, my dear." Channah accepted the gift with such royal bearing that Lisha wondered if she might have been a queen by birth. They'd never talked about her life back in Shemlon before she'd been taken by Amulon and the wicked priests.

"Yes, yes, yes," Amulon said, his eyes gleaming from his hard face. "We appreciate the gesture of ah...submission and servitude." He waved his hand at the small gift in a dismissive way. "But I assume you have some message from your husband? Some demand for kindness or mercy?" He laughed at his own attempt at humor.

"No, my lord," Lisha bowed her head. "Only a gift to honor you and your family."

"Well then, be on your way."

Lisha rose, hoping against hope that Channah would understand she needed a moment with her.

Channah did. After Lisha passed out the doorway, she heard Channah call out. "Oh, she forgot her clothes!"

Lisha waited outside in the dark, sheltering under a tree, her heart pounding. *Please, Lord, help her find a way to come out here.* She could hear their continued conversation.

"What does it matter?" Amulon asked. "They're barely rags."

"They belonged to her grandmother," Channah invented wildly.

"All the more reason to throw them out. Even better, toss them into the fire."

Lord, please. She needs you.

"You know how sentimental those Nephite women are. She'll be bawling and moping around for weeks. You think I want to see that? I need her to clean our cottage tomorrow. And what do these rags mean to me? Nothing."

Channah rushed out the door, calling after Lisha. "You forgot these!" She spotted her under the tree and hurried over.

Lisha took the proffered napkins, barely casting them a glance. "Channah," she whispered. "The Lord has promised to deliver us."

"Yes," Channah replied, looking earnest. "I know. And I know the waiting is even harder for you and the others than it is for me."

Lisha shook her head. "You're in as much danger as we are, perhaps more." She grasped Channah's hand. "But not anymore. The voice of the Lord came unto Alma. We must prepare tonight. Deliverance will come tomorrow. Tomorrow, we escape."

Color drained from Channah's cheeks, but she looked determined. "I will be with you as well as Lemish and many others. But first, my husband needs a drink." She glanced back to his silhouette in the doorway. "Perhaps several. We will come to your camp in the early morning."

ALL NIGHT LONG, the people of Helam gathered their flocks, their essential belongings, grain, and food. Lisha wondered at the intensity that filled their people, the fierceness of their faith. Gathering the flocks was difficult. The sheep were not accustomed to moving at nighttime. A few already had lambs, but miraculously, the small creatures remained quiet and calm. The ground was soft and wet from an early thaw, and the river continued its sluggish movement along the borders of Helam. It sometimes glazed back at night or carried chunks of ice from the north. Their journey to Zarahemla would be cold, wet, and challenging. But no one minded that at all. Hope-filled faces shone in the moonlight as they all worked together to gather the flocks.

When morning came, exhaustion should have bowed their shoulders, but they stood tall. Lisha and Alma stood side by side with Evi, Alma the Younger, and his small family. Zilpah carried their youngest in a wrap on her chest.

"Lemish is coming." Alma the Younger said, nodding his chin toward the edge of camp. "And his mother."

True enough, Channah and the other Lamanite believers hiked into camp, their backs laden with goods. Lisha rushed over and hugged her friends.

"My husband sleeps heavy this morning," Channah said. "All the warriors do and not because of drink. I believe the Lord has caused a deep sleep to fall on them all."

"I'm frightened," Channah's friend, Isa, said.

"The Lord will deliver you, just as He is delivering us all," Alma promised.

She nodded, exchanging a strained look with Channah.

"Our husbands stole us from our families," Channah explained. "They were cruel, heartless. But sometimes, they were also kind. They're all we know. As strange as it seems, it's difficult to leave them."

Lisha gathered the woman's hands into her own. "You are one of us now. You all are. And the Lord has promised His help. You will find peace and comfort; I am sure of it."

The woman buried her head in Lisha's shoulder, drawing on her strength.

Meanwhile, the whole company gathered, awaiting Alma's orders. He turned to face them. "We went through terrible things at the hands of Noah," he said. "When we fled the Land of Nephi, all we had was our faith, our belief that the Lord was there for us, that He would keep his promises. The Lord commanded us to leave, and we obeyed. Now, He commands us to leave this place we have built with our own hands – this haven we have sacrificed to create, this home that has been taken from us. He delivered us from Noah and his wicked priests. He will deliver us now."

They offered a shared prayer. Channah's eyes met Lisha's with quiet determination. Channah held the hand of her only living child, Lemish, and he held the hand of his wife, Miriam. Together, they rallied the families around them and followed Alma as he led them away from the City of Helam. Miraculously, the sheep, goats, and chickens seemed to move relatively quietly through the crisp morning air, gathering dew on their hooves and feathers as they walked through the tall grasses. The sounds were not out of place: lowing, bleating, shuffling.

At first, the backward glances came every few seconds as if each step brought them closer to being discovered instead of being freed. As time passed, so grew their confidence, and the company moved swiftly. Babies taken from their slumbering beds were lulled back to sleep while children settled into a cadence of a fast walk. Fewer people glanced back, but Alma made his way forward and backward, checking their path. It was obvious that a large group had passed through.

"We must change our path from time to time, cross the creeks and rocky riverbeds to disguise our tracks," Alma spoke in a hushed voice to Lisha.

She turned to gaze for a moment at the trail they were leaving. Grass was trampled, and the path was evident. "When Amulon sees we are gone, he will easily track us." For a moment, her eyes held fear. Then peace settled over her again. "God delivered hundreds of thousands of Israelites from Pharaoh. Surely, He can deliver our small band from Amulon."

Alma took Lisha into a firm embrace and whispered, "Your faith is beautiful. You are beautiful." Alma took her strong and calloused fingers into his and kissed them tenderly.

He had given several men charge over groups of refugees and called them over for a quick meeting. Lisha remained by his side while most others made their way to the shade of the trees beside the river and sat down for a rest. Alma clapped each of his men on the shoulders and looked into their faces. There was a mixture of excitement mingled with some anxious smiles.

"Have faith," he said, "like our fathers of old when Moses led them out of bondage. Pharaoh pursued them, but God protected the people with His mighty hand. He has delivered us this day and will cover us as well. Asher and Rafa," he continued, "send your fastest runners ahead. We will need a report. In the meantime, I will find a good place to cross to the other side of this creek and set up camp."

Asher and Rafa gave curt nods and left to complete their assignment. Lisha smiled at Alma, and he continued, "The Lord is leading us. You see to the needs of the people, my love."

"Of course," Lisha said. She made her way through the group huddled under the trees, sharing words of encouragement, hugs, smiles, and quiet song. She found Evi helping Zilpah tend her small children while Alma the Younger spoke in quiet tones with Lemish and his wife. Channah offered her a water skin and some dried fruit, which Lisha accepted gratefully.

"Are we really free?" Channah asked. "Will we ever really be free?" She looked wistful. "It's been so long; I almost can't imagine."

Lisha squeezed Channah's arms. Chirping melodies rose around them of birds taking in the warmth of the day. "We will be free, Channah," she said. "The Lord has promised, and He always keeps His word."

Channah's mouth tightened, and her eyes sparkled as she held back tears. "I'll never see my father again." Lisha embraced her. Channah wept bitter tears.

Moments later, Alma returned with a jubilant smile. "There's a valley up ahead where we can stop this night. It has one entrance and will be easy to guard and difficult for Amulon to find."

He rallied the people and led them through the creek and into a pristine valley filled with grasses for the animals to eat and soft ground for the people to sleep. A shout rang out. "The valley of Alma, for He led our way in the wilderness." Cheers of agreement echoed from the group.

Lisha and Channah came to stand beside Alma. "Today, God has delivered us. We prayed for this day. Even our Lamanite friends prayed for this day. We have made a covenant and promise to do all God has asked of us. We will live in thanksgiving from this day on for His goodness and mercy in freeing us from slavery."

Channah grasped Lisha's hand. "We too have been slaves, taken from our families when we were young girls, and made to bear children and become wives to men we did not love." Tears began to fall from her cheeks. "We feel love from you and from your God, and it brings us a joy we have never before felt." She glanced over at Lisha. "You are our people now."

Lisha pulled Channah into a tight embrace in view of the entire group. "Let us thank God for His mercy on us this day."

All bowed their heads, and Alma spoke the words they all felt in their hearts: gratitude, mercy, freedom, deliverance, and thanks. A song began in the back of the crowd and quickly spread as each voice joined in unison, expressing love and praise unto God.

IT WAS EARLY when Alma stirred. Lisha's eyes opened sleepily as she heard the rustling of grass and the burbling of the river that wound through the valley. She reached out to grasp his sleeve, and he turned. His expression was all she needed. "The Lord is speaking to you."

Alma nodded.

She watched him walk away from the camp and make his way up the steep rocky hillside. His silhouette slowly ascended till he stood atop the bluff. He knelt. He was there for some time, and Lisha's heart swelled in her chest. She loved him more than life. She reminded herself to tell him that more often. A large moon gave light to the valley of Alma, and she wrapped her arms around her knees and looked out over the camp that slept beneath a blanket of stars. She loved her people too. Memories of their escape, her trials, loss, hardship and then a change of heart. Faith and peace. Light and joy. Love and acceptance. And a new friend.

Alma stood and ran back to the camp. Slightly alarmed, Lisha began waking those around her. The sky was turning from inky black to a deep gray-blue. Clouds that were once dark, shapeless forms in the night sky were taking on a slight glow from a sun that was rising somewhere outside of their protected valley. Alma walked purposefully to Lisha and their family camp.

"It's time to move. The Lord has told me that Amulon and his men are coming. But the Lord will stop him here in this place to pursue us no more. We must make haste and leave now."

Alma announced the news to the camp and it didn't take long for the whole valley to empty of its temporary guests. He set sentries at their rear to watch for the Lamanite army the Lord told him was coming.

Later in the day, a large, billowing cloud formed over the group and turned darker as they day wore on. As nighttime approached, the storm behind them filled the night sky with flashes of light and sent thunder rumbling past them to echo off the surrounding hills. The nearly constant lightning and sounds of a terrible storm kept them up all that night. In the morning, Alma's men returned from their watch of the valley.

Aaron looked grim. Lisha grasped Alma's arm in concern. Alma the Younger stood with them, alert and wary. But Aaron's news brought swift relief.

"The river flooded the valley," Aaron said. "Much of Amulon's army was swept away. The rest are prevented from pursuing us by the raging water. We have some time."

Relief swept over Lisha. "Thanks be to God," she said, gratitude rising in her. She turned to her husband. "So often, I thought I knew what I needed. We believe we should be delivered from suffering, oppression, pain or struggles in the moment. But the Lord sees and understands things we cannot." She felt her son's gaze. "If we had fought for our freedom or even fled before now, we would have suffered great loss. Many of our people would have died at the hands of the Lamanites. Instead, the Lord has delivered us, and not one of us is lost or harmed. Praise Him." Then almost as an afterthought, she added. "He did it this time with a terrible storm."

She gazed back the way they'd come. The grass, trampled by their group, now stood straight and tall. Any sign of their passage had been erased in the rain. "Even if they pass through the river, they'll never track us now." She took her husband's hand and confidently walked with him as he led the people, by the hand of the Lord, toward Zarahemla.

As they made their way forward, one of the runners rushed up to them, sweaty and out of breath. He bent double, his hands on his knees. Once he regained his strength, he looked up, his chest still heaving. "Alma, we see it off in the far distance," he gasped, shaking his head. "You won't believe it."

"What is it, son?" Alma asked.

He shook his head again. "I've never seen the like...homes, buildings, wells; they stretch on forever."

LISHA, DINAH, CHANNAH 120 BC, CITY OF ZARAHEMLA

*L*isha couldn't believe her eyes. Zarahemla sprawled before them, a huge city teeming with families, shopkeepers, and a standing army of Nephite warriors ready to defend it all. An exhilarating blast of the Shofar horn rang out. As they neared the city, the gates flew open, and a host of people poured out.

At the front of them all strode Limhi, accompanied by a gentle-looking woman. Helam walked alongside them, holding a young girl's hand, his hair grayer and his movements slower than when they'd last seen him decades before. But there was no mistaking those square shoulders and that determined face. Lisha's breath caught in her throat. She and Alma shared a delighted look. She ran forward, eager to see her friends and to find Tamar and her long-lost sister, Sarai.

She met Limhi in the middle of the group and threw her arms around him. "This must be your wife!"

Limhi nodded proudly. "Dinah, meet Lisha," he said, "a great friend of my mother."

Dinah gave Lisha a tight hug, knowing she'd made another new friend. Nearby, Alma and Helam were catching up. Helam threw his arm around Alma the Younger. "You're a father now?"

Alma the Younger beamed at Helam. "I named my oldest after you.

Helaman," he called. "Come meet your namesake." Their boy came running up, eager to meet the man his family had so many stories about.

Lisha turned back to Limhi and Dinah. "Where is Tamar? I want to show her our family."

"I'm right here," the little girl with Helam piped up.

"Oh!" Lisha flushed with pleasure, looking to Helam. "Well, hello there!" She knelt before the girl. "And where's your Momma?"

The girl's shoulders shrugged, and, with a shy dip of her gaze, she responded. "She's with the angels."

Lisha felt the joy drain out of her. She rose and shared a sorrowful gaze with Helam and Alma.

Helam's face took on a look of pained joy. "Tamar and I wed a decade ago, although it seems not long ago. In a miraculous gift from the Lord, she conceived and bore twins. Our son, Helam the Younger, never took a breath, and Tamar failed to recover from the ordeal. Tamar is the surviving twin and becomes more of her mother each day." Tamar squeezed his hand and smiled up at him, wiping a tear from her cheek.

Lisha embraced him, feeling comfort in the tightness of his hug and hoped he felt the same.

"We had many good years," Helam said as Lisha stepped back. "She is never far from our hearts and finds ways to show us she is nearby. We feel her presence." He looked down at Tamar. "Doesn't she?"

Tamar nodded vigorously, then reached her slender hand out to grasp Lisha's. "You knew my Momma?" With a sincere whisper, she added, "Will you tell me stories, too? Papa tells me at night before I sleep, but I want to hear about my mother from you too."

"She was, is, my friend. A dear sister, and I would certainly like to tell you what I remember about her. About why I loved her."

"I know Momma is happy where she is because she gets to be with little Helam. He was born with me but didn't get to grow up with me."

Lisha couldn't hold back the well of tears that began to overflow. Her heart hurt and it felt as if a strap of leather was circling her throat and tightening with each new revelation. She began to weep, still clutching little Tamar's hand while reaching her arm around Helam's shoulders. His face pulled into a pained grimace, his breath came ragged and halting.

"Papa, Momma is here," Tamar said as she tugged on his hand, looking over at the temple steps. She pointed, then dropped his hand and waved. "She is smiling and standing next to a man."

Limhi and Dinah turned where Tamar had pointed.

Tamar dropped Lisha's hand and ran toward the temple, stopping at the bottom stair and gazing upward. No one dared move, they all just watched her. She stood there with her back to the group, nodded, and appeared to be having a conversation.

Alma the Younger shook his head. He turned to Helam. "I'm sorry for your loss, truly, but her stories about angels make her sound a little crazy."

Lisha's tear-stained face snapped back to Alma the Younger as he began to walk away from the group. "You may not see what she sees, but I believe her. I feel Tamar's spirit. She is here."

Alma shrugged and continued on his way.

THE INVITATION HAD COME from the king. Mosiah sent messages to each community in Zarahemla, inviting all to come to a feast honoring the reunification of their people. The city had grown over the decades, but they never forgot those who left with Zeniff so many years before. The people wearied him with questions of where they had gone. The expedition to seek out the lost ones had been successful. Limhi's people were now free and had joined their families in Zarahemla. Alma's people had found freedom as well, bringing many of the daughters of the Lamanites and their children. King Mosiah welcomed each new group with open arms and the city celebrated each new family.

Channah felt nervous. People had been very kind, but she heard the whispers. She and the other Lamanite women were dark and their young men looked much like the warriors that had battled the

Nephites, enslaved them, and caused so much pain and heartbreak. People wondered why they were there. She wasn't sure how to share their story in a way that would help the people of Zarahemla understand -- she had seen the hand of the Lord. She knew about Him; she *knew* Him. And she needed Him as much as any of them. Lisha had told her the color of her skin was a beautiful thing, different from others, true, but beautiful nonetheless, almost as beautiful as her spirit. Channah had come to believe her.

At the feast, King Mosiah spent several hours reading from the records Limhi and Alma's people brought back. The only group without a record was Channah's.

Mosiah placed the final record on the table. He rose and stood for a moment as if in deep thought. "Our loving Father in Heaven knows where each of His children are. Many years ago, when our people separated from those of our brothers, the Lamanites, His love for them never wavered. He has seen fit to bring some of them home with Alma's people, and we are blessed to have them here with us this night." He turned to Channah and motioned for her to rise. "Would you share the story of your people?"

Lemish stood and helped her to rise from the woven matt. She moved through the crowd until she reached the front, then turned to face the gathering. Mosiah placed a comforting hand on her shoulder before sitting. She took a deep breath and began at the beginning: their day at the lake. She talked about her parents, her Lamanite family, and how she wished to share what she knew about a loving Heavenly Father with them. Her joy overflowed as she expressed her love for the people of Alma and now those in Zarahemla.

As she finished her narrative, she saw her son, Lemish, rise up. He stood tall, with tears flowing down his face. She saw the pain in his expression. After a few moments, his wife rose to stand beside him.

He steadied his voice. "We never knew the story of our mothers. How they were taken from their home..." He paused, then, with difficulty, continued, "...ripped from their families." Admiration glowed in his face as he looked at his mother. "We honor our mothers and what they taught us. We no longer wish to be known by the name of our fathers."

King Mosiah stood and moved to stand beside Channah. "How many are there that are descendants of the King of the Lamanites?"

"We are twenty-three, with our children," Channah replied.

"You are one of us now, believers in the Lord who delivers," said King Mosiah. "Henceforth, you shall be known as Nephites. You have been a great leader among your people. We honor you as the royal daughter you are and ask that you represent your people and their needs here in Zarahemla."

Channah nodded and waited as he continued.

"The families who have arrived will each receive a plot of land where they can rebuild their lives. That includes your people."

Channah gathered her courage again. "We desire one thing more."

King Mosiah looked a little surprised but waited for her words.

"We desire to be baptized."

Limhi spoke before Mosiah had a chance to answer. "We have long desired to be baptized as well."

Mosiah turned to Alma. "Will you guide our people in this? Organize churches throughout the land? Ordain priests and teachers?"

Lisha squeezed Alma's hand. He nodded, his expression a mix of joy and determination. "Of course. Thank you."

SUNLIGHT ARCED through lacy branches that formed a canopy over the spring. Channah's heart was full as she joined with the people of Limhi, the people of Alma, and the long-time residents of Zarahemla in a sheltered cove. The waters were cold. But she and the others refused to wait.

When her turn came, she shared a joyful glance with Lisha, who stood arm-in-arm with a woman who looked just like her—her sister? Reunited at last? The thought warmed Channah's heart, and she longed for a similar reunion with her mother and father. Perhaps that day would come. In the meantime, she would follow the call of the Lord—into the waters of baptism, into a new life.

Once, she had been stolen, tormented, and enslaved. Now, she was redeemed.

Channah's gaze fell on her son and his little family, and hope blossomed within her.

We are finally free.

ABOUT THE AUTHORS

Mechel Wall is married to Barry Wall and together they have raised 8 wonderful children, gained more through marriage and have been blessed with 16 grandchildren as of publication. Mechel has been a flower farmer, florist/shop owner, biophilic designer and has contracted the building of a dream home she designed in drafting class in high school. They live in the bustling NW Arkansas area. She has been a writer all her life, and is just now emerging as a published author. www.writingonmechelswall.com is where you can find her.

R.H. Roberts lives in rural Oklahoma, raising kids and cattle at the same table. She majored in psychology and mastered in health at Brigham Young University before embracing her true love—literature. She has written several award-winning short stories and novels, which serve as a remedy for a life of devotion to family and faith. She loves hiking, traveling and attempting foreign languages. Visit her at RHRoberts.com for book extras and life insights. She'd love for you to join the conversation.

f